W9-BVD-711

Davita's Harp

CHAIM POTOK

Davita's Harp

Alfred A. Knopf   New York

Manufactured in the United States of America

TO THE MOTHERS

Mollie Friedman Potok
and
Sonia Leona Brown Mosevitzky

They said, "You have a blue guitar,
You do not play things as they are."
The man replied, "Things as they are
Are changed upon the blue guitar."

WALLACE STEVENS

Wilderness is a temporary condition
through which we are passing to the
Promised Land.

COTTON MATHER

BOOK ONE

One

My mother came from a small town in Poland, my father from a small town in Maine. My mother was a nonbelieving Jew, my father a nonbelieving Christian. They met in New York while my father was doing a story for a leftist newspaper on living conditions in a row of vile tenements on Suffolk Street on the Lower East Side of Manhattan, where my mother worked. This was in the late 1920s. They fell in love, had a brief affair, and were married.

Save for his sister and one uncle, none of my father's family attended the wedding. They were all staunchly devout Episcopalians, sturdy and elitist New England stock whose ancestors had come to America before the Revolution. They had lost sons in America's wars: in the Revolution, in the Civil War—two fell in that war: the first at Bull Run, the second at Gettysburg—and in the First World War, in which the eldest was badly wounded at Belleau Wood; he returned home and died soon afterward. My father's family—except for his uncle and sister—did not attend his wedding because he had left home against the will of his parents to go to New York to become a journalist, and because he was marrying a Jewish girl.

My mother had made the journey to New York from Europe soon after the end of the First World War. During the war she had attended a prestigious school in Vienna, where she had concentrated in English literature and modern European philosophy. She was about nineteen when she arrived in America. Her only relatives on the American side of the ocean were an aunt and a first cousin, her aunt's son. She moved into their small Brooklyn apartment. Her aunt, who had inherited some money from her late husband, the owner of a small garment-district sweatshop, saw her through college and certification as a social worker, and then suddenly died.

My parents' wedding was attended only by their friends, an odd assortment of leftist writers, editors, poets, theater people, journalists—and that one New England uncle and my father's sister. It was, my mother told me years later, a very noisy wedding. Angry neighbors called the police. My father's uncle, who was responsible for much of the noise, invited them in for a drink. He was from Maine and had little knowledge of the humorlessness of New York police.

Seven months later, I was born.

Our family name was Chandal. My parents named me Ilana Davita —Ilana, after my mother's mother, who had died some months before my mother left for America; and Davita, the feminine equivalent of David, after David Chandal, my father's raucous uncle, who had drowned in a yachting accident off Bar Harbor a few weeks after the wedding.

In later years I discovered that my father's uncle had been named after my father's grandfather, who had left home in his early twenties, wandered for a time through New Brunswick, bought a farm in Point Durrel on Prince Edward Island, worked the land for nearly five decades, and returned home to Maine to die.

I asked my mother once, years after my father was gone, what the name Chandal meant. She wasn't certain, she said. She had searched and inquired; her efforts had yielded nothing.

"Didn't you ever ask Papa?"

He hadn't known either, she said.

For as long into the past as I am now able to remember, there hung on a wall in my parents' bedroom a glass-framed nine-by-twelve colored photograph of three white stallions galloping across a red-sand beach, hooves kicking up sand, two racing neck in neck, the third following close behind. They are running along the rim of a pale green surf that is broken by two low parallel lines of curling waves. The water beyond is deep green. The sky is gray. White birds hover over a nearby sandbar. In the distance a line of reddish cliffs reaches across the horizon from the upper left until about halfway into the picture, then drops off into the sea. The caption, printed in a fine hand in black ink in the lower left-hand corner, reads, *Stallions on Prince Edward Island.*

And for as long as I am able to remember, a door harp hung on our front door. It was pear-shaped, nearly one inch thick and twelve inches long, and made of butternut wood. Its width was about six inches at the top and nine inches at the bottom. Four maplewood balls were suspended at the end of four varying lengths of fish line from a thin strip of wood near the top and lay against four taut horizontal wires. The lines were 8-lb.-test fish line and the wires were .027-gauge piano wire. We mounted the harp on the back of the front door and when we opened or closed the door the balls struck the wires and we would hear *ting tang tong tung ting tang*—the gentlest and sweetest of tones.

The photograph and the door harp hung in every New York apartment we lived in during my childhood. And we lived in many apartments.

We moved often, every year or so, from house to house, from neighborhood to neighborhood, on occasion from borough to borough. In each of the apartments in which we lived, we would be visited from time to time by a tall courtly man in a dark suit and a dark felt hat. Mostly he came when my father was not home. He would stay awhile in the kitchen with my mother, and they would talk quietly together. For a long time I did not know who he was. "An old friend," my mother would say. Once I heard her refer to him as her cousin. "His name is Ezra Dinn," she responded hesitantly to my question. Yes, he was a relative, her dead aunt's son, the only relative she had in America.

One winter we moved twice in three months. I remember the second move. The photograph of the beach and the stallions had been hung on a wall in my parents' bedroom; the harp had been set on a nail on the inside of our front door, and I could almost reach it if I stood on the tips of my toes—but we were barely out of the big moving barrels, cartons still lay about unpacked, and suddenly there were movers once again in the apartment, burly men treading noisily and grunting as they lifted onto their backs our heavy mahogany furniture, the open crates with my parents' books, the large cartons with my father's papers and magazines. I remember that move because my small room had been bitter cold and bedbug-ridden, and I was happy not to have to sleep in it again. I remember too that one of the movers, a tall man with a large belly and a fleshy face glistening with sweat, let his eyes slide over the titles of some of my parents' books—and his face went stiff and his jaws clamped tight. He shot my mother a look of disgust. She came to below his shoulders in height but met the look defiantly, craning her neck and staring straight at him until he turned away.

Very early I became a wanderer. I would walk the streets of each new neighborhood like some hungrily curious fledgling. My parents were frightened at first, for I seemed able to slip away in the blink of an eye, and vanish. They scolded me angrily and repeatedly, but it did little good. I needed the streets as antidote to the pernicious confines of the apartments in which we lived. I possessed an uncanny sense of timing and direction and seemed always able to return before serious parental panic set in. In the end my parents grew accustomed to my goings and comings, and left me alone.

Where did I live during those early, barely remembered years? I can recollect pieces of a surrealist landscape. Tracks high overhead on tall squat pillars and the iron thunder of elevated trains. Long lines of silent men waiting on sidewalks for food. Dimly lit staircases, malodorous hallways, quarreling neighbors, wet cobblestone streets, grimy hillocks of snow, wailing children, the smell of cooking cabbage and salt water, the yellow-white sand of high dunes, the swelling and crashing of waves —and always the music of the door harp and the silent galloping of horses across the red sands of a remote beach.

One winter we moved to a tenement near a river. In the apartment next to us lived the leader of the local street gang. He was in his teens, tall and grimy. He wore dark corduroys, a navy blue pea jacket, and a fisherman's cap, and he smelled of herring and onions. I would shy away from him whenever I saw him. Once he came by as I was jumping rope on the street with some girls. He put a foot into the wide swing of the rope and broke its rhythm and laughed as he walked off. He chanced to walk by one afternoon as I hid in the dim cellarway of our tenement during a game of hide-and-go-seek and frightened me with his leering look and glittering eyes and pimpled face. One night I heard his voice through the walls of my room. He was laughing shrilly. My heart hammered in the darkness.

One Saturday morning I was in the corner grocery store with a penny my mother had given me and was searching for a candy when he came in, tall, gangly, dirty, his cap set at an angle over his dark eyes. A cold wind blew in with him.

"Close the door," the grocer called from the counter. "I don't need the winter inside my store."

The boy banged the door shut and took some steps inside. He spotted me. I tightened my fist around my penny.

He came over to me. I stared up at him. He was so tall!

"My old man said he heard you lived down near the bridge a couple years ago and over on Broome Street before you moved here."

Vaguely I remembered a towering bridge and dark water and the stench of bloated things near barnacled pilings.

"There's a gang on this block that beats up little kids who ain't protected. You want protection?"

I did not know what to say because I did not understand the word protection.

The boy bent toward me. I saw his dark gleaming eyes and pimpled features and moist lips, and felt in that instant his contempt for my weakness.

"Hey, I'm talking to you. Girls need protection on this block. You give me a penny a week, and I'll—"

From behind the counter came the voice of the grocer, a big-chested man with thick arms and callused hands. "Izzie, you do your business in my store and I'll break your head. Leave her alone."

The boy straightened, tipped his head back, glared at me from under the peak of his cap, then turned and left the store, banging the door shut behind him.

That evening during supper I asked my mother what the word protection meant.

My mother explained words to me in a special way. She would give me the present meaning of the word and a brief account of its origin. If she did not know its origin she would look it up in the dictionary in the bedroom near my father's desk.

She told me that the word protection came from a word in an old language and had once meant to be covered in front. Now it meant to guard someone against attack or insult.

She wanted to know where I had heard the word, and I told her.

"Ilana, you see how the exploited working class lives?" she said. "Look at what happens to their children."

"He sounds like a very indecent fellow," my father said. "I think I'll have a talk with his father."

I lay awake that night listening to the beating of my heart. The radiator made loud banging noises. My mother had explained to me once that the janitor let the furnace burn down and the radiators go cold so the landlord who owned the house could save money. Landlords were capitalists, she said. Exploiters of the working class. But that would end soon. The world would change. Yes. Very soon.

Her dark eyes burned when she talked like that.

In the darkness of my room I heard a shout. The boy's voice pierced my wall. "I won't bother her. No, I won't go with Uncle Nathan to Newark! He's nothing! *Nothing!*"

Through the wall came the sounds of a man's angry voice and flesh striking flesh and a muffled cry.

About a week later my mother told me that we were moving again.

The apartments we lived in changed often, but my parents' friends seemed to remain the same. Sometimes there were meetings in the apartments. Adults hugged me, kissed me, tickled me, ignored me. A fog of cigarette smoke would collect in the air. Almost all the talk was noisy and about politics. Strange words and names would fly about like darting birds. Dialectical materialism, historical materialism, tools of production. Hitler, Stalin, Roosevelt, Mussolini, Trotsky. Brownshirt gangsterism, blackshirt murderers. Unions, bosses, capitalists. On with the struggle!

The meetings always ended with singing. I liked the singing and would listen to it from my room. My father had a rich baritone, and sometimes I would hear his voice above the others. They sang, "I dreamed I saw Joe Hill last night, Alive as you and me." They sang, "Solidarity forever, Solidarity forever, Solidarity forever, For the union makes us strong." They sang, "And just because he's human, A man would like a little bite to eat; He won't get full on a lot of talk; That won't give him bread and meat." Sometimes the singing was so loud I was sure it could be heard all through the house and perhaps even in the street. I would lie awake in my dark cold room and listen to the singing and to the beating of my heart.

Once someone went past my door, and I heard, "What the hell are they doing living in this place? Don't they have money?"

"I don't know," a second voice said. "Maybe they want to live with the proletariat."

Over breakfast the next morning I asked my mother what the word proletariat meant.

She said it was an old word from another language and it originally meant a worthless person who had nothing to give to his country except his children. Now it meant the lowest and poorest of people.

I was not sure I understood, and asked her with a child's exasperation why she always needed to give me the old meanings of words, why couldn't she simply tell me what a word meant today? And she said, patiently, in her slightly accented English, "Everything has a name, Ilana. And names are very important. Nothing exists unless it has a name. Can you think of something that doesn't have a name? And, darling, everything has a past. Everything—a person, an object, a word, everything. If you don't know the past, you can't understand the present and plan properly for the future. We are going to build a new world, Ilana. How can we ignore the past?"

At those meetings, my father, with his loud voice, ruddy features, wavy brown hair, and amiable nature, seemed nearly always at the center of talk that made people laugh; and my mother, with her scholarly demeanor and lovely features and long dark hair and soft musical voice, was almost certain to be at the heart of talk that turned people somber. Everyone liked my father; everyone seemed awed by my mother.

One morning, after a meeting that had ended in shouts, arguments, threats, and the sounds of things breaking, I lay in my bed in my cold room and heard the doorbell ring. My father's footsteps echoed through the apartment hallway. I listened to the soft tinkling of the door harp and to a brief conversation I did not understand. Two weeks later we moved again.

My mother was pregnant. I touched her hard belly. She went to a hospital and gave birth to a boy.

My father went around looking dazed. He prepared our meals. I set the table and helped him clean up. I lay awake in the darkness, listening to scurrying mice.

I walked to and from school on snow made brown with city grime and frozen to ice on the sidewalks. One afternoon, to shorten the walk, I cut across an empty lot, a miniature wilderness of dead grass, gray shrubs, rusted cans, and dog droppings atop a thin cover of snow and ice. I walked quickly through the lot to the parallel street. An icy gale blew through the streets. On a bleak side street a boy in my class spotted me and called out from his doorway, "Hey, Ilana, don't go into the next block. The gang there don't like it if you ain't a goy."

I didn't understand what he was saying and went on. The gusting wind brought tears to my eyes. Was my mother warm in the hospital? Did the landlord of the hospital turn off the heat at night? I walked quickly along the gray, late afternoon streets, needing badly to go to the bathroom and expecting the sudden appearance of a raging horde of boys. Nothing happened.

"What's a goy?" I asked my father that evening.

"That's what Jewish people call someone who isn't a Jew. It's the Hebrew word for Gentile. To Jews, I'm a goy."

"Am I a goy?"

"No, my love. Your mama is Jewish and so you're Jewish. Jewish people go according to the mother."

"According to you, am I Jewish?"

"According to me, Davita, all of you is Jewish, all of you is Gentile, all of you is Marxist, all of you—"

"Papa!"

"—is beautiful, and all of you is my special love."

He tickled me and I laughed and hugged him.

My mother returned home. She looked pale and was very weak.

They named my brother after my mother's grandfather. He looked red and scrawny and cried a great deal. There seemed to be something wrong with his stomach and his breathing. He made queer coughing sounds and could not eat or sleep.

A darkness settled upon my mother's lovely features. My father went softly about the apartment, speaking in a murmur.

There was a snowstorm. I walked to school in the snow and, on my way home, cut across the lot and went along white winter streets that were nearly empty of traffic and pedestrians.

One day three boys came out of an alley and stood in front of me, blocking my way. They wore winter jackets and dark caps. One of them had a cigarette in his mouth.

"You live here, kid?" he wanted to know.

"She don't live here," another said. "I know everyone that lives here."

"What're you doin' on this block, kid?" the third one asked.

I said, in a voice I did not recognize, "I'm going home from school. I'm in first grade."

There was a brief pause.

The one with the cigarette said, "You Jewish?"

They stood there looking at me, and waiting. I shivered in the bitter wind. A car went by, spraying dirty snow.

"My father isn't Jewish," I heard myself say in that voice that I did not recognize.

"We don't like strangers on our block, kid," the third one said. His tone was no longer hostile. He was talking now to impress the others.

The one with the cigarette said abruptly, "Your old lady, is she Jewish?"

I said nothing.

They stood there in the wind, waiting.

"Hey, kid," the one with the cigarette said. "You deaf or what?"

"My mother is Jewish," I said in that same strange voice.

They stood there, indecisive, and would not let me pass. The wind blew through my clothes. I needed a bathroom. I held my books and stood shivering. Then I was crying and no longer able to control myself. I stood crying and urinating into my clothes, feeling the wet warmth spread through my panties and down along the insides of my thighs and into my snowsuit.

One of them said, "Ah, shit, let her go. She's only a kid."

The one with the cigarette said, "She's got some Jew in her and she's on our block."

The third one said, "Aw, come on, Vince. For Christ's sake, she's only a little girl."

"Okay," the one with the cigarette said. "Okay. Get outa here, kid. And stay off our block."

"Yeah," the second one said. "You won't be so lucky next time."

I ran. Behind me I heard them laughing. I remember that laughter. The wetness was cold now, clammy, a pool of secret shame.

I let myself into the apartment with my key. The door harp sounded its gentle tune. No one was home. I changed my clothes and said nothing and wondered why the apartment was empty.

My mother had gone with my brother to the hospital. That night he died.

My mother cried and my father held her. I could hear her through the walls of my room. I don't know where we lived then, but I remember my mother crying and my father trying to soothe her and the radiators in the apartment contracting with cold and a voice in the darkness saying, Hey, kid, you Jewish? and my heart like an animal struggling against its prison inside my chest.

A few weeks later my mother began once again to pack up our apartment.

Soon after that last move my mother fell ill. She could not leave her bed. A doctor came. The tall courtly man in the dark suit and dark felt hat came too; I heard him talking with my father but could not understand what they were saying. From time to time I caught glimpses of my mother through the partly open bedroom door. She lay still on her white pillow, her long dark hair across her face and shoulders. An infection, I heard my father say to a neighbor. A women's sickness. Oh yes, a high fever, very high. Yes, serious, very serious.

One afternoon a few days after my mother took ill, I came back to the apartment from school. I closed the door and stood still for a moment, listening to the music of the harp. Out of the kitchen came a woman I had never seen before. I was very startled.

"Hello!" the woman called out in a cheerful voice. "You're Ilana Davita. I'm your Aunt Sarah, your father's sister. It's about time we met. Dear Jesus, aren't you a beauty! Put down your books and take off your coat. How about a glass of milk and some cookies?"

I looked at her suspiciously. "How did you get in?"

"Dear child, your father let me in and then went off to work."

"Papa didn't tell me you were coming."

"He never knows when I'm coming. I never know when I'm coming. But here I am! Do you want the milk and cookies?"

She was tall and thin and flat-chested and had pale skin and blue eyes and long fingers. Her hair was short and straight and flaxen. She was about my mother's age. She settled into the apartment and went around in a white nurse's uniform—dress and cap—and house slippers, and spoke in low, cheerful tones. She had many of my father's features and mannerisms: the corners of her thin lips seemed drawn up in a perpetual smile; she walked about in a loose-jointed sort of way; she would slide into a chair and drape herself over it, leaning back, deeply relaxed. She pronounced her words as my father did his. There was a carefully restrained fervor about her manner and a sharp light in her eyes—like the light in the eyes of my father when he wrote about strikes or talked about Communists and Fascists.

She slept on the studio couch in our living room. She cooked and did the laundry and swept and mopped the floors. Each morning she woke and dressed and read for a few minutes from a book, speaking the words softly. She read from that book after each meal and before going to sleep. Sometimes she sang songs with odd words and melodies. "English folk songs," she said in answer to my question. "And songs about Jesus. Aren't they lovely?"

She spent a great deal of time in the bedroom with my mother. I wondered what they talked about. Was my mother able to speak? No, my aunt said. My mother just lay in the bed and stared at the ceiling or the picture of the beach and played with her hair. Mostly she slept a lot. My aunt stayed with her so she would remember there were other people around her; it was important for everyone to know all the time that they weren't alone, my aunt said. I asked my aunt what she did all the time she was there. Oh, she kept herself busy, she said cheerfully. There was plenty to do. "Sometimes I read from the Book of Psalms," she said.

I did not know what that was.

At the start of the second week of my mother's illness my father was sent out of New York by his newspaper. "A strike," he said over his breakfast coffee, trying to make his voice sound light. "Back in a few days, my love. Be a good girl and listen to your Aunt Sarah."

That Sunday morning my aunt woke very early—as she had the Sunday before—put on a green woolen dress and low-heeled brown shoes, and left the apartment. The door harp woke me. She was gone for about an hour. The harp sounded its tones upon her return. I was in the kitchen, eating cereal. My aunt's cheerful face was flushed with cold. I could smell the cold coming off her clothes.

"A delicious Maine day," she said happily. "Cold clean air. Is your mother still asleep? Good. Dear child, why don't I make us some hot cocoa. Let me slip out of these Sunday clothes. Have you ever been to church? And Christmas? Do you celebrate the birth of our Lord? No, I suppose not. I'll be back in a moment."

She would put me to bed at night, turn out the light, and tell me strange stories in her throaty, expressive, somewhat nasal voice. She told me about a Pilgrim man named Smith and an Indian woman named Pocahontas. She told me about the woman writer George Sand. "One hundred years ago she was the most famous woman in Europe. Are you asleep, Davita?" I was not asleep. She told me about pioneer women who left comfortable homes to go west with their men. "The west was a terrible wilderness then. The women settled in houses that were miles apart. Bare earth, no trees, cruel winds. The sun burned you in the summer and the snow blew endlessly in the winter. Those were the prairies. Miles and miles of flat emptiness. Can you picture it, Davita? Flatness and emptiness all around you, and overhead the enormous sky. The men would go off hunting and trading and be gone for weeks. It's terrible to be alone, terrible. What do you think the women did in all that lonely time? Are you still awake, Davita? Are you listening? They used their imagination. That's right, their imagination."

I listened. In the chill darkness of my room I lay in my bed and listened to my Aunt Sarah from Maine telling me those stories about Pilgrims and Indians and lonely women who used their imagination to fight their loneliness. My mother never told me stories like those; her stories were about Poland and Russia and sometimes about an evil witch named Baba Yaga. I listened to my Aunt Sarah's stories and sometimes I saw the women inside my eyes.

One night she told me about a pioneering woman who would lie down among her sheep for company. "Can you imagine that, Davita? There was no one around her for miles and miles. Her husband was away and she was alone. How horrible loneliness can be! She lay among the sheep, looking up at the sky and feeling their warmth. She did that through most of the winter and into the spring. All alone in that small house on that vast prairie with only the sheep. One day in the spring the water began to rise in the stream near the house. She saw that the sheep were on the other side of the stream. She hitched horses to one of the wagons and went back and forth across the swirl of rising water, transferring the sheep. The water came up to the bed of the wagon. She was terrified. But she saved all the sheep."

That was an exciting story! I liked that story. Back and forth across the rushing water to save the sheep.

Aunt Sarah told me many such stories in the weeks she stayed in our apartment, tales about women who had helped to settle places with names like Kansas, Oklahoma, Montana, Wyoming, Arizona, Colorado —names with an echoing music that I would continue to hear each night long after she thought me asleep and left my room.

One night I asked her what she did. Was she a journalist like Papa? No, she said. She was a nurse. "A nurse for the Church and for our Lord Jesus Christ."

I didn't understand what that meant.

My mother began to walk about the apartment, white-faced and laden with grief. It was early spring now. The snows were gone from the streets.

Four weeks after my aunt arrived, she packed her bags. I watched her. "Time to go home," she said briskly, cheerily. "A time for everything under the sun. A time for this and a time for that. Now it's time to go home. Where did I put my slippers?"

I stood in the doorway with my parents and my Aunt Sarah. She bent to kiss my forehead and I felt in that instant her warmth and burst into tears. "No tears," she said. "Aunt Sarah does not like tears. A waste. Did the pioneer women cry? Don't forget my stories, Davita."

My father carried her bags out the door. The harp played softly its sweet and simple tune.

For weeks afterward I would wake at night thinking my Aunt Sarah was in my room. I would lie in the darkness and imagine myself listening to her stories. Some months after my aunt left we moved again.

Now we lived in a four-story red-brick apartment house on a narrow street on the West Side of Manhattan. My father was away often. There were many strikes that winter and he wrote about them for his newspaper and for magazines.

At breakfast one morning I asked my mother, "What does strike mean, Mama?"

She gazed at me somberly and said it was a word with many meanings.

"What does it mean where Papa is?"

"That strike is when people stop working in order to force the owners to give them more money or a better place for working."

She gave me some of the other meanings of the word. I did not understand how one word could have so many meanings. To stop working. To make someone afraid. To hit someone. To enter the mind. Strike.

"Were you ever in a strike, Mama?"

"Yes, darling. Years ago. And my grandfather, when he was young, once organized a strike in Russia, in a city called Odessa." Her dark eyes grew dreamy whenever she mentioned her grandfather. She talked about him often.

"Is your grandfather dead?"

"Yes."

I had begun to realize that all living things died. Often I lay awake at night trying to understand that. All living things died.

"Can a strike hurt people?"

"Sometimes."

"Will Papa be hurt?"

"I don't think so."

"Mama, where do dead people go?"

She told me.

I could not grasp it. Endless unimaginable darkness in the earth or as scattered ashes.

"Is my little brother dead like that?"

"Yes," she said, after a moment.

"Will you and Papa die?"

"Yes. But I hope not for a long, long time, darling. Now finish your breakfast. I don't want you to be late to school."

My father returned home two days later, tired and grimy. He bathed and slept and sat at his desk, writing. Outside my window snow fell silently on the streets and cars moved by on muffled wheels.

I asked my father over breakfast the second morning he was back, "Were people hurt at the strike, Papa?"

He sat hunched over his food, lost in thought. Often when he was writing he did not hear people speaking to him. He did two kinds of writing. One he called his special writing; that he did at home at his desk, often far into the night. The other he called his regular writing, which he did somewhere in a newspaper office in Manhattan. His regular writing appeared in the newspaper for which he worked; his special writing was published in magazines.

I asked my mother, "Is Papa still doing his special writing?"

She looked at my father and nodded.

He was unshaven and seemed not to have slept. He was then in his middle thirties, a tall and handsome man with wavy brown hair and blue eyes, straight nose and strong chin, and a mouth given easily to laughter. Save when he was doing his special writing, he seemed possessed of a singing geniality of spirit that buoyed the hearts of those around him. He had a way of coming lightly into my room at night and sitting down on my bed and saying, "It's talking time, my love." It was from him that I first heard of Paul Bunyan, Johnny Appleseed, Baron Munchausen, and other such gentlemen of fabled accomplishment. He especially loved telling me about Paul Bunyan. And it was from him that I learned about Maine and its lakes and hills and coastal villages and islands.

He said to me that morning after I asked my question again about the strike, "Yes, people were hurt. One was badly hurt."

"No one was made dead?"

"No."

"I'm glad."

"Eat your cereal, Ilana," my mother said quietly.

"I don't like anyone to be dead, Papa. It's dark like a big forest and it goes on and on and never ends."

My father slowly turned his head and looked at me.

"What does it feel like to be dead, Papa?"

"I don't know, my love. No one has ever come back to tell us about it."

"You can talk to Papa about it another time, Ilana," my mother said. "Papa has to finish his article today."

Often they worked together on his special writing. My father would come into the living room or the kitchen and read aloud what he had written; he wrote in longhand and my mother sometimes had difficulty with his handwriting. Softly she would make suggestions. My father would return to his desk.

"I was afraid Papa would be made dead in the strike."

"Wrong, my love. Wrong. Come here and give me an ocean of a hug. That's right. Harder. Yes. *That's* a hug!"

From where she stood near the stove my mother said, "You'll be late to school, Ilana. And your father has work to do. Let's finish breakfast. Do you want another cup of coffee, Michael?"

My father completed his special writing that night. Two nights later about twenty people came to the apartment for a meeting.

I lay in my bed and listened to the meeting. How noisy it was! From time to time, above the tide of noise, I would hear the boom of my father's voice. I would imagine him laughing and his eyes filled with light. He was a strong man with muscular arms and shoulders. I lay in the darkness, listening to my father's voice. It seemed inside my room, his voice with its New England music.

Abruptly the noise faded and the meeting grew silent. My mother had begun to speak. How quiet they all became whenever my mother spoke. I listened to the silence, the occasional cough, the soft music of the door harp that accompanied the entry of a latecomer. My mother mentioned the name Stalin. She said, "We are not slaves to a universal idea," and, "In the capitalist family, the husband is the bourgeois, the wife is the proletariat." She talked on for a while. I heard someone quietly interrupt her to say, "Comrade, we don't take orders here the way they do in the Bronx." I could not hear my mother's response. My room was icy cold, my bed a frozen lake. On and on my mother spoke. I fell asleep.

In the morning over breakfast I asked my mother what the word idea meant.

"That's a good one," my father said cheerfully, looking up from his newspaper. "Work on that one, Annie. That'll keep you busy for a while."

"Your eggs are getting cold, Michael."

He put down the paper. I saw his name beneath the headline on the right-hand column of the front page: Michael Chandal.

"I heard you using idea last night, Mama."

"Don't you ever sleep, my love? You're acquiring my bad habits, becoming a night person. Beware of the night people, Davita. Avoid us like the plague."

"I'll try to explain idea to you, Ilana. Eat your cereal while I talk."

The word idea, she said, came from an old word that originally meant to see. An idea was something that existed in a person's mind. It could be a thought, an opinion, a fantasy, a plan of action, a belief. It used to mean an image in the mind, a picture of someone or something, a likeness. But no one used it that way anymore.

"Davita, my love, did we understand any of that?" my father asked genially.

"Mama, is what you call Stalinism an idea?"

My father stopped chewing and looked at me.

"Yes," my mother said, smiling faintly.

"Is my being cold in bed at night an idea?"

"No, darling. That's a feeling."

"That's an exploiting capitalist landlord, is what that is."

"Is when I hear the door harp an idea?"

"No, darling. That's hearing. That's one of your senses, like seeing and touching and smelling. An idea is in your mind, your head. When you think about the door harp, it's an idea."

"When I think about the cottage and the beach and the ocean, is that an idea?" I had suddenly remembered the seaside world where we spent our summers.

"Yes, Ilana."

"Do ideas become dead, like people and animals and birds?"

"Sometimes."

I sat at the table in our small kitchen and gazed at the pale winter sunlight that shone through the window.

"Well," my father said, pushing back his chair and getting to his feet. "This has certainly been one of my more enlightening breakfasts. Now I've got to go to work. There's an idea for you. Work. A powerful idea. Annie, you'll remember to call Roger about Jakob."

"I'll remember," my mother said.

My father turned to me. "Davita, a writer named Jakob Daw will be coming to stay with us for a while. I'm telling you now so it won't be the shock it was when you walked in on your Aunt Sarah."

"Is Jakob Daw from Maine?"

"Jakob Daw is from Austria. He's an old friend of your mother's." I saw my mother look down at the floor, her face without expression.

"Does Jakob Daw write ideas?"

"I don't know. Does he write ideas, Annie?"

"Yes. You could say that he writes ideas." My mother's voice sounded unusually subdued. "And about things from his imagination."

"Well," said my father, "this has been an interesting breakfast. Will my girl give her dad a hug? A big mountain of a hug."

I saw my mother looking at us, her eyes troubled.

Mama is thinking something, I told myself. She is having an idea.

"*That* was a hug!" my father said.

Two days later my father went off to cover a strike in a textile mill in northern Maine. He was gone nearly a week. He returned with a deep cut on his scalp and a painfully wrenched left shoulder.

He sat at his desk, writing.

I wandered silently about the apartment, frightened. One afternoon I passed by my parents' bedroom and saw, through the partly open door, my father lying on the bed, his hands over his eyes, the light from the desk lamp falling upon his papers and the black Waterman's fountain pen with which he wrote. On the wall over the desk was the glass-framed photograph of the beach and the horses. I gazed a long time at the photograph. I imagined I could hear the sand-muffled sounds of their beating hooves. Then I heard my father say clearly, in a voice I did not recognize, "Ah, Christ, what the hell is it all about? How can it be anything? It's not a damn thing. It's nothing. That's what it is. *Nothing!*"

I backed away quietly from the door and went to my room and stood by the window staring out at the street. Hillocks of dirty snow lay upon the curbs. A few lone people walked stiff as toys through the wind.

The front door opened. My mother was back from shopping. The door closed. The harp played softly. I went from my room into the kitchen to help my mother with the groceries.

On occasion my mother would tell me an old Russian tale about a sister and brother fleeing from the evil witch Baba Yaga. Two lost children running through a vast open wilderness of barren stony earth. The boy carried a little leather pouch in which were three magical objects: a pebble, a kerchief, a comb. They could use each item only once. One night the witch drew dangerously close, and from the pouch the brother removed the comb and threw it to the ground. A tangled forest sprang up between them and Baba Yaga. The children journeyed safely on. Days later they again saw Baba Yaga close behind them, dark-garbed, green-skinned, hideous. The boy drew out the pebble and threw it to the ground. A towering mountain rose suddenly between them and Baba Yaga. On they wandered, seeking their home and their parents. Weeks passed. One day they again saw Baba Yaga, in fierce pursuit. Quickly the boy drew out the kerchief and placed it on the ground. A wide, swift river appeared, blocking the path of Baba Yaga. The river swirled and hissed along its banks and was filled with treacherous crosscurrents and whirlpools. The witch Baba Yaga stood along the far bank, screaming and cursing. The children held their ears and fled. That day a farmer found them asleep on a haystack and recognized them and brought them home to their parents. What a joyous reunion there was! And soon the children forgot the evil witch Baba Yaga and their long flight through the wilderness.

She told me that story again one night in the early spring of that year. I lay half asleep in my bed, listening. When she was done, I asked, "What does magic mean?"

"It's too late now, Ilana."

"Is there a meeting again tonight?"

"Yes, darling. But we'll try to be quiet."

She kissed me. Cool and dry on my forehead. Not like my father's kiss, always warm and moist and on my face. Lips coming toward me and lips going away. Cool and dry, warm and moist. Mama and Papa.

From the kitchen came the sound of my parents' voices. I could not make out their words. The doorbell rang. I heard my mother's footsteps in the hallway. The singing of the harp was drowned by a rush of voices. The apartment filled with noise. I fell asleep finally to the sounds of the ringing telephone.

The meeting woke me. It was unusually noisy. "What's the alternative?" someone kept shouting. "Tell me what the alternative is." A surge of voices drowned out his next words, sharp voices, angry voices. The air in my room vibrated faintly with the din of the meeting. I heard the word Spain many times. I had never heard that word before. Spain. It was a long while before I was able to fall back asleep.

At breakfast my father sat reading his newspaper and my mother stood at the stove in her pink house dress and white apron. The apartment seemed tense with the atmosphere of last night's meeting. My father looked tired. He read to my mother a news story about Spain, and they talked about that briefly. I did not understand what they were saying. My mother's voice sounded strained. I played with my cereal.

My mother put a plate of eggs and meat in front of my father and sat down at the table. They continued talking about Spain.

I looked up from my cereal. "Mama."

They ignored me. Now they were talking about the writer Jakob Daw.

"Mama!"

"One minute," my mother said.

I said, "Last night Baba Yaga ran after me in a dream and I used a door harp like the one we have, only smaller, and it became an ocean. What is magic, Mama? And what is Spain?"

My mother said, after a pause, "Later, Ilana."

My father said, brightening, "No, go ahead, Annie. I want to hear this."

My mother said, after another pause, "Magic is a very old idea, Ilana. If you want it to rain and you say certain words, and if each time you say those words it rains, that's magic. Words or things that control other things or people or nature. That's magic."

"Is magic real?"

"Only in stories, darling."

"Can magic stop people from being dead?"

She hesitated. "Only in stories."

"We could use some magic in Spain," my father said. "Azaña could use some magic."

"I like the idea of magic," I said. "What else is magic?"

"If I could clean up the mess you make at the table just by a wave of my hand, that would be magic," my mother said.

"Yes, my beauty," said my father. "That would be very strong magic, indeed."

"If I could stop my room from being cold at night by saying, 'Cold, go away,' is that magic?"

"Yes, darling."

"If I could stop us from moving all the time by saying, 'Moving, stop,' is that magic?"

"That would be magic, all right," my father said quietly.

"Finish your cereal, Ilana," my mother said. "I don't want you to be late for school."

My father pushed back his chair and got to his feet.

"What is Spain, Papa?"

"I am off to the newspaper, my love. A brief explanation. All right? You remember the ocean near our beach? Spain is a country on the other side of that ocean. People there hate one another. Terrible people called Fascists may try to take over the country, like they're trying to take over another country called Ethiopia. I'll tell you more another time. Give your dad a big mountain of a hug."

"Michael, will you find out about Jakob's itinerary?"

"As soon as I get to the paper."

"Don't forget you promised Philip a piece on the Toledo strike."

"How can I forget, Annie? You won't let me."

The winter was gone. Grass began to grow in the empty lots and backyards of the neighborhood. Sometimes on Sunday afternoons my mother would take me on a long walk to a park. We went to that park one Sunday that spring, walking along side streets that sloped gently toward green fields and woods and the silvery sheen of a river. Narrow dirt paths wound through the fields and trees. Park benches were set like beckoning laps here and there alongside the paths and in playgrounds. I sat on a bench with my mother and watched thin white clouds sail across the blue sky. Small birds flew by overhead. An early spring wind blew through the trees and brought with it the scent of the river.

I got down off the bench and played for a while in a sandbox with a girl my age. There were few people in the park. My mother sat on the bench, her face to the sun. She wore a coat and a beret. She had said little to me during our walk to the park. She had a way of withdrawing from time to time: her eyes would dim and she would stare straight ahead and I had the feeling she was looking at memories and images that she would not share with anyone. She was that way that Sunday afternoon in the park.

I grew weary of the sandbox and went over to the bench and sat next to my mother. Absentmindedly, her face still to the sun, she put her arm around my shoulders and hugged me to her. I inhaled the scents of her coat and skin and sat nesting in her embrace. Then I asked her, "Mama, when is Jakob Daw coming to stay with us?"

There had been talk of him again during breakfast that morning. And that strange distant look had entered my mother's eyes.

She kept her face to the sun as she answered. "I don't know, Ilana. Soon."

"Why is he coming to America?"

"Certain people are bringing him here to lecture at our meetings in New York and other cities. And to help us raise money for people in Spain."

"I hope he won't stay with us long. I don't like a strange man in our house."

"Jakob Daw is not a stranger, Ilana. He's an old friend. I knew him in Europe a long time ago. He's a great writer, though not too many people in America have heard of him or understand what he writes. Darling, listen, I want to sit quietly for a while and think. If I let you play on the bars will you be very careful and not be mischievous and fall as you did the last time?"

"If I start to fall and I say, 'Stop,' and I don't fall, is that magic?"

"Yes. But I don't advise you to try it, Ilana."

From the bars near the sandbox I saw my mother on the bench staring down at the gravel path, her eyes wide and moist and dark. I wished she would wear nicer clothes and put on makeup. What was she remembering? A sailboat went by on the river, gliding slowly along like a lazy wide-winged white bird. I hung upside down from a bar, watching my mother.

Suddenly that night the winter returned and snow fell on the spring grass. My room turned cold again. I saw my breath on my window and wrote my name with my finger, using the penmanship I was learning in school. Ilana Davita Chandal. My name written clearly on a window against the cold night. I returned to my bed.

The winter cold remained. Nights felt endless; days were gray, leaden. People went about as if weighted. There were many meetings in our apartment. Again and again I heard the names Roosevelt, Hitler, Stalin, Mussolini, Franco. I heard strange words. Republic, militia, rebellion, coup d'état, garrison. And more names. Ethiopia, Germany,

Spain, England, France, America. And names with menacing sounds. Anarchist, Falangist, Fascist. And words that frightened me. Murder, bombing, air raid, execution. All the world's peoples and politics seemed to crowd into our apartment at those meetings.

After each meeting my parents would stay up late in the kitchen, drinking coffee and talking. The sounds of soft music would come from the radio. Sometimes they would go into the living room and put a record on the phonograph and continue their talking. As they talked, my father's voice would rise with excitement and my mother would remind him I was asleep and his voice would drop. I wished I could be with them, my room was so cold, the nights were so dark, the winter a wilderness without end.

Then the cold was gone and the weather turned permanently warm. Suddenly something was wrong with my eyes. Headaches and slow dissolvings of the world. My parents' faces grew tight. My mother took me to a doctor. He was a bald and cheerful man. He peered into my eyes through a glistening instrument. Could he see the ideas in my head? "Well, young lady, you read a lot, don't you. Not many girls your age read so much. It's glasses for you, my dear. To be worn all the time. And make especially sure that you have them on when you read and write. Unless you want to continue straining your lovely blue eyes and end up bumping into walls. Do we want to do that?"

My parents were relieved to be told that all I needed for my eyes were those glasses. The lenses were thin, mounted on gilded metallic frames. When I put them on the world leaped into a clarity that was startling. I saw people and objects in sharp outline: the boys who lounged around the street lamp in front of our apartment house and hooted at me as I came and went; the owners of the grocery and laundry and candy store on our block; the weary faces of men and women; the headlines in the newspapers on the corner stand; the dust that blew through the streets; the picture of the beach and the horses in my parents' bedroom; the books and magazines on Spain my father was bringing home.

The days lengthened. One day in late April my father was sent to Boston by his newspaper. I lay in my bed that night, reading a children's book about Spain. I looked at pictures of long valleys and sun-baked mountains and wide rivers and hill villages and Moorish castles. I especially liked the pictures of the castles.

Later, asleep, I heard softly from a corner of my room the sibilant voice of Baba Yaga. My child, my child, come to me. Why are you afraid? How can I hurt you? I am an old lady. Come.

I ran across a meadow into a dense wood. Birds leaped from the trees, darkening the sky. I ran listening and heard only silence. I stopped and put my ear to the ground. There! I could hear the heavy thumping footfalls. I jumped to my feet and fled, leaving my glasses on the ground. Baba Yaga followed close upon my heels. And as she sped past the glasses the lenses burst into flame and a chasm opened in the earth. Into this black and bottomless chasm plunged Baba Yaga, twisting and turning as she fell. I could hear her receding scream.

Over breakfast the next morning I asked my mother, "Do dead people ever come back to life?"

"No."

"Never?"

"Never."

Calmly I ate my cereal.

A moment later I asked, "Will I ever have another brother?"

"Perhaps."

"Why did my brother die?"

"Because he was sick."

"Why did he get sick?"

"I don't know, Ilana. He just did."

I finished my cereal and drank my milk.

"Mama, why did you tell me the story about Baba Yaga?"

"My mother used to tell it to me. Did I frighten you? It's important to know about evil people and how to protect yourself against them."

"Baba Yaga won't bother me anymore. Baba Yaga is dead and will never come back. I'd better go to school now so I won't be late."

My mother stood at the sink, gazing at me, her eyes dark and troubled.

I walked quickly to school in the early morning sunlight, the world sharp and clear through my new glasses, the magic glasses of Ilana Davita Chandal.

In class I raised my hand. The teacher had been talking about different kinds of relatives and asked if anyone had an aunt or an uncle. "My Aunt Sarah is in Ethiopia," I said. "Ethiopia is a country in Africa."

I sat in the third row on the side of the room near the wall of tall windows. Heads turned toward me.

The teacher, a heavyset, middle-aged woman who wore her graying hair in a bun, smiled patiently and said, "What does your Aunt Sarah do?"

"She's a nurse."

"Your Aunt Sarah is a nurse in Ethiopia? Does she work in a hospital?"

"Sometimes she works in a hospital. Mostly she works in villages. She helps the Ethiopians who are hurt by the Italian Fascists in the war."

The class was quiet.

"The Italians invaded Ethiopia last year and are bombing villages. They kill women and children. And Fascists are going to start a war in Spain. They're going to rebel against the government and try to take over the country."

The class was very still.

"Well," the teacher said with a thin smile, "we certainly know a great deal about politics, don't we. Do we know who Mr. Adolf Hitler is?"

"Adolf Hitler is the Fascist leader of Germany. He's an evil person."

"And Benito Mussolini?"

"He's the Fascist leader of Italy."

"And Stalin? Do we know about Stalin?"

"Stalin is the leader of Russia."

"Is Stalin a Fascist?"

"Stalin is a Communist. He is not afraid to use his power for good purposes."

The teacher stood behind her desk, looking at me. Her round face seemed a pale floating disc above the darkness of her dress, which began just beneath her chin and reached to well below her knees.

"Where are you hearing all these things, young lady?"

"From my father and mother and their friends."

"I see. Well. All right. Let us leave the subject of politics. We were talking about aunts and uncles. Would anyone else like to tell us about his or her aunt or uncle? Robert? Yes. Go ahead."

I stopped listening and sat bored, gazing out the window at the cement expanse of the school yard and thinking about Aunt Sarah.

During the recess a boy came over to me in the yard as I played alone on the bars. He was short and heavy, with olive skin and lusterless eyes. He sat two rows behind me in class.

He said, "Hey, listen, kid. Watch out what you say about Italians."

I swung myself into a sitting position on one of the bars and looked at him.

The boy said, "My father says Mussolini is a great man. You watch your mouth."

Another boy came over, lanky and flaxen-haired, with cold blue eyes and a sharp chin. I had never seen him before.

He looked up at me sitting on one of the bars. "Hey, you, four eyes."

I looked around. The yard was crowded and noisy. Along the far side near the chain-link fence a group of teachers stood talking to one another.

"You little bitch," the flaxen-haired boy said. "My kid brother told me what you said about Adolf Hitler. You better watch it."

"That's what I told her," the first boy said.

"My father says Adolf Hitler is the best thing that ever happened to Germany. He's gonna get rid of all the Commies and Jews. You better keep your mouth shut or you won't make it back home one day."

I climbed down from the bars. The flaxen-haired boy stepped in front of me.

"Are you Jewish?" he asked, bending toward me, his eyes bright with hate.

The other boy stood by, watching.

My legs trembled. "My father isn't Jewish. My mother is Jewish."

He seemed not to know what to make of that.

"Watch your mouth," he said, after a moment.

"Yeah," the other one said. "Watch what you say."

They sauntered off in different directions and were gone into the crowds of playing children.

I leaned heavily against the bars, my heart thundering. I had not thought words could be so dangerous. Cold and murderous blue eyes. He had really wanted to hurt me. I would have to be careful of what I said in school from now on.

A whistle blew. I came out of the yard into the crowded corridor and went to my classroom. I sat stiffly in my seat. Behind me sat the boy who had warned me to watch what I said about Mussolini and Italians. I sat very still, gazing out the window and listening vaguely to the teacher and thinking of my Aunt Sarah in the villages of a place called Ethiopia.

That night I woke from dream-filled sleep and lay in my bed listening to the soft music of the door harp. I heard a voice I did not recognize, a man's voice, hoarse and raspy, speaking quietly in a language I did not understand. My mother said something to him in that same language. The man coughed. Then my father said loudly, in a tone of exasperation, "You can't imagine what a pain in the behind that was, Annie. You'd think we were bringing in Karl Marx or Lenin. All very polite, you understand. The bastards."

"They were merely doing their job, Michael," I heard the man say in accented English. "It is your State Department and immigration people in Washington whom you must blame."

"Anyway, Jakob, you're here," I heard my mother say.

"Yes, Channah," the man said. "I am here."

"It is so good to see you again after so many years. Can I get you a cup of coffee? And something to eat. Mocha coffee. See, Jakob? I remembered."

"Yes, please. It was a terrible trip. We were in a storm three whole days. Terrible."

I listened to their voices for a while longer and then drifted back into sleep.

Pale morning sunlight woke me. I lay in my bed listening to the sounds of the street. Cars and trucks and the distant clang of a trolley. After a while I put on my slippers and went from my room. Walking past the living room, I saw a man asleep on the studio couch. I stood there a moment looking at him, then went back to my room for my glasses. Standing again in the entrance to the living room, I peered closely at the man on the couch.

He lay beneath a blanket and I could see only his face and head. He had a wide forehead, straight dark hair, thin arching dark eyebrows, and an aquiline nose that seemed almost knifelike. Faint movements of his small nostrils signaled his silent breathing. Beginning in dark corner wedges, the wide thin upper lip rose delicately to a small pink petallike plateau at the center of the mouth; the lower lip was full, effeminate. The chin was pointed, the cheeks slightly concave. His smooth face and forehead were shockingly pale. I had never before seen anyone with such chalky features. I moved nearer to him and stood watching. A moment passed. Then, like a doll that is turned this way or that, his eyelids abruptly slid open, and he was looking directly up at me.

I drew back, frightened by the suddenness of his waking and ashamed at being caught looking at him as he slept.

His eyes were black and large and shiny. The heavy lids gave them an owllike hooded look. He gazed at me and did not move.

My heart beat loudly in my ears.

Lying there, moving only his lips, he said quietly, "Is it morning already? Yes, I see it is." He coughed briefly, a wet soft cough. "Good morning, dear child."

"Good morning," I heard myself respond.

"You are Ilana Davita."

I nodded.

"I am Jakob Daw."

He began to sit up. I moved away.

"Dear child, where are you going?"

"To the toilet."

I went quickly through the hallway to the bathroom near the door to the apartment. I saw the harp on the door, its gentle curves, its wooden balls, its circular hollow beneath the strings and taut wires. Standing on tiptoe, I touched the balls gently and watched them strike the wires. Soft sweet music filled the silent hallway. *Ting tang tong tung ting tang tung.* I went into the bathroom.

When I returned to the living room, Jakob Daw, dressed in baggy dark trousers and an old rumpled white shirt, stood near a window gazing out at the street. He turned as I entered. He was a small man, not much taller than my mother, thinly boned, with delicate fingers and white hands and narrow shoulders. He looked fragile and infirm.

He said to me in his hoarse, raspy voice, "Again, good morning, Ilana Davita. Your parents did not do you justice when they told me about you. A Viking beauty. Clearly your father's side dominates, at least on the outside. How old are you?"

"Eight."

"A lovely age, an innocent age." He put a hand to his mouth and coughed delicately. "Excuse me. You go to school, of course."

"I go to public school."

"And you read? Good. Very good. Now for what may be a more difficult question. Can you show me where things are in the kitchen so I can make for myself a cup of coffee? I am lost in the morning without my coffee. Yes? Thank you. But first I will go to the washroom. It is at the end of the hall, if I remember correctly. Yes. Is it all right to call you Ilana Davita? Good. It is very important to call people by their correct names."

A few minutes later we sat at the kitchen table. Jakob Daw smoked a cigarette and sipped from the cup of hot mocha coffee. He seemed tense, distracted, and kept glancing out the window at the red-brick wall of the adjacent apartment house. The hand holding the cup trembled slightly as he brought it to his lips. Sitting close to him, I noticed the network of small bluish veins on the backs of his white hands and along his temples.

I asked him, "Do you wear glasses, Mr. Daw?"

He said, "I wear glasses when I write."

"I just got new glasses."

"Do they help you?"

"I see things very clearly now. And I don't have headaches."

"Must you wear your glasses all the time?"

"Yes. But sometimes I forget."

"You must not forget. It is important to see clearly all the time."

"Mr. Daw, do you write stories?"

"Yes."

"Do you write stories like Baba Yaga?"

He inhaled on his cigarette and gazed at me curiously over the rim of his cup. "I am afraid I do not know that story."

"It's about an evil witch who chases a girl and boy, and they have three magic things with them to protect themselves against her."

"Ah," he said. *"That* Baba Yaga. Yes. Well, my stories are only a little like the story of Baba Yaga."

"I hate Baba Yaga. But she's dead now."

He looked at me through his hooded eyes.

"The dead don't ever come back, you know. My mother told me that."

He put down the cup. "That is true," he said. "And also not true."

"Do you know Adolf Hitler?"

"Do I know Adolf Hitler? Personally? No."

"Have you been to Spain?"

"No. Not yet." He raised his cup and drank from it. "There will soon be a war in Spain."

"What does war mean?"

He looked at me. A sad smile played briefly along his lips. He said, "War is a fight between large groups of people or between countries. War is terrible. It is one of the most terrible things that man does."

"Do people become dead in war?"

"Yes. Many people."

"Mr. Daw, do you have children?"

"No, Ilana Davita. I have never been married."

"I had a baby brother once, but he died."

"Yes," he said. "I know. I think I will have another cup of this very good coffee."

He started to rise, then stopped. There were footsteps in the hallway. My mother came into the kitchen, wearing her pink house dress. Her long dark hair lay loosely over her shoulders and back. Jakob Daw looked at her, then looked away, then looked at her again.

"Well," my mother said, "you two have met."

"We have met and are having a splendid conversation," Jakob Daw said.

"Mr. Daw taught me the word war, Mama."

"The child asked about Spain," Jakob Daw said.

My father came breezily into the kitchen. "Good morning, my love." He kissed my cheek and I smelled his shaving lotion. "Good morning, Jakob. You look terrible. Have you had your coffee? I see you have. You look like that *after* your coffee? I want to review your itinerary, and then I've got to get over to the newspaper. Christ, we've got to get you looking better, Jakob. You can't go around the country talking to people and looking like that. Annie, what can we do to put some life into our Jakob?"

The three of them sat around the table, talking. I could not understand most of what they were saying.

I said, "How long will you be here, Mr. Daw?"

They looked at me. Jakob Daw said, "Ten days. Perhaps two weeks."

"Do you have ideas, Mr. Daw?"

"Ideas?"

"Do you see ideas in your head?"

"Oh, yes. I have ideas. Yes. Listen. May I ask of you a favor? Please do not call me Mr. Daw. Call me—" He stopped and looked at my mother. "Channah, what should Ilana Davita call me?"

"Perhaps Uncle Jakob," my mother said.

"Good idea, Annie," my father said.

"That is fine," Jakob Daw said. "Is that all right with our Ilana Davita? Good. I am going out now with your father and I will return later in the day. Good-bye, Ilana Davita."

"Good-bye, Uncle Jakob," I said.

In the park the following Saturday afternoon I asked my mother, "What does Uncle Jakob write?"

"Stories. Articles." She sat with her eyes to the sun. Her face had a worn and haunted look. "He is a great writer, and one day the whole world will know about him."

I could not understand why a great writer had to sleep on the studio couch in our living room.

"What kind of stories does Uncle Jakob write?"

"Strange stories. Wonderful stories."

"Why doesn't Uncle Jakob stay in a hotel?"

"He's not well and doesn't want to be by himself."

"Did you and Uncle Jakob grow up together?"

"No, darling. We went to school together in Vienna."

"Were you good friends?"

"Yes. We were very young. And the war was everywhere. We were—friends."

She lapsed into silence, her eyes brooding.

I sat on one of the swings, and my mother pushed me. Back and forth, gently, sunlight on my face, oaks and maples with young leaves overhead, earth with young green grass below. Back and forth, like the wooden balls of our door harp. Back and forth, my mother pushing.

That night the weather was strangely warm. My father opened the windows and breezes pushed against the curtains and shades. There was a meeting in our apartment, noisy and tense, though there was also some singing and my father's barking laugh. Jakob Daw spoke about Germany, Russia, and Spain. His voice was quiet, hoarse. I watched people straining to hear, leaning forward to catch his words. A quality of intense power seemed to radiate from his fragility, from his hooded eyes and hoarse voice, from his occasional cough. I found myself often staring at him, fascinated, unable to take my eyes from his face.

I asked my mother the next day after school, "Does Papa know that you and Uncle Jakob went to school together?"

"Of course."

"Did Papa know Uncle Jakob before he came to stay with us?"

"Only through his reputation," she said. "Through his name as a writer."

In the first week that Jakob Daw was with us, he and my father traveled together a number of times to different parts of the city. Meetings, my mother explained. Jakob Daw would return from those trips looking exhausted.

"A vast and ugly city," he said one night over supper. "The heart of decaying capitalist power. A city without hope and without compassion."

"Capitalism and compassion are incompatible," my mother said.

"You won't find too much compassion among my New England Episcopalians," my father said. "Except for my sister Sarah, and a few others."

At times that week I woke in the night and put on my glasses and went into the living room where Jakob Daw slept. By the light of the street lamps I could make out dimly his straight dark hair and pale features. I would stand there, staring at him, entranced in a way I could not understand. One night I woke and went into the living room and he was not there. I heard voices from my parents' bedroom. The three of them were talking quietly together; I could not make out their words. Two nights later I was awakened by a loud, piercing cry, a single brief scream that ended in a choking sob. I rushed into the living room and saw Jakob Daw sitting up on the studio couch, his knees drawn up to his chin, his eyes wide, his hands over his ears. "Ah, you cannot do this!" he cried. "How can you think to do such a thing?"

My mother was suddenly in the room. "Ilana, go back to your bed immediately," she said to me in a voice I did not recognize.

In the morning I thought it had all been another of my bad dreams and did not talk of it with anyone.

One night my father went alone to a meeting in a section in Philadelphia called Strawberry Mansion. I woke to go to the living room and Jakob Daw was not there. His clothes were on the chair near the studio couch. I went quietly through the hallway to my parents' bedroom and saw him through the partly open door. He was sitting at my father's desk. On the wall above the desk was the framed picture of the horses on the red-sand beach on Prince Edward Island. I saw them galloping against the wind, manes flying, sand spraying out behind their thundering hooves. Jakob Daw had on spectacles rimmed in silver metal. Somewhere in the room with him was my mother, but I could not see her. Jakob Daw was writing with a black fountain pen. The only light in the room came from the desk lamp; it bathed his features in soft lights and shadows. He sat bent over the desk, writing. He turned his head slightly. The spectacles flared; his dark eyes burned.

I went quietly back to my room.

That image of Jakob Daw writing, his face bathed in warm lights and shadows, his glasses flaring, his eyes burning—it lingered in memory. I fell asleep with that image fixed in my mind. A picture. An idea. Jakob Daw writing.

The following day Jakob Daw and my father went to an evening meeting in Brooklyn. Then they began to travel to places outside the city. I heard names like Newark, Jersey City, Long Island, Baltimore, Washington, D.C., Philadelphia, Wilmington.

One night I lay in bed reading another book about Spain that my father had brought home for me. Someone tapped on my door. It was Jakob Daw.

He stood hesitantly in the doorway. "May I come in?"

I sat up in my bed and put down the book. "Yes."

He came slowly into the room and sat down in the chair near the head of the bed. The light of my reading lamp fell upon his pale, almost feminine features, bathing them in lights and shadows. Beyond him the room was a blur of dim and shapeless forms.

He asked with a quiet, apologetic smile, "Did I interrupt your reading? I am sorry. What book is it?"

"It's about the Spanish people and their cities and also their castles, especially the castle called the Alhambra."

"The Alhambra. A beautiful castle." He hesitated, looking down at his hands, which lay limply on his knees. "Well, I thought I might, that is if you are interested, I might, well, tell you a story." He gazed at me hesitantly, the apologetic smile still on his lips. "Are you interested?"

Yes, I was very interested.

The smile widened. "Good," he said. "Good." He peered at me a moment, then looked down at his hands. He raised his eyes and looked at me directly. "The story is about a bird," he said. "A little bird with black feathers and short wings and a small red spot under each of its large dark eyes. Are you ready, Ilana Davita? Here is my story.

"The bird woke one day from a long deep sleep and found himself in a strange land. How had he come to this land? From where had he flown? The bird could not remember. It was a beautiful land—lovely soft green hills and leafy trees and dew on the flowers and grass and cooling breezes and the sun always shining but never too hot and at night a full moon and a gentle wind. There were animals in the land and they were like animals everywhere, peaceful when left alone, hunting and killing only for food. The people of the land lived in small groups that were often at war with one another. Some people were cruel; others were kind. They were like people you meet everywhere. But the land itself was like no land the bird had ever seen or imagined. It seemed enchanted, a magical land, filled with crystal lakes and fields of wheat and corn, with rolling sunlit meadows and deep forests—and music. A soft haunting music could be heard everywhere. It seemed to come from the earth itself, a low enthralling tinkle of sound, like joyous bells far off beyond the blue hills, beyond the green meadows, far, far away. Music.

"The little bird loved the land and did not like the people. He wondered why the people made war, why they were so cruel. He thought it might be a good idea to try and change them. Now, how could a little bird do that? One day as he sat on the branch of a tree in the cool green shade of overhanging leaves, he had an idea. It occurred to him that in some way it might be the music that was the cause of the cruelties he saw. People hurt one another, killed one another, made war with one another—and instead of feeling sorrow and regret, went ahead and were soothed by the music. Perhaps if the music came to a stop; perhaps if there was no music to soothe a person who did someone harm—perhaps then the harm itself might come to be felt as intolerable and be brought to an end. And so the bird set out to discover the source of the music. He began to fly back and forth across the land, back and forth, and back and forth."

Jakob Daw stopped. There was silence.

I asked quietly, "Did the bird find the music?"

"He is still searching."

I thought a moment. "I don't think I like the story."

Jakob Daw smiled sadly and sighed. "So many people do not like my stories."

"Mama said you're a great writer."

"Did she? Your mother is very kind."

"The bird is still searching?"

"Yes."

"Will he ever find where the music comes from?"

"I do not know."

"Is the music a kind of magic?"

"Magic? Perhaps. Yes. It might be a kind of magic."

"I've never heard a story like that before, Uncle Jakob. It doesn't even have an ending."

"Yes. I see. No ending. Perhaps you would like me to tell you another story."

"Not now, Uncle Jakob. I'm tired."

"I thought you might be."

"Why do people read your stories if they don't really like them?"

"I ask myself that very often. I do not know. Good night, Ilana Davita."

"Good night, Uncle Jakob."

He went quietly from the room.

I lay in my bed. What a strange story! It was a long time before I was able to sleep.

I dreamed of the bird that night, flying, flying, to find the source of the healing music and wake the world to its befouling cruelties. A little black bird flying, a small red spot beneath each of his glittering eyes. Jakob Daw's story had been very confusing and I had not understood it. Yet I was dreaming about the little bird flying to find the source of the music. What would he do if he ever found it? Flying, flying across the blue hills and crystal lakes and sunlit meadows of my enchanted land. Flying, the magical music a warm solace. Flying.

Jakob Daw was with us for two weeks. Then he packed his bags to go away for a while to a country called Canada. He would be back in the summer, he said. He stood at the door to the apartment with me and my parents. He shook my mother's hand, gently, and I saw pass between them a look that seemed burdened with memories. My father saw it too, and a deep pity entered his eyes. Jakob Daw bent to kiss me, and I felt his gentle shyness. It was a dry kiss, briefly delivered to my forehead. His fingers brushed my cheek. They felt hot.

I dreamed often of the little bird. I could not grasp the story; yet I kept dreaming of the bird. How strange to be so affected by a story I did not understand!

One night over supper, a week or so after Jakob Daw had left, I told the story to my parents. They did not understand it, either.

"There's something hidden in it," my father said. "But I don't know what it is. I wish more of his stuff was out in English. What's it like to read him in German?"

"Extraordinary," my mother said.

"He's a strange guy. Was he this way when you knew him in Vienna?"

"Yes," said my mother. "But he wasn't ill in Vienna. That came later."

Flying. The little black bird flying to find the music of the world.

A letter came from Aunt Sarah. She was still in Ethiopia. My father read it to us at the kitchen table. She described the heat and the suffering of the Ethiopians and the horrible medical facilities. She prayed a great deal and read often from the Book of Psalms. It was difficult to do the work of our Lord in this dreadful land, but she was certainly trying. "And how is Ilana Davita? I must see her again and tell her more of my Maine stories."

"Is the war in Ethiopia over?" I asked.

"Yes," my father said, frowning.

"The Italians think it's over," my mother said. "It isn't over for the Ethiopians."

"It's over," my father said with an uncharacteristic scowl. "Chalk up one more for the Fascists."

The weather had turned very warm. I walked alone through the neighborhood now, seeing streets clearly, remembering them. I had words for most of the things I saw, and it was the words that I remembered. I began to like the streets and the people. In school a boy who sat near me in my class and whose father hated Mussolini came over to me during recess, and we played together on the bars. I liked the neighborhood and the school and the walks to the park with my mother and the scent of the river. We received no more mail from my Aunt Sarah and heard nothing from Jakob Daw.

One morning in early June, as I was washing in the bathroom, I heard our doorbell ring. My father went through the hallway and opened the door.

A man's voice said, "Mr. Michael Chandal?"

"Yes."

"My name is Sloane. I own this building."

"Well, hello. Come on in."

"No, thanks. Mr. Chandal, I have to tell you that you're in violation of the terms of your tenancy."

"What?" my father said.

"The meetings you hold in your apartment are a gross disturbance to the peace and quiet of the other tenants. Also, I'm told you've taken in someone to live with you. That's another clear violation."

"That individual is no longer here," my father said.

I heard my mother call from the kitchen. "Michael, what is it?"

"I'll handle it, Annie," my father called back.

"I've got to ask you to vacate the premises," the owner of the building said.

There was a pause.

"I'll do you this favor," the owner of the building said. "I'll give you thirty days. After that the sheriff will be here to evict you."

"For Christ's sake—"

I heard the door close.

The harp sent warm, soft, shivery music through the air.

"Capitalist son of a bitch," my father said.

He went back along the hallway. I flushed the toilet and washed my hands and went quickly through the hallway to the kitchen, my heart pounding.

"I want to call Ezra," my mother was saying.

"We don't need Ezra," my father said.

"I want to call him anyway," my mother said.

The door harp came down. The picture of the horses on Prince Edward Island came down. My mother's cousin appeared one evening in his dark suit and dark felt hat and spent a long time in the kitchen, talking to my parents. I helped my mother pack the large barrels and cartons. My father packed the books and magazines and papers. The apartment filled with shadows and echoes. I had bad dreams about Baba Yaga, who had somehow returned to life.

Early one morning burly men climbed the staircase and appeared at our door. Neighbors hung from windows, watching. The men grunted and sweated as they carried our furniture out of the house and loaded it into a van. We moved across the river into the second floor of a narrow two-story brownstone house in a distant part of the city called Brooklyn.

About one week later we moved again—not with furniture and barrels, but with summer clothes, pots and pans, towels and bedding, the door harp, the picture of the horses, and some of my parents' papers and books—to the cottage in the shore section of New York City called Sea Gate, where we had spent the past few summers. My mother had written earlier to Jakob Daw in Canada, giving him our new address in Brooklyn and inviting him to join us in the cottage. He did not reply.

Two

The cottage—three small bedrooms, a kitchen, a small dining room, a parlor—looked out on the sand and the sea. It had a screened-in front porch and a back lawn where grass and scrub brush grew from sandy soil. From the porch I would look eastward and see Rockaway Beach in the distance to my left, and the Atlantic Ocean, and Sandy Hook almost directly before me, and Staten Island to my right. I would come out the front door onto the porch—the front of the cottage faced the beach; the rear of the cottage faced the street—and hear the song of the door harp. Then I would come down off the porch onto the dunes, skirt the wild deutzia shrubs with their white blossoms and green leaves, and walk along the smooth clean yellow-white sand of the sloping beach to the rim of the sea. And there I would often stand for long minutes, looking at the water—at the rhythmic roll and crash of the waves, at the sparkles of sunlight on the curling crests, at the rush of foaming surf. The water was dark green near the shore and deep blue along the horizon. Ships sailed in the blue distance toward the line of sea and sky, freighters moving with such ponderous slowness they seemed fixed in the water. I watched them often that summer and wondered where they were sailing. To the Austria of Jakob Daw? To defeated Ethiopia and my Aunt Sarah? To the Spain that my father and mother and I were now reading about in newspapers and books and magazines?

My room faced the dunes and the sea. In the mornings, through the narrow line of high uncurtained clerestory windows came the pale brightness of dawn and then the fires of the new sun. What enchantment there was in the light and the warmth and the scent of the sand

and the sea! I would listen to the wind in the giant poplars and the young sycamores; to the cries of gulls in the morning stillness; and to the occasional loud, ringing call of a strange bird, a call that sounded like a woman's voice: *Hoo hoo hoo hoo hoo.* I remember waking on our first morning in the cottage in that burning summer of 1936, the sense of newness sharp and pure, and hearing that bird's call, and wondering if it was the bird in Jakob Daw's story. *Hoo hoo hoo hoo,* the bird called as I lay in bed bathed in the morning sunlight. *Hoo hoo hoo hoo ha ha ha.*

Later that morning I went for a walk along the shaded streets of Sea Gate. The air was warm, the sun white in a blue sky. There was little traffic and no concern about unwanted strangers: Sea Gate was fenced and protected. I walked beneath the poplars and sycamores past the empty lots with their dwarf forests of wild grass and low bushes, past the small frame houses built in the twenties and the large, old, wealthy homes with their cupolas and dormer windows and deep wrap-around porches—the homes designed by Stanford White and William Van Allen for the very rich. Sea Gate was a small community, a few hundred homes, a few thousand people, and it contained in the summers I was there—the summers before my father went to Spain and our lives changed—the last remnants of that legendary set of upper-class Protestant pirates, along with the first of the Italians, Greeks, and Jews, as well as atheists, Socialists, Communists, writers, editors, theater people, and their various wives, mistresses, and children.

We were in a small world of sand and sea about ten miles from the heart of Manhattan. A trolley ran through the area to a ferry. The ferry brought you to South Street at the tip of Manhattan. My father would take the trolley and the ferry to the newspaper where he worked. Almost always by the time I woke in the morning he was gone. But he was always back in time for a swim and supper—unless he needed to go out of the city on a story. He would come home carrying three or four newspapers in addition to the one for which he worked, get into his bathing suit, and head across the beach to the water. He was a fine swimmer and would swim very far out, his arms and shoulders and face flashing in the afternoon sunlight. Sometimes my mother would swim with him and I would watch them moving together smoothly in the sea.

I loved the beach and the surf. In front of our cottage a small stone jetty came off the beach at a sharp angle and, together with the low wooden jetty that ran straight from the beach into the water, helped form along the water's edge a shallow tidal pool of gentle surf and smooth wet sand. I would wade in the pool, feeling the tugs of the surf; or I would sit for hours, building tall castles in the sand. I spent much of that summer building castles, sometimes with friends, often alone.

Sometimes in the mornings after breakfast or at night while my parents were talking quietly together, I would look at the newspapers my father brought home. At first I did not understand most of what I read. But certain words and phrases became quickly familiar to me that summer: heat, drought, dust bowl, weather bureau alarmed, rain is needed. Repeatedly I saw the names North Dakota, South Dakota, Minnesota, Montana, Illinois, Virginia. I imagined fields and meadows and hills burning beneath the relentless sun. The same sunlight that I loved to play in here was killing people out west. And the names of all those places were like the names in the stories about westering women told me by Aunt Sarah. How would those women have used their imaginations to save themselves from this cruel sun?

At the end of the first week in July the newspapers said that the temperature in the Midwest had reached 120 degrees. More than one hundred people had died of the heat. My father told us when he returned from the newspaper that day that the heat had begun to move eastward. I sat in my little pool, rebuilding the castle that had been attacked by the night tide and waiting for the heat.

The next day the heat in New York climbed to over 100 degrees. In the late afternoon I stood on the screened-in porch gazing at the beach and the sea. The air was still and hot. Gulls circled slowly overhead, calling. The surf rolled lazily in and out across the sand. There were many people on the beach and in the water. I heard my father's voice from somewhere in the cottage: he had just returned from his work in Manhattan. I heard my mother's voice return his greeting. Then I heard a third voice. I went quickly into the cottage.

"He looks awful," my father was saying to my mother. "Look at him, Annie. We've got to do something about how he looks."

"You chose such a hot day to return," my mother said. "Can I get you a cold drink?"

"The heat in Canada was unimaginable," Jakob Daw said. "To me it seemed the air was burning. Birds would not fly."

"Uncle Jakob!" I called from the kitchen doorway. They had not seen me standing there.

Jakob Daw turned, his pale face startled. Then he broke into a smile.

"Ilana Davita. How good to see you again. Look at your suntan! A Viking with a golden suntan!"

"Here's something cold for you, Jakob," my mother said.

Jakob Daw took the glass from my mother. He arched his gaunt body slightly forward from the waist, put the glass to his mouth, and drank thirstily. His Adam's apple moved up and down on his thin neck. His face was wet with perspiration.

"We have to sit and talk," my father said. "Tanner wants a report on Canada for Tuesday's meeting."

"There is much to talk about. Canada was—interesting."

"How long will you stay with us, Uncle Jakob?" I asked.

"I do not know."

"Will you stay a few days?"

"Oh, yes. At least a few days."

"Can I get you a real drink?" my father asked.

"No, thank you. Another iced tea would be very pleasant, Channah."

"Would you like to see the sand castle I made?"

"I will be happy to see your sand castle, Ilana Davita."

"Let Uncle Jakob sit down and relax now, Ilana," my mother said.

"Would you tell me another story later?"

He looked at me, a weary smile on his pale face. "Of course I will tell you another story. Of course."

That night he was up late with my parents. I could hear them talking quietly on the screened-in porch. The air was hot and humid. I lay in my bed, moist with heat, listening to the distant roll of the surf. Insects lurched wildly against the screens of my windows; I thought the heat must be driving them mad. I slept fitfully and had disquieting dreams, though when I woke I could not be certain what they had been about.

Jakob Daw remained inside the cottage all day. From my castle on the beach I saw him talking with my mother on the screened-in porch. My father had gone to work at his regular writing. During lunch, which my mother served us on the porch, Jakob Daw was silent and withdrawn. He ate very little. How pale and weary he looked. My mother moved about quietly. He fell asleep at the table, breathing raspingly, woke with a start, and glanced quickly around, a frightened look in his eyes. My mother put her hand on his shoulder. He slumped in his chair. A few moments later, he went to bed.

Very late that night—the second Saturday night of July—I was awakened by the sounds of a car pulling into the driveway between our cottage and the empty house across from us. I was bathed in sweat and dazed by the heat. I got out of bed and went to the side window. The shade was up, the curtain open. I peered through the window and saw a long dark car near the side door of the wood-and-brick house that adjoined the driveway. As I watched, the car lights and the engine were turned off. Two men, a woman, and a boy about my age came out of the car. The woman held a baby and went directly into the house, followed by the boy.

The two men began to move cartons and boxes from the car into the house. Lights were being turned on in some of the rooms of the house. By the small light over the side door of the house I saw dimly that one of the men was heavyset and bearded and the other was tall and thin. After a while the tall man climbed back into the car and drove off. The bearded man went into the house.

There was silence. The night pulsed rhythmically with the insect life of the sea's edge. Then the light on the screened-in porch across the way came on. I heard a door open and close and saw the boy come up to the front of the porch and look through the screen at the dark beach. There was a small high curving sliver of blue-white moon. The deep night was bathed in stars. The boy stood there a long time, gazing out at the darkness. He raised both his arms over his head and moved them back and forth a number of times. It was an odd sort of gesture, a pleading of some kind. He lowered his arms to his sides and stood still a moment longer. Then he turned and went back into the house. The porch light was extinguished. The ocean seemed loud and near in the darkness.

I went back to bed. The heat was stifling. Insects flew against my windows. In from the beach drifted low voices: people lay on the sand near the water, driven from their homes by the heat. I thought I heard a muffled cry, and I trembled. *Nothing!* Was it that word again? *Nothing.* And was that my mother's voice now, barely audible, soothing?

A long time later I fell into an exhausted sleep.

The sounds of a door opening and closing woke me. It was early morning. From my window I saw the man and the boy who had come during the night leave the house by the side door and walk toward the street. They wore dark trousers, white shirts, and fishermen's caps. I went back to sleep.

Sunlight woke me. I found my mother in the kitchen. She looked tired. My father and Jakob Daw had gone into Manhattan, she said. What did I want for breakfast?

A letter arrived from Aunt Sarah. The kitchen was too hot and my parents and I were having breakfast on the porch. Jakob Daw was still asleep. My father read the letter aloud. Aunt Sarah was back in Maine, working in a hospital in Bangor. Ethiopia had been very, very bad. She was certain we were aware of what would soon transpire in Spain. How was Ilana Davita? "Be careful of the heat. Drink lots of water and take salt tablets." Maine was cool in the mornings and evenings and lovely even in these very hot days. If the heat of New York ever became intolerable, my parents should consider packing me off to Maine. She sent her love to all of us and a special kiss to Ilana Davita.

"Your sister keeps herself very busy," my mother said.

"She's telling us that she may go to Spain."

"Yes," my mother said. "I understood that."

Jakob Daw came out onto the porch, looking as if he had not slept. "Good morning," he said, and coughed briefly. "The heat is terrible."

"It's terrible everywhere, Jakob," my mother said.

"Except in Maine," my father said.

"Sit down and I'll get you some breakfast," my mother said to Jakob Daw. "Did you sleep at all?"

"No. Early in the morning I fell asleep and was awakened by your neighbors. They seem to be very devout people. They go to synagogue every morning."

"How do you know where they're going?" my father asked.

"The man carries a prayer shawl."

"They're distant relatives of Annie's," my father said.

"The boy is my cousin's son," my mother said. "The man and his wife are the brother and sister-in-law of my cousin's wife, who died recently. They are very religious people. The boy is saying Kaddish for his mother."

"What does Kaddish mean?" I asked.

"A prayer that's said in synagogue every morning and evening for about a year when someone close to you dies."

There was a brief pause.

"Did you know they were coming here to the beach?" I asked.

"Of course. I suggested it. The boy is very upset by his mother's death. His father asked if I would help keep an eye on him. From a distance, of course. What would you like for breakfast, Jakob?"

I looked out our screened-in porch at the empty porch of the adjoining house.

"Michael, are you going to the hunger march?" Jakob Daw asked. "Yes? Then I will come along."

"We can make the noon train to Philadelphia if we leave here inside half an hour."

"I will eat quickly," Jakob Daw said.

"Jakob, you're exhausted," my mother said.

"Yes," Jakob Daw said. "But I will go anyway."

My mother and I spent most of the day on the beach. We swam together for a long time—my father had taught me to swim—and then I worked on my castle. My mother sat on a chair nearby beneath a beach umbrella, reading. She wore a yellow, wide-brimmed sun hat and a dark blue bathing suit, and she looked trim and full-breasted and lovely. I saw the boy who had moved next to us walking across the beach with the bearded man. They wore white short-sleeved shirts and dark trousers rolled up almost to the knees and were barefooted. I watched them step into the edge of the surf. The boy's face broke into a smile. The man bent and embraced him. I turned my attention back to my castle.

We ate supper that evening on the porch in air so sultry it seemed weighted. During our meal we saw the boy and the man come off the porch of their house and start quickly along the driveway, talking in a language I could not understand.

I asked my mother what the word religious meant.

She said it came from an old word that meant to bind, to tie. "Religious people feel bound to their ideas," she said.

I asked her what language the man and the boy had been talking.

"Yiddish," she said, after a moment.

"Is that the language our neighbors use where we moved in Brooklyn?"

"Yes. I spoke it until I came to America. It was the language of my childhood."

"I never heard you speak it."

"I used to speak it sometimes where I worked. There's no need for me to speak it at home."

Later that evening I saw the man and the boy come back up the driveway. The man went into the house through the side door, and the boy climbed up the short flight of wooden stairs to the screened-in porch. The boy stood on the porch, looking thin and pale, and gazed out at the beach and the sky, his nose and mouth pressed against the screen. He raised his arms again in that strange gesture of supplication —lifting them over his head and waving them back and forth. Then he seemed to sense that someone was watching him, and he looked quickly around and saw me. He lowered his arms.

He stared at me a moment, his face pale and without expression. Then he turned and went quickly inside.

That night my mother and I slept outside on blankets on the dunes. There was no breeze and no sound of birds; birds did not fly at night, my mother had once told me. I lay still beneath the stars and listened to the surf. There were many people on the beach that night. I huddled against my mother and imagined I was the ocean. Would the westering women have done that in this heat? Imagined that they were the ocean? I was the waves and the surf, sliding smoothly back and forth, wet and cool, across the moist sand, in and out of the tidal pool where my castle stood. All that hot night I slept with the rhythm of the surf in my ears. Once I thought I heard the sand-muffled beat of horses' hooves, but I knew that had to be a dream. When I woke it was light and gulls circled overhead, crying into the silent air. The ocean was a vast shimmering sheet of silver, and above it the hazy blue sky was piled high with masses of white luminous clouds. There was a faint humid breeze and the strong scent of brine.

My mother stirred and moved against me. She murmured in her sleep, words I did not understand but that sounded like the Yiddish she said she no longer spoke. She opened her eyes.

"Good morning," she said. "How hot it is! Did you sleep well? I had a dream about my grandfather. Did I say something before I woke? Look at the sky, Ilana. How beautiful it is!"

We had breakfast on the porch. I helped my mother with the dishes. The cottage felt large and empty without my father and Jakob Daw. They were away at the hunger march. Starving people were marching on the capital city of Pennsylvania. There was no more money to keep them on relief. About sixty thousand families. My mother had explained it to me. It was the end of capitalism, she had said. The end of a cruel and heartless system. Soon we would see the beginning of a new America, a kinder America, an America under the control of its working class, an America that cared for its poor.

I came out on the porch. Behind me the door harp played its soft melody. The sky had turned pale and there were tall whitecaps now far out on the water. Heaving waves rolled onto the beach, breaking, churning. I looked over toward my private world of tidal pool and castle. Standing near the castle and peering down at it was the thin pale boy from the house across the driveway. I went quickly out of the porch and along the dunes and the beach.

He must have seen me crossing the dunes. He straightened and turned and stood stiffly, watching me hurrying toward him.

"That's my castle," I said. "Don't touch it."

He turned his head slightly so that he was looking past me at the sea. He was about my height. He wore a fisherman's cap and a short-sleeved white shirt and dark trousers rolled up to a little below his knees. His face had a stiff, pinched look. He was barefooted.

"I wasn't going to touch it," he said. His voice was thin and quavery.

"I don't like anyone to touch it."

"But the water goes over it at night."

"No, it doesn't. It only reaches the bottom part."

"Doesn't that get broken?"

"So I build it again. I still don't like anyone to touch it."

"You built this by yourself?" he asked. All the time he talked he did not look at me directly but gazed past me at the sea. "Where do you get ideas for such a thing?"

"From books and magazines. From my—imagination."

"Such things really exist?"

"Sure they exist. In Spain. It's a castle."

"Is Spain a country?"

"Spain is a big country in Europe. Don't you know about Spain? Don't you see the newspapers?"

He looked faintly uncomfortable. "The castle looks like pictures I've seen of places in Yerusholayim. You've never heard of Yerusholayim? It's a very holy city. Jerusalem. The city of King David."

I thought I had heard of Jerusalem.

"You're my neighbor," he said. "I see you on your porch. Do you come here every summer? I don't like it here. There's nothing to do."

"You can go to Coney Island and the boardwalk. You can swim."

"I don't know how to swim. I don't like to swim."

"Why did you come to a beach if you don't like to swim?"

"Everyone said I needed a rest. I needed—air. I needed to get away. Everyone said that."

"Do you live in New York?"

"I live in Brooklyn."

"We just moved to Brooklyn. Just before we came here."

"My name is David," he said, still looking past me to the sea. "David Dinn."

"My name is—Ilana."

"Ilana," he said, then repeated it. "Ilana. That's a Jewish name."

"It was my grandmother's name."

"Are you Jewish?" he asked, turning to look directly at me.

"Yes."

He seemed surprised. "I didn't think you were Jewish."

"Well, I am. Is the baby a boy or a girl?"

"The baby? Oh. A boy."

"I had a baby brother once. But he died. He got sick and he died."

"He's not my brother. He's my cousin. I'm here with my aunt and uncle. My father is too busy with his work to come to the beach. My mother is—my mother is dead." His voice broke and his eyes brimmed with tears. "My mother was a great person and now everyone says she's with the Ribbono Shel Olom, she's with God."

"What does your father do?" I asked.

"He's a lawyer. He works in a big office in Manhattan."

"My father works in Manhattan. He writes for newspapers and magazines."

"Where do your parents come from?"

"My mother is from Europe. My father is from Maine."

"Maine?"

"The state of Maine. It's a state north of—"

"Your father was born in Maine? Where were his parents born?"

"In Maine, too, I think."

"Your father is Jewish?"

"No. My mother is Jewish."

He stared at me.

There was a brief, tense silence.

"I have to go back," he said finally.

"All right," I said.

He turned and went up along the beach and across the dunes to his house.

During lunch I asked my mother if she had said Kaddish when her mother had died.

"Yes."

"And your father?"

She hesitated. "Yes."

"Did you say it when my brother died?"

"No. I didn't believe in it anymore."

We swam together a long time in the afternoon, and then I worked on my castle. I did not see David Dinn. Just before supper Jakob Daw returned, looking white and drained. He had left my father in Harrisburg and had come back alone because he felt ill. His hands trembled and his cough was loud. He was running a fever. He went to bed in the room next to mine and my mother brought him food and medication. I sat on the porch and saw David Dinn and his uncle come out of the house and go along the driveway together and turn into the street.

From the porch that night I watched flashes of lightning over the horizon. Distant thunder rolled in from the sea. The air lay heavy and still. A gust of hot wind stirred the shrubs and trees into life. Then the wind blew in hard and brought with it large, pelting drops of rain. The rain fell with dull thudding sounds on the sand and the trees and the roof of the cottage.

It rained most of the night. I lay in bed and listened to the roar of the wind-lashed surf and wondered how far up the beach it was. I thought I could hear it just below the dunes, foaming and boiling and reaching for our cottage. My mother came into my room and held me and cradled me in her lap and sang to me softly in a language I did not understand. I fell asleep inside her warmth.

In my sleep I thought I heard a man cry out and the soft and soothing voice of a woman. There was a sudden lurid flash of lightning and a booming roll of thunder and again a man's voice cried out, in a language I did not understand. I heard my mother in the room next to mine. Then lightning and thunder followed one upon the other for a long moment in a blinding and deafening cascade of crackling blue-white luminescence and pounding drumbeat noise. I sat up in my bed and stared into the darkness, listening. Whispery sounds came from the corners of my room. I felt again all the old terrors of all the cold nights in the time of our winter wanderings. Lightning crackled and the room leaped into view. The thunder that followed rattled the windows and my bed. I lay in my bed and could not sleep. The whispers went on for a long time. Sometime in the night the storm subsided and became a dull and softly drumming rain. I fell asleep finally to the rhythm of the rain on the cottage and the trees.

I woke early in radiant sunlight. The air was cool, the cottage very still. Somewhere nearby a bird called. *Hoo hoo hoo hoo.* I got out of bed and dressed quickly and went out on the porch. The door harp played softly upon its taut wires.

The sky was clear and blue. Droplets of rain clung to the trees and deutzia shrubs. On the horizon the sun glowed deep red through a low bank of dazzling clouds. The floor of the porch was wet. The air smelled of brine and clean wet sand. All the world of beach and sky and sea lay fresh and clean to the fair day. I walked across the sodden dunes and beach to my tidal pool and my castle.

The walls and turrets had crumbled. The battlements were gone. Towers and ramparts and casements had been reduced to heaps of sand. The wharf and water gate had collapsed. The moat and bridge were indiscernible. The castle which I had built to nearly three feet in height was a flattened ruin.

I was the only one on the beach save for the wheeling gulls. I bent over the wrecked castle and put my fingers into the wet sand. I would build it again. I got down on my knees and began to work the sand.

I worked a long time. The sun climbed high above the horizon and the air grew warm. I had forgotten my dark glasses and felt the sun stinging my eyes. I raised my head at one point and looked across the dunes and saw David Dinn watching me from the porch of his house. Then someone was standing over me. I glanced up and saw Jakob Daw. He wore baggy pants and a rumpled shirt and old shoes encrusted with wet sand. His face was pale and his eyes were dark and weary. He stood there squinting in the sunlight and gazing down at the castle I was trying to rebuild.

"Good morning, Ilana Davita. Your mother and I saw you from the porch. That was a terrible storm."

"It wrecked my castle."

"I see. I am very sorry."

"I have to rebuild it now."

"Your mother asks you to come to breakfast."

"Not now. Are you feeling better, Uncle Jakob?"

"Yes. The fever is gone. It will take you a long time to rebuild this castle, Ilana Davita."

"It's our protection against the Fascists on the other side of the ocean, Uncle Jakob. I have to rebuild it."

He said nothing. I felt his hooded eyes looking at me.

"It's our magic protection. We'll live in it and never move from it. That's why I can't let it be wrecked."

I felt him standing there and looking at me. I worked on the sand. The ocean rolled quietly and rhythmically upon the shore.

Jakob Daw coughed and cleared his throat. Then I heard him ask in his soft and raspy voice, "Ilana Davita, may I help you?"

"Yes," I said.

He bent stiffly over the castle and put his white hands into the sand. His delicate fingers kneaded the sand, shaping it, smoothing it. Overhead in the enormous sky birds wheeled and screamed. A distant freighter moved ponderously toward the horizon. Jakob Daw and I worked together rebuilding my castle.

During those summers in Sea Gate my parents and their friends would meet together regularly in different homes. The night after the storm my mother went to a meeting alone and left me with Jakob Daw, who was tired and did not wish to go out. When I went to bed he was on the porch, writing. From the window near my bed I saw him seated at the table, hunched over his pad. The spectacles he wore when writing gave his face a scholarly look. Insects, attracted by the light, flew against the screen walls of the porch. Through the darkness came the monotonous sounds of the surf. I returned to my bed and sat propped against my pillow, reading a children's book about Spain that I had found during my weekly trip with my mother to the local public library.

There was a faint knock on my door. I called out and the door slowly opened and Jakob Daw came hesitantly into my room. He had seen my light burning, he said. Wasn't I tired from the day's work on the castle? He had promised my mother I would not stay up late. Was there something he could get me? Perhaps a glass of milk? Water? Perhaps I would like to hear a story. People sometimes said that his stories put them to sleep. Yes? A story? Good. Very good.

He sat on the edge of my bed. I put the book down and lay back on my pillow and listened. He spoke quietly in his hoarse voice and sometimes I had to strain to hear his words.

"There was a horse that lived in a narrow valley at the foot of a tall range of mountains. This was a young horse, a beautiful horse, gray in color, all gray, even its eyes and mane and hooves and tail were gray. The grayness had about it a special quality: it glowed with a warm, soft light. Can you imagine such a horse, Ilana Davita? A young, strong, gray horse, shining as it galloped about during the day, shining as it stood asleep during the night. A very beautiful horse.

"In the mountains along the valley lived a herd of black horses. These were powerful creatures who always went racing about in the gulleys and crevices and along the shoulders of the hills. Often the gray horse, hearing the distant beating of their hooves, would look up and see them running along a high ridge, silhouetted against the sky. They were entirely black; their manes were black, their eyes and hooves and tails were black. And the black was a deep black, with no glow, no light, a flat, strong black, like a night without moon or stars. Sometimes it stormed in the hills and the gray horse would see the black horses running in the rain and outlined against the sky when lightning flashed. They were awesome seen like that, running in the lightning and the rain.

"The little valley where the gray horse lived emptied onto a broad, sandy plain. Here lived another herd of horses that grazed peacefully in the oases that grew out of sand watered by underground streams. White was the color of these horses, a white that hurt the eyes. Every part of them was white—their eyes, their manes, their tails, their hooves. Pure, clean, dazzling white. On dark nights their whiteness was seen for miles, each horse a pulsing glow of light. The gray horse would look at the white horses on dark nights and at the black horses during the day and in lightning storms.

"As the years went by, he began to feel more and more disturbed by the thought of being forever between the light of the peaceful white horses and the darkness of the powerful black horses. He did not understand why living that way should disturb him; but he knew it did. Perhaps he felt that he was living in a very dull between-world, and the older he grew the less inclined he was to remain in this state of betweenness. Often it seemed to him that what was especially bad about his own world was the way the horses of the other two worlds went about ignoring his presence. Sometimes the horses from the mountains would gallop through the valley and meet with the horses from the plain. Sometimes the horses from the plain would go roaming through the valley and climb the hills to be with the horses from the mountains. On occasion those meetings would end in whinnies of anger, in bites and kicks. Despite this, they appeared to need one another's presence and continued their visits. But no one seemed to need the gray horse, and all treated him with utter indifference. Sometimes he managed to have a conversation with a white or a black horse and conveyed to them unusual ideas that came to him as he grazed peacefully in his little valley. On occasion he would overhear white or black horses discussing his ideas without letting on where they had originated. He was lonely. Perhaps that was the reason for his unhappiness. There is no feeling more terrible than loneliness, no feeling worse than the sensation of being locked inside your own heart. And so one day he decided to leave his little valley and go off in search of other gray horses like himself."

Jakob Daw fell silent. I felt him very silent on the edge of my bed.

I asked, "Is he like the bird, Uncle Jakob? Is he still looking?"

"No. He is no longer looking."

"What happened to him?"

"He searched a long time and could not find another gray horse. He returned to his valley."

"Is that where he is now?"

"No. He decided one day to join the black horses in the mountains. One night during a terrible storm he was struck by lightning. The lightning burned him black, all black. He was killed. That is the end of the story."

There was a silence. Through my open windows came the murmurous sounds of the surf.

"I don't like that story," I said finally.

Jakob Daw said nothing. He sat on the edge of my bed, one leg crossed over the other, his hands holding his knee. He seemed a faint, wraithlike presence.

"I didn't understand some of the words," I said.

"Ah," he sighed. "In many of my stories the words are complicated."

"And I didn't like the ending."

He sighed again, softly. "Some people do not like my stories when they are without endings; others do not like them when they are with endings. It appears that you do not like them either way. I am very sorry. But never mind. One day I will tell you a story that you will like."

"Why couldn't the horse use magic to change his color?"

"Why couldn't he use magic? Because, Ilana Davita, he lived in a world that was without magic."

"But why was he hit by the lightning, Uncle Jakob?"

"Yes. Why?"

"I liked the gray horse."

"Yes? I liked him, too."

"I wish he didn't have to be hit by the lightning."

"So do I." He got to his feet and stood near the bed and looked down at me. "Now I think I will say good night and you will go to sleep."

"Good night, Uncle Jakob."

I watched him recede into the shadows that filled the corners of my room. The door closed softly.

I dreamed about the gray horse that night. He came into my room, his hooves strangely silent on the wooden floor. He clung to the corner shadows, glowing faintly, his eyes dark, forlorn. Then he moved slowly and soundlessly through the hallway and the living room to the porch and the dunes. He whinnied softly and shook his head, his long mane flowing, his muscled skin rippling. Over the beach flew a small black bird, circling, searching. The gray horse moved down the dunes to the beach and abruptly broke into a gallop. Along the end of the beach there rose a range of dark hills. The gray horse ran along the beach toward the hills. Clouds gathered swiftly over the sea and moved inland. The horse entered the range of hills and began to climb. Drops of rain struck the ground. I heard the rain pelting the sand and falling in the hills. A jagged bolt of lightning tore apart the night sky and struck the gray horse. I heard his cry, saw him stagger, watched him fall to his knees. He lay very still. Overhead the small bird circled for a while over the body of the blackened gray horse. Then it flew off toward the sea and disappeared.

I woke shivering and bathed in sweat. My nightgown was soaked. I pulled it over my head and dropped it on the floor near my bed. Naked, I got out of bed and went out of my room and past the room of Jakob Daw. The door was partly open. He was not in his bed.

I went to the bathroom and returned to my bed. How dark the night was! No moon, no stars. Hot air pulsing with insect life, ocean winds stirring the poplars and the deutzia shrubs. Noises moved through the darkness. The night seemed airy with soft, rhythmic, musical sounds that came drifting in from the other side of the cottage, sounds like wings fluttering, like cicadas singing, like distant laughter, like horses galloping on the yielding sands of a fabled beach.

In the morning the heat was gone and the air was cool. I came out of my room and saw that the door to Jakob Daw's room was closed. I ate breakfast alone and went down to the beach.

An unbroken layer of gray clouds covered the sky. The sea was the color of slate; the beach looked desolate. I worked on my castle. Once I glanced up and saw David Dinn standing on the dunes and watching me. He turned away and went down toward the water, a thin melancholy figure, walking alone on an empty beach, gulls calling overhead, dull gray water breaking and rolling across the smooth wet sand at the ocean's edge.

All that morning my mother and Jakob Daw remained in the cottage. I saw them on the porch, talking together. In the afternoon my mother came out for a swim and Jakob Daw sat on the porch, writing. I played with a few girls my age on the beach. I did not see David Dinn.

My father returned home before supper, tired, grimy, bringing with him newspapers and magazines and the news of serious rumors of revolution in Spain. From the porch I heard him talking inside the cottage with my mother and Jakob Daw. He came out to the porch. "Hello, my love. Why are you out here? How about a hug for your weary dad? No, an ocean of a hug. That's right. *That's* an ocean of a hug!"

All through supper the three of them talked as if I were not there. They talked about a senator who was killed in an automobile crash, about the king of England's near narrow escape from assassination, about a new workers' party that had just been organized in New York State. After supper they went out on the porch and continued talking.

Through the window of my room I saw David Dinn and his uncle emerge from their house and start up the driveway to the street.

I told my mother I was going out for a walk.

"Take along a sweater," she said, and went back to her conversation with my father and Jakob Daw.

I went quickly out of the back door of the cottage and walked to the edge of the sidewalk and looked both ways. There they were, almost a block away, walking together, David Dinn holding his uncle's hand. I waited until they had reached the end of the block. Then I followed, keeping close to the trees in case they should turn suddenly to cross the street. Between the trees and houses I caught glimpses of the beach and the ocean, dull-colored and deserted. The chill air was heavy with the briny scent of the sea.

They stopped at a corner and turned to cross the street. I slid behind a tree. There was no traffic. They crossed and continued up the side street. I crossed carefully and ran to the corner where they had crossed. I turned cautiously into the side street and saw they were nowhere in view.

A long black car went slowly by. A gray cat gazed at me warily from the stoop of an elegant turn-of-the-century house. From somewhere nearby came the voice of a radio announcer. I started quickly up the street. A wind blew in from the sea and I heard it in the trees. I wore a light summer dress beneath my sweater and the wind chilled me as it ran across my legs.

At the next corner I stopped and looked up and down the street and could not see them. I turned to start back to the cottage and saw, coming toward me, two men in dark suits and dark felt hats and dark beards. I let them pass. They turned right at the corner. I went to the corner and saw them enter a beige-colored house.

The house was a small one-story frame building. It stood on a street of empty lots and scraggly trees and similar small houses, some white, others pale brown. Lights shone from its windows. I walked past it and saw over the entrance a sign that read BETH ELOHIM. A narrow porch encircled the building. I heard voices from inside and climbed the stairs to the porch and went to the side of the house. There I stood at an open window, looking in.

I saw a small hall-like room crowded with wooden folding chairs arranged in two sections and separated by a narrow aisle. The chairs faced a podium covered with a purple velvet cloth. On the far wall, facing the chairs, was a closet of some sort covered with a long purple curtain. Near the rear wall stood a curtain seven or eight feet in height and made of muslin held in place by unpainted two-by-fours. The three or four rows of chairs between the curtain and the wall seemed separated from the rest of the room. There were about fifty chairs in the room, and three boys and a dozen or so men, all standing. A middle-aged man stood in front of the podium, chanting in a toneless voice. A lengthy silence followed the conclusion of the chanting. In the front row of chairs David Dinn stood next to his uncle, swaying slightly back and forth as he read from the book in his hands. The man at the podium began to chant again. From time to time there were responses from the others. All were now seated. The man at the podium fell silent. Then two elderly men and David Dinn stood and recited something in near-unison. Again there were responses from the others. David Dinn sat down and leaned his head on his uncle's shoulder. I saw his uncle put an arm around him and hold him in a gentle embrace.

I moved quietly away from the window and down off the porch. It was nearly night. I walked quickly beneath the trees in air that was dark and cold. The trees whispered and moved as if alive in the wind. When I returned to the cottage Jakob Daw and my parents were still on the porch, talking. A huge leftist parade in Paris; Hitler and his accord with Austria; Roosevelt leaving Maine for a two-week vacation cruise aboard his yacht; the Fascists ready to move against the government of Spain. I went into my room to go to bed and through my window saw David Dinn and his uncle come up the driveway and go into their house. My parents and Jakob Daw were still on the porch talking when I fell asleep.

All the next morning my father sat at the kitchen table, writing about the hunger march in Pennsylvania, and Jakob Daw sat at the table on the porch, writing a story. From my castle on the beach I watched Jakob Daw writing. He was in his middle thirties, about the same age as my father, but seemed at times almost an infirm old man. He would remove his spectacles often and rub his eyes. For long periods of time he would stare off into space. He was like my father then: writing and yet not writing. What did he see when he sat staring like that? Ideas? Images? Dreams? His birds and horses?

I asked him over lunch what his new story was about. He smiled tiredly.

"I do not know. There is a young woman in it and a bird and a river. But I do not know what it is about. I have not yet completed it."

I didn't understand how anyone could begin to write a story and not know what it was about.

"In Vienna you wrote stories that even your classmates understood," my mother said.

"I was very young in Vienna," Jakob Daw said. "So was the century."

"My story is about hungry and angry people," my father said. "It's about the beginning of the end of capitalism."

"Perhaps I will not know what my story is about even after I complete it," Jakob Daw said. "Others may have to explain it to me."

"But what kind of story is it if you don't know what it's about, Uncle Jakob?"

"Indeed," Jakob Daw said. "Many ask me that question. I do not have an answer."

In the afternoon my father swam alone for a long time while my mother sat on a chair beneath an umbrella on the beach, writing a letter to Aunt Sarah, and Jakob Daw lay on the bed in his room, resting. I worked on my castle, enlarging it. From time to time my mother would stop writing and gaze out at the sea and I knew she was remembering things from her past that I knew nothing about. It seemed strange to know so little about your own mother. She had had another life across this ocean and in this city before I was born and she never talked of it with me. I watched her sitting on her beach chair gazing at the sea and the sky and the gulls that circled and called overhead.

My father came out of the water and walked up the beach to my mother, his muscular body wet and glistening. He rubbed himself briskly with a towel and lay down on a blanket in the sunlight. I saw my mother look at him and then continue her letter to Aunt Sarah.

Later, working on my castle, I looked up and noticed David Dinn wading in the surf a few yards from the far jetty. He wore dark trousers and a white shirt. He seemed fearful of the water and, hitching up his trousers as far as they would go, danced quickly back from an onrush of surf in the wake of a sudden tall wave. I watched him for a while and turned back to my castle.

A shadow fell across the sand near my fingers. I looked up. David Dinn stood gazing down at the castle.

"It's nice," he said. "It's very nice."

"I'm not done with it."

"I like the way you did the tops of the walls." He was pointing to the embrasures in the parapets. His voice was shy, hesitant. His trousers were rolled up and I could see his thin, pale, sand-encrusted feet. "What's this on the outside?"

"A turret."

"And this?"

"A tower."

"And what do you call this?"

"A wharf."

"And this?"

"That's called a drawbridge."

"How do you know all those names?"

"I saw them in books."

A vaguely approving look came into his eyes. "In books," he echoed softly, then was silent a moment, looking down at the castle. "What do you call this thing here?"

He was pointing to the carving I had made in the large door over the drawbridge.

"That's a door harp."

He gazed uncertainly at the carving.

"It plays music when you open and close the door. It gives you a good feeling."

"Do castles have door harps?"

"I don't know. My castle does. We have one in our house. It belongs to my father."

"Is it like a mezuzah?"

"What's that?"

"It's something we put on the side of a doorpost. It reminds us of God."

"A door harp has nothing to do with God. It just plays nice music. We don't believe in God."

He turned from the castle and fixed his eyes on me. He said nothing. His eyes were dark and sad. I was reminded of the sadness in my Aunt Sarah when I once told her we never celebrated Christmas.

"I have to go back," he said.

"Okay."

"I really like your castle."

"Thanks."

"You made it bigger this time."

"That's for protection against another storm."

"Did the storm scare you?"

"Yes."

"The last time there was a storm like that, we were in the mountains. A year ago. My mother came into my room. That was a nice summer." He stopped and stared at the castle. He grimaced and for a long moment held his lower lip between his teeth. "I miss my mother. It hurts inside me. Everyone says it will go away, but it doesn't."

I didn't know what to say.

"I have to go back," he said. "My aunt will worry about me."

"Listen," I said. "Do you know that your father and my mother are cousins?"

"Sure I know. I have to go back and eat supper and go to shul to say Kaddish. You really don't believe in God?"

"No. My mother says that God is—"

"I'm going," he said. "I really like your castle."

He turned and walked off. I watched him go back up the beach to the dunes, thin-shouldered and a little stooped. He looked like a small Jakob Daw.

The evening was warm. Insects droned in the darkening air. We had been invited to a supper meeting in one of the elegant homes on nearby

Highland Avenue. My father had on a suit; my mother wore a lovely pale blue summer dress with half-sleeves; even Jakob Daw was dressed in a suit and tie. I felt uncomfortable and out of place in a blue dirndl skirt and white blouse.

The house—old, white, gabled, and three-storied—had a deep encircling red-brick porch and tall dormer windows. The woman who met us at the door was tall and bony and very old. She had large watery blue eyes and networks of wrinkles on her cheeks and lips. Her name was Mrs. Greenwood. She wore a long dark cotton dress and a string of white pearls. She greeted my parents warmly and seemed a little flustered in the presence of Jakob Daw. "So good of you to join us, Mr. Daw. An honor to have you in my home. Do come in. There are others so eager to meet you. And how are you, young lady? Ilana Davita. What a charming name. There is a young girl here from Spain, about your age, I believe. Do come in, please."

We went through the entrance hall into a spacious living room furnished with ornately carved mahogany chairs and sofas. A wine-colored carpet covered the floor. On the walls were gilt-framed oil paintings and a large rectangular mirror which hung from the ceiling molding by two tasseled cords. A yellow cat lounged on a cushion before the stone fireplace and regarded the crowd out of enormous green eyes.

Seated alone on a sofa in a corner of the living room was a girl about my age. She was olive-skinned, had long dark braided hair and large dark eyes and wore dark shoes and a light purple dress with a white lace collar. She sat primly on the sofa, looking lonely and forlorn, her feet dangling above the carpeted floor.

I wandered about by myself. From the living room came my father's loud voice. I went through rooms with leather chairs and deep sofas and tasseled portieres and tall heavily draped windows. No one noticed me going up the carpeted staircase. I wandered through neat sitting rooms, lovely dressing rooms, resplendent bedrooms. There were no bookshelves anywhere. I wondered where the books were kept. I couldn't remember ever having been in a house that had no books.

I was startled by a burst of applause from downstairs. I went quickly through the carpeted second-floor hallway and down the staircase and slipped unnoticed into the living room. Guests stood about in a rough semicircle in front of Mrs. Greenwood, who was introducing Jakob Daw. "He has come from Europe on a special mission, and we are so pleased to have him in our home tonight." There was more applause. "We have with us too," Mrs. Greenwood went on, "Mr. Michael

Chandal, the renowned journalist, and his wife, Anne Chandal, an acknowledged authority on the writings of Marx and Engels. We will be hearing from our guests later this evening. But now I should like to invite you all to our buffet supper. Please, do help yourselves."

People moved toward platters of food decorously arranged on marble side tables along two walls of the dining room. A crystal chandelier glowed over the huge, elegantly set center table. I heard talk about Roosevelt and his cruise off the coast of Maine. Someone said, "Debs? Debs was a great man and a great thinker." Someone else said, "That's right, a thinker and a drinker." I heard my father's loud barking laugh. My mother was talking to a small group of men and women who were listening intently to her words. Someone brought me over to a small table in a corner of the dining room where the children were to sit. Three boys and the olive-skinned girl sat at the table. The boys were older than I and talked among themselves.

The girl sat staring down at her food and not eating.

"Hello," I said. "My name is Ilana Davita."

She looked at me. "I am called Teresa," she said in an accent I had never heard before.

"Where are you from?"

"Madrid."

"Where's that?"

"España."

"What's España?"

"Spain."

I stared at her. "When did you come?"

"Tres días—three days ago. I come here only three days ago con mia madre y padre—with my mother and father. A long ride on a boat. A very bad storm."

"Is there war in Spain?"

"I am—how you say?—I am afraid all the time in Madrid. There is shooting. All day and all night men with guns on our street. I see this. Men—how you say?—yelling and shooting their guns. My cousin is killed on the street in front of our house. Twenty years old. I see his body."

She lapsed into silence and gazed down at her food, her eyes dark and expressionless. Loud words from the center table moved through the large room. Franco. Rebellion. War.

Later, the people went with their coffee cups into the living room and sat down in the folding chairs that had been arranged in neat rows. In the dining room servants quickly cleared the remnants of the buffet supper from the tables.

Mrs. Greenwood stood in front of the guests and thanked them for coming. She wanted them to meet a young girl who had just arrived from Spain, she said. Her parents were now in Washington because of some difficulty with the immigration people and therefore could not be with her tonight. "Friends, this is Teresa. Please tell us about yourself, dear child."

Teresa was sitting in the front row between me and Jakob Daw. She slid down from her chair and went slowly over to Mrs. Greenwood and turned to face the group of thirty or so people in the room. She looked frightened and frail and she spoke in a hesitant voice, her head lowered, her eyes fixed on the carpeted floor.

"I live in España, in Madrid. I am afraid all the time. There is shooting in Madrid. My father says the Fascists will kill us all. All night there is shooting. My cousin is killed by Fascists on the street in front of our house. I see the holes in his face. He is twenty years old. My mother screams and cries and says we must go to America or the Fascists will kill us. My father says to tell you he hopes we will—how you say?—we will remain in America and not be sent back to Spain. My mother says to thank you for your—como se dice?—for your hospitality. Muchas gracias."

She stopped. There was silence. She looked up at Mrs. Greenwood.

"Thank you so much, dear child," Mrs. Greenwood said very quietly.

Teresa sat down between me and Jakob Daw and put her hands in her lap. She looked straight ahead, blinking her eyes rapidly. A sheen of sweat lay upon her face and wisps of her hair looked pasted to her forehead. She kept looking straight ahead and blinking her eyes.

Mrs. Greenwood asked my father if he would say a few words to the meeting. My father rose and faced the group. He was an awkward and halting speaker, unable to carry over his normal joviality into the formality of a public talk. He never knew what to do with his hands; he kept moving them in and out of the pockets of his pants. He cleared his throat and said he would try to fill everyone in on the latest news. Telephone service between Spain and Paris had been cut, he said. This was true also of telephone service between Spain and London as well as Spain and Lisbon. There were reports that a revolt had broken out. No one knew as yet how serious it was. "My own feeling is that we're seeing the start of a long civil war. I think that Germany and Italy will probably come in on the side of Franco. The only power that will stand against the Fascists will be Russia. The British, the French, the Americans won't lift a finger to help Spain. The alternatives are going to be an active alliance either with communism or with fascism, or neutrality—which will be the same as a passive alliance with fascism. And we know what choice decent people will make. That's the way things look to me. I'll be happy to try to answer your questions."

There were some questions. After a while he sat down. I saw he was sweating. My mother put her fingers on his arm. He slumped back in his chair.

Mrs. Greenwood was introducing my mother and talking about a man called Angelo Herndon and some people named Scottsboro and about the Unemployment Insurance Bill and the Social Workers Conference. "Here is our own very special Anne Chandal," she said.

My mother stood and faced the audience.

I almost never understood anything my mother said when she spoke before a group. She would be seated in a chair or, like tonight, be standing, and she would start by saying something like, "Capitalism and humanism are contradictory concepts," or, "Marx states that the bourgeoisie tends to regard the wife as an instrument of production," or, "Engels makes the point that the modern family is based on the domestic enslavement of the woman"—and I would be unable to follow her words. My father, normally effusive and gregarious, talked dully and drily about facts; my mother, normally gentle-voiced and reticent, talked dramatically and excitedly about ideas.

My mother had begun to speak. I glanced at Teresa. She sat stiffly with her hands in her lap, her face impassive. Her eyes had ceased their nervous blinking. What was it like, guns and screams and shooting and your cousin dead on the street? I could not imagine it. I put my fingers on her arm and pressed gently. She stared at me in sudden alarm and jerked her arm away.

I looked at my mother. "Let no one misunderstand us," she was saying. "When the proper time comes we will be as prompt with action as we are now with words. Thank you for your attention."

There was a loud burst of applause. My mother returned to her chair, her face flushed. The applause went on for another minute or two, then came to an end.

Mrs. Greenwood introduced Jakob Daw. "He has come to America from Europe on a special mission to raise funds for an international anti-Fascist organization which he and other writers are establishing to help writers whose lives have been shattered by Hitler. Mr. Jakob Daw."

Jakob Daw rose slowly and stood before the group. He put on his silver-rimmed spectacles and removed from an inside pocket of his jacket a sheaf of papers.

"I am a writer of stories," he said quietly in his raspy voice. "A writer is a strange instrument of our species, a harp of sorts, fine-tuned to the dark contradictions of life. A writer is uncomfortable making speeches. I have made many speeches these past weeks. You will please forgive me if tonight, instead of making another speech, I read you a story I have just completed." He coughed and put his hand to his lips. "A very brief story. Is that acceptable to you? Yes? Thank you."

He peered at the papers in his hands, bending over them. His hands shook slightly. I glanced at my mother and saw on her face awe, anticipation, eagerness. She noticed my glance and turned her head away. A deep crimson flush rose from her neck and spread across her face. My father sat slumped in his chair, his arms folded across his chest.

"Here is my story," I heard Jakob Daw say. "Please forgive my occasional cough. It is an old cough and seems not to have improved despite your sunshine and warm weather.

"Now for my little story.

"A young woman lived alone on the grassy slope of a wide river. She had come to this slope after an immense journey from the dark lands of her childhood. She was a lovely woman, a girl really, with legs naked and slender as those of a crane, with skin the color of ivory, with hair long and yellow as the sun, a girl gentle and kind and outwardly at peace on this slope beside this wide, clear, calm-running river.

"Along the slope grew an unusual lilylike flower. Its outer leafy sepals were dark blue, its inner whorl of scented petals were pale blue, its stem was light purple. When dried and crushed, this flower yielded an exquisite fragrance. The girl would gather these flowers, dry them in a large ceramic dish, grind them between two smooth white stones, and sell the powder to the matrons in the nearby village.

"No one in the village knew where she had come from. No one in the village could remember when the little cottage in which she lived had been built. Nor could anyone recall who had built it. They would watch her come along the village street of an afternoon with her straw basket filled with the little paper packets of fragrance. She asked next to nothing for the packets and would soon be returning along the village road with her basket empty. She would follow the road along its curving path through a meadow of tall grass and wild shrubs. Then the grass would fall away and the ground would begin to slope downward toward the river. And there in the midst of the sloping earth, in an expanse of emerald grass that grew thick and never too tall, was the cottage. She would go inside and not be seen until the following morning when she would emerge and once again pick the flowers which she would then crush into the fragrant powders she brought daily to the village.

"One day a small black bird flew over the village. He circled the village twice, searching carefully, for he was on a quest. He had reason to believe that the eternal inner music of the world was the cause not of joy, as nearly all believed, but of great harm. For by comforting the pangs that often come in the wake of harm, the music dulled the conscience of man, eased the commission of evil. So this little bird believed, this bird with the shiny black body and the tiny red dot under each of his eyes. If he could find the source of the music he might discover a way of bringing it to an end and thereby awaken the world to the horror of truth and the need to live by its demands.

"On that day, as the bird circled the village the second time, he saw the girl. It seemed to him that she gave off a light visible even in the brightness of day. He circled again, watching as the girl sold her packets of fragrance, watching the trail of light she left behind: the very air through which she passed seemed to brighten by her presence. And the music seemed especially strong in the landscape around the village. He followed the girl to her cottage, and there the music was stronger than he had ever heard it before. Could this girl and her cottage be the source of the world's eternal music? The bird alighted on the roof of the cottage, prepared to wait and see.

"Many days passed. Each morning the girl picked and ground her flowers. Each afternoon she sold her packets in the nearby village. But as the days went by, the bird began to notice that she went to the village later and later each day. He noticed a weariness coming upon her shoulders, a slowness in the way she picked and ground the flowers, a reluctance to walk the path to the village, a heaviness in her legs as she moved about the slope, a growing darkness in the sockets of her eyes. And one day she rose and came out of the cottage and did not pick any flowers. Instead, she went down to the edge of the river and gazed into its clear, gray-blue, silently rushing water. She turned and with dark and solemn eyes stared up the slope at her cottage. Then she turned again and looked deeply into the water. And once again she turned and looked yearningly toward the cottage. She seemed to be measuring the steepness of the slope. Then the bird heard her murmur sadly, wearily, 'I cannot endure the slope.'

"She thrust her hand into the water.

"The surface of the water congealed, turned brown and bracken. An odor rose from it, a foul and stinking putrescence. The girl turned and walked slowly up the slope and along the path through the meadow and the street through the village and was never seen again.

"The little bird understood that this lovely girl was not the source of the world's eternal music and flew off to continue his search."

Jakob Daw stopped and looked up from the papers in his hands. "That is my story. Thank you."

I saw the tremor in his hands as he folded the papers and stuffed them back into the inside pocket of his jacket. In the large room was a silence so palpable it had the density of stone. I glanced around. People were staring at him in utter bewilderment. Mrs. Greenwood sat in a front row chair with her lips fixed in a tiny frozen smile.

Jakob Daw went slowly to his chair and sat down. His face was white. He was removing his spectacles when my father and others began to applaud. My mother sat white-faced and motionless. The applause died away.

Mrs. Greenwood rose and stood before the group, looking very old and full of authority. She began to talk about the need to help the government of Spain. She said that in the coming months more and more meetings of this kind would take place all over the country. "If Spain falls to the Fascists," she said, "Hitler and the others will soon attempt further conquests and our very civilization will be threatened. We are at a crossroads and we need your help."

Behind me a man stood and began to talk about Franco. He said he was giving money to stop the Fascists in Spain now and to keep them from infesting America. A woman rose and spoke about the Italian invasion of Ethiopia. They had used poison gas, she said. And terrible explosives. Against tribesmen on horses.

Teresa slid down off her chair and went from the room. She went quickly into the entrance hall and up the staircase. I watched her legs climbing the staircase—the rest of her cut off by the top of the living room doorway; spindly legs in knee-length white socks and shiny black shoes.

I listened to another brief talk and the announcements of contributions. Jakob Daw was sitting with his eyes closed. From time to time a tremor ran across his face. My father was slumped back in his chair, arms folded across his chest, his long legs stretched out before him. My mother sat very still, staring straight ahead, her face flushed.

I whispered to my mother that I needed to go to the bathroom and slipped quietly from my chair and went upstairs.

I went from room to room and could not find Teresa. There was no one in the hall bathroom. I started back toward the staircase. Passing the open door of a bedroom into which I had looked before, I heard a low, keening sound. I stopped and listened. It was coming from behind the open door. I stepped inside and peered behind the door and saw her sitting on the floor against the wall near the corner of the room, her arms around her legs, her chin on her knees, her eyes closed. She was rocking slowly back and forth, hugging herself tightly. A low, soft, tremulous wail came from her lips and filled the dimness of the large bedroom like an icy mist.

I was frightened and didn't know what to say. She seemed unaware of my presence. I called her name.

Her eyes flew open. She stiffened and immediately ceased her rocking.

"Can I get you something? Are you all right?"

She sat there, staring at me.

I put a hand on her arm. Her skin felt hot and moist. She was trembling.

"No touch me!" She pulled her arm away. Her eyes were wide and wild-looking. She pushed herself back against the wall.

"I won't hurt you," I said. "I'm sorry if you thought I would hurt you."

"No pity me!" she said in a high, thin voice.

"What?"

"Puta Americana!" she said, her eyes raging. "Hija de puta! Santa María, ayúdame!"

I backed out of the room and went down the stairs. I was cold and could hear clearly the pounding of my heart.

The meeting had ended. People were standing about. I moved slowly through the living room, listening to the talk. Some were beginning to leave.

"Ilana, my dear!" Mrs. Greenwood called. "Your mother is looking for you."

I thanked her. "Is Teresa sick?" I asked.

"Sick? Why?"

I told her what I had seen upstairs.

"Thank you, Ilana. I will tend to her."

"Hello, my love," I heard my father call. He came up to me. "Where have you been? Your Uncle Jakob is tired and wants to leave."

People stood all around us. I listened to them talking. We were near the door.

"So good of you to have come," Mrs. Greenwood said. "A most successful evening. You must come over again soon, Mr. Daw, and explain your little story to me. Thank you so much."

Jakob Daw nodded and bowed slightly, his face ashen. I had never seen him so tired.

I took my mother's hand. Her skin was hot.

We came out onto the street. A moist warm wind blew in from the sea and stirred the leaves of the poplars. There was no traffic. We walked four abreast in the street beneath the embowering trees. The street lamps threw queer shadows onto the asphalt.

"I'm very tired, Michael," my mother said.

"It's just another couple of blocks," said my father.

"What does raped mean?" I asked.

I saw them look at me.

"I heard a man say Teresa was raped."

They did not respond. We walked along beneath the trees.

"Mama?"

"It means to hurt someone very, very badly," my mother said in a voice I could barely hear.

"Is it an old word?"

"One of the oldest," said my father.

"She was so scared," I said. "She made strange sounds."

We walked on awhile longer together in silence.

"I'm terribly tired, Michael," my mother said.

"Almost home, Annie," said my father. "One more block."

"Ilana Davita," Jakob Daw said abruptly. "Did you like my story?"

"I think I did, Uncle Jakob. But why did the girl go away from her cottage and the village?"

"Indeed, why?"

"I liked the part about grinding the flowers and then selling them in the village."

"Yes?"

"But I didn't understand the part about the slope."

"A slope is the most difficult of things to understand, Ilana Davita."

We continued along together on the dark, humid street. My mother held tightly to my father's arm. We walked in and out of the shadows of trees and I could not clearly see her face.

"We raised a lot of money tonight," my father said.

There was no response. Approaching the cottage, we heard the sounds of voices singing. We went up the path to the back door of the cottage. The singing was coming from the narrow driveway.

My mother stopped at the door and listened. Then she opened the door and we went inside.

I came out onto the screened-in porch and listened to the wind and the surf. I looked at the porch of the house across the driveway and saw four people seated around a table: David Dinn, his aunt and uncle, and a man I did not recognize at first. He wore a dark suit, a white shirt and dark tie, was clean-shaven, and had thick dark hair and chiseled features. David Dinn's uncle too had on a dark suit and tie. His aunt wore a white dress with a high lace collar and long sleeves; a kerchief covered her hair. They sat around the table singing a slow and mournful-sounding tune. David Dinn, wearing a short white-sleeved shirt open at the throat, sat with his eyes closed, swaying slightly back and forth in his chair. He had a high, thin voice. I could hear him clearly above the deeper voices of the men and the soft, subdued voice of his aunt.

My parents and Jakob Daw came out onto the porch.

I asked my mother what the people on the other porch were singing.

"Zemiros," she said. "They sing special songs with their Shabbos meals."

"Isn't that Ezra?" asked my father, peering through the screen.

"Yes."

"Is he up here for the weekend?"

"Yes."

"How is the boy?"

"Not good."

They were speaking quietly so as not to disturb the singing. The tune came to an end and another followed. Moths fluttered against the screens. The dunes and the beach were dark and murmurous with the sounds of the wind and the sea.

"I used to sing like that," my mother said.

"That's a nice picture, Annie," said my father. "You and your father singing together like that and swaying."

"Not my father. My grandfather. Shall we go inside?"

As we came into the cottage the music of the door harp mingled softly with the singing from the next house.

My mother asked me to put myself to sleep. The three of them sat in the kitchen, drinking coffee and talking. I went over to the small book-case in the living room where my parents kept the books they brought with them for the summer and took down my mother's dictionary. I went through it carefully, as she had taught me earlier that year when we had searched for the meaning of the word utopia. I found the word I had heard the man use about the girl called Teresa. I read carefully and did not understand and looked up some more words. It took a while before I was able to form some image in my mind of what I thought the word meant. All the time I was going through the dictionary I heard the loud voice of my father and the weary voices of my mother and Jakob Daw.

I closed the dictionary and went into my room and lay on my bed. I did not really understand the word but I knew it was something terrible and I wondered how your imagination helped you if you were hurt that way. After a while I got off the bed, undressed, and went to the bath-room. My parents were still in the kitchen with Jakob Daw. I heard the words Spain and correspondent a number of times, and the most dread word of all: war. I washed, brushed my teeth, and went back to my room. In my bed I lay thinking of Teresa and listening to the singing from the nearby porch.

The next morning my father and Jakob Daw took the ferry to Man-hattan. Later I walked with my mother to Coney Island. The air was hot and the beach was jammed. We sauntered along the crowded board-walk, took some of the rides, had taffy and cold drinks. I rode on the carousel with my mother, both of us moving up and down on our horses. I thought of the picture of the horses in my parents' bedroom. We ate hot dogs and in the early afternoon saw Charlie Chaplin in *Modern Times.* The movie theater was crowded. I saw Charlie Chaplin caught in the gears of the giant factory machine. "That's how bosses treat their workers," my mother said to me when we came back out into the eye-stinging afternoon sunlight. "Like pieces of machinery, not like human beings."

We walked together in the sunlight and tumult of the hot afternoon.

Later we returned to Sea Gate and swam together and I came out of the water and worked on my castle. I looked up and there was David Dinn a few feet away, dressed in dark trousers and a white short-sleeved shirt, watching me.

"Hello," I called to him. "Come on over."

He came hesitantly, glancing over his shoulder, his bare feet looking white and bony on the moist sand.

"I heard you singing last night. I liked the melodies."

His face looked blotched. Skin was peeling from his nose.

"Did you go to your synagogue this morning?"

"Yes."

"I was asleep. Don't you want to go in for a swim? There are long bathing suits you can put on if you don't want to look too naked."

He stared at me.

"I'll take you in if you're afraid. I'm a good swimmer. My father taught me to swim."

"I can't swim today. It's Shabbos. A Jew doesn't swim on Shabbos. It's a holy day."

"I'm sorry, I didn't know that."

"A Jew shouldn't build castles out of sand on Shabbos, either."

I looked at my castle, tall and golden in the afternoon sunlight. "I'm not a religious Jew."

"Shabbos is for all Jews," he said.

"I'll take you in swimming tomorrow, if you want."

"My father is leaving tomorrow."

"I'll take you in after he goes."

"I won't feel like it." He turned abruptly and started up the beach. Still walking, he pivoted and called out to me, "You shouldn't build your castle on Shabbos. It's wrong. You keep the Messiah from coming."

I watched him cross the dunes and go into his house. He seemed to leave behind him a heavy wake of sadness.

My father and Jakob Daw returned from the city and came down to the beach. It was late afternoon and still hot, the sun high and pale orange in a milk-white sky. My father, wearing his bathing trunks, called out, "Hello, my love!" and went into the water with my mother. Jakob Daw, dressed in baggy pants and a shirt, watched as I shaped some final towers on my castle.

"It is beautiful," he said. "I have never before seen such a sand castle."

"Uncle Jakob?"

"Yes?"

"Will there be a war in Spain?"

"There already is a war in Spain."

"Are you going back to Europe?"

"Yes."

"When?"

"Very soon."

"But there's a war in Europe."

"Europe is my home, Ilana Davita."

"Uncle Jakob, were you religious when you grew up in Europe?"

He did not answer. The sun shone full upon his face, giving his pale skin a yellowish translucent look. He seemed ghostlike, insubstantial.

"Uncle Jakob?"

"I was once very religious," he said.

"Was my mother?"

He looked off toward the sea. There were many bathers in the water. I could not see my parents.

"You will have to ask your mother." He coughed briefly. "Now I think I will take a little walk along the beach. It is a beautiful day."

"Did you know my mother in Europe?"

"Yes. We were good friends."

"Was that when she went to school in Vienna?"

He looked surprised. "Yes. We were together in Vienna, in the high school, the gymnasium. Your mother told you about that? It was during the World War."

"There was another war?"

"Oh, yes. There have been many wars."

"Were you in that war, too?"

"Yes." He coughed again. "Now I will go for my walk, Ilana, before the sun sets and the air becomes too damp. We will talk more later if you wish."

He went off across the beach toward the distant jetty, walking stiffly in the pull and yield of the sand, his hands clasped behind his back. I watched him until I could no longer make him out. Low overhead a biplane flew languidly along the shoreline and, off in the distance, freighters sat heavily upon the line of pallid horizon. The surf lapped at my feet, cold and foamy and dense with seaweed. I thought, If the ocean ends in Europe, then I'm now connected to Europe. I stepped back out of the surf and stood looking out across the ocean at the far-off freighters. After a while I felt tired and went back across the beach and the dunes to the cottage.

All through supper they talked about Spain and social fascism and the third period. I sat quietly, listening to the urgency in their voices, and then no longer wanting to hear anything. Standing on the porch, I saw David Dinn and his father and uncle leave their house. I recognized his father as the urbane and courteous gentleman who had visited my parents now and then in our various apartments. David Dinn noticed me and raised a hand in greeting. They went along the driveway and turned into the street.

My mother came into my room that night as I was getting ready for bed.

"You were so quiet during supper, Ilana. We didn't pay much attention to you. I'm sorry, darling. Were you upset by all our talk about war?"

"Yes."

"I'm so sorry."

"Is Uncle Jakob going away soon?"

"Yes. On Monday."

"To Europe?"

"Yes."

"But there's a war in Europe."

"He has work to do, Ilana. We each have work to do."

"Did Uncle Jakob fight in that other war?"

She hesitated. "Yes."

"Was it a bad war?"

"There are no good wars, Ilana."

"I mean, was Uncle Jakob hurt in that war?"

"Yes. He was gassed. They poisoned the air. His lungs were badly hurt."

"Like they did in Ethiopia?"

"Yes."

"Mama, were you religious in Europe? Uncle Jakob said he was very religious in Europe."

"Yes," she said after a moment. "I was religious when I lived in Europe."

"The religious boy next door said I shouldn't build my castle on Shabbos. It's a very special day."

"I'll have to ask my cousin to talk to his son. What did you tell him?"

"I said we weren't religious."

"That's right, Ilana," my mother said. "We'll build the new world in our own way. The old way is false."

"I like their songs, though, Mama."

"Yes? That's nice, darling. Now I want you to go to sleep. It's late."

"Their songs are pretty, Mama."

"There is a lot more to them than their songs, Ilana. The ideas they live by are false."

I was very tired. The boardwalk and the carousel and the movie and the swimming and the castle. A long day in the sun on the margin of the sea.

"Good night, Mama."

"Good night, darling."

I felt her kiss. Cool and dry. She went from my room.

In my sleep I heard a cry and the shuffle of feet and the opening and closing of doors and a man's voice calling and my mother responding. Through my window I saw lights in the next-door house and my mother hurrying across the dunes with David Dinn's father and disappearing into the house. I was very sleepy. I heard the roll of the ocean and the whispers of the wind. I slept again. A shout woke me. I heard the voices of Jakob Daw and my father and thought they were on our porch. My head felt weighted; I could not lift it from my pillow. My room seemed to fill with whispers and shadows from the world of Baba Yaga. I was still awake when my mother came back to the cottage. I heard her talking on the porch with my father and Jakob Daw about David Dinn, but I did not understand what she was saying. I fell back asleep. In the morning it all seemed a dream and no one said anything about the strange dark music of that night.

David Dinn came down to the beach that afternoon. He wore a cap and a full-length bathing suit over which was a white cotton garment that was open at the sides. It hung over his shoulders and came down across his chest and back. From each of the four corners of the garment dangled a long woolen fringe. He looked pale and thin. He was carrying a large towel. He walked over to where I was completing my castle and said nervously, "Hello. I can go swimming. Can you go in with me?"

"Sure," I said, glancing back up across the beach and the dunes. His father was watching us from inside their porch.

David Dinn spread the towel neatly on the sand and put his cap on it. He removed the white garment, folded it with care, and placed it next to the cap. The air was hot and the beach was crowded. I walked into the surf and felt the chill touch of the water on my legs. I turned and saw David Dinn hesitating on the edge of the ocean, staring at the water. I went back and took his hand. He looked surprised and tried to shake free. I held on and pulled him with me.

"Come on," I said. "It's cold at first, but you get used to it. Come on! I'll show you how to ride the waves."

He let me lead him into the water. He shivered with the cold and cried out as a wave broke too high against us and nearly knocked him off his feet. His face was white with fear. But I held on to him and soon the sea felt warm and we went deeper into the waves and I showed him how to ride the crests, how to anticipate the swells, how to jump as they billowed, what to do when they crashed and came rushing toward us in a charging cascade of foaming water. We held hands and jumped up and down in the water, riding the waves. Then a wave broke high over our heads and I stood poised, facing the beach, waiting for the wall of water. It struck us solidly and I was caught in its churning thrust and saw David Dinn go under, come up gasping, and go under again. I pushed against the swirl of the water and stood and looked quickly around. There he was, a few feet away, coughing. I ran over to him through knee-high water.

"Are you okay?"

"I swallowed some water." He coughed again. "I'm fine. We better go out."

"All right."

On the beach he asked me to hold his cap and cotton garment as he quickly dried himself. His lips were blue and he was shivering. He wrapped the towel around himself and took the cap and garment.

"Thanks," he said. "That was fun. I liked it."

He started up the beach toward the dunes. I looked at the house and saw his father still standing on the screened-in porch, watching.

We ate supper on the porch. I sat quietly and listened to my parents and Jakob Daw talk about Hitler and Franco and the rebellion in Spain. They talked about Roosevelt sailing his yacht off Nova Scotia—"That's not far from Prince Edward Island," my father said—and about something that had taken place in a city called Danzig.

A car came up the driveway and stopped. In the adjoining house the side door opened and David Dinn and his aunt and uncle stepped out. My parents and Jakob Daw went on talking. David Dinn's father was dressed in a dark suit and a dark felt hat. He put down the suitcase he carried and embraced his son. They were locked in that embrace a long time. Then he climbed into the car and it drove off. David Dinn stood awhile with his aunt and uncle, looking at the empty driveway. He turned and saw me watching him. He was crying. He followed his aunt and uncle back into the house.

My father went into Manhattan after supper and my mother and Jakob Daw sat on the porch, talking. I wandered alone on the beach, my bare feet in the cool sliding surf. The ocean rose and fell with fearful and monotonous power. Along the line of the horizon the day had already become night; stars shone, a crescent moon was rising. From the trees beyond the dunes came the call of the bird I was never able to see. *Hoo hoo hoo hoo hoo.* I passed my castle. The tide had filled its moat and now surged against its bastion and outworks. I would repair it in the morning. A chill wind blew in from the sea. I returned to the cottage.

Jakob Daw knocked on the door of my room that night and came in and sat on the edge of my bed. He looked very tired and the tremor was still in his hands.

"I came in to say good-bye to you," he said quietly. "I am leaving very early in the morning."

I sat up in my bed. "Are you going back to Europe?"

"Yes."

I was quiet.

Jakob Daw coughed briefly. "Ilana Davita, it has been a pleasure to meet you and get to know you. I wish you a good life."

"Will you come back to America?"

"I do not know. It would be pleasant. But I have never done the pleasant things. Still, it would be very pleasant to return to America. This is a great land. But Americans do not know what to do with its greatness. It will all be wasted." He looked at me. "Do you understand what I am saying? Sometimes I forget that you are only a child."

I said nothing.

He leaned toward me and gave me a shy, awkward embrace. I felt the fragile gauntness of his body. He got slowly to his feet.

"Good-bye, Ilana Davita. I admire your castle very much. It is a fine and formidable castle. Good-bye."

He moved into the shadows of the room and was gone.

I lay back in my bed and closed my eyes and listened to the night. I slept and woke and slept again. Sounds woke me, a long whispering, a sigh, the roll of the ocean, the pulsing of night insects. The surf seemed immediately outside my windows, lapping at the dunes and curling toward the cottage. And there were the horses, racing along the beach, beating the sand with their flying hooves. They were so near I thought they would break through the walls of my room. I felt the thunderous beating of my heart and got out of bed and stood at a window. The moon was gone. The sky seemed washed with stars. The beach lay deserted. Distant sounds of a woman crying drifted faintly into my room.

In the morning Jakob Daw was gone. During breakfast my mother told me that my father had come very early with a car and had taken Jakob Daw to the pier in Manhattan where his ship was docked. I wondered why the car had not awakened me. On the kitchen table were the newspapers my father had brought back from Manhattan. I saw the headlines. REBELS GAIN IN SOUTH SPAIN; CIVIL WAR RAGES IN CITIES. My mother looked pale and distraught. Her eyes were red. She stayed inside the cottage most of that day.

I went down to the beach and the castle. The air was warm and bright. David Dinn came over to me and we went into the water together. He rode the waves grim-faced and fearful. I taught him how to breathe out with his face in the water and how to move his arms and legs. He seemed astonished by his sudden ability to move through water. Later we sat near the castle in our wet bathing suits, and I said, "I'm going to build another castle."

He stared at me. "You're going to wreck this one?"

"I want to build a second one." I paused a moment. "Will you help me?"

He hesitated a moment. "Sure," he said. "All right."

We started on the second castle. All that week we worked on it together. Sometimes I found myself looking off at the ocean and thinking of Jakob Daw. I would touch the surf. His ship was on this water and now I'm touching his ship.

On Saturday David Dinn would not work on the castle. I didn't work on it, either, because I didn't want to do any of it alone anymore. We were still working on it together and it was almost done when he, too, went away.

There were meetings in the cottage. Many of the people at the meetings were strangers to me. Some spoke to one another in languages I did not understand. Mrs. Greenwood came to one of the meetings and bestowed upon me her small, fixed smile. I asked her about Teresa. "Why, as far as I know she is fine, just fine." On occasion people traveled in from the city for those meetings. Words flew through the air of the cottage. Revisionism. Trotskyists. Popular Front. Trials. Comrade Stalin. There were loud arguments.

Once a week three or four people came to the cottage and together with my mother they would study a book by Karl Marx. My father was working at his special writing. I played on the beach with boys and girls my age and worked on the castles. Sometimes it rained. I watched the rain from our porch as it fell upon the beach.

Strange and fearful events were being reported. Off the coast of New Jersey the pilot of a small plane swerved to avoid hitting a bird, and the man in the rear seat fell to his death in the sea. I dreamed about that: hurtling through the air to the sea. I imagined it was the bird in the story by Jakob Daw. I saw a headline that read AMERICAN WOMAN WOUNDED IN SPAIN, and thought of Teresa. On the cover of the magazine *New Masses,* for which my father wrote, I read MASSACRE OF AMERICAN JEWS SET FOR SEPTEMBER! I did not talk to my parents about that but lay awake nights in my bed thinking of David Dinn and his family, and waiting.

A letter came from Jakob Daw. He was in Zurich for the time being and would probably soon be going to Spain. Europe was darkness. He had written a story during the crossing to Europe and would read it to us the next time we were together. Very good wishes to Ilana Davita.

My Aunt Sarah showed up suddenly one Friday afternoon and stayed the weekend. She looked thin and there were circles of darkness around her eyes. I watched her on her knees by her bed, praying, and saw her on the porch, talking to my parents about Ethiopia. She hated the Italians and called them lustful for empire and thin-blooded throwbacks to the ancient Romans. "Look how tan you are, darling!" she said to me. "I burned and burned in Ethiopia. You certainly appear to be having a good summer. Yes, I do think I'll be going to Spain fairly soon. They'll need nurses in Spain. Did you celebrate Easter at all? How sad!" She left on Sunday afternoon to catch a train north.

My father told me one evening as I lay in bed, "My paper may send me to Spain."

I sat up. "Will you be away long?"

"Don't know, my love. Not too long."

"But there's a war in Spain."

"That's why they're sending me. To write about the war."

Jakob Daw. Aunt Sarah. My father. Europe was devouring the people I loved.

The summer was coming to an end. I dreaded the oncoming winter. How many times would we move? Who would protect me and my mother?

One morning in the last week of August David Dinn's aunt and uncle loaded their summer belongings into a car, closed the house, and drove away. A few days later I helped my mother pack. The harp came down off the door; the colored picture of the horses on the beach came down off the wall. From our porch I looked at the ocean and the beach and the wheeling gulls. I stood near my castles a long time, gazing out across the sea. The next morning we returned to our apartment in the city.

BOOK TWO

BOOK TWO

Three

On a warm and sunny Friday afternoon in late September, with the trees still in full leaf and no hint of autumn in the air, my mother and I traveled with my father by cab to a pier in Manhattan. I remember my mother wore a dark gray crocheted beret and a light gray cotton summer dress and her long dark hair fell upon her shoulders and down her back and picked up highlights of the sun that shone through the windows of the cab. Her eyes burned with apprehension. We said almost nothing to each other during the long ride to the pier.

I stood on the stone pier and stared in awe at the ship: vast, mountainous, painted a dazzling white, festooned with flags, crowded with passengers, and named the *Lisbon.* How does it stay afloat, it's so huge? And it's taking my father across the ocean to the darkness on the other side.

We went up the canopied gangplank and through winding corridors to my father's stateroom. It was a small room with a narrow bed, a desk, a closet, a porthole, and a tiny bathroom. It reminded me of my rooms in the apartments in which we had lived over the years. Would it turn cold at night?

My father and mother stood near the porthole, talking quietly. I went over to them.

"Will you see Uncle Jakob in Europe?"

"I told you, Davita. Maybe."

"Will you see Aunt Sarah?"

My father gave me a patient smile.

"Ilana," my mother said.

"I don't want you to go, Papa."

"I know that, my love."

"Europe is a place where people are made dead."

"I'll be careful," he said. "I promise. Now give us a decent hug, my love. It's got to last me for a while."

I clung to him with all my strength.

"That's a decent hug!"

I watched as he and my mother embraced. He held her a long time. He was a handsome man, tall and ruddy and with wavy brown hair. My father, Michael Chandal.

Later my mother and I stood on the crowded pier and he waved to us from the deck. The ship slid slowly away, gulls circling overhead. I watched my father become smaller and smaller. Then he was gone. The ship moved downriver toward the sea. It looked like the freighters I had watched all summer, not seeming to move at all but getting smaller and smaller. I stood on the pier, frightened and crying.

"Now is not a time for crying," my mother said, sounding like my Aunt Sarah. "Now is a time for working." She gazed across the pier at the river and the ship. "Always they go off and we wait." A deep sadness was in her eyes and on her face. "It's for something worthwhile. But we wait." She turned to me and blinked her eyes rapidly. "We should go home. I feel cold."

A hot wind was blowing in from the river.

We took the subway back to the Brooklyn brownstone where we lived.

The apartment was still in disarray from our June move. The door harp was up; the picture of the horses had been hung on the wall over my parents' bed. But bulging cartons stood everywhere; windows were without curtains; books were still in crates; not even all the dishes had been unpacked. I wondered how long it would be before we moved again.

Inside the apartment that early fall afternoon after our return from the pier, my mother stood at her bedroom window looking down at the small grassy yard and at Ruthie Helfman, the redheaded girl about my age who lived on the floor below and who sat on a chair, reading. She stood by the window a long time. Then she removed her beret and slowly shook her head, and I watched the shimmer of sunlight in her long dark hair.

"Work," she murmured to herself, but distinctly. "Work, work, work." She turned from the window and went through the room into the hallway. I heard the bathroom door close behind her.

I stood near the window. There was a sycamore along the rear boundary of the yard and small birds sang and played in its leaves. I looked at the redheaded girl and wondered why she wore a long-sleeved dress on a hot day. Her mother, a short, plump woman in her middle or late thirties, also wore long-sleeved dresses, and always kept her hair covered with a kerchief. I thought of David Dinn and his long trousers and white shirts. That had been fun, swimming and building the castle with him. I imagined him going to synagogue every morning and evening to say—what was it?—Kaddish for his mother. Did he still go now that school had begun? Up so early every morning? And in the winter too? Awake in the darkness and cold?

I stood near the window looking at the girl and thinking of David Dinn. Then I thought of the white ship sailing on the ocean to the war in Spain. The papers were talking about the siege of Madrid. Big guns and airplanes and bombs. And tanks? Had I read about tanks? And my father and Jakob Daw in Spain. I stood at the window and looked out at the sycamore and the ocean and the bombs and the redheaded girl and wondered when my father would come home.

I heard a woman's voice. The girl's mother was calling to her in a mixture of English and a language I could not understand. I watched the girl read on awhile longer, then slowly close the book. As she stood, she raised her eyes and saw me looking at her and waved. I waved back. She had a freckled face and a pug nose and cupid's-bow lips. I watched her climb the stairs to the wooden back porch and go into the house through the back door.

I sat on the windowsill, looking at the yard. It was a small rectangle of grass bordered by a picket fence, with yards on either side and the sycamore beyond that separated us from the backyard of the house on the parallel street. The houses on these streets were nearly all of brownstone, either two or three stories high, some colonial style or mock Tudor, others boxlike and nondescript. The two-story brownstone into which we had moved had two front-facing windows on each floor. As you approached the house, the window to my room was to the left, the bay window of the living room was to the right. On the second floor— our floor—each of the windows was flanked by a turretlike structure that seemed an architect's afterthought and gave the house an odd castlelike appearance. I came out of my parents' bedroom and went through the long tunnellike hallway past the kitchen and the bathroom to my room.

The room I lived in now was long and narrow. Its single window looked out onto the tops of the trees that lined the street. Opposite the window was the door that led to the small narrow hallway that separated my room from the spare bedroom where a window faced the cellarway and the grassy backyard.

I stood in the doorway and looked at my room: the narrow bed, the small dark-wood chest of drawers, the chair, the old table that was my desk, the small bookcase, the bare pale-blue walls. I was very tired. I lay down on my bed and put my hand over my eyes. The street was still, the trees silent in the hot afternoon. The odors of cooking chicken and soup rose from the apartment below. I remembered the odors on some of the streets in Sea Gate on Friday afternoons. From somewhere in our apartment came my mother's voice singing a slow dirgelike tune I had never heard before and in a language I could not understand. The tune abruptly ended. The silence returned.

I heard the downstairs hallway door of the house close. The door had a lock that snapped shut with a loud, echoing click. I went to my window and saw the redheaded girl's father go quickly down the front stoop and turn up the street. I had talked to him once, briefly, a short, round-faced man with small round merry eyes and an ebullient voice. Now he wore a dark suit and tie and a dark felt hat, and he walked briskly up the street. There was about his stride a certain taut hurried purposefulness that reminded me of the way David Dinn and his uncle would leave their beachside house day after day in the mornings and evenings. It was nearly sundown; the sharp edges of the street were beginning to soften and blur. Maybe my mother and I would go to the movies tonight. *Modern Times* was showing in a neighborhood theater. I wanted to see it again. I went back to my bed and lay down and put my hand over my eyes. A vague memory surfaced. Somewhere in the past my mother and I had waited outside a movie theater. When had that been? It was snowing. An icy gale blew in from the nearby river. The lights of a towering bridge winked through the snow. Along the bank under the bridge, men lived in shanties. I had once seen them: ghostly figures in tattered clothes huddled around trash-can fires. My mother was handing out leaflets to people emerging from the theater. Most ignored her. One man called her a vile name. An old woman spat at her, the spittle blown away by the wind. My mother stood defiantly in her thin coat and dark beret. I had shivered in the cold and tried not to cry. What movie had been showing in that theater that night? I couldn't remember. Now I wanted to see *Modern Times* again: Charlie Chaplin caught in the cogs, rollers, cams, and gears of the runaway factory. Was that like someone caught in a war? War. Sailing. Spain. I lay on my bed imagining the huge ship and my small stateroom and the ocean outside my porthole and waiting for the darkness of Europe.

We did not go to the movies. After supper my mother went to her bedroom to work on another pamphlet and I wandered idly about the apartment, looking out open windows at the street and the adjoining houses, listening to voices and music from the radios of neighbors and to the family in the apartment below singing Sabbath songs together— their zemiros—like the melodies I had heard David Dinn and his family sing that night in Sea Gate after we had returned from the meeting about the war in Spain. I undressed and washed and got into bed. How far does a big ship travel in one day? Spain. Teresa. War.

My mother came into my room and stood near the door. The room was dark and I could barely see her.

"Are you awake?" she asked softly.

"Yes."

She came over to me. "I had no idea it was so late. You put yourself to bed. I'm sorry, darling."

I raised myself on an elbow. "How long will it take Papa to get to Spain?"

"About a week or ten days, I think." I could see her only dimly. Her voice was low.

"I feel very lonely."

She said quietly, "We have to work hard, Ilana. That way most of the time we can forget the loneliness. I learned that from my mother."

"Did your father go away, too?"

"Yes. Often."

"Did he go to war?"

"No, darling. My father was a member of a group of very religious Jews called Hasidim. He used to go away almost every Saturday and holiday to the city where the rebbe, the leader of the group, lived."

"Your father went away? Why did he do that?"

"He went to pray in the rebbe's synagogue with the others of the group."

"He left you alone with your mother?"

"Yes. Very often."

"Your father didn't care?"

"I suppose he didn't care enough. After all, we were only women. The only other man in the house was my grandfather, my mother's father. I don't know, darling. I never talked to my father about it. My mother would keep very busy while my father was away. She ran a flour mill with my grandfather. But Shabbos was very hard. She couldn't find what to do because she couldn't work. It was very hard."

"Were you angry at your father?"

"Was I angry? Yes. I was angry."

"I'm angry at Papa for going away."

"Ilana, your father is a fine journalist and he'll be doing something very important in Spain, important for the world."

I lay back on my pillow. I was beginning to feel sleepy. I asked, my eyes half-closed, "Mama, would you have married Papa if Jakob Daw had been in America?"

I heard her draw in breath. There was a brief silence. Then she said in a cold voice, "I don't like if questions, Ilana. They're upsetting and turn your head away from your work. I don't have time for such questions. 'If this' and 'if that.' They are not helpful questions."

"Mama?"

"I think you ought to go to sleep, Ilana."

"Did you hear them singing downstairs?"

"Yes."

"It sounded very nice. Like David Dinn and his family. In Sea Gate. Remember?"

"Yes."

"Good night, Mama."

"Good night, Ilana."

She kissed me on the forehead. I watched her go out of the room. I was very sleepy and closed my eyes and was quickly asleep. I thought I heard the door of the house click shut but I would not leave my warm sleep with the breeze coming through my open window and the whispering of the trees. The door fell shut again and I opened my eyes. Brilliant morning sunlight lay upon the floor and walls of the room. For a long moment I thought I was in the cottage on the beach. Then I got quickly out of bed, went to the window, and saw, coming down the front steps, the redheaded girl and her mother, both wearing light-colored summer dresses, the mother also in a pink flowery hat. They turned up the street and walked together in the direction the girl's father had gone the evening before and with that same brisk and purposeful stride.

A letter arrived from Jakob Daw addressed to my parents and to me —"Mr. and Mrs. Michael Chandal and Ilana Davita." It was postmarked Bilbao, Spain. I brought it upstairs from our mailbox near the front door of the house. My mother opened it quickly, scanned it, then read it aloud.

"My Dear Chandals. Germany deadly and menacing, a viper testing its poison in Spain. Switzerland antiseptic, aloof, paring its nails. Exhausting journey through France to Bilbao. Hot and dusty bus ride terrible for cough. When does Michael leave for Spain? Wrote nothing these past weeks. Cough a bit worse. Bilbao a loyalist stronghold thick with bureaucrats, generals, writers, journalists. A large city with very old churches, arcaded squares, a few museums, and squalid huddles of white cubelike houses on narrow winding hilly streets, and also a wild dark riverfront, where I have taken a room. I will remain in Bilbao a week or so to rest and meet certain people, then move on to Madrid. Rumored to be very bad in Madrid now. Must see for myself. Heavy involvement with party friends, but that is not for a letter. Remember with fondness the cottage and the beach and Ilana Davita's castles. With affection. Jakob Daw."

Jakob Daw was now living on the riverfront in a city called Bilbao. Hadn't there been a riverfront once in the early years of my life amidst all the moves from apartment to apartment? Tugboats, barges, garbage scows, vast rising blocks of stone, a tangle of steel girders, wet cobbled streets, a block-long crowd of silent men waiting in line for soup and bread? Where had that been? My mother going from house to house, apartment to apartment, handing out party leaflets, talking about the cruelties of capitalism, the need for unions, and I walking with her through the grimy snow, and the river up ahead running beneath the awesome rise of the bridge, dark cold water with things floating in it, one of the things a small skeletal black bird with socketless eyes, beak wide open, floating along the scum-green bank amidst orange rinds and apple cores and bits of wood and the effluvia of human waste. "People are good by nature, Ilana," my mother would say to me on those walks. "But this goodness is now blocked by social, political, and religious barriers. We are struggling to throw down those barriers. Then you'll see a new day for all mankind. It will happen soon, Ilana. Soon. Capitalism is dead. You can see its corpses everywhere." Or she would say, "You can't imagine how much cruelty there is in this world, Ilana. Man against man. Cruelty and injustice. We're fighting this cruelty to make a better world." Her face was red from the icy wind. "Remember what you're seeing, Ilana. Remember what I'm telling you." Unshaven, hollow-cheeked men, exhausted-looking women, pale dark-eyed children—they would respond to her knocking and some would slam the door in her face and others would stand in the doorways as she talked of the need to fight the bosses, to organize the working class, to make a new dawn for the poor and the laborer, and she would urge them to come to the next public meeting of the local party branch, and she would hand out leaflets and pamphlets or stuff them into old mailboxes in decaying hallways, and we would be out on the wet street again near the river, the icy wind stinging my eyes, my mother's hair blowing wild beneath her black woolen beret. What section of the city had that been? Where had we lived during those winter months I accompanied my mother day after day through snow and wind, watching her work for her new world? I could not remember.

"A wild dark waterfront, where I have taken a room," Jakob Daw had written. With wet dark streets and a towering bridge and garbage scows and ragged men living in shanties along the bank and dead birds floating in the water?

In the months that followed my father's departure to Spain, my mother began to travel two or three times a week in the evenings to Manhattan. Committees were being formed to help Spanish war refugees; there were meetings she had to attend, people she had to meet. She tried to explain it to me one evening over supper.

"Do you understand, Ilana?"

"I think so, Mama."

"Are you big enough for me to leave you alone?"

"Yes, Mama." I was afraid of being alone at night, but I would not let her know it.

"If you need anyone, go down to Mrs. Helfman. I'll leave you a telephone number where you can call me if you feel you need to. You can spend the time doing your homework or reading your father's articles on the war. I'll show you how to use the phonograph so you can listen to music. You're sure I can leave you by yourself?"

"Yes, Mama."

"There's a lot of work that has to be done now for the people in Spain. And I can't do it from here."

We would eat an early supper together and do the dishes. Then my mother would put on her coat and beret and leave the apartment, and I would hear our door harp and the click of the downstairs lock and see her through my window, walking quickly beneath the autumn trees to the subway station on the parkway. I did my homework, wandered aimlessly about the apartment, put myself to sleep. Sometimes I read the newspaper in which my father's articles on the war had begun to appear. It seemed to me he was moving around a lot. He wrote about things he had seen in places called Salamanca, Segovia, Toledo, Valencia, Barcelona, Guadalajara, Madrid. I found the names on the map of Spain my mother had cut out of a newspaper and put up with thumbtacks on the kitchen wall near our table. I would sit at the table and look at Spain. Soon I knew its shape by heart: Spain and Portugal, a boxlike contour of land jutting into the Mediterranean and the Atlantic with knoblike protrusions here and there. I could not understand the war. My mother had tried to explain it to me, but I could not grasp it. Rebels against Reds, Fascists against Communists, aristocrats and middle class against workers, landowners against peasants. A brutally divided world. It seemed as if an ocean of blood had rolled across that land. None of my classmates talked about the war; few even knew about it. But somewhere in Spain was my father amidst bombs and shells and burned-out villages and fields littered with dead horses and human corpses. I was able to understand many of the words that I read in his articles, but I could not imagine a ruined village or a field of dead horses and men. After a while I stopped reading my father's stories when I was alone at home at night.

One night I went into my parents' bedroom and found on my mother's dresser the letter Jakob Daw had sent us from Bilbao. I wished I could read German. I went out of the bedroom and into the kitchen and searched the map of Spain for Bilbao. I found it in the north, near another place called Guernica.

Sometimes when I was done early with my homework, I would go downstairs and play with Ruthie in her apartment, which was almost a duplicate of ours. Once I came down and they were in the middle of supper. Her mother invited me into the kitchen. Ruthie's father sat at the table with a small dark skullcap on his dark hair. They were a cheerful family and spoke noisily among themselves, sometimes in English, most often in Yiddish, which I did not understand.

One evening Ruthie and I were playing together in her room when she asked me when my father was coming home. I said I didn't know.

"I'm glad my father doesn't go away on long trips," she said.

"What does your father do?"

"He teaches in a yeshiva."

I didn't know what the word yeshiva meant, but before I could ask her, she said, "Where'd your father go?"

"To Spain."

"Is that a country?"

"Spain is a country in Europe. It's below France and near Italy."

"I know about Europe. That's where my parents came from. It's across the ocean. My father says that Europe was like Gehennom for Jews."

"What does Gehennom mean?"

"It's—it's where you get punished for your sins. You know, after you die. Gehennom."

"Is it like a war?"

"I don't know."

"That's where my father is. In the war in Spain."

"Is there a war in Spain?"

"A terrible war. Don't you see the newspapers?"

"My father doesn't want me to read goyische newspapers. He says I shouldn't fill my head with garbage and leave no room for important things."

The next morning over breakfast I asked my mother, "When is Papa coming home?"

"I don't know, darling. Did you read your father's story from Barcelona?"

"No."

"It's an excellent story, Ilana."

"Why doesn't Papa write to us?"

"When he comes back, ask him."

"Are you going to a meeting again tonight, Mama?"

"Yes."

That evening someone rang the bell to our apartment and when I opened the door there was Ruthie. The harp sang merrily from its place on the door.

"My mother said I could come up and play with you," she said.

I closed the door. Again the wooden balls rose and fell, and the music of the harp filled the apartment hallway.

Ruthie looked at the harp in fascination. "What's that?"

"It belongs to my father. Someone gave it to him. It's like a good luck charm."

She asked me to open and close the door a few times. Then she opened and closed it herself. She seemed enchanted by the random play of the swinging wooden balls, by the music that came from the taut wires.

"My mother wants us to have a piano, but my father says we don't have the money. I like this—what do you call it?"

"It's called a door harp."

"I really like it," she said.

We played awhile in my room. Outside an autumn wind blew through the nearly naked trees on the street. Later I invited Ruthie into the kitchen for a glass of milk and cookies. She said she couldn't eat our food.

"What do you mean?"

"My father says you aren't kosher. We can't eat in your house."

"I don't understand. What does kosher mean?"

"It means your meat has to come from certain animals and be prepared in a certain way, and you have to have separate meat and milk dishes."

"You mean I can eat in your house but you can't eat in mine?"

"It's from the Torah," she said. "It's the law of God."

I didn't understand what Torah meant, but I didn't ask her.

At the door she said, "Will you come down and play with me next time?"

I hesitated a moment, then nodded.

She put a hand on the knob and opened the door. The harp came to life. She swung the door gently back and forth. The harp sang and sang. She gave me a smile and went downstairs.

I came into the kitchen, poured myself a glass of milk, and ate some cookies. The apartment was silent. I sat at the kitchen table, eating the cookies and looking at the map of Spain.

One night while my mother was away I began to unpack some of the cartons that lay stacked about the apartment. I remembered where some things belonged—certain clothes in this dresser or closet, certain books or papers on this shelf or in that drawer. If I could not remember where something belonged, I chose a drawer or shelf for it and put it there neatly. The emptied cartons I piled in a deep closet out of sight.

My mother seemed not to notice what I was doing. One night I asked if I could help her put up the window curtains. She was too tired, she said. I asked her again the next night. We put up the curtains together.

Ruthie came in one evening as I was emptying a carton in my parents' bedroom and began to help me. We worked together for a while, sorting pamphlets and books and clothes. At the bottom of the carton I found an album of old black-and-white photographs. One was of a family I did not recognize: a man, a woman, two boys, and a girl. They were sitting on a lawn near a huge white house. Behind the house was a tall sky and a grove of spruce trees. I thought one of the boys resembled my father and the girl looked a little like my Aunt Sarah. The man in the picture was thin and tall and stern-looking; the woman was dark-eyed and gaunt and unsmiling. Other photographs were of a small rectangular house on the edge of an open sea, taken at various angles and at different times of the day. There were birds in those photographs, white-winged terns that circled about and strutted along the wet sand of a curving beach. I saw photographs of my parents and their friends, some of whom I recognized from the many meetings in the different apartments in which we had lived. In one of the photographs my parents looked very young and my mother was pregnant. I looked at that photograph a long time. Was that I inside my mother? Or my brother, who was dead? There was a brittle sepia-colored photograph of my mother—very young, her hair in braids—with a woman and an old man with a long unkempt white beard. I thought they must be her mother and grandfather. The woman was short and slight of build and had dark, burning eyes. There was no photograph of my mother's father.

Ruthie and I looked at the photographs together. Then I put them in a neat pile on my father's desk. The next day they were gone. My mother said nothing to me about them.

One Saturday morning in early November I rose early and dressed and ate breakfast. My mother was still asleep. I went back to my room and sat on my bed, waiting to hear the click of the downstairs hallway door. There it was! I went quickly out of the apartment and down the stairway and out into the chill autumn air.

The street was ankle-deep in dead leaves. I followed behind Ruthie
and her mother, keeping a distance of nearly a block between us. A cold
wind blew the leaves in aimless arabesques along the ground. Ruthie
and her mother turned up a side street in the direction of the parkway. I
went by the grocery store where my mother and I shopped and the
candy store with the newspapers on the stand outside. Heavy black
metal weights held the papers down against the wind. I glimpsed a large
headline as I passed: GOVERNMENT TO QUIT MADRID WITH CITY'S
FALL IMMINENT. A smaller headline read PANIC SEIZES CAPITAL. What
had I seen a day or two earlier on my way back from school? Yes.
CENTER OF MADRID IS REPORTED AFIRE. "Is Papa in Madrid?" I had
asked my mother that night. "Yes," my mother had said. "Aren't you
reading his stories?"

I saw Ruthie and her mother turn into the parkway. I followed,
keeping behind the trees that lined the wide street. There was little
traffic along the six center lanes of the parkway. I saw Ruthie and her
mother turn into a four-story red-brick building set far back from the
curb and fronted by an open cemented area that looked like a school
play yard. They went up a short flight of stone steps and through a wide
wooden double door into the building. Over the door was a large sign
with blue letters on a white background: RABBI ISAAC DINN TORAH
ACADEMY.

I stared at the sign. Three boys about my age came out the door and
stood near the steps, talking and laughing. They fell silent as I went past
them up the steps and through the door. I could feel them looking at
me.

I was in a wide entrance hall. The air was warm. Lights glowed from
a ceiling chandelier and from fixtures on the walls. The floor was covered with worn brownish linoleum. The walls were bare and painted a
cream color. At the far end of the hall a wide staircase ran up into deep
shadows. To my left a corridor formed a long narrow tunnel between a
double row of closed rooms.

I heard a rush of voices to my right as a wide door swung open and
two men came out. They were bearded and wore over their dark suits
some sort of dark-striped cloth garment from which dangled long white
fringes. They went past me into the corridor. Behind me two women
entered the building and went quickly through the wide door. Again I
heard voices as the door opened. I pushed against the door and felt it
open easily. I slipped inside and stood very still against the wall near the
door.

I was standing in an aisle formed by the wall and a low wooden partition. Men and women moved past me in and out of the door. Beyond the partition was a large room with a single wall of tall windows that faced the street. The room was crowded with chairs and divided nearly in half by a wall seven or eight feet high, its lower half made of plywood, its upper of sheer ninon. Men sat on the window side of this wall, women on the other. Many of the women wore kerchiefs or hats. The men had on either felt hats or skullcaps. On the men's side, near the wall across the room from me, was a small lectern at which a man now stood, his back to the room, his white-fringed garment drawn over his head. A large ornate red velvet curtain covered a section of the wall that he faced. The room was crowded. I saw girls my age on the men's side of the room, but they all seemed to be with their fathers. Most of the older men wore the dark-striped white garment. The men's side of the room looked like a lake of white water.

I slipped into an aisle chair in the back row on the women's side of the room, first removing from the chair and holding in my hand a dark-bound book. I opened the book and found it was printed in a language I could not read. I looked up and found I could see only dimly through the curtain that divided the room. Next to me sat an elderly woman with a kerchief over her white hair and brown spots on her face. She handed me her open book, pointing a bent finger at the page, took my book, opened it, and brought it up to her nearsighted eyes. I watched her carefully out of the sides of my eyes, turning the pages with her, rising and sitting together with her and the other women. I could not see Ruthie or her mother. Then I saw them, in front, seated near the curtain. On the other side of the curtain I heard a man's voice chanting against a background of murmured response and low talk. I sat very still, listening carefully and waiting.

There was a momentary pause. Then I heard it, the soft tuneless recitation I had once heard briefly before. I peered through the curtain but everything looked distorted. I went from my chair to the back of the room and stood on tiptoe, peering over the partition. There he was, standing next to his father in one of the front rows and swaying slightly as he recited the Kaddish; there was David Dinn.

I went back to my seat. A few minutes later I followed the crowd out of the room and the entrance hall through the double doors to the wide cement area in front of the building. There I waited near a tree at the edge of the sidewalk.

The area became dense with people standing around and talking.

There was heavy traffic now along the parkway. A cold wind blew through the trees, sending leaves to the street. Ruthie and her parents came out of the building together. I saw them greeting people and laughing. After a while they started along the parkway, Ruthie walking between her parents and holding their hands. Then David Dinn emerged alone from the building and went over to some boys his age. I waited. It was cold. He kept on talking to the boys. I moved through the crowd and came over to him.

"Hello," I said. "Do you remember me?"

He looked at me in surprise.

"The beach," I said.

He seemed not to know who I was.

"The ocean. The castle."

His pale face lighted with recognition. "Ilana," he said. "I didn't recognize you in—without—I didn't recognize you."

He became flustered. The boys in the group were staring at me.

"Is this your building?" I asked.

"What?"

"The name is the same as yours. Is it your building?"

I heard laughter.

He looked embarrassed. "It's named for my father's grandfather. He was a great rabbi in Germany."

"It's nice to see you again, David. Do you live near here?"

"A couple of blocks away."

"Do your friends always laugh at someone who makes a mistake?"

"What?"

They were all staring at me and grinning.

"Good-bye. Have a nice—how do you call it?—Shabbos. Have a nice Shabbos."

I turned to walk away, feeling their eyes on my back.

A man had come through the crowd. He was tall and finely tailored in a dark coat and suit and felt hat. It was David Dinn's father. He came over to us.

"Hello, Ilana," he said. "How are your parents?"

I stared at him. "They're—" I stopped. "My father is in Spain."

He nodded as if he knew all about my father.

"In Madrid."

"Yes," he said. "I know."

"My father is a journalist and his newspaper sent him to write about the war."

They were all staring at me. No one was grinning now.

"My father wrote about the battle for Toledo. You know, the castle there, the fortress. The—" I couldn't remember the name.

"The Alcazar," David Dinn's father said.

"That's right. The Alcazar. It was on the front page of his newspaper."

"I'm afraid I don't read that newspaper," David Dinn's father said. He spoke in a kindly way. There was a polished and courtly manner about him. "I'm afraid we have to go now, Ilana. Someone is expecting us. I wish you a good Shabbos. And your mother, too. I hope your father returns home soon and in good health. Come, David."

I watched them walk away.

When I got home I found my mother seated at the kitchen table, listening to the radio.

"Where were you?" she asked.

"Out for a walk."

"They expect Madrid to fall today," she said.

I said I didn't understand.

"It will be captured by the Fascists," she said.

The radio announcer was talking about the fighting for the bridges and roads leading to Madrid.

"Where is Papa?"

She said nothing.

The announcer was describing a reporter's eyewitness account of a battle for a crucial bridge. Fifty Moors stormed a seven-story apartment house near the bridge. The Moors were professional soldiers from Morocco, Franco's best troops. They raced inside the building, throwing hand grenades and firing their machine guns. They fought their way to the second floor and then the third, killing the defenders. As they kept climbing higher, their pace grew gradually slower. Each floor slowed them more. They had succeeded in killing every one of the occupants; but no Moors had come out of the building.

The announcer went on to other news about Madrid.

"I saw David Dinn," I said. "I passed by his synagogue. I saw his father."

The announcer was describing Madrid as a doomed city. Franco and his Moors were ready for the kill, he said.

"Mama, what does David Dinn's father do?"

"What? Oh. Mr. Dinn is a special kind of lawyer. He helps people who come to America with immigration problems."

"Like Teresa and her parents?"

"Teresa? Oh. Yes. Like Teresa."

"Did you tell Mr. Dinn to rent the cottage next door to us on the beach?"

"Yes, Ilana. He needed a place close to the city so he could visit David. And he wanted David to be near me in case something happened. The boy was—he was very upset by his mother's death."

"Did Mr. Dinn help us get this apartment?"

She looked surprised. "Yes," she said. "You *are* clever. You have my mother's head. Now be quiet, please. I want to hear the news."

I left her at the kitchen table and went into my room. Through the white lacy curtains on my window I saw the thinly leaved trees and the street and children playing stoopball a few houses away. A car went up the street, scattering leaves. I wish you a good Shabbos, Ilana. And your mother, too. I hope your father returns home soon and in good health. I stood there gazing through my window curtains at the cold November street.

One cold afternoon that week I went with my mother by subway to Manhattan. The train was crowded, the ride noisy and jarring. My mother said little to me during the ride. We came out of the station into chill air brown with mist and smoky with burning charcoal from hot pretzel and roasted chestnut stands. We walked along crowded streets lined with stores and cafeterias and turned into an cavernous loft building with tall ceilings and echoing corridors. An ancient elevator took us up; through its folding metal gate I saw the iron entrails of the shaft. We went along a wide corridor with light green walls that sorely needed painting and entered through a door whose top frosted glass panel had painted on it in large black letters the words AMERICAN COMMITTEE FOR REFUGEE AID.

We were in an enormous, high-ceilinged, barnlike room. A wall of tall wet windows looked out at the brown buildings of the street. The room was crowded with desks and chairs and noisy with talk. At each desk sat a man or woman, writing or talking into a phone or to someone seated at the desk. Along one of the walls were rows of wooden folding chairs occupied by men and women who sat quietly, waiting. In the front row, one woman sat slowly twisting a handkerchief; another held in her fingers a rosary; a man with a scar on his face sat with his eyes closed and his arms folded across his chest, the scar a livid white line between two smooth planes of olive-colored skin.

My mother directed me to a chair next to a middle-aged woman and told me to wait until she was done with her work. I sat quietly in the chair and watched my mother go over to one of the desks and sit down and pick up the phone. From time to time a name was called out over a loudspeaker and someone rose from one of the chairs and went toward the desks. I looked around at the faces of others seated near me. Were they all from Europe? From war? My father and Uncle Jakob and Aunt Sarah had gone to Europe and all these people had run away. Europe. I disliked the sound of the word. It was the land of Baba Yaga.

It seemed to me I was in that room a long time. The air was cold and damp, and tense with misery. I watched my mother talking to the man with the scarred face. After a while he left, and an elderly woman took his place at my mother's desk. The minutes passed slowly. I had taken a book along but could not read. I watched the faces of the people in the chairs.

War.

Later I walked with my mother through crowded evening streets. A din rose from the dense traffic. The brown sooty air was spectral with garish fluorescents and plumes of steam rising from grates. We went into a small restaurant and sat at a small round table near the window, looking out at the people and the traffic. We ordered supper. A light rain began to fall. I saw it on the window and the street. Halos of mist formed around the lights of the street lamps. My mother sat in her dark dress and beret, eating slowly, the distant look in her eyes.

I asked her what the play she was taking me to see was all about.

"It's about the big war in Europe and someone who tries to stop it."

"Does he stop it?"

"No."

"I don't want to see a play about war."

"It's a fine play, darling, and I want us to see it."

We finished supper and walked through the rain to the theater. It was crowded. Our seats were in the balcony. I had a good view of the stage. My mother sat quietly, her face pale with apprehension.

I leaned over to her. "Are you all right, Mama?"

"I'm fine, darling."

"Is anything wrong with Papa?"

"No, no."

I sat back. A moment later the curtain rose.

The play was about a simple, good-hearted man named Johnny Johnson who enlists in the army during the big war to fight the Germans. He joins up only because the girl he is going to marry insists that he be patriotic and kill Germans. He doesn't want to kill anyone. He gets sent to Europe. On the front lines he befriends a German soldier. The two of them are amazed that they wanted to kill each other. The German says his friends really don't want to fight. Johnny Johnson says they should all stop fighting. He very nearly succeeds in stopping a major offensive against the Germans. But the American officers in charge of the offensive arrest him. He is sent to a lunatic asylum. Many years later he is released. He spends the rest of his life selling toys on the street. "Toyees for sale!" he cries. "Toyees for sale!"

There were songs in the play and an odd kind of music. I remember best a speech against war that Johnny Johnson makes to the officers planning the big offensive. "End this killing—end it now. . . . Do it! Do it! . . . But you don't listen. . . . You don't want to end this war. There's something black and evil got into you—something blinded you —something—"

I remember too an American priest and a German priest, both of them chaplains, praying together to God and to Jesus Christ, "Save and deliver us, we humbly beseech thee, from the hands of our enemies"— as two squads of gas-masked soldiers, Germans and Americans, are locked in hand-to-hand combat; and an American and a German fight each other with bare hands; and two soldiers, a German and an American, lie tangled and dying in barbed wire, their hands clasped in friendship; and surrendering German soldiers are machine-gunned by Americans; and surrendering American soldiers are machine-gunned by Germans; and Johnny Johnson holds in his lap the head of a dying soldier and offers him a drink of water—and the two priests saying together in the same breath, "Amen."

We came out of the theater into the November night. A cold mist hung in the air. I walked beside my mother, still seeing the play and hearing the music. We crossed a street. I could see the subway station at the end of the block.

"He wasn't crazy," I said. "The others were crazy."

My mother said nothing. She was huddled deep in her coat as if it were an arctic night.

"I didn't understand it," I said. "And I didn't like the ending."

We walked down into the subway station. The train came roaring out of its black tunnel. On the way back I fell asleep, my head against my mother's shoulder, and woke with a stifled scream. People looked at me. I had dreamed of severed arms and legs scattered on a muddy field. War. My mother held me. I thought the ride would never end—the stops and starts, the lurching and rattling, the screaming metal wheels. I felt myself swooning with exhaustion when the train at last pulled into our station.

We climbed the stairs to the parkway and started home. The streets were deserted. Sodden leaves lay underfoot and made watery sounds beneath my shoes. We went into the entrance hall and started up the stairs. Behind me I heard clearly the loud closing click of the hallway door. The harp played as we entered our apartment. We had barely put away our coats when someone knocked on our door. My mother went to it quickly. It was Mrs. Helfman.

She thought she had heard us come in, but hadn't been sure. She had decided to come up and find out if we were back. She sounded out of breath. A cable had arrived for my mother in the late afternoon. She hoped it wasn't bad news.

My mother thanked her in a quiet voice. Mrs. Helfman said again that she hoped it wasn't bad news and turned and started for the stairs. The harp played as my mother closed the door. Standing near the door, my mother tore open the cable with trembling fingers. She scanned it, then read it to me. It was from my father, from Madrid. He was coming home.

That Saturday morning I rose early, dressed, and left the apartment. My mother was still asleep. I walked through streets deep in leaves to the building on Eastern Parkway named after David Dinn's great-grandfather. Inside the room with the dividing wall, I sat in a chair directly against the curtain and searched for a loosened seam that might afford me a clear view of the men's side of the room. I had to change seats three times before I found one.

Frayed edges of ninon fabric framed the view. A boy stood at the lectern, chanting. He seemed very young. I did not know what he was doing or saying: the book in my hands was all in Hebrew, which I could not read. The room was crowded. Abruptly everyone stood. The red velvet curtains along the far wall were parted; doors were opened; a long scroll-like object, garbed in a brocaded and beaded red cloth and topped with a silver crown, was removed from a wide closet set deep into the wall. The scroll was paraded around the men's side of the room. Many of the men placed a fringe of their white woolen shawl on this scroll and then touched the fringe to their lips. There were a number of young girls in the room, and they put their fingers on the scroll and then kissed their fingers. The scroll was placed on the podium that stood near the center of the room.

For about an hour, the same boy who had led the service read aloud from the scroll, in a rhythm and chant I had never heard before, his voice high and clear. All sat silent as he read. From time to time he would stop and one of the men at the podium would chant something and a hum of talk would fill the room. Then the scroll was raised high in the air and all stood. With everyone once again seated, the boy remained alone at the podium, chanting, swaying slowly back and forth, a thin pale-faced boy in a suit and tie and a small dark skullcap and the fringed white and dark-striped woolen garment over his narrow shoulders. Then he was done and a shower of small brown bags and bits of candy flew through the air amidst shouts of "Mazol tov! Mazol tov!" Children scurried about for the bags. A swelling rise of laughter and talk accompanied the rain of candy and the scampering of the children. Some minutes later the scroll, carried by the boy, was again paraded through the men's side of the room and brought up to the closet in front of the room. All sang in response to the boy's singing. I liked the music and tried to sing along.

Later, everyone stood in silence a long time, praying. And still later, David Dinn and his father rose together and recited the Kaddish. Others stood too, but I could not see them all for the narrowness of the open seam.

Afterward on the sidewalk in front of the building I moved slowly through the noisy throng to where David Dinn was standing with his friends.

"Hello," I said.

He turned to me and said quietly, "Hello, Ilana."

"Was that a celebration?"

"Where?"

"Inside. This morning."

"That was a bar mitzvah," he said.

"My God," one of the other boys said. "She doesn't know what a bar mitzvah is."

"Are you Jewish?" another asked me.

"She's Jewish," David Dinn said. "Leave her alone."

"Why is that curtain in the room?" I asked. "Why do the men and women sit separately?"

They all looked at me. One of them snickered loudly.

"It's the law," David Dinn said.

"What law?"

"Jewish law."

"She's not one of us," a boy said.

"Where does she come from?" another asked.

"Can I ask one more question?" I said to David Dinn.

"Sure," he said, looking a little uncomfortable.

"Is it the law that instead of helping you're supposed to laugh at someone who's trying to learn?"

They stood there, staring at me and saying nothing. All around us the crowd moved and surged, joyous, boisterous.

David Dinn's father came out of the crowd, looking tall and courtly in his dark coat and dark suit and hat. "There you are," he said to David. "And there *you* are, Ilana. How are you and how is your mother?"

"My mother is fine. My father is coming home."

"He is? I'm glad to hear that. Is he well?"

"No. He was wounded in Madrid. He's coming home to rest. My Aunt Sarah is a nurse in Spain. She's bringing him back."

His face darkened. "I'm very sorry to hear that, Ilana."

I saw David Dinn staring at me, his mouth open. The others had fallen very silent. The noise of the crowd rose and fell all around me like the back-and-forth rushing of surf in a storm.

Mr. Dinn said, "Why didn't your mother—?" then abruptly stopped. He was silent a moment, his fingers tapping rapidly upon one of the buttons of his coat. He ran a finger along the inside of his shirt collar. Then he said to me, "Have a good Shabbos, Ilana. I wish your father a speedy recovery. We must go now. Come, David."

"Good Shabbos," David Dinn said.

They stepped into the crowd and were gone.

I stood a moment amidst David Dinn's friends. They all looked alike in their dark coats and hats and pale faces, all standing there and staring at me in silence.

I turned up the parkway and walked home alone.

A letter arrived from Jakob Daw. He was in Madrid.

"My dear Channah. I write in English to show you I have not forgotten the language we once studied together. I write to tell you that I have entirely ceased writing stories. Here things happen daily for which there are no words. One hears sounds that language cannot name: sounds from children and animals as the shells fall, sounds later when the shelling has stopped. Michael was with La Pasionaria at the Segovia Bridge. He will be hurt if he is not more careful. I tell him he has a beautiful wife and a lovely, sharp-minded daughter to go home to and care for. He answers that all the world is in peril now and if the Fascists win we are all doomed. He washes his face with water from a dirty basin in our bombed-out hotel and gets something to eat and rushes back to the front. And the front is everywhere, everywhere, all around Madrid. He is handsome, your Michael. How do you say it? Dashing. Yes. He has friends wherever he goes. I sit alone in my room. I have a drink sometimes with an officer who comes to visit and talks to me about my stories. Here there is a hell beyond the ability of even a Dante to depict. No words for it, no names. Kazantzakis said the other night that an officer told him the Spaniard has many souls inside himself and is all full of unreconciled and contradictory desires; he is a mixture of many races still uncrystallized. He loves life, but something in him cries out, 'All this is nothing!' Then he hungers for death. He goes from extreme to extreme, yearning, suffering. He has too much blood inside him. Blood must be taken from him. He has a need to burst into violence. There is inhuman joy and passion in this war. And at the root of this passion is the despair at the possibility that all is nothing. Kazantzakis says that here there is madness. Spaniards talk of death as if it were a neighboring land where all go to visit sooner or later. Madness. Convulsions of hatred. Anarchy. A time of apocalypse. Can an entire people become insane? Can all of mankind go mad? Chaos is king in Spain. Here little children carry flags and guns. Here priests urge on the killing. All the air is filled with the song of a dying bird. Journalists watch the bombing raids with curled lips and sarcastic smiles; others are cold, indifferent. All is a prologue to a great catastrophe. How can one write stories? I saw a child Ilana Davita's age lose her legs to a shell. Stories! How lovely Vienna was when we were there in our dream time. How sad that we did not know we were leaving forever our youthful lives. We might have bade good-bye in some appropriate way to those early years. How much there is to regret! What a cruel century we now live in! The cough is better in Madrid than it was in Switzerland. I shall try hard to restrain your impetuous Michael. You will please give Ilana Davita my most affectionate greetings. Jakob."

The letter had been addressed to my mother, who had not told me about it. I found it on the desk in her bedroom one evening that week as I wandered about the apartment while she was in Manhattan. There was much in the letter I could not understand. But I understood enough.

Later that evening I stood at my window gazing down at our darkening street. How quickly the green life had gone from the trees! Would my room be cold again in the coming winter? Probably we would move again soon. The lamp-post lights came on, sudden yellow-white pools in the evening's shadows. Behind me the apartment seemed to pulse with menacing words. Death as a neighboring land. I did not understand that. All the air is filled with the song of a dying bird. What did that mean? Perhaps I should not have read the letter. Perhaps I really hadn't understood it. But no more stories! I understood that. What would happen now to the little bird?

Through my window I saw Mr. Helfman walking along the street on the way back from work. He taught Hebrew and Bible at the school named after David Dinn's great-grandfather. He went up the front steps. I heard the clear echoing click of the closing hallway door. I lay down on my bed and thought of Jakob Daw.

On Saturday afternoon in the first week of December a cab pulled up at our house. My mother and I went racing downstairs. Aunt Sarah stood on the curb, wearing a nurse's uniform and a wide dark-gray cape. She was helping my father out of the cab. He seemed unable to move his right leg.

"Hello, Annie!" my father called out when he saw my mother. "I'm back in one piece!"

My mother bit her lip and held back her tears. She did not kiss him. I saw Ruthie and her parents looking at us through the bay window of their living room. All up and down the street people were looking at us.

"Hello, my love!" my father said to me. "Christ, how you've grown! Look what's happened to your old dad. Be very careful, love. No hugs now. Give us a hand, Sarah. The steps will be tricky."

My aunt and the cabdriver helped him up the stairs and into the apartment. He glanced at the singing harp as he came through the door.

"Hello!" he said to the harp. "Are you glad to see me? I'm damn glad to see you!"

My aunt and my mother took him into the bedroom and closed the door. The cab drove away.

I waited in the hallway outside the bedroom. I had almost not recognized him. He had lost a great deal of weight and seemed smaller now than when he had left. His face had a yellowish cast that accentuated and darkened the blueness of his eyes. His wavy brown hair had been cut very short and I could see clearly the stark whiteness of his scalp. Later my mother explained to me that he had been ill for a while in Spain with a stomach sickness called dysentery. Now he was recovering from a sickness of the liver called jaundice and from a deep wound in the hip caused by the fragments of an exploding grenade.

He lay in the double bed in my parents' bedroom. My mother, white-faced, rigidly calm, borrowed a cot from Mrs. Helfman and placed it next to the double bed. Aunt Sarah moved into the room across the hallway from me.

The last of the leaves fell from the trees. The weather turned bitter cold.

Strangely, my room remained warm.

In some houses in the neighborhood little candles burned in the windows. Ruthie told me one night as we played together in her living room that the candles were in celebration of a Jewish holiday called Chanukkah. There had been a war a long time ago, she said, to free the Jews from pagan conquerors. The candles were for the miracle that had happened during that war when the temple in Jerusalem had been recaptured from the pagans and rededicated to God.

She talked as if from memory and not from understanding.

I asked her when it had all happened.

"About two thousand years ago, I think."

"Who were the enemies of the Jews?"

"I think they were called Syrians."

"Who were the Syrians?"

"I don't know. Maybe it was the Greeks."

"I like the candles. They're pretty."

"Ilana, is your father very sick? Why does the doctor come so often?"

"I don't know."

"Is he getting better?"

"My Aunt Sarah says he's getting better. She's a nurse."

"Was she in Spain, too?"

"Yes. She was in Badajoz and Toledo and Madrid."

"I don't know any of those places."

Behind her on the windowsill the little candles burned in the bronze candelabrum she called a menorah. The curtains of the bay window had been pulled aside and the candles cast warm and golden light against the blackness of the street. Small and pretty orange candles burning in the darkness of the enormous night.

Aunt Sarah bought a little pine tree and placed it in her room. She began to leave her door open during the day and I could see the tree small and green and glittery with tinsel.

I asked her one day what the word Christmas meant.

She looked astonished. "Dear child, do you know nothing about Jesus Christ, our Messiah, our Prince of Peace, the Son of God?"

I said I knew only what I had heard and learned in public school. And school was very boring, I added.

"Dear, dear child."

Briefly she told me the story of the child Jesus and the three wise men.

"Why is there a war in Spain if Jesus is the Prince of Peace?"

"We must pray to Jesus Christ for peace, Ilana. He is our Lord."

I didn't understand. And she had not explained to me the meaning of the word Christmas. In my public school the tree was tall and decorated with lights. It felt comforting to have had the candles of the menorah the week before and to have the green life and lights of the trees now in a time when the streets were raw and cold and the nights were long and often filled with odd and fearful sounds.

Sometimes in the blackness that followed midnight or in the dimness of early morning I would wake to the sounds of my mother singing. Her voice moved softly through the darkness, and always I thought I was dreaming: a haunting, melancholy rise and fall of melodies I had never before heard and words I did not understand. Sometimes it seemed there were no words at all to her songs but only sounds like ai dai dai and bim bim bom. Once I heard her repeat a word a number of times with a sad and defiant tone in her voice. "Guttenyu," she said. "Ai, Guttenyu." Another night she said, "Mamaleh. Mamaleh." She said that over and over again that night. "Mamaleh."

That was the night my father lay burning with a fever that had come suddenly during the day. The doctor had been in again that afternoon.

He was a short, thin, bald-headed man with a slight stoop and a heavy accent of some kind. He had treated me often during my early child-hood illnesses and was—as my father had once put it—"one of our people." He remained in the bedroom a long time with my father and Aunt Sarah and my mother, and when they all emerged he looked dark and serious. "Hot compresses, hot, hot, must clean it out," he said. He saw me in the long narrow hallway near the kitchen. "Ilana Davita," he said. "How are you? How are you? Your papa will be fine. Look who his nurses are. Look. How can he not be fine? You take after your father. You will be a big help to us one day with those Scandinavian looks of yours. Help us to organize the Swedes."

My mother stood in the doorway to the bedroom, looking over her shoulder into the room. Her face was ashen.

My father cried out that night and I woke in terror. I thought his voice was coming at me from the walls of my room. Who had cried out like that once, the words coming through my walls? Someone in one of the many buildings in which we had lived. I lay rigid in my bed. "Dear Christ!" he screamed. "What kind of a country is this? It's all nothing! Can't you see? It's *nothing!*"

I heard my Aunt Sarah's slipper-shod feet going quickly through the hallway.

The next morning I asked my mother, "Did Papa have a bad dream?"

"Yes," she said and looked away.

One afternoon in early January I came into my parents' bedroom. Aunt Sarah was there on a bed near the chair. My father's brown hair was growing back and formed a dark halo against the whiteness of his pillow. He looked frail and shrunken beneath the covers. I wanted to hold him.

He turned his head to me. "Hello, my love. Come to visit me again?"

"How are you, Papa?"

"Under repair. Your mother and aunt are splendid mechanics of the flesh."

"Papa, did you see castles when you were in Spain?"

"Castles? Oh, yes. I saw castles, my love."

"Were they pretty?"

"Was what pretty?"

"The castles."

"Nothing in Spain is pretty these days, Davita."

"Weren't the castles pretty?"

"No, my love. The castles I saw were full of holes and people were dead in them."

He turned his head away.

"Are you going back to Spain, Papa?"

He said nothing.

"I don't want you to go back."

"It's a hell," he said, not looking at me. "But it's the only place to be. A decent person knows where he belongs now."

"Papa."

"Davita," Aunt Sarah said. "Enough."

I went from the room.

When I returned from school the following day the harp was gone from the front door. My father had asked that it be moved to the bedroom. It hung directly in his line of vision on the inside of the door across the room from the galloping stallions.

Once or twice a week Mrs. Helfman cooked a pot of soup and brought it up to us. She would not leave the pot but transferred the soup to one of my mother's pots and took her pot back down. I met her on the parkway one cold Saturday afternoon in mid-January. She was out for a walk with Ruthie.

"How is your father, Ilana?"

"Better, thank you, Mrs. Helfman. He says he likes your soup."

"Yes?" She smiled with pleasure. Then she said, "Listen, Ilana, you don't have to sit by yourself in shul. You can sit up front with us. All right?"

"Sit up front with us," Ruthie echoed. "You don't have to stay in the back against the curtain."

Snow fell. Visitors came through the snow to see my father. Some of the visitors had attended the meetings in the many apartments in which we had lived. The discussions; the words that had flown about; the singing. I remembered. One of the visitors was a short, thick-chested man who wore a wool stocking cap, a brown leather jacket, and dark gray work pants. He had hard gray eyes and a small white scar that ran down from a corner of his mouth to the end of his chin. Once I saw him take off his jacket and roll up the sleeves of his flannel shirt. Garish tattoo marks rippled along the bulging muscles of his arms. He came often and each time sat alone with my father for hours.

"What do they talk about?" I asked Aunt Sarah in her room one

night after the man had gone. The room was neat, clean. The pine tree
had long ago been removed. Outside the window snow fell onto the
garbage cans in the cellarway.

"The revolution," she said with a bitter tone in her voice.

"I heard Mama say the man is going into industry. What does that
mean?"

"I have no idea. I wish my brother had more sense. I wish he had
never gone to Centralia. I wish—"

"Aunt Sarah?"

"Yes, Davita."

"Don't you want a better world? The revolution will make a better
world. I don't like this world, Aunt Sarah. I think Baba Yaga is everywhere in this world. How will it ever become better?"

"Dear child—"

"Is Jesus Christ going to make it a better world?"

"Yes! Our Lord is the Way and the Truth and the Life!"

"Will Jesus Christ bring a revolution?"

"He will come again and everything will be changed."

"He *will* bring a revolution!"

"Dear child, it will be our Lord's doing, not man's. Our Lord will
bring a new world of the spirit."

"Aunt Sarah, if you don't believe in what Papa and Mama believe in,
why did you go to Spain?"

"I am a nurse, Davita. I have a religious duty to go wherever there is
suffering. I despise both communism and fascism. But I despise fascism
more."

"Did you meet Jakob Daw in Spain?"

"Yes. In a hotel in Madrid. He was surrounded by friends and admir-
ers."

"Did he look all right?"

"He was ill."

"He wrote to us and said that he won't write any more stories. I don't
like his stories, but he shouldn't stop writing. My mother knew Jakob
Daw in Vienna when she was very young. Did you know that? Do you
hear my mother singing at night sometimes? She frightens me when she
sings like that."

"Take good care of your mother, dear child. Special care. Your father
is not the only one in this family who has been wounded."

"Jakob Daw was wounded in the big war in Europe. Mama says he
was gassed."

Aunt Sarah was quiet.

"I don't understand what that means."

She turned her head to the door of the room. "Was that your father?"

"I didn't hear anything."

"It's your father."

She got up and went from the room, leaving the door open. I listened to her walking through the long hallway in her house slippers. The door harp sounded. I sat on the edge of her bed, staring at the partly open door. My mother was away in Manhattan. The apartment was silent now, its corners filled with shadows. I went to the window in Aunt Sarah's room and peered through the darkness and the snow at the cellarway. The narrow cement walk was lit by a dim bulb; it reminded me of the driveways between many of the cottages in Sea Gate. The dunes the beach the castles the surf the ocean. David Dinn and Kaddish. The two of us together in the waves. The sun and the warm wind and the water. What had Jakob Daw called the years in Vienna with my mother? The dream time. Yes. The dream time.

I said to my mother one night in late January, "Will Papa ever write again?"

She had come into my room while I was reading at my desk and had sat down on the edge of my bed.

"Yes," she said. "Of course. He has to get well first. What are you reading?"

I showed her the book: *A Christian Child's Bible.*

"Aunt Sarah gave it to me. I like the stories. Abraham and Joseph and Moses. And Sarah and Rebekah and Rachel. I like Rachel. And Mary and the child Jesus."

"I don't care for religious books."

"It's only stories," I said.

There was a brief silence.

"Mama, will Uncle Jakob ever write stories again?"

"I don't know."

"Are you going away again tomorrow to Manhattan?"

"Yes."

"I miss the meetings we used to have. I miss the songs. Where are all the people?"

"The people in Manhattan can't come here for meetings."

"Why not?"

"I meet with people in Brooklyn now, Ilana."

"I don't understand why—"

"Is this the first book Aunt Sarah has given you?"

"No. There were two others. One was about Christmas in Maine. I liked that one. The other was about Jesus and King Herod and a massacre of little babies when King Herod was told the messiah was born."

"A massacre?"

"All the Jewish babies were killed. Did you know that? And King Herod was Jewish."

"So was Jesus."

"Jesus was Jewish? Aunt Sarah never told me that."

We were silent a moment. The door harp sounded softly through the hallway. I heard Aunt Sarah's footsteps. She entered the kitchen. The radio came on to the sounds of laughter. It was the Jack Benny program.

"I don't like to see you reading Christian books," my mother said quietly. "Christians once hurt me. I don't—" She stopped and looked at the window. Falling sleet tapped lightly on the panes.

I stared at her. "Christians hurt you?"

"During the big war. Cossacks and Poles. Christians." She seemed to shrink into herself, to grow smaller and smaller before my eyes.

"Mama."

She was silent, lost in her darkness.

"Mama."

She stirred. "It's a frozen rain," she said as if to herself, but clearly. "Must we go out in this frozen rain?"

"Mama!"

She looked at me. "I'm all right, Ilana."

"It's only stories, Mama."

"Yes? All right. Read whatever you want, Ilana. You'll find your own way. Isn't your room too warm?"

"I like it this way. All my other rooms were cold. I miss the meetings in the other places, but I don't miss the cold."

"The Helfmans keep the house warm. This is their house." She rose from the bed. "Good night, darling. I have some work to do. Listen to that rain! How nice it is to be in a warm room."

She kissed me on the forehead and went from the room. I continued reading the book of Bible stories my Aunt Sarah had given me.

On the parkway the next afternoon on my way home from school I met Mrs. Helfman. She was carrying a copy of *The New York Times.* In her heavy dark-brown winter coat and her woolen hat with its long scarf, which she wrapped around her neck and tucked into the beaver collar of her coat, she looked a little like a short round bear. It had snowed briefly in the morning and cars now moved cautiously along the wide parkway, trailing plumes of smoke. Mrs. Helfman, her face red with cold, greeted me cheerily.

"Hello, Ilana. Isn't this weather terrible? Worse than I ever remember in Poland. You are coming home from school? This isn't out of your way? How is your father?"

"Better, thank you. He's beginning to walk around."

We went past the yeshiva named after David Dinn's great-grandfather. A few boys and girls milled around outside, their breath vaporizing in the freezing air. I did not see David Dinn.

"You walk this way all the time?" Mrs. Helfman asked. "It adds at least two blocks. You look frozen, poor child."

We turned off the parkway into the side street and walked beneath trees that glistened with ice. The wind gusted fiercely between the tall apartment houses that made a tunnel of the street. It cut through my leggings, touched icily the insides of my thighs, and moved between my legs. I needed to go to the bathroom. The briefcase I carried was very heavy. There was our street with its brownstones and sycamores and the sky open and dull gray through the naked swaying trees. The houses looked shrunken and cold in the wind. We walked along quickly, skirting patches of frozen snow that lay upon the sidewalk.

Mrs. Helfman was talking to me but I had barely heard her.

"I asked if your mother is home."

"No. Mama is in Manhattan. She helps refugees from the war in Spain. She's not paid for that. But tomorrow she works on a job as a social worker. She says that's to help pay our rent. My father can't write now. Can I see the headline in the paper?"

She unfolded the newspaper, holding it against the wind. The headline read REBELS CLOSE ON MALAGA AFTER HARD 2-DAY BATTLE. A smaller headline read HEART OF MADRID SHELLED. She tucked the paper back under her arm.

"My father says he's going back to Spain as soon as he gets well."

Mrs. Helfman did not respond.

We stepped carefully around a hillock of grime-encrusted ice that had collected around the exposed roots of a sycamore. There was our house up ahead with its front stoop and glass and metal double door and the turrets on the sides that gave it the appearance of a castle. And there was my room in the turret, the window shade raised, the curtain drawn aside as I had left it that morning when I had stood there looking out at the street.

We came into the vestibule.

"Mrs. Helfman?"

"Yes, Ilana."

"Is David Dinn's father a relative of yours?"

"Yes. I'm his aunt."

"I see you talking to him when you come out of synagogue on Saturday morning."

"Yes," she said. "He is my nephew and a very good and decent person. Well, here we are." We had come into the downstairs hallway. The door closed behind us with its loud clicking. "Go upstairs and drink something hot right away, Ilana."

"Mrs. Helfman, do you have a book I could read that would help me with the words? I can't read the words. The Hebrew words in the synagogue, I mean."

She looked a little surprised. "Yes, we have many such books. I will ask Mr. Helfman to find a good one for you. Ruthie will bring it up. Now go and get something hot to drink."

Inside our apartment my father was asleep and Aunt Sarah sat dozing on a soft chair in the living room. I went to the bathroom and then made myself a cup of hot chocolate. I walked very quietly through the hallway to my room and sat at my desk. How silent the apartment was. My room was very warm. The wind blew against my window. I sat at my desk a long time, listening to the wind.

One night that week I found my father in the living room gazing out the bay window at the snowstorm blowing through the city. He wore a robe and slippers and his crutches stood near him leaning against the wall. The ruddiness had begun to return to his face, but his weight was not yet back and his flesh hung loosely beneath his chin. He saw me in the doorway to the living room.

"Hello, my love. Where do you keep yourself these days? Yes, a little hug. That's fine. Why do you look so sad? Sure, I'm getting better. Can't you tell? Tell me about school. Tell me what you're reading."

We talked for a while about my schoolwork, which I found boring, and about my classmates, who seemed to go out of their way to avoid me. The work was too easy, I said. The questions the teacher asked were always so simple, I said. No one seemed to like it when I knew all the answers, I said; not even the teacher. I was reading a book of Christian Bible stories, I said. And another book that was teaching me how to pronounce Hebrew letters and words. I wished the winter would be over, I said. I wanted to go back to the cottage on the beach. Was the door harp going to stay always on the bedroom door? I missed it when I went in and out of the apartment now, I said.

"I didn't know it meant so much to you, Davita," my father said. "I'll ask your mother to put it back."

"I like the music. I like the way the balls bounce up and down and music comes from the wires."

"Do you? That's what *I* like about it, my love. It was a gift from my brother to me. He brought it back with him from Europe after the big war. I'll ask your mother to put it back up on the front door as soon as she comes home."

"Did your brother bring the photograph of the horses on the beach?"

"No. My grandfather gave me that. He owned a farm near a beach on an island in Canada. He lived there a long time and when he became old and sick he came back home and gave me that picture before he died. That was just before the war. I was about thirteen or fourteen. He was a strange old man. Loved to be by himself. Very religious man. Went to church, read the Bible. Loved being alone. He left the farm to me and your Aunt Sarah."

"Was your brother a soldier?"

"Yes. He came home badly wounded."

"Did he get well?"

"No. He died. He was my older brother and he died. We were two brothers and one sister. We'll certainly put that harp back on the front door, my love. Can't abide seeing you so sad. Did your aunt give you the book of Bible stories?"

"Yes."

"She keeps trying. Where is your Aunt Sarah, anyway?"

"She's asleep in her room. Papa, what happened to you in Centralia?"

He looked startled. "What? Where did you hear about Centralia?"

"Aunt Sarah said something happened to you in Centralia. Where is Centralia, Papa?"

"It's a town in the state of Washington, on the other side of the country. My love, we won't talk about Centralia tonight, if you don't mind. As a matter of fact, we won't talk about Centralia until you're really grown up. All right? Do you like the Bible stories?"

"Yes."

"My mother used to read Bible stories to us every Sunday afternoon in our living room. My father would start a big fire going in the fireplace and we'd all sit there and my mother would read to us from the Bible."

"Why don't your mother and father come to see you? All your friends come, but not your mother and father."

He was silent and sat gazing out the window at the snow. "They don't want to have anything to do with us, Davita. Let's not talk about it. All right?" He turned to me again. "Why are you reading a book about Hebrew?"

"So I can read and understand the words when I go to the synagogue on Saturday mornings."

That startled him to the point of astonishment. "What?" he said, staring at me. "What are you talking about, Davita?"

"Sometimes I like to go to the synagogue on Eastern Parkway where Ruthie Helfman goes. It's nice there and I like listening to the songs. I don't like the curtain though. But I found some openings and I can see through it. The synagogue is in the school where Ruthie goes. And David Dinn goes there too. Do you remember David Dinn?"

"Of course I remember David Dinn. Ezra Dinn's boy."

"Mrs. Helfman told me Mr. Dinn is her nephew and he's a nice man."

"He's a fine man," my father said, a strange tightness entering his voice. "A decent person. Very helpful. And very religious. So you go to a synagogue. Christ, what happens here when I'm away? Listen, how about a cup of tea and some cookies for your tired father?"

"Did Mama know Mr. Dinn when you met her?"

"She knew him. They're cousins. Didn't she tell you? She lived with his mother when she first got to America."

"Uncle Jakob knew Mama in Vienna, and Mr. Dinn knew Mama in New York."

"That's right," my father said. "The three of us were in love with your mother, and she married me. How about the tea and cookies, my love?"

"Yes, Papa."

"We'll put that harp back up on the front door right away. I don't need it anymore now. Your old dad is going back to his writing. My brother used to call it a magic harp. Got it from some old European family. The magic didn't work for him, though. Now go and get me my tea. And for Jesus' sake, stop looking so sad. Come on, Davita, give me a smile. A real smile. That's right. Yes. Now *that's* a smile!"

We were eating supper in the kitchen on a Friday night in February when I heard through the walls and floor of the house the faint sounds of singing from the apartment below. The Helfmans were singing their zemiros together. Like the Dinn family in the cottage on the beach. I sat in my chair, listening to the singing, and heard my mother say, "You're not well enough, Michael. You're not. Is he well enough yet, Sarah?"

"We'll let the doctor decide," my father said.

"That commissar?" Aunt Sarah said. "He'll send you back too soon, Michael."

The melody came distantly through the walls and floor, sweet and slow and joyous. And Ruthie's high voice and the deep nasal voice of her father, softly singing the Shabbos songs.

"Sarah, did you read the piece I finished last week? The *New Republic* bought it. John called me today. I've got my strength back. We'll see what the doc says. It'll be another two or three weeks, at the most."

"You'll go back when the doctor says you can," my mother said.

"Agreed," my father said.

"I don't trust that commissar," Aunt Sarah said.

"Ilana," my mother said. "What on earth are you doing? You'll tip the chair."

I was leaning back to be closer to the wall and the music. I brought the chair forward. The music was now barely audible.

"If I can get off those crutches and onto a cane, I'll be all set," my father said.

"Michael, why don't you come up to the farmhouse for a few weeks?" Aunt Sarah said. "You've been wanting to write a book. You can start it there."

"Now is not a time for writing books, Sarah. We'll have Hitler on our front lawns one day soon if he's not stopped in Europe. You were there. You know what's going on."

I tipped my chair back again and listened at the wall.

"Michael," Aunt Sarah said, an imploring tone in her voice. "You're the only brother I have, the only relative I can really talk to. I don't want you to get hurt."

"We'll see what the doctor says," my father said.

"Ilana, please sit straight," my mother said. "What's the matter with you tonight?"

"Talk to him, Anne," Aunt Sarah said. "He listens to you."

"But I want Michael to go back," my mother said. "He ought to go back. People trust his stories about the war. He went there at my urging. It's the right thing for him to do."

"Absolutely the decent thing," my father said.

"We will go by what the doctor tells us," my mother said.

"I don't like that doctor," Aunt Sarah said. "I don't trust him."

"Ilana, what are you doing?" my mother said. "I asked you not to tip your chair."

"I was listening to the music, Mama."

"What music?"

"From the Helfmans downstairs."

The three of them looked at me.

"Mama, if Papa goes back to Spain, can we have Friday night dinner sometimes with the Helfmans?"

"We'll talk about it another time, Ilana. Are we done? Can I bring dessert?"

They went on talking about Spain. After a while the music downstairs came to an end. My father went to his desk in the bedroom to work on another article. My mother sat in the living room, reading and listening to the phonograph. Aunt Sarah went to bed.

I sat at my desk, studying the book of Hebrew letters and words the Helfmans had given me. The winter wind rattled my window. Downstairs the Helfmans were singing again. If there was no snowstorm tomorrow morning, I would go again to the synagogue. That was better than sitting home listening to all the talk about Spain and Franco and Hitler and Stalin and the Abraham Lincoln Brigade and the bombing of Madrid and the battle for the Jarama and seeing in my mind pictures of arms and legs everywhere. It was comfortable in the synagogue and people sang together. And I liked being in the same room with David Dinn and imagining myself back on the beach with him and in the water waiting for the waves. And I knew a few of the Hebrew words now. And the door harp would sing as I went from the apartment. My door harp. Singing.

I sat in the synagogue behind the curtain and watched David Dinn and his father recite the Kaddish. The large room was crowded, the air warm. On the men's side the windows were foggy with condensation. The murmurous voices, the incantatory tone of the man at the lectern before the ark, the rhythms of the congregation's singing—I felt a drowsy languor wash over me, felt myself afloat in a warm and calming sea.

On the wintry sidewalk outside after the service I saw David Dinn and four or five of his friends and came over to them.

"Hello, David. Good Shabbos."

"Hello, Ilana." He still looked a little embarrassed whenever I came over to him. He wore a heavy dark-blue jacket and a woolen cap that covered his ears. A bitter cold wind blew along the parkway.

"What does the word yiyaw mean?" I asked. "I saw it in the prayerbook. Am I saying it right? Yiyaw?"

"I don't ever remember seeing a word like that, Ilana," David said. "Where is it?"

"I saw it a lot of times. Maybe I'm not saying it right. I was reading slowly to myself because I can't follow everyone else, and I kept seeing these same two letters. I think you say them—"

"Oh," David interrupted. "Wait!"

"Don't say it!" one of his friends said loudly. "It's the name of God!"

"It's pronounced Adonoi when you pray," David said. "And you say HaShem when you're just using it in talk. You never pronounce those letters as they're written, Ilana."

"Why not?"

"The name of God is too holy to be pronounced."

"I don't understand."

"She doesn't understand," one of his friends echoed.

"That's the law," David said. "That's the way you're supposed to say it."

I saw his father coming over to us through the crowd.

"Adonoi," I said. "And HaShem. Is that right?"

"Yes," David said, looking uncomfortable.

"Then why do they write it with those two letters?"

"I don't know."

"Good Shabbos, Ilana," David's father said. He wore a dark winter coat and a dark felt hat. "How is your father?"

"Much better, thank you. He's going back to Spain in a few weeks."

"Back to Spain? So soon?"

"My mother says he can go back if the doctor says it's all right. My mother says he should go back."

Mr. Dinn stood there, looking down at me, sadness in his eyes. He seemed not to know what to say.

"Mr. Dinn, can I ask you something?"

"Of course."

"Am I Jewish?"

He looked startled. "Of course you're Jewish," he said.

David turned his eyes away and gazed down at the ground. His friends had become suddenly very still.

"Some kids in my school say I'm half-Jewish."

"According to Jewish law, Ilana, there is no such thing as someone who is half-Jewish. If your mother is Jewish, you are Jewish."

"That's what my father once said. But I wanted to be sure."

"Your father was correct."

"But how can I be all Jewish if my father isn't Jewish?"

"That is the law, Ilana," Mr. Dinn said quietly.

"Her father isn't Jewish?" one of David's friends said in a loud voice.

"Be quiet, Yankel!" David said, visibly angry.

Mrs. Helfman came out of the crowd. "Ezra, forgive me. The Liebermans are waiting. Good Shabbos, Ilana. How is your father? Ezra, Mrs. Lieberman has a cough and this wind is not good for her. Can we go? Give your parents and your aunt my regards, Ilana."

"Good Shabbos, Ilana," David said.

They went off into the crowd.

David's friends stood in a small tight huddle, staring at me. Then they turned and walked away.

I went quickly home.

That week my father stopped using his crutches and began to walk with a cane. The cane gave him a jaunty look. Twice he traveled to the newspaper where he worked. His old barking laugh had returned. He took my mother out one night to see a Russian movie. Aunt Sarah moved about the apartment in her house slippers, quoting the Bible to herself and murmuring under her breath. One evening as she dozed on the couch in the living room I looked closely at her legs and realized why she walked about in slippers: her legs were swollen from all the hours she stood upon them as a nurse. She dozed fitfully, her thin frame looking taut even in sleep. She seemed a melancholy figure now that her task here was coming to an end. Where would she go now?

In the first week of March the doctor informed my father that he had fully recuperated from the jaundice and the wound. He would have a slight limp but that would disappear in time. We celebrated that night with dinner and wine in the kitchen. My aunt cried and drank too much and had to be helped to bed. "My only brother," she kept saying. "Who else do I have? Dear Jesus, be kind to us."

One week later my father bought a steamship ticket to Lisbon. I overheard him telling my mother one night that he was having difficulty renewing his passport.

"Immigration is giving me a hard time. I don't think they want me to leave the country."

"Shall I ask Ezra to help?"

"I'll handle it myself, Annie. I don't need Ezra."

"All right, Michael. You know how kind he is. Please don't be nasty."

"I get the jitters sometimes with him so close."

"What do you mean close? I saw him more often when we were moving from place to place in Manhattan than I see him now. He's a very kind and considerate man. He knows to stay away."

"Is he still my competition, Annie?"

"Oh, you foolish, foolish man. How could you think that?"

"Because I love you. Because I'm getting edgy about going away. Am I doing the right thing?"

"Yes. I would tell you if you weren't."

"You always have."

"Promise me, no heroics, Michael. Please."

"No heroics, darling. I promise."

"Shall we go to bed now?"

"God, I love you."

"My sweet darling Michael."

I went silently back down the long tunnel of our hallway to my room.

One night toward the end of that week Aunt Sarah came into my room as I sat at my desk, reading. She asked if she could sit on my bed. She had on a plain dark woolen dress and looked tired and pale. She had not worn her nurse's uniform since the day the doctor had announced my father's recovery. She sat primly on the edge of my bed, a tall thin woman with blue eyes and short blond hair and a somewhat too long face that was handsome on my father but somehow didn't seem to belong on a woman.

"Well," she said. "Your Aunt Sarah is going home."

I said I would miss her.

She asked if I would mind her sending me a book from time to time. I said I would like that very much.

"Are you going to Spain?" I asked.

"Not right away. I may go up to the farmhouse for a week or two. I'm very tired. You would love the farmhouse, Davita. You might come to visit me in Maine one day, and I'll take you up. It's a long trip, but it's so lovely there. There's a beach and the sea and birds."

"And horses."

She smiled. "And horses." She was silent a moment, and sad. "I'll miss you, Davita. I will pray to our Lord for you and your mother."

"Will you pray for Papa, too?"

"I pray for your father all the time. I wish he—I wish my brother would—" She broke off, her voice quavering. "We have to trust in our Lord," she said. "We must have faith in Jesus Christ. I am going to pray for all of you right now. Will you pray with me?"

I didn't know what to say or do.

She rose from the bed and got down on her knees in the center of the room.

I went over to her and got down beside her. She closed her eyes and brought her hands together. Her lips moved. She was saying something that I could not hear. Then I heard her say, "Yea, though I walk through the valley of the shadow of death . . ." I closed my eyes and brought my hands together and remained on my knees, listening to my aunt pray. My knees hurt. I heard her say, "Amen."

"Amen," I said.

We rose.

She kissed me gently on my head. As she bent toward me I caught a sharp sense of her sadness and fervor. Then she went from my room. Later I heard her talking with my parents in the kitchen. She left early the next morning before I woke.

That Saturday afternoon my parents and I walked beneath the trees along Eastern Parkway to Prospect Park a few blocks away. It was a cold windless day, the air clean and sharp, the sky so blue it seemed inside a summer day's dream. My father walked with his cane. We passed some boys from the synagogue where David Dinn and his father prayed. They ignored me. There was little traffic on the parkway and few people in the park. We walked together through the park to the lake, where about a half-dozen people were ice-skating. The sun spangled the frozen water and gave it a hard opalescent sheen. We sat for a while on a bench and I watched small winter birds playing in the trees.

Then my mother grew cold and we walked on, circling the lake and then heading out of the park and back onto Eastern Parkway. We talked very little. I held tightly to my father's free hand. My mother's eyes were dark, burning.

That night my father came into my room as I was at my desk and sat down stiffly on my bed, straightening his right leg with care.

"Well, my love," he said. "How are you feeling?"

"I'm not feeling good, Papa."

"I see that," he said.

"I don't want you to go away."

"I know you don't, my love. But I'm going anyway because I have to. Listen, Davita, I want to tell you something. I'm not sure you're old enough for this. I'm going to tell you a story. It's not a Jakob Daw kind of story. And it's not about our friends Johnny Appleseed or Baron Munchausen. It's about your father and someone who was a little like Paul Bunyan. Are you interested? Yes? Good girl. Okay.

"When I was about seventeen years old I caught pneumonia and almost died. This was soon after my brother died and a few weeks after I graduated from high school. I lay sick in my bed all summer, coughing and sweating, and when I recovered I was too weak to go to college. I had been accepted into Harvard. My father thought I ought to spend a few months with one of his cousins in the state of Washington. Clean air and healthy farm work would restore my strength, he said. His cousin also owned forests and lumber mills. So they put me on a train. I thought the ride would never end. Hills and valleys and lakes and plains and mountains and deserts. When I got off the train I found myself in a beautiful green world. My father's cousin had a large farm near the town of Centralia. I loved it—the farm, the forests, the work, the animals—that cool green rainy world on the other side of the country.

"In November I went into Centralia with my father's cousin and his family to celebrate Armistice Day and watch the parade. A terrible thing happened that day. Are you listening, my love? This is not a nice story. This is about a different kind of America. Listen."

I listened.

That was the night he told me about what happened in Centralia, Washington, on November 11, 1919. But he did not tell me everything.

He told me about a man named Wesley Everest, who worked at logging—a kind of small Paul Bunyan, he said. He had been in the army in Europe during the war and had won a medal for sharpshooting. He was from Kentucky and Tennessee, and after the war he wandered west and ended up as a lumberjack in the great forests of the Pacific Northwest. He joined the union called the Industrial Workers of the World—nicknamed the Wobblies. This union wanted workers to have good food, decent working conditions, no more than eight hours of work each day. They wanted things that a lot of people thought were bad for America. The owners of the forests and the mills hated the men who belonged to this union and called them Communists and Reds. They paid other men, who had also been in the war, to beat up those helping the union. This union had a hall in Centralia. There were rumors that the hall would be attacked on Armistice Day. But those ex-soldiers marched right past the hall and didn't stop, and it looked like the rumors had been all wrong.

"I remember I stood watching them. It was cold and foggy. We felt good that nothing had happened and we stood in the crowd, laughing and having a good time. But on the way back, the parade suddenly stopped in front of the union hall and some of the men broke through the door. I heard shooting. There was a lot of screaming and yelling. My father's cousin said we had better get out of there and get back to the farm. The next day we found out that Wesley Everest had shot one or two of the men who had followed him as he had run out of the hall and the town and tried to cross a river. The river was too strong and too cold and he couldn't make it across. They brought him to the town jail. That night some men broke into the jailhouse and took him out and killed him."

My father fell silent and looked down at the floor. He said, a moment later, "Davita, listen. There are two kinds of America. That's what I realized that day. And I knew which kind I belonged to. That's why I'm going back to Spain, my love. I don't want fascism in my country, and the place to stop it is Spain. I'll miss you. Be a big girl and listen to your mother. She's a very special person, your mother. You'll find out about that as you grow up."

"Papa?"

"Yes, my love."

"What does your father do?"

"He's in the lumber business. My whole family is in the lumber industry. Now I want you to give your father a big hug, an ocean of a hug. It's got to last me a long time. That's right. *That's* the hug I had in mind!"

He kissed me on my face and held me a long time. He was tall and strong and I loved him, my father, Michael Chandal.

The next afternoon my mother and I rode with him in a cab to a pier in Manhattan. It was a cold clear day, the sky a brilliant blue. My mother and I stood in the crowd on the pier and watched the ship move slowly away. My father stood on the deck, waving his cane. Gulls circled and screamed overhead. The river looked burnished beneath the late afternoon sun. Along the shoreline the water was frozen and out in the wide clear channel large blocks of ice floated on the surface and glistened in the sunlight. My father grew smaller and smaller. Then I could no longer see him.

My mother stood huddled inside her coat, gazing down the river at the receding ship, her eyes wide and moist, her hair long beneath her beret. "It's time again for being alone," she said in a low, clear voice. "I hate it."

We took the subway home.

That week a letter arrived from Jakob Daw, from Spain. It was addressed to me.

"Dear Ilana Davita. Recently I thought I would not be able to write anymore. But what does a writer know? The story tells me: Write. And I write. I will write very slowly and with care so you will be able to read my terrible handwriting.

"We return now to our little bird. He crossed the stormy ocean and suddenly found himself in an even stormier land. All the earth was filled with the storms of war. Our bird flew back and forth across the burning land. And he was astonished to find that wherever he went he heard music. How strange that in the midst of war there was music! Men marched and fought and killed and sang. Our bird saw the war and listened to the songs and thought this must be the land where the source of all the world's music was to be found. He flew to battlefields and watched men running and falling; he saw shells exploding, bombs falling, buildings crumbling, children dying. He saw men and horses dead in fields and alongside rivers. Sometimes he flew in the rain and still the war went on. Once he came to a small valley that lay between a range of mountains and a wide plain that bordered on a sea. And there in that valley he found a white horse, dead in a field of grass, killed by an exploding shell. What a lovely horse it must have been! Dead in the grass from the war. It seemed to our bird that all the beautiful things in the world were dying in this war—and still the music was going on, giving strength to both sides, soothing the dying and those left to grieve.

'Make an end to the music!' our bird cried. 'Cover the world in a pall of silence! Let all see the truth without the false veil of this eternal welling music!' He flew about in a frenzy, searching. He watched as the land grew darker day by day with the war. And still the music.

"One day, while flying over a mountain, our bird saw soldiers from one army enter a small village and kill old men, women, and children who were reported sympathetic to the other side. The next day he flew over a valley and saw soldiers from the other army enter another village and kill old men, women, and children who were sympathetic to the first side. In the weeks that followed, our little bird saw that happen in many villages and towns. His eyes grew dull, his wings grew weary. How could the source of all the world's music be in such a land? Impossible! And he decided to end his search in the land of blood and bombs and return across the ocean to the land of mountains and rivers and plains and great forests. He thought wearily that the source of the music might well be somewhere in that new land. He would search for it there. And he began his westward journey back across the great sea.

"That is my story.

"How are you, Ilana Davita? Did I frighten you with my words about war? The really bad things about this war have no words as yet and I told you only those things that you are probably seeing in the newspapers. Does my story have an ending this time? I am very tired. It is easier to write a story with an ending than to write one without an ending. Is your father well? Send him my kindest regards. And to you and your mother, my affectionate good wishes. Jakob Daw."

I showed the letter to my mother and watched as she read it.

"Is Uncle Jakob coming back to America?"

"Yes," my mother said in a barely audible voice, staring at the letter.

"Where will he live?"

"I don't know."

"Why is Uncle Jakob coming back to America?"

"I don't know. Are you finished with your homework?"

"Yes."

"Help me make supper."

"I wanted to read the Hebrew book Ruthie gave me."

"I need someone's company in the kitchen now, Ilana. Please help me."

Four

My father cabled us from Paris. Smooth crossing, safe arrival, hip holding up. He cabled us again from Barcelona. Daw around somewhere. Am searching. Hip okay. Then he cabled us from Madrid. Found Daw. He and Madrid in bad shape. Hip doing nicely.

We heard nothing from Jakob Daw.

We began to receive mail from my father every two or three days. He told us that he loved us and missed us. He wrote about the weather—cold and wet—and the activities of some of his fellow journalists—flamboyant, contemptible, noble, cowardly. He himself was being careful. The hip was fine and he had discarded the cane. He sent on gossip about Hemingway and Malraux. He wrote about a Canadian doctor who had perfected a technique for giving blood transfusions on the battlefield—the first time this had ever been done. He wrote about some Jewish combat pilots he had met, a couple of them from Brooklyn, and the large number of Jews in the Abraham Lincoln Brigade. He wrote that he had come across some members of the family of the girl named Teresa. Did we remember little Teresa? We had met her in Sea Gate last summer. Then he wrote that the weather was turning warm.

I asked my mother one morning, "Why is Papa writing so much now? He didn't write us before."

"Sometimes things happen to people and they change," my mother said.

"They do things they didn't do before?"

"Yes."

"Like when I started going to synagogue after I met David and Ruthie?"

She hesitated a moment. "Yes, Ilana. Something like that."

"And like what happened to Papa in Centralia?"

She gave me a sudden sharp look across the breakfast table and said in a tight voice, "Your father spoke to you about Centralia?"

I nodded, a little frightened by the anger in her eyes.

"What did he say?"

I told her.

She relaxed a little. "Yes," she said softly. "Like what happened to your father in Centralia."

"I'm glad Papa changed and is writing to us," I said.

My mother was changing too. A sadness had settled upon her. Those moments when her eyes turned inward became more frequent and intense. Sometimes she went about the apartment talking to herself in words I didn't understand. One afternoon I went past her bedroom and noticed the door open and peered inside and found her standing at the window that looked out onto the backyard. The soft light of early spring lay upon her lovely features—the small lips and slightly pointed chin and high cheekbones and dark eyes and the long startling spill of her raven hair. She stood sharply outlined against the window—trim, thin-hipped, full-breasted, her head nearly touching the pane. She was speaking softly to the window, her lips almost on the glass. "You know what it is, don't you. You see through us the same way that we see through you. It's the loneliness. That's right. It's Mama waking to no husband on Shabbos and yom-tov. Yes, that's right. It's zaideh alone with us at the table. Yes, yes. It's the sounds in the darkness during the night, for which I need the strength of my man, and my man isn't here. It's pogroms that might come at any time. Yes, pogroms. Can anything be worse than this black plague of loneliness?"

She went on talking that way awhile, then began to use words I didn't understand. I moved quietly back from the door and went to my room.

Now she worked half-days five days a week as a social worker in an agency in Manhattan and also taught English four nights a week to new immigrants in a nearby night school. She said to me one Saturday afternoon, "Please don't be upset that I'm not home at night or that sometimes I get home late from the agency. You're a big girl. Besides, I'm a very good social worker and a very good teacher of English, and I like what I'm doing. That's right. I had very good teachers in Vienna and in Brooklyn College. I can see you're upset. There isn't much we can do about it, Ilana. We need the money to live."

On the nights when she was home she would come into my room and sit in the light padded living room chair she had moved near my desk. She would help me with my homework or sit quietly, reading. I had the feeling on those nights that it was less our need for money that drove her to work than it was her dread of being long hours alone.

One night in the second week of April I woke trembling and went fearfully through the dark hallway to my parents' bedroom and climbed into bed next to my mother, who lay still and warm, breathing lightly, her hair in disarray over her face and the pillow. I lay against her, trembling, and she stirred and woke and turned her head to me.

"What is it, darling?" Her breath was stale and dry.

"A nightmare, Mama."

"Poor darling. Let me hold you. You're shivering. I'm here, Ilana. Your mother is here."

She soothed me and I slept inside her warmth. Through my sleep I felt her holding me, stroking my face and hair, whispering against my cheek words in a language I did not understand.

One Friday my mother remained in Manhattan after work in order to attend a party-sponsored rally in Madison Square Garden. That evening I went out of the apartment and stood for a long moment on the landing outside the door, listening to the song of the door harp. The house sounded eerily silent. I went down the stairs, my capped shoes echoing softly through the hallway. In the air were the distinctive odors of chicken and soup; I remembered Friday afternoons on certain streets in Sea Gate. I had on a pale blue light woolen dress with a white collar and long sleeves—my best dress. I went to the door of Ruthie's apartment and rang the bell.

Ruthie opened the door. "Hello, Ilana," she said. "Good Shabbos. You shouldn't ring the bell on Shabbos. It uses the electricity. Remember?"

"I'm sorry."

"Come in. I like your dress. Is that for us?" She wore a white long-sleeved woolen dress which accentuated her red hair and freckled face.

"From me and my mother."

"Is it Ilana?" I heard her mother call from the kitchen.

"Yes, Mama. And she brought a present."

"Come in and say hello. My husband will be home soon from shul."

We entered the kitchen, a hot white room thick with the embracing odors of soup and meat.

"What a beautiful plant!" Mrs. Helfman said, taking the gift I had brought. "A pothos. I like the green and white leaves. My husband is a gardener. Did you know that?" She had on a dark blue long-sleeved dress, over which she wore a white apron. A white kerchief covered her red hair. Her eyes were soft and wide and brown, and her roundish face, flushed by the heat in the kitchen, was smooth and happy-looking. "I like your mother's taste, Ilana." She put the plant on the windowsill near the kitchen table. "It will get the afternoon sun," she said. "Ruthie, take Ilana into the living room."

"Can't I help with something, Mrs. Helfman?"

"You want to help? Sure you can help. I'll tell you what you can do. But first put on an apron. I don't want you to spoil such a pretty dress."

We made a salad. We brought dishes from the kitchen to the living room, where a console table had been moved away from the wall, opened and widened and covered with a white cloth. On the buffet stood a polished triple-branched silver candelabrum. White candles, their drip pans still clean, cast soft yellow light and pale shadows throughout the room. The table gleamed with its six settings of dishes and glasses and silverware and silver wine cups. On the wall over the buffet was a dark blue velvet hanging on which was painted in gold a representation of the Old City of Jerusalem. Above the city, in a flaming nimbus from which spokes of golden light radiated in all directions, were Hebrew words which Ruthie had once translated for me: "I believe in perfect faith in the coming of the Messiah; and even though he delays, still I believe in him." There were no other pictures or drawings anywhere in the apartment. On the righthand lintel of each door, at about eye level for adults, was a little box which Ruthie called a mezuzah. There were holy writings inside each box, she said. The box reminded you that God was in your house. The silver filigree mezuzah on the front door had been carried by her father to America after the big war. It was one of the few possessions left in his house in a small town in Poland after the pogrom in which his parents and his two sisters had been killed. No one could understand how the mezuzah had survived the pogrom. It was a miracle, Ruthie said.

I knew that word: pogrom. Ruthie had explained it to me during one of the many times we had played together. The organized killing of Jews by a mob. The word frightened me. Pogrom. Like the word war.

Ruthie would talk to me often about her parents' European beginnings. Her father was a descendant of teachers and rabbis; her mother's father and both grandfathers had been merchants. Ruthie's parents had been introduced to each other in America; and Ruthie had been born two days before me. We had laughed with delight when we discovered that coincidence in dates. Often, as I listened to her talk about her parents, I wondered why I knew so very little about my mother's life in Europe. She had been born in Poland and educated in Vienna. Her father was a Hasid and on Sabbaths and festivals was often away from home visiting the leader of his sect. She had been raised by her mother and grandfather. Sometimes I wondered what it was like to have your mother's father acting as your father. It had to be better than having no father at all.

The three of us stood around in the kitchen, engaged in warm and idle talk. Mrs. Helfman wanted to know what kind of rally my mother was attending. When I told her, she raised her eyes to the ceiling, shook her head, and sighed. Ruthie wanted to know what a Communist party was like. Mrs. Helfman asked her to take the braided bread called challah into the living room and put it on the table; the men would be here soon, she said. I asked which men. I had seen the six settings but did not know who else was coming. "My husband and my nephew and his son David," Mrs. Helfman said. "Take this challah cloth out to the table, Ilana, and give it to Ruthie. She'll know what to do with it."

I went through the hallway to the living room and handed the white embroidered cloth to Ruthie. I heard a knock on the door. Mrs. Helfman went to open it. For a moment I expected to hear the soft tones of the door harp. I heard instead Shabbos greetings and the voices of Mr. Helfman, David Dinn, and his father as they entered the apartment.

I stood in the doorway to the living room, looking down the hallway. They all wore dark coats and suits and dark felt hats. Mr. Helfman, short and portly, was talking in what I thought was Yiddish to Mr. Dinn, whose tall, spare figure seemed to dwarf the presence of his son.

David saw me and raised a hand in greeting. Mr. Helfman was putting the coats away in a closet near the door. Mr. Dinn kissed Ruthie's mother on the cheek.

They all came up the hallway into the living room, the men wearing dark skullcaps now. David appeared thinner than usual in a dark suit that seemed a size too large for him.

"Good Shabbos, Ruthie," Mr. Dinn said in his urbane and courtly manner. "Good Shabbos, Ilana. I understand your mother is busy tonight." As he said this, a faint note of disdain entered his voice. "Well, it's certainly nice to see you, Ilana. What a lovely dress on such a lovely girl! Two lovely girls! We must not forget our Ruthie. What do you hear from your father, Ilana?"

"Papa and Uncle Jakob left Madrid and are going to the north of Spain."

"Uncle Jakob?" Mrs. Helfman asked.

"Mr. Jakob Daw. Mama's friend."

"Jakob Daw, the writer?"

"Yes."

"Jakob Daw is one of Channah's friends from her Vienna days," Mr. Dinn said. "My cousin has very interesting friends. She has other friends as well, but we won't talk about them."

Again, that tone of disdain entered his voice. He had pronounced the first consonant of my mother's name with a guttural sound on the first letter, like someone clearing his throat. Uncle Jakob called her by that name. Some called her Hannah. My father called her Annie. Most called her Anne. What did it mean when a person was known by many different names? Channah, Hannah, Annie, Anne. Like my mother calling me Ilana, and my father calling me Davita, and Uncle Jakob almost always calling me Ilana Davita, and Aunt Sarah—

"Now and then I read your father's stories on the war," Mr. Dinn was saying. "He's a very good writer, when he gives us facts. But he's not very good when he starts in with the Communist propaganda. Is Jakob Daw also writing about the war? It seems every writer of importance is in Spain now writing about that war."

"How do you know so much about the war?" Mr. Helfman asked.

"I read the papers and magazines. I see refugees in my office. Don't you read what's going on?"

"I read. But it doesn't interest me. I refuse to fill my head with it. Who cares about goyische wars? A head has just so much space in it, and if you fill it with junk you have no room for important matters."

We had all taken seats in the living room. Ruthie and her mother sat together on the blue upholstered couch, Mrs. Helfman leaning against the tufted side cushion at her right, her plump fingers playing idly with the ornament of the curved wooden scrolled arm of the couch. I sat next to Ruthie, who had on her face the blank look she wore when she was bored. Mrs. Helfman listened with interest to the conversation but said little. Mr. Helfman sat in an easy chair across from David and his father.

"We all ought to care very much about this war," Mr. Dinn was saying. "If Franco wins, Hitler has a green light."

"I don't believe it for a minute," Mr. Helfman said. "What green light? What? Hitler is a clown and a yold. What will he do?"

"Hitler is not a clown," Mr. Dinn said quietly. "It would be a dreadful error if we thought he was."

"What can he do?" Mr. Helfman asked. "You think America and England and France will let him do what he wants? Not a chance."

"They have been letting him do what he wants for years," Mr. Dinn said. "That's why Franco is winning in Spain. That's why we have the choice we have today: fascism or communism. What a choice! It's like choosing between Sedom and Amorrah."

David sat in an easy chair next to his father. From time to time he raised his eyes and glanced at me. His eyes were sad and dark in the milky whiteness of his face, and his neck, sticking out of the collar of his too-large shirt, gave him a scrawny, birdlike appearance.

"I don't know if Uncle Jakob is still writing about the war," I said to Mr. Dinn. "Uncle Jakob wrote to us that he's tired of the war."

"Is he?" Mr. Dinn said without apparent interest.

"He wrote that both sides in the war are terrible and that he wants to come to America."

"Jakob Daw wants to come to America?" Mrs. Helfman said.

Mr. Dinn turned to me. "When is he coming?" There was a vague tightness in his voice.

"He doesn't know. My father wrote that the Americans won't give him a visa. So they're going together to Bilbao. That's a city in the north of Spain."

"Yes, I know where Bilbao is, Ilana. Why are they going to Bilbao?"

"I don't know. Mama says maybe Papa wants to help Uncle Jakob get back across the border into France."

There was a brief silence.

"Perhaps we should make Kiddush and wash and eat," Mrs. Helfman said quietly. "Everything is ready."

We moved to the table. Mr. Helfman poured wine from a silver beaker into the silver cups. He and Mr. Dinn had large cups; the other cups were small. We stood in front of our chairs as Mr. Helfman, holding up his cup, began to chant the prayers in a thin, unmelodious voice. I could make out some of the words; I had seen them in one of the books Ruthie had given me and in the synagogue prayerbook. "Boruch atuh Adonoi, elohainoo melech hu'olum. . . ." He chanted slowly, and when he was done, everyone said, "Amen." He sat down and drank from his cup. Then he stood again as Mr. Dinn began to chant the same prayer. David stood next to his father, his head turned slightly sideways, gazing up at him. I could see his lips mouthing the words.

Mr. Dinn finished. We all said, "Amen," and sat down in our chairs and drank from our cups. Then we all filed into the kitchen. Ruthie showed me how to wash my hands with the special two-handled beaker. I didn't know the blessing for washing one's hands; nor did I know the blessing over bread; but when Mr. Helfman made the blessing and cut the challah, I answered, "Amen."

The challah was warm and light and had a sweet taste.

We sat around the table, eating and talking. I had been placed next to Ruthie and across the table from David and his father. Ruthie's parents sat at opposite ends of the table. The talk among the adults was about the yeshiva and its new principal, a devout young man from England; about its English and Hebrew teachers and board of directors; about something called the Akiva Award; about the run-down condition of some of the classrooms; and about the school's serious money problems. "People don't have jobs, how can they give to a yeshiva?" Mr. Helfman said. I didn't understand most of what they were saying. Ruthie sat eating quietly, her face a blank. David listened but said nothing.

Between the soup and meat courses, Mr. Dinn steered the conversation back to the war in Spain until Mr. Helfman said, "It is against the law to talk of matters that might disturb one's Shabbos." Mr. Dinn broke off. We did not talk of Spain again during the meal.

Two of the three candles on the buffet sputtered and died.

Mr. Helfman asked me what I was studying in public school and began to compare my subjects with those taught in the yeshiva. There was haughtiness in his voice as he went along claiming superiority for the yeshiva curriculum.

"How are your grades, Ilana?" Mrs. Helfman asked.

"I get nineties and hundreds," I said.

"I'll bet you do," said Mr. Dinn. "So did your mother."

From across the table David was looking at me as if he were seeing me for the first time.

On the buffet the guttering flame of the third candle suddenly flared, leaped upward, flickering wildly, and was gone. A thin column of dark smoke spiraled slowly toward the ceiling.

"Ilana, would you like to help me bring in the dishes?" Mrs. Helfman asked.

From inside the kitchen, which was now cluttered with dirty pots and dishes, I heard David and his father and Mr. Helfman talking together about something I didn't understand. They spoke briefly in English, then slipped into Yiddish. Mr. Dinn and Mr. Helfman went on talking Yiddish, but David kept going from one language to another.

Mrs. Helfman saw me listening and said, "They are discussing tomorrow morning's sedra—the reading from the Torah."

"David knows almost all the Torah by heart," Ruthie said proudly. "David is a genius."

"Bring in the cake," Mrs. Helfman said to Ruthie. "And don't brag so much. You'll bring upon us the evil eye, God forbid."

Later, as we sat around the table near the end of the meal, Mr. Dinn leaned back in his chair, cleared his throat, and proceeded to deliver a little sermon. His forefingers tucked inside his vest pockets, he began in his sonorous voice to describe how God came down to Mount Sinai thousands of years ago in order to give the Torah to the Jewish people. The mountain was all covered in smoke, he said. There was thunder; lightning flashed from the clouds. The Torah was written in fire on tablets and the tablets were then wrapped in fire. Moses' face shone with light as he held them. "Only Moses could touch that sacred fire," said Mr. Dinn. "And that sacred fire could not be tampered with. The Sanctuary in the desert also had a special sacred fire, and only on that fire was one permitted to offer a bird or an animal as a sacrifice to God. Tomorrow's sedra tells us that the sons of Aaron the high priest brought their own fire into the Sanctuary and were killed. A strange fire must never be brought into the heart of the Sanctuary where the sacred fire of God is found. From this we can learn that we must preserve with care the sacred fire of our Torah, its laws, its words, and never permit it to be mixed with strange fires from the outside."

As he spoke I noticed David and Mr. Helfman and his wife glance at me from time to time as if to gauge my reaction to his words. But I could not understand much of what Mr. Dinn said. Mr. Dinn and Mr. Helfman then talked awhile longer about the mysterious deaths of the sons of Aaron. David joined their conversation. Ruthie and Mrs. Helfman sat listening. Then they all began to sing zemiros. There were phrases in the zemiros that I recognized. Mr. Dinn seemed surprised to see me join in the singing. I sat quietly through the many songs I didn't know, listening, trying to memorize the lines that were being repeated. Sometimes I just sang the melody without the words. Nine months earlier, on a sultry Friday night, I had listened to David and his father joyfully singing these songs on the porch of their house in Sea Gate; now I was singing with them. I had no idea what the words meant; I just enjoyed the music, the lilt and rhythm of the melodies, now slow and now fast, now melancholy and now joyous.

At a pause in the singing Mr. Dinn leaned forward and placed his long arms on the table and said, "Well, I see you enjoy singing, Ilana. You know, there's an interesting story told about King David and his harp." He adopted again that serious and sonorous tone. "King David was a great musician. When he slept his harp hung from the wall over his bed. The winds are strong in Jerusalem. Each night the wind would blow through the strings of the harp and the harp would begin to sing. King David would wake and listen awhile to the music of his harp, and then spend the rest of the night studying Torah so he could be a strong and wise king. An interesting story." He smiled down at me in his distant and courtly manner. "Let's sing some more."

The air in the room grew warm. Mr. Dinn and Mr. Helfman and David removed their jackets and sat in their shirt sleeves, singing. There was color on David's normally pale face and his eyes were shining. He sang in his high, thin voice, with his eyes closed and his body swaying back and forth. We sang for a long time. Then they sang and chanted the prayers that ended the meal. And when the singing was done, Mr. Dinn and David and Mr. Helfman got into a discussion about a point raised earlier concerning the sons of Aaron. They were deep in this talk a few minutes later when, suddenly, jarringly, the doorbell rang.

Mr. Helfman looked up, surprise on his round face. A shadow passed over Mr. Dinn's abruptly stony features. Mrs. Helfman said, "It must be your mother, Ilana."

Ruthie went to the door.

I heard my mother's voice and her footsteps in the hall. She came into the living room with Ruthie. She looked weary and ashen. Her hair was in disarray beneath her dark beret. She stood blinking her eyes in the brightness of the living room and gazing at the people around the table.

"Hello, Ezra," she said evenly. "How are you?"

"I'm well, Channah," Mr. Dinn said, after a pause. "And you?"

"I'm very tired."

"Your rally went well?"

"Very well."

"You spoke?"

"Yes."

"I'm glad for you that it went well." His manner was stiff and polite. There was a brief silence.

"David, how are you?" my mother asked.

I saw a slight stiffening of David's thin form. "I'm okay," he said with some sullenness in his voice.

My mother said to Mrs. Helfman, "Thank you for taking care of Ilana."

"A pleasure and a joy," Mrs. Helfman said.

"Anytime," Mr. Helfman said. "A smart girl, a bright girl." He said something in a language I didn't understand. My mother smiled wearily.

"Channah," Mr. Dinn said.

My mother turned to him.

"Call me Monday morning about Jakob Daw's visa. There are people in Washington I can talk to."

My mother looked at him, then looked at me.

"If you want me to, I'll help," Mr. Dinn said.

My mother nodded slowly, wearily.

"Good night, Channah," Mr. Dinn said.

"Good night, Mrs. Chandal," Mr. Helfman said.

"Good Shabbos, Ilana," David said.

At the door, Mrs. Helfman said, "You're sure you don't want a cup of tea? You look exhausted."

"I want to go to bed," my mother said.

Ruthie said, "Good Shabbos, Ilana."

"Good Shabbos, Ruthie. Maybe I'll see you in shul in the morning."

"Good night, Mrs. Helfman, Ruthie," my mother said.

We started along the hallway to the stairs. A dull heavy silence brooded over the house. I could hear the echoes of our footsteps.

"Mama?"

"Yes."

"You shouldn't ring their doorbell on Shabbos. They don't use electricity."

She paused for the briefest moment on the stairs, then continued along beside me. "I'll try to remember, Ilana."

"Were there lots of people at the rally?"

"Thousands. Many thousands."

"And you gave a speech?"

"Yes."

We were on our landing but not yet at the door, and she was already removing her coat and beret.

"Mama, did you go to school with Mr. Dinn?"

"We went to Brooklyn College together a long time before you were born." She fumbled in her purse for the key, hampered by her coat, which she had thrown over one arm. As she put the key into the door, she murmured to herself, but clearly enough for me to hear, "I am so tired. . . . Who can get used to this? After so many years together, to come home alone and go to bed alone and wake up alone. . . ."

The harp sang softly as we entered the apartment.

The web of sunlight upon my curtain woke me. I dressed and ate quickly. In a dream during the night I had heard my mother crying. I peered into her room and saw her curled up in sleep, looking frail and small, her mouth slightly open, the morning light giving her smooth face an ivory pallor. I went from the apartment and the house and walked in the cool April morning air to the synagogue.

Some days before, I had wandered about the apartment in an aimless and brooding reverie and had found myself in my parents' bedroom looking at the bookcase that stood alongside the desk. I discovered an English Bible. I took it along with me. Inside the synagogue, I found my seat near the curtained wall. An old woman helped me find the Torah reading. I read slowly and carefully the ninth, tenth, and eleventh chapters of Leviticus. The English was very difficult and I did not like the parts about killing a calf and dipping a finger in the blood and pouring the blood on the altar. I wondered if that was how everyone once worshipped God. I was not surprised that my parents did not believe in God or prayer. Blood and altars and burning kidneys and fat! I read carefully how the sons of Aaron were killed while bringing strange fire before the Lord. A fire went out from the Lord and killed them. I could not understand why they had to be killed for that. I read slowly about the animals the children of Israel were permitted to eat and about those they were prohibited from eating. There were creatures whose names I didn't know: coney, ossifrage, ospray, kite, cormorant, gier eagle, and lapwing. But I knew hare and swine and vulture and owl. I read very carefully and slowly but didn't understand what cloven-footed and cheweth the cud meant. But I understood about creeping things that went about on the belly and had more feet among all creeping things that creep upon the earth: I thought those words meant anything that had lots of legs. I understood about that. I remembered the roaches and bedbugs in our past apartments and the insects on the screens of the porches in Sea Gate: flying, crawling, whirring, buzzing, tapping.

Outside in front of the building after the service I went over to David and wished him a good Shabbos and said I couldn't understand why God killed the two sons of Aaron just because they were using strange fire. It seemed a very cruel punishment, I said.

David stood among his friends and gazed at me out of his large dark eyes. Dusty sunlight came through the early spring trees of the parkway and fell upon his face, giving his skin a translucent appearance and revealing the veins in his cheeks and along the sides of his head.

"They died because they were very bad," he said.

"What did they do?"

"The midrash says they would be marching along behind Moshe and Aharon, and the children of Israel would follow, and all the time the sons of Aharon would keep saying to each other, 'When are those two old people going to die so we can become the leaders?' They had evil hearts."

"Where does it say that? I didn't see it in my book."

"It's in the midrash. Those are stories that explain the Torah."

"But why isn't that story in this book?"

"Because it isn't. Not everything—"

"What kind of book is that?" one of David's friends suddenly interrupted.

"It's a Bible book," I said. "I found it in—"

One of the boys had come alongside me and was peering at the spine of the book. "It's the King James Bible," he said in a tone of horror.

They all backed away a step or two as if I were holding in my hand a specimen of forbidden vermin.

"That's a goyische Bible, Ilana," David said. "It's used by missionaries."

"Did she bring it into shul?" another boy asked.

A rush of heat swept across my face. They stood before me in a tight semicircle, about a half-dozen of them, in dark suits and hats, gazing at me out of dark accusing eyes. I felt myself swiftly judged and instantly impaled upon their cold and demeaning stares.

"I'll get you a different Bible," David said. "You shouldn't bring that one to shul. You shouldn't even read from it. There's my father. Good Shabbos. I'll give the Bible to Ruthie and she'll bring it to you."

He stepped into the crowd and was gone. I walked quickly home.

A letter had arrived from my father. He was in Bilbao with Jakob Daw. Hip okay. Daw okay. Visa not okay. War very definitely not okay.

Over lunch I asked my mother what the word missionary meant. She said it meant a person who was sent by a church to some area to do educational or hospital work and to win followers for the church. "It comes from an old word meaning to send off," she said.

"I took your Bible to shul today and David said it was a Bible for missionaries."

"Missionaries use it, yes."

"He said I shouldn't bring it to shul anymore."

"I'm not in the least bit surprised."

"Why do you have such a Bible?"

"It's a lovely work of English literature, Ilana. I read it for the pleasure I get from its language."

"Is Aunt Sarah a missionary?"

"Yes."

We ate for a while in silence.

"Are you going to ask Mr. Dinn to help Uncle Jakob get a visa?"

"Yes."

"Is the war very bad in Bilbao?"

"The war is bad everywhere in Spain."

"Can we go for a walk in Prospect Park later?"

"Yes."

"I want to go for a walk and see if there are flowers and watch people rowing on the lake."

"You'll see tulips and daffodils, Ilana. Those are lovely flowers."

"Mrs. Helfman said that Mr. Helfman plants flowers in the backyard in the spring."

My mother said nothing. She seemed abstracted, elsewhere in her thoughts.

After a while I said, "David's friends are pretty nasty, you know? I don't like them."

"Boys are nasty sometimes."

"They laugh at me. They're cruel."

"Men can be like that too sometimes," my mother said.

"They're mean and evil. They're like the sons of Aaron."

"Finish your lunch, Ilana."

"I wish God would send a fire and kill them."

"Ilana!"

"I hate them."

"Please finish your lunch, Ilana. Then you'll help me clean up and we'll take our walk."

I did not go back to that synagogue for a long time.

The weather turned warm. There were days of brilliant sunshine and clear blue air. Young birds played in the budding trees outside my window. The sycamore in our backyard took on a soft and lacy look. One Sunday afternoon I saw Mr. Helfman turning over the earth near the far fence of the backyard and planting seeds. I watched him from the window of my parents' bedroom, a short, pudgy, genial man wearing an old sweater and pants and a dark skullcap. He worked a long time, pausing frequently to wipe his face with a handkerchief. That was the afternoon three strangers—two men and a woman—came to the apartment and sat with my mother in our living room, studying. They looked to be in their middle or late thirties. I stood in the doorway to the living room and listened. They sat in the afternoon sunlight that came through the bay window. Each held a book and each read from it in turn. From time to time they would discuss a passage at length. My mother would respond to their questions in her quiet, determined, authoritative tone. Her face, bathed in sunlight, wore a soft gauzy luminous look. After a while I returned to my room and lay on my bed gazing at the sunlight coming through my window and listening to my mother's voice coming through the wall and thinking of Sea Gate and the sunlight on the beach and wondering where Jakob Daw and my father were. The war was now in the mountains all around Bilbao.

After the people had gone I asked my mother who they were.

"Friends."

"What were you doing?"

"Studying a work by Karl Marx."

"Will they come back?"

"Every Sunday afternoon."

By filling all the hours of her days with work she was removing from her life the hollows of what she called empty time. Empty time led to loneliness, she had once said to me. And sometimes one might do strange and hurtful things out of loneliness. Loneliness was to be prevented as one prevents the spread of a plague.

The following Sunday afternoon the strangers returned and sat with my mother in our living room, studying Karl Marx. They studied the text sentence by sentence, stopping often to ask questions of one another and to listen to my mother's explanations. Sometimes my mother would answer by quoting from the original German. I lay on my bed listening to my mother's voice through the wall.

Four letters had arrived from my father that week. He wrote that Jakob Daw had a visa waiting for him in Lisbon and would soon be leaving Bilbao. Hip fine, war bad, visa large surprise and small miracle. I thought of Jakob Daw and my father in the war that was all around Bilbao. Pieces of arms and legs and the corpses of horses and people and the fires of shells and bombs. War.

I spent the rest of the day reading a book Ruthie had given me. It was about an ancient plague that had struck the students of a great rabbi during a revolt of the Jews against the Roman empire. The rabbi's name was Akiva. Thousands of students died of that plague. Suddenly the plague stopped. This happened about two thousand years ago, the book said, and Jews still celebrated the day the plague began to come to an end. There were color pictures of boys and girls picnicking and playing at racing games and with bows and arrows.

My mother and I went to the movies that evening and saw a long newsreel on the war in Spain. We watched Madrid being bombed and the fighting in the hills around Bilbao. There were fiery explosions and huge columns of boiling black smoke and collapsing buildings and men lying dead in tall grass beside a swiftly flowing river.

I became ill that night in my bed and vomited and my mother changed my nightgown and my sheets and held me and sang me to sleep with a lullaby in Yiddish. I was running a high fever and later in the night had a dream. There was a sudden rustling noise and I looked and Baba Yaga was in the sycamore tree outside my window, peering at me through the branches, green-visaged, monstrous. A shock of terror pierced me. I found you, dear child, she said. Now you will go with Baba Yaga. Abruptly she sprang from the tree through my window and stood at the foot of my bed, laughing hideously, her mouth huge and black, her eyes red and burning. I was paralyzed with terror and could not scream. I felt myself wanting to scream, tried to push the scream from my throat, but my throat was tight, nothing would come from it. She moved toward me, a vile stench rising from her. How loathsome and grotesque she was! She stood beside me and reached out. I felt her touch my face. Icy cold and burning and an image of dead things floating in the green scum of a river's edge. I screamed and woke. My mother was immediately in my room. I cried and shivered. She held me and remained with me until I fell back asleep. In the morning the fever was gone but I lay shivering and my mother stayed with me all that day, nursing me as Aunt Sarah had once nursed her and my father. That night my temperature was still normal, and the next morning I returned to school.

I felt weak all that day. The weather was alternately cloudy and sunny, the air suddenly cold each time clouds slid across the sun. The cold prickled my skin and I would find myself shivering. On the way home from school I went past the yeshiva but saw no one I knew in the front yard. My mother was at her work in Manhattan. I let myself into the apartment and stood near the door a moment, listening to the harp. In the kitchen I had a glass of milk and some cookies, then wandered listlessly through the rooms and hallway. From the window in the spare bedroom I saw cats playing among the garbage cans in the cellarway. I thought of Aunt Sarah and wondered where she was. Had she come back from Spain? What did she do in her work as a missionary: nurse sick people to health and ask them to believe in Jesus Christ? Did she ask them to get down on their knees with her? I remembered myself on my knees in this room. It seemed an awkward position for prayer—and yet strangely comforting in a way I could not understand. On your knees with your hands together. I felt myself sliding to my knees and raising my hands. I knelt at the window a foot or so from the bed in which Aunt Sarah had slept. I didn't know what to say or to whom to say it. Finally I said, "Please protect my father and my Uncle Jakob. Please. Please. My name is Ilana Davita Chandal. Please protect them. I love them very much."

I got to my feet, feeling cold. The apartment was warm but my feet and the tips of my fingers were icy. I went out of the spare bedroom and walked slowly through the hallway to my parents' bedroom. From the window I saw that someone had suspended a bird feeder from a branch of the sycamore. Birds perched on the feeder and fluttered about it, pecking at the seeds. It seemed far enough away from the branch to prevent a cat from getting at the birds. The earth of the garden bed lay scraped and naked to the sky. In the east the sky had begun to empty of color. I walked back slowly through the dim hallway. Entering my room, I heard, echoing through the silence that lay heavily upon the house, the clear loud click of the lock on the downstairs hallway door. Someone was quickly climbing the stairs. I went to the door and opened it and saw Mr. Dinn come onto our landing.

He wore a dark spring coat, a dark suit, and a dark felt hat, and he carried in his hand a copy of *The New York Times.* He seemed startled by my appearance at the door.

"Hello, Ilana. Is your mother home?"

I stared at him and said my mother was in Manhattan and would be home soon.

"I was on my way back from the office and thought your mother might be home," he said, trying to make it sound light and matter-of-fact. Then he said, "How are you feeling? Are you over your fever?"

I told him I was feeling fine, and wondered who had told him I had been ill.

"Please tell your mother I was here," he said. "Ask her to call me."

I watched him start back down the stairs, a tall thin man, walking straight and stiff, and had a sudden image of the way my father used to sit slouched against the back of a chair with one foot draped across its arm. At the foot of the stairs Mr. Dinn turned and went through the hallway to the Helfman apartment. I heard him knock, heard the door open, heard Mrs. Helfman's voice. I went back into the apartment. The wooden balls of the door harp pinged softly upon the taut wires.

A while later, from the window of my room, I saw my mother walking up the street. What a sweet and lovely sensation that was each time, watching my mother moving toward the house and toward me! I heard the lock click shut. I waited but did not hear my mother's footsteps. I waited a while longer and went to the door and opened it. I heard my mother and Mrs. Helfman talking together quietly in the downstairs hallway. Then my mother started up the stairs. I came out onto the landing and she saw me. She looked very pale.

"Mama, Mr. Dinn was here and asked you to call him."

"I know, darling. Mrs. Helfman told me."

"What's the matter, Mama?"

"Let me come inside and close the door. There was a very bad bombing near Bilbao yesterday and Mr. Dinn wanted to know if your father was all right."

She removed her light coat and her beret and placed them in the closet.

"Is Papa all right?"

"If anything had happened, the paper would have called us. I'll phone Mr. Dinn. Then I'll make us something to eat. I'm sorry I'm so late today. The office was jammed. I have to go out later and teach my English class. I'll call the paper in the morning. Come inside the kitchen, Ilana, and help me with supper. First, let me call Mr. Dinn."

Her voice sounded strange. I watched her go along the hallway to the telephone on the stand between the kitchen and her bedroom.

During supper we heard a radio news broadcast about a bombing raid by rebel aircraft against a small unprotected town in northern Spain.

"Fascist barbarians," my mother said venomously. "Like the Cossacks. Barbarians!"

"Mr. Dinn could have trusted me to remember to tell you. I'm not a child."

"He was being very kind, Ilana. He wanted to make sure."

"He doesn't trust me because I'm a girl. David is the same way. They think I have no brains."

"It's very difficult for me to imagine anyone thinking that you have no brains. What's troubling you, Ilana?"

"I'm afraid about Papa," I said, after a pause.

"I'm sure your father is fine," my mother said. "He's taking good care of himself these days. Will you do the dishes, please? I must run to my class."

I cleaned up the kitchen and turned off the light. The apartment was dim and still, deep shadows hovering in the hallway and in the corners near the door. I wandered into my parents' bedroom and stood near my father's desk. Suddenly I had a sharp image of him sitting there working at his special writing, brown wavy hair, pale blue eyes, ruddy complexion, a genial man working for a better world for everyone. Why did he run around so much? Why did my parents *care* so much? No one else's parents seemed to care much about the world. Mr. and Mrs. Helfman didn't seem to care about the world; nor did the students in my public school class and their parents. Mr. Dinn cared a little about the world; he helped people who were in trouble over immigration laws. But most people had jobs and came home at night and played with their children. How could a single event like what happened in Centralia change a person so much? And what had changed my mother from an observant Jew to a Communist? I could not imagine events that would so change an individual.

The image of my father faded and was gone.

I went to my room, undressed, and got into bed. I fell asleep reading the book about Rabbi Akiva and his students and the plague and the revolt against Rome.

Through my sleep I heard someone enter my room and come quietly over to my bed. I didn't know who it was and found I could not wake. I sensed the warmth of someone standing next to me and heard soft slow breathing. Then I felt a warm, moist kiss on my cheek, felt the dark sadness of the silent presence that was leaning over me, felt it clearly through my sleep but was still unable to wake. Then strange and musical words were said but I could not understand what they meant. Then whoever it was drew away from me and stood silent for a long moment and turned and went softly from my room.

Later my mother entered my room. She kissed my forehead, her lips cool and dry, and turned off my light and went out. I woke suddenly into the darkness and heard my room filled with whispers. I listened to distant talk and through the haze of dread and half-sleep thought I recognized the voice of Mr. Dinn. The harp sounded softly. I dropped back into sleep.

During breakfast the next morning I told my mother of my dream.

"I also dreamt of your father last night," she said. "It isn't unusual for that to happen."

She looked down into her coffee cup as she spoke. She seemed not to have slept. She had on her pink housecoat. Her eyes were red and puffy, her long hair uncombed.

"Was Mr. Dinn here?"

"Yes. He came to tell me about Jakob Daw's visa."

"When will Uncle Jakob come?"

"I don't know. But when he does come he'll have trouble remaining."

"Why?"

"There are people in Washington who don't like his politics."

"I don't understand."

"It means there are powerful people in the government who won't let him remain in America more than a few months because they think he's a threat to the country."

"Where will he go?"

"I have no idea, Ilana." She paused and stared down into her coffee cup. "I'm so tired," she said, quietly but clearly. "Why don't they leave us alone?"

"Do we know where Papa is?"

"I called the newspaper. As far as they know your father is still in Bilbao. I think you should get yourself ready for school. I don't want you to be late. Go ahead, darling. I'll clean up the dishes. It will give me something to do."

On my way to school that morning I went by the candy store and saw the headlines. With some of the money my mother gave me for candy I bought a copy of *The New York Times.*

Crossing a street against the light, I was almost hit by a car. Sitting in the classroom and listening to the droning voice of the teacher, I kept looking down at the newspaper on my lap. During recess, I went off to a corner of the yard and stood alone, reading. A boy ran past, chasing a ball, saw me reading, and snickered. I glanced up for a moment and noticed my teacher, a graying middle-aged woman, standing with another teacher a few yards away near the schoolyard fence. They were both watching me. The yard was filled with the high happy sounds of playing children. I envied them and wished I could be like them. Playing in the warm dusty late morning sunlight unaware of the dark world beyond the school and the neighborhood and the city and the country and the ocean. Unaware of Franco and Hitler and Mussolini. Unaware of Spain and Madrid and Bilbao. Unaware of the destruction by airplanes of the little town of Guernica a few miles from Bilbao where my father and Jakob Daw now were. Unaware of the headline that read HISTORIC BASQUE TOWN WIPED OUT; REBEL FLIERS MACHINE-GUN CIVILIANS. Unaware of the story beneath the headline: "BILBAO, Spain, April 27.—Fire was completing today the destruction of Guernica, ancient town of the Basques and center of their cultural tradition, which was begun last evening by a terrible onslaught of General Francisco Franco's Insurgent air raiders. The bombardment of this open city far behind the lines occupied precisely three and one-quarter hours. . . . At 2 A.M. today, when the writer visited the town, the whole of it was a horrible sight, flaming from end to end. The reflection of the flames could be seen in the clouds of smoke above the mountains ten miles away. Throughout the night houses were falling, until the streets were long heaps of red, impenetrable ruins." I looked beneath the lower headline and saw the writer was someone called G. L. Steer. I wondered if my father had written about the bombing. My mother always brought home the paper for which he wrote; the candy store in our neighborhood did not carry it. I opened the newspaper and looked inside for the continuation of the story. The pages flapped in the cool April wind. The writer described the survivors who had fled from Guernica to Bilbao "in antique, solid-wheeled Basque farm carts drawn by oxen. The carts, piled high with such household possessions as could be saved from the conflagration, clogged the roads all night long." I didn't know what the word conflagration meant but thought it might have to do with destruction and fire. "Other survivors were evacuated in government trucks, but many were forced to remain round the burning town, lying on mattresses or searching for lost children or other relatives."

A whistle signaled the end of the recess. I skipped down to the next paragraph. "The object of the bombardment seemingly was the demoralization of the civil population and destruction of the cradle of the Basque race. This appreciation is borne out by the facts, beginning with the day when the deed was done. Yesterday was the customary Monday market day in Guernica for the surrounding countryside. At 4:30 P.M. when the market was full and peasants were still coming in, church bells rang an alarm for approaching airplanes. . . ."

I looked up. The yard was empty. I ran to my class and was late. I slid into my seat beneath the withering look of my teacher and amidst the grins and whispers of my classmates. Yes, how nice to be aware only of games and gossip, of dresses and parties, and not of airplanes, bombs, and Bilbao, and my father and Jakob Daw somewhere near the fires of Guernica.

The apartment was empty when I returned home. I sat in the kitchen and went on reading the newspaper. "The whole town of 7,000 inhabitants plus 3,000 refugees was slowly and systematically pounded to pieces. For a radius of five miles around, the raiders bombed separate easerios, or farmhouses. In the night these burned like little candles in the hills. It is impossible to state the total number of victims. . . ."

I heard my mother come in the door. She had a copy of the newspaper for which my father wrote and there was a story in it by my father about the fighting around Bilbao. The story had been written the day of the bombing of Guernica. The paper also carried a story about Guernica that had not been written by my father.

"Mama, did you call the newspaper again?"

She had called the newspaper. No one there knew exactly where my father was. They assumed he was in Bilbao and were expecting additional stories by him from there.

Late that night I woke and heard my mother singing in the living room in a low haunting voice that chilled me. What strange music came from her, what soft yet piercing tones, a subdued rise and fall of minor-key melodies and wordless songs that held me frozen to my bed. Then she stopped and began to talk in a language that sounded like Yiddish. And suddenly an image of Jakob Daw's little black bird flew across my mind. I saw it clearly, flying and circling, searching for the source of the music of the world. And I asked myself: What would the bird do if he ever discovered that source? Would he swoop down and bomb it?

The next day after school I walked quickly beneath the spring trees along Eastern Parkway on my way home. The air was golden with sunlight, but I felt chilled. Passing the yeshiva, I saw a crowd of children in the open area in front of the building. I stopped for a moment. It seemed a festive crowd. The double door of the building was wide open and children kept streaming in and out, some carrying pieces of cake. I started to walk on, then stopped again. David Dinn had just emerged from the building with some of his friends, all with cake in their hands. I stood on the sidewalk near the curb, watching them talking and eating. Then I saw David look past his friends and notice me. He said something to his friends and came quickly toward me.

"Have you heard anything about your father?"

"No."

"That was a terrible bombing."

"Did you see the newspapers?"

"My father told me about it."

"Is today a holiday?"

"It's Lag Ba'omer. The day the plague stopped. Do you know the story about Rabbi Akiva and his students and the plague?"

"Yes. The revolt against Rome. Is it very cold?"

"It's not cold."

"I should have worn my heavy sweater."

He gave me a look of concern. "Do you want me to walk you home?"

"Two nights ago I dreamed my father came into my room and kissed me. Do you ever have dreams like that about your mother?"

A shadow passed over his pale face. He did not answer.

"David?"

"Sometimes," he said in a low voice, and glanced quickly around. "Look, let me tell my friends I'm walking you home."

He went over to his friends. I saw them staring at me. The wind blew cruelly. The newspaper, folded and tucked under my arm, seemed strangely burdensome.

David Dinn came back to where I stood.

"I'm very cold," I said.

"Come on," he said.

We walked together along the parkway.

"Your father came over to my house the other day."

"I know."

"Your father helped my Uncle Jakob get a visa."

"I don't know anything about what my father does."

"I know what my father does."

David did not respond. He walked bent forward, a little stooped. We left the parkway and turned into the side street.

"Do you want some of this cake?" he asked.

"No, thanks. I'm very cold. Could I borrow your jacket?"

"It's a man's jacket," he said, hesitating.

"I'm very cold, David."

"You're not—" He broke off and slipped the jacket from his thin body and draped it over my shoulders. "Let me carry that for you," he said, and took the *Times* from under my arm.

"Do you celebrate Lag Ba'omer every year?" I asked.

"Yes."

"And it happened two thousand years ago?"

"That's right."

"I wonder if anyone will remember Guernica that long."

"Jews would remember if it happened to them."

"What do you study in your school?"

"All kinds of subjects."

"There's my house. Thanks for your jacket."

One of our neighbors, a gaunt old woman with rheumy eyes and a lame leg, stood on the top step of her front stoop and regarded us curiously.

"David, do you still say Kaddish for your mother?"

"Sure."

"Every day?"

"Yes."

"Thanks for walking me home."

"Ilana, will your parents be going back to Sea Gate this summer?"

"I don't know."

He stood there a moment, looking down at the sidewalk. I had the feeling he was reluctant to leave.

"I'm very cold," I said. "I'd better go up."

He watched me climb the stone stairs and go inside. The lock clicked shut behind me. I went up to the apartment.

My mother was in the kitchen. She sat at the table, her head in her hands. She had on her light spring coat and her beret. She looked up at me as I came inside.

"Ilana," she said. "I just got home a few minutes ago. Sit down. I have to tell you something." She stopped. "Ilana," she said again. Her voice broke.

"Mama?"

"Are you cold? Why don't you take off your sweater?"

"Is Papa dead?" I asked.

She stared at me. The blood left her face.

"Mama?"

"No, darling. Of course not. Your father is not dead. But no one seems to know where he is."

A cold hand seized my heart. "Was Papa in Guernica?"

"Yes. But no one knows how long or even if he was there during the raid."

"Mama—"

"We will be very brave, Ilana. We will not act like hysterical women. We will be brave and calm. Won't we? Won't we, my darling?"

"Yes, Mama."

"He could not have been so foolish as to go into such a bombardment. Not my Michael. Oh, no." She stopped and blinked her eyes a number of times. Then she noticed her arms. "Look at me, darling. I'm still wearing my coat. How silly! Let me hang it up and I'll make us supper. It will be all right. We mustn't worry. Will you help me make supper? Don't cry, Ilana. You promised me you wouldn't cry. Please, Ilana. Please."

My father had disappeared.

The headlines in his newspaper read OUR CORRESPONDENT PRE-SUMED LOST IN GUERNICA RAID. Guernica lay in a valley about fifteen miles east of Bilbao. Correspondents in the Bilbao hotel where my father had been staying remembered having seen him leave with a car and a driver about two hours before the raid had begun. He was doing a background story on Basque culture and needed to find in Guernica a six-hundred-year-old tree and the parish church of Santa Maria. Jakob Daw had left Bilbao a few days before and was presumed to be on his way to Lisbon for his visa and steamship ticket to the United States.

April moved slowly into May. My room was very cold. In the nights I woke crying and shivering. I wet my bed and lay curled into a tight ball. There was comfort in that position. My mother changed my sheets and held me and stroked my face and hair. She went stiffly about her work, her face controlled and without expression. I did not once see her cry.

People began to visit us. They came in the evenings and on weekends and stayed for hours. Many of them I recognized from the meetings with which I had grown up in our previous apartments. They chucked me under the chin, remarked how grown up and brave I was, told me I was beautiful, and warned me to be careful of the sons of bosses and capitalists. Some were strangers to me, quiet men and women who seemed to give off a radiance of power and yet were hesitant and deferential in the presence of my mother. The two men and the woman who studied the works of Karl Marx with my mother came one evening and stayed for more than an hour. From time to time Mrs. Helfman would suddenly appear at our door with a pot of soup or meat, which she would transfer to my mother's pots and dishes before quietly leaving.

The door harp sang incessantly.

In my school only a few seemed aware of my father's disappearance. A pimply-faced boy came over to me in the yard during recess one afternoon and said, "Your old man was a Commie, serves him right he's dead." I turned and walked away from him. My teacher took me aside and said to me, "Is there any way we can help you, dear? If there is, be sure to let us know." I found I had nothing to say to her.

Sometimes Ruthie would come up and invite me down to play with her. Often I stood near the window in my parents' bedroom and watched Ruthie's father tending the flowers in the backyard. On occasion Mr. Dinn would appear in the apartment. He and my mother spent long periods of time talking together in the kitchen or living room.

On the Saturday of the first week in May, David walked me part of the way home from the synagogue. He was pale and solemn and for a while could find nothing to say. Then, in a thin and hesitant voice, he said that he didn't know what to say, it was reminding him of last year when his mother had died and the world felt black and cold and he didn't want to get up in the mornings. "But I got up anyway," he said. "I had to get up. I had to say Kaddish."

People continued to come and go. Slowly I began to find unendurable the endless music of the door harp. Pinging each time the door opened. Pinging each time the door closed. The harp grated against my ears and tightened the cold hand around my heart. One afternoon I taped the wooden balls to the wires with stripes of adhesive and the harp fell mute. My mother said nothing to me about that.

Early in the second week of May my mother traveled to Manhattan to talk to some of the people on the paper for which my father worked. She was told that someone had news about my father: an American writer for the Hearst chain who had known him in Bilbao and had just returned to the States. Briefly they recounted his story and then said that he wanted to talk privately with my mother.

One night that week a tall, heavily built man with a dark mustache and a thin voice came to our apartment. He had dark straight hair and wore steel-rimmed spectacles and a rumpled tweed jacket and light-colored creased trousers. We sat in our living room. My mother brought him a Scotch-and-water. He held the glass, peered at it, sipped from it, and began to talk. He spoke a bit hesitantly and with an accent I had heard before only in movies. He had needed to be in the States anyway right about now, the man said, and had decided he would come see us rather than write. A priest he knew had been to see him in Bilbao, he said. This priest had heard a strange story from another priest, a Basque, who had survived the air raid on Guernica. The planes had used carefully planned tactics, the man said. He sipped from his glass. His voice became cool and clinical. First, small groups of aircraft had appeared and randomly dropped heavy bombs and hand grenades all over the town. They proceeded from one section of the town to the next in an orderly manner. Some of the bombs made holes twenty to thirty feet deep and drove the people out of their dugouts and shelters. Immediately after those planes came wave after wave of fighter aircraft, swooping very low and machine-gunning the people who had run from the shelters. This drove the people back into the shelters. Then came another wave of bombers that dropped heavy bombs and incendiaries on the shelters, burying those who had fled from the machine guns. "Clever bastards," the man said. "Very methodical. Made military history. Opens up a new chapter in the annals of war. Could I trouble you for another drink, Mrs. Chandal?"

My mother took his glass and went from the living room. He sat looking at me through his steel-rimmed spectacles.

"How old are you, little girl?"

I told him.

"What's your name?"

"Ilana Davita Chandal."

"You got any brothers or sisters?"

"I had a little brother once but he died."

He looked at me and was silent.

My mother returned with his drink. He resumed his story.

A young Basque priest had been driving to the railroad station in the center of Guernica when the first bombs fell near the Mundaca River. He saw one of the bombs knock down the front of a four-story hotel not far from the station. Women and children had been standing around in front of the building and when the bomb fell he saw a rain of arms and legs and heads. He ran toward the station to help. More bombs fell in the distance.

The man paused. "You sure you want the little girl to hear this?"

"I want her to hear everything," my mother said.

"All right," the man said, and took another sip from the glass. Then he went on.

As the priest was running toward the station, the man said, a car suddenly appeared out of a swirl of dust, and a tall, brown-haired man jumped out. Two aircraft swooped down and began a strafing run. The priest turned and raced toward the river and found concealment under a paved bridge that rested on metal beams and cement pillars. Machine-gun bullets struck the car in which the brown-haired man had ridden, and it exploded. The man was knocked to the ground. He scrambled to his feet and began to run toward the river and the bridge. In front of him a nun was hit in the strafing run and fell. The man lifted her in his arms and went on running for the bridge. Behind him came a wave of bombers. He would have made it but his right leg suddenly seemed to collapse under him and he fell near the bank of the river. The priest started toward them when the first bombs fell, knocking him backward into the ankle-deep water at the river's edge. He saw the man and the nun disappear in the explosion. When the earth settled, there was nothing except—

The man stopped, glanced briefly at me, and sipped from his glass.

"There was nothing," he said.

A long silence went by. I looked at my mother. Her face was composed. Around my heart the icy hand squeezed until I thought I would cry out. I sat very still.

The man went on.

It was only a long time afterward, when the driver, who had jumped before the car exploded, began making inquiries about a brown-haired journalist, that the priest realized the man had been an American correspondent. The priest learned of these inquiries from a nun in the Carmelite convent outside Guernica and had no way of locating the driver. He informed his superior, who in turn told a number of officials as well as the Hearst correspondent in Bilbao, whom he had befriended some months before during a particularly bad night of shelling in Madrid.

"There's no certainty, you understand," the man said. "There was chaos that day. The priest could be mistaken."

"He is not mistaken," my mother said in her firm and quiet voice.

"How do you know?"

She told him about the wounded right hip.

There was a brief silence.

"I see what you mean," the man said. "Yeah. Real sorry."

There was another silence.

The man finished his drink and put the glass down on the coffee table near the pile of copies of the newspaper for which my father had written. He looked first at me, then at my mother.

"Anything I can do?" he asked in a quiet voice.

"It was good of you to come," said my mother.

"No trouble," said the man, getting to his feet.

My mother walked with him to the door.

When he was gone my mother returned to the living room and sat down on the sofa. She sat stiffly and kept her knees tightly together. Her eyes were black, burning. "Michael?" she said in a strange small voice. "Michael?"

I felt the cold around my heart and now also on the nape of my neck and went quickly downstairs for Mrs. Helfman. To my astonishment, Mr. Dinn appeared at our door almost immediately after Mrs. Helfman came in. My mother did not cry. She sat on the sofa and kept calling my father's name. I lay in my bed in the darkness and did not cry, either. The room was very cold.

The next day my mother went out before breakfast and returned with the morning papers. One was the newspaper for which my father had worked; she had walked a long distance for that paper. My father's picture was on the front page. Wavy hair, eyes full of light, jaunty smile. My mother and I sat at the kitchen table, staring at my father's picture.

The headline read, in large letters, MICHAEL CHANDAL KILLED IN GUERNICA RAID. Beneath that, in smaller letters, I read, NOTED CORRESPONDENT DIES ATTEMPTING RESCUE OF WOUNDED NUN.

The story described my father as a well-known journalist devoted to workers' causes, as a loyal comrade and a tireless worker. It mentioned his family origins—"New England stock, aristocrats, heads of a timber empire against whom Chandal had rebelled in his early years." It talked of his writings, his travels, his journalistic style, his high reputation. Then it told how he had died—and it was the same story the man had told us the night before.

My mother turned the pages of *The New York Times*. Again there was my father's picture and a headline: JOURNALIST MICHAEL CHANDAL, 36, DEAD IN GUERNICA RAID.

"What does obituary mean?" I asked.

My mother corrected my pronunciation and explained the word.

The article described my father's New England origins. It said his family had pioneered the lumber industry in the United States. It mentioned the brother who had died in the last war and the change that had come over my father as a result of certain events he had witnessed during and after a riot against Wobblies on Armistice Day, 1919, in Centralia, Washington—"events described in *Nineteen-Nineteen*, the novel by John Dos Passos," the article added. It told of my father's journalistic career, his known association with Communists and Socialists, his "lean, nonrhetorical style," and the "possible permanent value of what Mr. Chandal used to refer to as his 'special writing.'" The article closed with the statement that Mr. Chandal left behind, in his immediate family, a wife and daughter, as well as parents and a sister. And it announced the time, date, and place of a memorial service.

The other newspapers carried similar stories. One of them, writing about Centralia, used the words "grisly events."

Once again the apartment filled with visitors. And once again Mr. Dinn appeared one night after I was supposed to be asleep and spent a long time in the kitchen, talking with my mother.

A few days later my mother and I took the subway into Manhattan. She wore a dark dress and a dark beret. She sat very straight and still in the train, gazing out the window into the tunnel through which we sped. Her lovely face was set in an expressionless ivory mask; her eyes were dark, shining. I had yet to see her cry over the death of my father. There was about her now a quality of grace, a regal poise; suffering seemed to have added to her reservoir of courage.

We came out of the subway and walked along a crowded downtown street in a warm rain. We turned a corner and entered a hotel and climbed a wide carpeted staircase to a carpeted hallway and a vast elegant ballroom. The wooden pillars of the room were of imitation marble and on the ceiling pink cherubs and bosomy maidens frolicked amidst flowers along the banks of a blue and misty river. The room was filled with chairs and crowded with people. Heads turned as my mother and I entered the room. We walked through a sea of stares toward the stage.

A man I had never seen before came toward us. He was of medium height, his head entirely bald, and he wore a dark brush mustache. He greeted my mother deferentially, nodded briefly at me, and led us onto the stage. My hands and feet and heart were cold. All around us on the stage people were shaking my mother's hand. I felt entombed by the darkness of their suits and dresses. And all the faces in the enormous room beyond the stage: silent now, raised, solemn, expectant.

A man stood and began to talk in a low voice about my father. The sound system sent his words back to the stage in a softly reverberating echo. He talked about Michael Chandal the comrade, Michael Chandal the journalist, Michael Chandal the writer, Michael Chandal the hero. My mother sat very straight, gazing fixedly at the speaker's back, her head raised and her hands in her lap. The speaker finished and there was a burst of applause. The speaker turned and started back to his seat. As he crossed the stage, I saw him glance furtively at my mother, as if seeking her approval for his words, and I saw my mother give him a single nod. He smiled faintly and slid into his seat and took out a handkerchief and wiped his face.

There were many speeches about my father that afternoon. There were speeches too about the party, about the menace of fascism, about the cause—*causa,* the speaker called it—about the glorious achievements of the Soviet Union. Someone quoted a poet who had been to Russia and had said, upon his return, "I have seen the future and it works." That received long and loud applause. Someone else quoted the words of a member of the Lincoln Brigade: "Men may die, but let them die in a working class cause. Men die and mean to die (if necessary) so that the revolution may live on. They may stop us today, but tomorrow we still take up the march." Again loud and long applause.

Then a heavy silence moved swiftly through the crowd. The bald-headed man had risen and was now approaching the podium. He stood for a moment and looked out across the room, bathing in its silence. Then, in a tone that seemed to require no loudness to assert its authority, he began to introduce my mother. He talked of her dedication to the party, her skillful writing, her brilliant teaching, her remarkable courage. His quiet amplified voice seemed to push against the walls of the room. Then he was done and he returned to his seat. There was respectful, subdued applause.

I watched my mother rise and walk to the podium.

Slowly and in a firm voice she thanked the people for coming to the meeting. Michael would have been so pleased, she said. She told about how she and my father had met in the twenties, how he had convinced her of the rightness of his views, how they had supported one another's work for the party, how they had raised a child together, sacrificed together. Her voice quavered and she stopped for a moment. I looked around the room. All the crowd was rigid with silence. Overhead the happy cherubs and maidens played along the banks of their misty blue river, and along the walls strange birds and animals conjured up from some mythic bestiary gazed at the crowd from tall leafy trees and a lush green meadow. I looked up at the ceiling and thought about joining the cherubs in their play. What would it take? Only a small leap. That's all. A small leap—and then the blue river and the cool water and the careless frolicking with the plump pink maidens. Then my mother said, loudly, in a voice I had never heard her use before, a tone so abruptly fierce with determination that I felt myself go cold, "In the name of my late husband, Michael Chandal, I pledge to you that I will continue to work for the party. I will continue to work for a better world. I will continue to work for a classless society and for the dream of Karl Marx. Long live the revolution!"

There was tumultuous applause. My mother returned to her chair. I looked up at her. Her eyes shone; a thin sheen of perspiration covered her flushed cheeks and forehead. Her face was expressionless. The bald man shook her hand. The applause continued a long time. Then the crowd burst into song. All stood at attention, singing.

Afterward we came down off the stage and people pressed densely around us. I thought I saw the tall, dark-suited figure of Mr. Dinn in the crowd. A woman moved across my field of vision. When I looked again he was gone.

Someone took us home in a car. I remember a dark river and a tall bridge and cobblestone streets and a wide parkway. I clung to my mother and smelled her warmth and the sweat on her face and neck. I fell asleep and woke later in my bed in the darkness of my room and heard the voices of my mother and Mr. Dinn. The room was cold. My bed was wet. A chill wind blew through the leafy branches outside my window. In the cellarway a cat wailed.

I said to my mother during breakfast the next morning, "What do you and Mr. Dinn talk about at night?"

She gazed at me wearily. "Don't you ever sleep, Ilana?"

"Do you talk about Uncle Jakob?"

"Yes. And other matters."

"Why did Papa die?"

"Why? I don't know. He just did, that's all."

"Like my little brother?"

"Yes," she said, after a brief pause. "Like your little brother."

"I hate it when there's no reason that people die. Will you do anything else for Papa?"

"What do you mean?"

"Will there be another memorial service?"

"No."

"Nothing else?"

"What else do you want, Ilana?"

I didn't know what to say and was quiet.

"Go get yourself ready for school," she said. "I don't want you to be late."

I left her in the kitchen, looking down into her cup of coffee, and went to the bookcase in my parents' bedroom and carefully searched the shelves. There was another bookcase in the living room and I looked through that one too. The book I wanted was not in my parents' library.

I was late getting out of the house and ran most of the way to school and came late to class. My teacher said nothing. My classmates tried to avoid looking at me.

During the morning recess I went into the school library and quickly scanned some shelves. After school I walked along Eastern Parkway and went into a large stone-and-glass building and climbed up a marble staircase. I waited awhile on line and then asked the librarian for a certain book.

She had white hair and metal-rimmed spectacles and gazed at me piercingly from across her desk.

"Who is the book for?"

I told her the book was for me.

"That isn't a book for a little girl. It's in the adult division."

I went home.

The next day after school I crossed Eastern Parkway very carefully, with the help of the lights, and walked some blocks to a bookstore. Inside I asked an old man with a lined face and a white mustache and heavy-lidded eyes if he could show me where to find a certain book.

"Why?"

I hesitated, my heart pounding. "To buy it."

"Who for?"

"My mother," I said.

He went over to some shelves and pulled down a book. Then he told me what it would cost.

I told him I didn't have enough money.

He put the book back on the shelf. "Come back when you do," he said.

The next afternoon I walked again down Eastern Parkway and turned into the library. I climbed the staircase to the adult division, went through wide glass-and-wood doors, and found myself in a vast hushed tall-ceilinged marble-floored room. Sunlight streamed through enormous vaulted windows onto long polished wooden tables and tall dark-wood bookcases. There were few people at the tables. I stood frozen for a long moment, awed by the silence and the light. It seemed a room without shadows, its furniture and books and reading lamps and catalogues starkly outlined by the brilliant sun. I stood very still. Coursing through me was the gently electric attraction of the books. I looked cautiously around. The librarians were busy at their desks. I slipped easily past their gaze.

I entered the maze of bookcases. So many books! So many more stories than in the children's section below! I did not know what to do.

Standing nearby, searching for a book, was an elderly man in thick glasses, baggy pants, and a sweater. I asked him where I might find *Nineteen-Nineteen* by Dos Passos.

"Hah?" he said, staring at me.

I repeated the question.

"I don't know that book," he said. "Why don't you ask one of the librarians?"

I said nothing.

"Who did you say is the author?"

"John Dos Passos."

"Try under P," he said. "Wait. Dos Passos? Try under D. Maybe you'll find it under D."

I told him I couldn't find the D's. He told me where to look.

I found Dos Passos. I did not find the book. I went out of the library and walked quickly home.

I returned the following day. The book was not there. Nor was it there the day after.

The next day was Friday. I walked in a drizzle to the library and climbed the marble staircase and went past the long counter behind which sat the librarians, working at their desks. I went to the bookcase and searched the shelf and there was the book.

I took it from the shelf and held it and had no notion how to find what I was looking for. I began to turn pages and found a page marked contents. It contained a list of names and something called Newsreel and The Camera Eye. I kept turning the pages and looking at the names. I found nothing about a place called Centralia.

I went through the contents page again. The third name from the end was Paul Bunyan. I turned the pages and saw what I thought were newspaper headlines: BAGS 28 HUNS SINGLEHANDED and GANG LEADER SLAIN IN STREET and REDS WEAKENING WASHINGTON HEARS. I couldn't understand why there were headlines in a book of stories. Was the book about true stories *and* made-up stories? How would I know the difference between them?

I found the page I was looking for and saw in large letters PAUL BUNYAN. I began to read.

"When Wesley Everest came home from overseas and got his discharge from the army he went back to his old job of logging." I read very slowly. There were many words I did not understand. "In the army Everest was a sharpshooter, won a medal for a crack shot." Some of the words were very long and seemed made up of two or more words. I couldn't understand why a writer would put words together like that. I read, "Wesley Everest was a logger like Paul Bunyan." I read about the Wobblies and the timber owners and Memorial Day, 1918, in Centralia and the way a group called the American Legion wrecked something called the I.W.W. hall, beat up everyone they found inside, and drove the rest out of the city. I read that the loggers hired a new hall and on Armistice Day, 1919, people broke through the door and there was shooting. Wesley Everest fired his rifle and ran for the woods. He was captured crossing a river and brought back to jail.

Then I read, "That night the city lights were turned off. A mob smashed in the outer door of the jail. 'Don't shoot, boys, here's your man,' said the guard. Wesley Everest met them on his feet. 'Tell the boys I did my best,' he whispered to the men in the other cells.

"They took him off in a limousine to the Chehalis River bridge. As Wesley Everest lay stunned in the bottom of the car a Centralia businessman cut his penis and testicles off with a razor. Wesley Everest gave a great scream of pain. Somebody has remembered that after a while he whispered, 'For God's sake, men, shoot me . . . don't let me suffer like this.' Then they hanged him from the bridge in the glare of the head-lights."

I read those last two paragraphs again. Then I finished reading to the end. "Nobody knows where they buried the body of Wesley Everest. . . ."

I returned the book to the shelf.

My hands were shaking and I could not breathe. I slid past the suspicious gaze of a librarian and hurried down the marble staircase to the street.

It was raining. I walked beneath the trees, trying to take deep breaths. A queer heaviness lay upon my chest. The rain came through the leaves and fell upon the puddles on the sidewalks. Along the darkly glistening asphalt of the streets, cars moved cautiously, tires hissing. People scurried along beneath umbrellas. I needed to go to the bath-room. I turned off the parkway into a side street and could no longer control my trembling. The strange heaviness still lay upon my chest. Then I felt the flow of urine begin to seep slowly from between my legs and into my panties and down along the insides of my thighs. I stood under a tree in the rain and felt the hot rush flow outward. The street was empty save for automobile traffic. I began to run. I ran along the side street and then through the street where I lived and up the stoop and through the doors and up the staircase into the apartment.

The singing of the door harp startled me. My mother must have untaped the wooden balls before leaving for work. She should have told me she would do that. Why hadn't she told me? I would have said not yet, I didn't want music yet, it was too soon for me to be hearing again the singing of the harp.

In my room I removed my clothes. Naked, I went to the bathroom and washed myself. Peering down at the ridges and valley between my legs, I felt suddenly nauseated and thought I would vomit. I sat down on the toilet. After a moment the nausea passed. I returned to my room and put on fresh clothes. I did not know what to do with my wet underpants. I went into the kitchen and threw them into the garbage pail under the sink. They would be in the alleyway that night with the cans of garbage and the roaming cats. I lay on my bed and put my hand over my eyes. What had they done with Wesley Everest's—? Paul Bunyan. What a sweet story that had been each time my father had told it to me. Tall Paul Bunyan, his huge ax, his blue ox. Through half-sleep I heard a great scream of pain and sat bolt upright on the bed, shaking. I lay dazed in a sleep of exhaustion when my mother came home.

During supper that night I said, "Did Papa see what happened to that poor man Wesley Everest in Centralia?"

My mother coughed and put down her knife and fork and stared at me.

"I read it in a book today. About what happened to—"

My mother broke sharply into my words. "I do not want to talk about that at the table," she said.

We ate in silence.

After supper I asked my mother, "Did they really do that to that man?"

"Yes," she said.

"How could they do that? What kind of people would do that?"

"Ilana, I wish you had not—"

"Did Papa see them do it?"

She hesitated. "Yes," she said. "He saw them hang him. But he was too frightened to tell anyone."

"It's not a story?"

"No, Ilana."

"But it's in a book that's a story."

"It happened," my mother said.

"I'm scared, Mama."

"Come here. Come to me. Let me hold you. Would you like to go to the movies tonight? Maybe there's a funny movie playing in the neighborhood. All right? Ilana, tell me something. How did you find that book?"

I told her. She stared at me and shook her head; but she said nothing. Later we went to a movie but I cannot remember what it was. I closed my eyes during the Movietone News and put my hands over my ears—and suddenly understood what the word Newsreel meant in the book by John Dos Passos. Sitting in the cavernous darkness of that theater, with my eyes and ears closed against the horrors of the war on the screen, I saw inside my eyes the words, "Wesley Everest was a logger like Paul Bunyan," and the words, "Wesley Everest gave a great scream of pain."

In the morning I walked to the synagogue and sat alongside the dividing curtain, peering through the distorting fabric at the boy who stood at the lectern leading the service, and then seeing him clearly through the tear in the ninon. The boy was becoming a bar mitzvah. Ruthie had told me about that. He was taking on all the obligations and privileges of an adult Jew. No, Ruthie had said in response to my question, girls didn't become bar mitzvah, only boys. And she had giggled.

The synagogue was crowded. Cool air blew in through the open windows on the men's side of the large room. I saw David and his father sitting together near the front of the room, watched them rise and say the Kaddish together and then sit down. No woman rose to say the Kaddish. I had noticed that over the weeks I had been coming here: no woman ever recited the Kaddish.

The boy at the lectern completed the service and moved to the podium to chant the Torah portion. He had a high sweet voice. The room was hushed as he read. All around me women sat beaming. He faltered once, was quietly corrected by one of the men who stood near him at the podium, and went on. Soon after he was done with the reading, the Torah scroll was lifted and wrapped and given to a boy about my age to hold; he sat on a chair, clutching the scroll tightly. The bar mitzvah commenced chanting aloud from a book. Candies were thrown when he was done. An elderly man in a long graying beard rose to continue the service. The Torah was returned to the ark. Someone gave a brief talk. All rose as the elderly man resumed the service.

I was very tired. My heart beat fiercely; I thought the woman sitting next to me would hear it pounding. I held the prayerbook tightly; I could read the alphabet. Many words were familiar to me now; I could speak them, though I understood almost nothing of what I was saying. It seemed strange to be deriving comfort from unclear words; I couldn't understand that.

We rose for the long silent prayer. I stood thinking of my father and the nun whose life he had tried to save. Then I thought of Wesley Everest and the events in Centralia—and I began to understand how it might be possible for a life to be changed in a moment by a single startling event.

I must have dozed. I sensed a silence about me and opened my eyes. Peering through the opening in the curtain, I saw David and his father rising to their feet. And then I was on my feet too, listening to the voices on the other side of the curtain and reciting faintly with the men the words of the Kaddish, which I found, to my astonishment, that I knew by heart. There was a surge of whispering, a soft surflike rush of sound from the women around me. Someone said, "What is she doing?" Another said something in Yiddish. I stood, quietly reciting the words. There has to be more for you, Papa, than just one memorial service. Can one recite the Kaddish for a father who wasn't a Jew? I didn't care.

I went on. The Kaddish ended. I sat down and closed my eyes, feeling upon my face the hot stares of all those nearby.

The service went on. Then, moments later, I heard again the words of the Kaddish, and I rose and began to recite them too, louder this time, and I thought I heard one or two of the women answer, "Amen."

Outside on the sidewalk after the service David came over to me and said, "Good Shabbos, Ilana."

I returned his greeting.

He fidgeted uncomfortably. "Ilana," he said. "Listen."

I looked at him.

"Girls don't recite Kaddish. Women aren't—"

"Does it make any difference that my father wasn't Jewish?" I asked.

"I don't think so. I'll have to ask my Talmud teacher. But that's not what I'm—"

"I'm very tired, David. I have to go home now."

I left him there staring at me as I turned and walked off.

I had no sensation of walking. The warm May sunlight seemed a perverse and malevolent counterpoint to my feelings and filled me with despair. I shivered with cold. The streets of the neighborhood were gray and unfamiliar. I walked as in a stupor, turning fearful corners like some blind and unthinking creature, coming upon my own street, filled now with playing children and old women on their stoops and young mothers with baby carriages and men washing their cars and others returning from the synagogues of the neighborhood. Out of habit I walked carefully beneath the trees, avoiding the cracks and roots in the sidewalk; out of habit I waved at neighbors and responded to their greetings; out of habit I raised my eyes to my window in the castlelike turret that formed the side of the house. And there in the window next to mine, the bay window of our living room, I saw my mother's face and, beside her, a pale visage that seemed an apparition. I stopped and stared and felt the surge of blood in my ears. I flew up the stone stoop and the inside stairway and through the apartment door, which my mother had opened for me. Behind me I heard distinctly the singing of the door harp as I flung myself into the gaunt arms of Jakob Daw. And I buried my head in his chest, saw out of the sides of my eyes the face of my mother, her wet eyes, her trembling lips, and felt suddenly the rush of all the weeks of grief and the ocean of pain pouring forth. And I wept like the child I was.

Five

That same day a letter from Aunt Sarah addressed to my mother arrived in the mail. Aunt Sarah was somewhere near Madrid. I asked Uncle Jakob if he had seen Aunt Sarah in Spain and he said no, he hadn't, because she worked in a battlefield hospital and cared for the severely wounded. The three of us sat around the kitchen table as my mother read the letter aloud.

"Dearest Anne. 'The Lord gave, and the Lord hath taken away; blessed be the name of the Lord.'

"I loved my brother. I find that I cannot believe he is dead. Unlike my parents, I did not think that politics should sunder a family. That belief is reinforced every day in this dark and tragic land. The hatred here of man toward man is boundless and unfathomable, the slaughter is unimaginable. We are a vile and cursed species and were it not for the grace of God all life would be a hopeless travail. I know such faith is for you a chimera, an illusion cast upon us by those in power so as to make existence bearable and their power impregnable. But, my dear Anne, isn't what you call an illusion simply someone else's dream with which you disagree? And what of your workers' revolution, your classless society, your dream of an early end to social strife, economic scarcity, individual degradation and misery? If faith in God is merely an illusion, then why not faith in man too? Anne, are your dreams too not an illusion? It seems to me that those who do not care what means are used to achieve their ends, indeed who justify all in the name of an end, need illusions far more than those others who see in mankind suffering and sin and the radiant power of faith in our Lord Jesus Christ.

"Forgive me, Anne. I did not mean to burden you with a homily in this time of grief but to say that though I despised my brother's political ideas, I loved him as a person; and I prayed that such love would be a possibility for us all. I prayed that with patience and compassion I would win him back to the true path, or, at the very least, learn to understand something of his path and thus not sever myself from him, from my only brother. 'Him that is weak in the faith, receive ye.' I did not lose him, and so at least to that extent my prayers were answered. But how naive I was to believe in the power of patience and love in all mankind! How foolish! The rivers of blood that now soak the soil of Spain are a testament to the unredemptive savagery of mankind. 'A time to kill, and a time to heal; a time to break down, and a time to build up.' How we love our killing time! We appear to need it. I do not know why. I realize now that events do occur to some of us that set us upon our life's path. I do not know exactly what it was that happened to Michael in Centralia and that changed him so. He never told me. I wish he had.

"Dear Anne, let us not sever the feelings between us because my brother is no longer alive. We are linked together by memories and by the lovely life that is Ilana Davita. It is my intent to return home this summer, a respite from the carnage that is Spain. The truth is that the Republican cause is lost, the Rebels triumph. Shall we somehow see one another? Yours in affection. Sarah."

My mother stopped reading and sat very still, gazing down at the letter.

"She is at least correct about the outcome of the war," Jakob Daw said, and coughed briefly.

There was another sheet of paper in the envelope: a letter to me. I took it from my mother and read it quickly to myself. Then I read it aloud.

"Dearest Davita. This is your Aunt Sarah writing. How I loved your father and how I shall miss him! What shall I say to you? Your father was a soldier; his weapons were words. He would have wanted you to have courage and to be strong. I shall be at the farmhouse this summer. Is the lovely picture of the horses on the beach still hanging on the wall? Perhaps Jesus will be good to us and enable us to be together for a while—your mother, you, and I. How I wish we two could pray together again as we once did, on our knees before Jesus Christ! I wish you strength, Davita. Remember your father's kindness and laughter and, more important, his love for your mother and you. I send you my love. I pray for you and your mother constantly. Aunt Sarah."

There was another silence. Jakob Daw put his delicately boned hand to his mouth and coughed.

My mother asked, "What did Aunt Sarah mean about your praying together on your knees?"

I told her about that and saw her exchange looks with Jakob Daw.

"It's late," my mother said. "I think we should eat lunch. Ilana, will you help me?"

"Uncle Jakob, where will you be living?"

"I do not know as yet." His voice was hoarse, raspy. He was thinner now than he had been before. There were blotchy bluish-black circles around his heavy-lidded dark eyes. His straight dark hair was combed back flat. All his features—the arching eyebrows and sharp-edged nose and concave cheeks and slightly pointed jaw—had become harshly angular and somewhat exaggerated in a face that was now nearly skeletal-looking. Yet I felt strength in him, felt a quality of being I did not understand, a strong and nearly overpowering sense of his presence as he sat there next to me at the kitchen table.

"You could live in the room next to me where Aunt Sarah stayed," I said eagerly.

Jakob Daw smiled. "We will see," he said.

"Help me set the table, Ilana. We'll talk later about where your Uncle Jakob will stay."

"Will you tell me more stories about the bird?"

"I shall first have to think if there is anything more to tell."

"You're putting the knives on the wrong side of the plate, Ilana," my mother said.

"Let me help you," Jakob Daw said. "We will have lunch and then I will lie down. I am very tired. It is a big ocean and it seems to get bigger each time I cross it." He coughed again, his thin shoulders shaking, his face as white as the paper on which Aunt Sarah had written her letters.

He slept the entire afternoon, woke briefly for a light supper, and slept again. My mother had to be out somewhere that evening and I wandered about the apartment, stopping from time to time at the window in my parents' bedroom and gazing out at the slowly darkening sky. I saw Ruthie standing in the backyard near the flowers her father had planted. I thought about the sunsets over Sea Gate and imagined the cottage and the dunes and the long gentle glide of the beach toward the surf and the castles I had built in the wet sands of the tidal pool. I stopped by the partly open door to Jakob Daw's room and peered inside. The light was dim. How thin he was, how frail-looking! The tiny quivering movements of his nostrils, the delicate rise of his thin upper lip, the full and feminine lower lip, the boniness and chalky whiteness of his face—a sticklike figure in baggy pants and rumpled shirt, lying still and softly breathing. He seemed the most fragile person I had ever known.

I came into my room and sat at my desk awhile, reading another of the books Ruthie's father had asked her to bring up to me. The doorbell rang. I went to open the door. The harp sang clearly in the silent apartment.

It was David and his father.

"Hello, Ilana," Mr. Dinn said solemnly, looking tall and austere. "How are you?" He said something that sounded like "Goot voch." David, not looking directly at me, said hello in a shy voice and repeated what his father had said.

I stood in the doorway, looking at them. They were dressed in their Shabbos clothes—dark suits, dark ties, dark hats.

"We came straight from shul," Mr. Dinn said. "Is your mother home?"

I told him my mother was at some kind of meeting.

"Did Mr. Daw arrive safely?"

"Yes. He's asleep."

"Good. I won't bother him. Please tell your mother—"

Jakob Daw came out of his room. His hair was disheveled and his eyes blinked repeatedly. He looked gaunt, untidy.

"The doorbell woke me," he said in his hoarse, phlegmy voice. He seemed a bit dazed. "Who is it, Ilana? Hello? Is it someone for me?"

"It's Mr. Dinn and his son, David."

"Dinn?" Jakob Daw said. He appeared to collect himself quickly and advanced into the hallway toward the door. "Come in, come in. Channah went to a meeting and will be back soon. I thank you for all you did. Please come in."

Mr. Dinn shook Jakob Daw's hand and I saw on his long narrow face a hint of deference and awe. "A pleasure to meet you," he murmured. "An honor. I apologize for waking you."

"No, no, I slept too much today. Ilana, can we make a glass of tea for Mr. Dinn? Or, better, perhaps a cold drink. Yes? Good."

They came into the apartment. Jakob Daw and Mr. Dinn started along the hallway to the kitchen. I closed the door. David turned, attracted by the play of sounds on the harp as the balls struck the taut wires.

"What's that?"

"A door harp."

"I never saw anything like that."

"It belonged to my father."

"It's pretty. I like the music."

"Do you want to see my room?"

The question flustered him. Behind me I heard a key go into the lock and the door opened.

My mother stood in the doorway. The harp sang. She saw David and looked astonished.

"Well," she said, coming inside and closing the door. "David. Hello."

I heard Jakob Daw call from the kitchen. "Channah? Dinn is here. We are in the kitchen."

"Can I bring David into my room?" I asked my mother.

"Of course," my mother said, removing her beret.

"Maybe another time," David said, looking uncomfortable, his eyes darting about.

"Oh, please, David."

"Go ahead," my mother said, and went quickly up the hallway and into the kitchen.

David followed me to my room and stood in the doorway, looking at my chair and desk and bed and bookcase.

"You're very neat," he said.

"Come inside," I said. "Why are you standing in the doorway?"

He took small halting steps into the room and slipped into the chair at the desk. He was still wearing his dark hat. I sat on the edge of my bed, keeping my legs together and tugging my dress down over my knees. I saw him look down at the Hebrew book on my desk.

"You read Hebrew?" he asked. "Where'd you get this book?"

"I'm teaching myself to read. It's not hard. Ruthie and her father help me. It's Mr. Helfman's book."

He scanned the shelves of my bookcase. "You like fairy tales?"

"I love fairy tales. I love stories. My—my father and my mother got me those books. Don't you like fairy tales?"

"No. Fairy tales are for girls."

"Where'd you hear that? Don't you like stories that come from your imagination?"

"No. I don't like my imagination. It keeps me awake at night. Sometimes it keeps me from studying. Sometimes it shows me things that scare me."

"What things?"

"Things. People."

"What people?"

"Sometimes it shows me my mother in her grave."

I stared at him and said nothing.

He gazed down at the floor, his face very pale, his lips trembling faintly. All the time he talked he would not look directly at me.

"I miss my mother," he said. "Every day I see her dead in my imagination."

I did not know what to say.

"I know my mother is with God," he said. "But I see her in her grave and I can't help it. I can't help how I see her." He was still not looking at me as he spoke. "It helps if I study a lot. That keeps my imagination away."

"I'm not afraid of seeing my father in my imagination. I love to see my father. There's a picture of three horses on a beach in my parents' room, and now sometimes I see my father riding one of the horses."

"Do you ever see him in his grave?"

"He doesn't have a grave. He was blown up by a big bomb and no one could find anything."

He looked at me then and his mouth fell open. Then he looked slowly away.

"I think imagination is a wonderful thing," I said. "My Aunt Sarah told me it helped the pioneer women who had to live alone when their husbands were away hunting. Sometimes it gives me very bad dreams. But it gives me nice dreams too. Especially in school. It helps me get through my classes."

"You don't like your classes?"

"They're boring."

"My school isn't boring."

"Sometimes I fall asleep in class and have dreams. Sometimes I dream with my eyes open."

"What do you dream?"

"All kinds of things. Stories."

"You wouldn't find my school boring."

"I couldn't go to your school, David. I don't know enough Hebrew."

"You could learn. We have students who don't know too much Hebrew when they come in. They learn."

"And I don't believe in God."

Once again he looked straight at me. "You don't believe in—? Why do you come to shul?"

"I like to be with everyone. I like to listen to the songs. I like it when the Torah is taken out and read. It's warm and nice. It feels good and everything feels like it's being changed into something very beautiful like when I was building the castles on the beach. Remember? I don't like the curtain though. I don't like having to sit behind the wall where I can't see clearly. Why do they have that wall? I don't like it when people are separated like that."

"It's the law," he said quietly, still looking at me.

"Someone should change it."

"You can't do that. God made the law."

"No He didn't. My mother says that people make the laws, then they say that God made them so that everyone will obey. My parents taught me—"

He broke in angrily, "Your parents are—" He stopped and fidgeted on the chair through a brief silence. Then he said, "Are you going to keep saying Kaddish for your father?"

"Yes."

"You really shouldn't, Ilana. You really don't have to. Everyone's talking about it."

"Will they tell me to leave the shul if I keep saying it?"

"I don't know. I don't think so."

My mother called us from the kitchen.

"I don't understand why a girl can't say it."

"A woman doesn't *have* to pray, she doesn't *have* to come to shul. Why are you doing it?"

My mother called us again.

"I have to do more for my father than just attend one memorial meeting. He was my father."

David said nothing. He rose from the chair and I slid off the bed. My mother called us a third time. We went from my room and along the hallway toward the kitchen, our footsteps echoing faintly on the wooden floor.

My mother, Mr. Dinn, and Jakob Daw looked at us as we came into the kitchen. They were standing at the table. Mr. Dinn held in his hand two new white candles whose tips had been scraped back, exposing additional lengths of wick; the wicks were bent toward each other. On the table was a small glass dish in which was a reddish substance; next to the dish was a shot glass filled nearly to overflowing with an amber liquid that, upon my coming close to it, smelled like my father's Scotch.

"David, we'll make Havdoloh here," Mr. Dinn said. His dark hat was tipped back on his head.

David looked very surprised. "Here?" he blurted out. "Why here?"

"Because Mr. Daw has requested it."

"For my dead grandfather," Jakob Daw said quietly. "It is the service he loved most. The Havdoloh. I would stand next to him while he said it. My father, you must understand, was first a follower of the ideas of Lassalle and later of Bakunin. Those names mean nothing to you, of course. And yet my father could never once bring himself to forbid me to listen to my grandfather's Havdoloh and to drink the wine afterwards."

"Tonight we'll have Scotch instead of wine," Mr. Dinn said. "We don't seem to have the proper wine in this house."

My mother looked down at the glass dish and the shot glass on the table and said nothing.

"In Madrid," Jakob Daw said in his raspy voice, "I once said to myself that if I came out alive I would do something that would make my grandfather happy. I said it again in Bilbao, and I said it three or four times in Barcelona. Once I said it very loudly in Barcelona so I should be heard above the machine-gun fire by whoever or whatever listens to such promises. I do not believe in God, you understand, but I do believe in my grandfather's Havdoloh."

Mr. Dinn handed the candles to David, who held them tightly together, his eyes fixed on the wicks.

"The word havdoloh means separation," Mr. Dinn said. "We separate the Shabbos from the other days of the week. First we light the candles as a sign of this separation, because you're not permitted to use fire on Shabbos."

The hand in which David held the candles shook slightly. Mr. Dinn struck a match and, a moment after it flared into life, reached over and turned off the kitchen light. Shadows danced on the ceiling and walls. My mother's eyes shone in the flame.

"At home we use one candle with many wicks," Mr. Dinn said softly. "It's a beautiful candle of many colors."

"I remember such a candle," Jakob Daw said. Lights and shadows played on his gaunt face as the wicks were fed by the match and became fused into a single tall flame.

"The spices in the dish help to make the service more beautiful by their aroma," Mr. Dinn said. "Some say their purpose is to strengthen you for the coming week's burdens. At home we have a special silver box for the spices. My wife, of blessed memory, bought it."

I saw David look up at his father, his mouth slightly open, his eyes wide and dark.

"I remember my grandfather's box," Jakob Daw said. "It was a filigreed silver box shaped like the tower of a castle."

"Yes," said Mr. Dinn. "Exactly."

I looked at David. He was staring uneasily at the flame. A narrow spiral of smoke rose upward from the candles and vanished into the ceiling shadows.

My mother stood very still, saying nothing.

Mr. Dinn raised the little glass in his right hand and began to chant. His eyes were closed and he swayed slightly as he sang the words. He had a rich baritone voice that rang out clearly in the small kitchen but did not assault our ears. The melody moved through the apartment, returning faintly from distant corners. Then David and his father chanted something briefly together, and Mr. Dinn went on alone. He put the glass down on the table and picked up the dish of spices. He said a blessing over the spices, sniffed them, and gave the dish to Jakob Daw, who sniffed and passed it to my mother. She put the dish briefly to her nose and gave it to David, who took a deep breath of the spices and passed it to me. The scent was sweet, heady, aromatic. I put the dish back down on the table.

Wax was running down the candle onto David's fingers. His hand continued its faint trembling.

Mr. Dinn cupped his hands together, knuckles down, and moved them close to the flame. He chanted a blessing and opened his hands so that the light of the flame bathed his palms. David repeated the gesture with his left hand. Jakob Daw, my mother, and I did nothing for a moment. Then I saw Jakob Daw extend his arms, cup his hands, and open his palms. How pale his hands looked, how dry and brittle! I could see ridges of bones, outlines of veins.

Mr. Dinn raised the glass again and went on chanting, his voice louder now. Then he was done and he sipped from the glass and put it down and David blew out the candle. The lights came back on in time for us to see a small column of smoke drifting upward from the extinguished candle and forming a thin cloud below the ceiling.

Jakob Daw stood very still next to my mother, his eyes closed.

"Goot voch," Mr. Dinn said. "I wish everyone a good week."

He kissed his son. He shook my mother's hand—with a special tenderness, I thought. He bent to kiss my head and I sensed in him a rush of gentleness and warm concern that surprised me; I had not thought him capable of deep feelings.

"Goot voch, Mr. Daw," he said, offering his hand.

Jakob Daw opened his eyes and for a moment seemed not to know where he was. He shook Mr. Dinn's hand.

"Some memories are good, most are bad," Jakob Daw said. "This was a good memory."

"You can make Havdoloh by yourself," Mr. Dinn said. "You don't need someone to do it for you."

"There are many things I cannot do by myself," Jakob Daw said, "and Havdoloh is one of them. I appreciate the memory. Believe me when I tell you that in Barcelona I did not think I would ever be in Brooklyn listening to a Jew make Havdoloh. It is all very strange. Nothing I write could ever be as strange as our real world."

"We must go," Mr. Dinn said. "I'll come over tomorrow and we'll talk some more. Keep in mind what I suggested. There will definitely be trouble. That much I know."

"It is probably someone who does not like my stories. I have been told that my stories often have strange effects upon my readers."

"It's not your stories, it's your politics."

"But I no longer have any politics. I have renounced my party affiliation. Stalinism is dead for me after Barcelona."

My mother gave Jakob Daw a piercing look.

"We'll have to convince the people at Immigration," Mr. Dinn said.

"Will that be difficult to do?"

"Yes," Mr. Dinn said.

"But what can they do to me? I have the visa. It was given to me by a fine gentleman in Marseilles. Can they revoke a visa?"

"They can come up with a visa charge. They can claim fraud. They can do a deep search and charge you with failure to disclose some petty offense. It's called material fraud bearing on admissibility. They can get you if they really want to. Or they can simply let the visa run out and not renew it."

"You are saying, if I understand you correctly, that I am in the clutches of a bureaucracy and now share the common lot of the working class. Perhaps it would have helped if I were a different kind of writer. What a pity! It would be so ironic to have come to America only to be sent back to Europe for something I no longer am. It would be a little like living inside one of my own stories."

"You won't be sent back," Mr. Dinn said. "I can promise you that. Come, David. We have to go. Say good night."

"Will you visit me again?" I asked David.

"I don't know," he said, not looking at me directly.

My mother accompanied David and his father to the door. I heard the harp. My mother came back into the kitchen and sat down at the table.

"What happened at the meeting?" Jakob Daw asked.

"Precisely what you expected. They were delicate but firm."

"Well," Jakob Daw said, "it is beginning. Barcelona or Brooklyn, they are the same Stalinists."

"I don't want to hear you talking like that, Jakob," my mother said.

"No? Listen to me, Channah. I was in Barcelona. My eyes saw this. They slaughtered anarchists, Trotskyists, P.O.U.M. people. Stalin's hand purged Barcelona. If it were not for Ezra Dinn and the visa waiting for me in Marseilles, I would have remained in Barcelona and would now be either in a jail or dead. It was more important for the Communists in Barcelona to kill anti-Stalinist workers than to kill Fascists. This my eyes saw, Channah."

"The party is my life, Jakob," my mother said in a small voice. "I don't know what to do."

"I am going to lie down," Jakob Daw said. "I am very tired."

He went out of the kitchen and along the hallway to his room.

I woke in the night to go to the bathroom and passed by the partly open door to Jakob Daw's room. He was at the small desk, writing. Later I woke again after a vivid dream about my father: he was swimming in the ocean off the beach at Sea Gate and three horses suddenly thundered across the sand and when I looked again for my father I could not see him. I woke with my heart beating fiercely and got out of bed to go through the hallway to the bathroom—and there was Jakob Daw at the little desk in his room, still writing, the desk lamp brushing his face with a soft and luminous wash of yellow light. He still had on his clothes of the day before, and I wondered if he had slept at all. He wore his spectacles and, in the moment or two that I stood there watching, the glasses flared in the light and it was as if his eyes were on fire. I heard nothing save the scratching of his fountain pen on paper and it seemed to me a wondrously musical sound. Words and ideas were coming from him through his fingers and pen onto paper, and a story was being created! I was seeing it but I could not understand it, this act of creating a story.

My mother went out early the following morning. Jakob Daw was asleep. I wandered about the apartment. In my mother's bedroom I stopped to gaze at her large bed and wondered what she must feel like sleeping alone and knowing my father would never return. I opened her closet, saw her few clothes and shoes: skirts, dresses, a cardigan sweater, spectator shoes, pumps, walking shoes, slippers. On a shelf were her berets and two purses. Then I opened my father's closet. His clothes and shoes were still there. That was a strange feeling, standing there and staring at my dead father's clothes and shoes. All seemed to be waiting patiently for his return. I closed the closet door. The bed had been neatly made with its pale blue flowered spread. Near the bed I saw an open carton with a white label on which were printed the words SPECIAL WRITING in my father's hand. My father's desk was clean; my mother used it now for her own writing. I stood in the doorway and it seemed to me my father was everywhere in that room—on the bed, at the desk, by the window, in the corners. I went back through the hallway to my room and spent the rest of the morning at my desk, reading.

My mother returned home shortly before lunch. Jakob Daw woke coughing and came out of his room in the same clothes he had worn the day before. His door was across the hallway from mine and I saw him stagger a little as he went from his room. He appeared haggard, exhausted. His eyes were swollen, his face unshaven. He saw me looking at him and said something in a language I could not understand and went along the hallway, coughing. The bathroom door closed.

In the kitchen my mother dropped something: the noise of shattering glass was abrupt and jarring. Angry words exploded from her, uttered, it seemed to me, in the same language Jakob Daw had used a moment before.

In the early afternoon the three of us walked along the parkway to Prospect Park. For some fresh air, my mother said. We all needed fresh air. We watched people rowing on the lake. There were small fish in the lake and they made tiny rippling circles along the surface of the water as they fed off the bread crumbs people threw them. The park was crowded. We sat on a bench with our faces to the sun. Birds flew high overhead against a cloudless sky. My mother and I had come to this park with my father the day before he had sailed back to Spain. That seemed a long time ago. When had that been?

I asked Jakob Daw if he knew how to row a boat. He smiled tiredly and said in a brooding tone, speaking not to me but to the sky and the air, that it was another of the many things he could not do.

"There were other things to do in Vienna when I was growing up. Many other things. I rowed through Schnitzler and Hofmannsthal. And through Marx and Freud and others. Those were deep and beautiful lakes. Sometimes they became wide rivers. Once I even rowed through Theodor Herzl, but it proved uninteresting. But I did not learn to row in ordinary water." He coughed. "Another of my many failings, along with ineptitude in the trenches and in—" He stopped, glanced at my mother, and looked quickly away. "In other matters."

He leaned back on the bench, his hands clasped behind his head. He had changed into different clothes, as baggy and as wrinkled as those he had worn before. I was sitting between him and my mother and felt a gray sadness rising from him and, at the same time, felt myself drawn to him as if by some dark mesmerizing force. He had cut himself while shaving; a clot of blood lay on his bony chin. I wanted to touch the blood, wash it away, dress the wound. The afternoon sunlight accentuated the network of small lines around his eyes and showed clearly the flecks of gray in his hair. I could not remember having seen gray in his hair when I had first met him last year in our apartment in Manhattan.

My mother had been sitting quietly, looking at the lake. She wore a white beret and a dark blue skirt. "I used to go rowing," she said. "With my grandfather. We lived near a wide river. He used to take me rowing when I was a little girl. I was too young to row the boat myself. And then the war came and we ran from the town—it was a border town between Russia and Poland, and we were told the Russian cavalry was coming. We hid in a forest. I remember the forest. That was all the rowing I ever did."

"Didn't you ever go rowing with your father?" I asked.

"I never did anything with my father. Once my mother took me out on the river and we almost overturned the boat. My mother was a very modern woman, but she didn't know anything about boats. Your father had an uncle once who knew about boats. But he died in a boating accident. I don't like boats. Boats frighten me. People I love keep going away from me on boats."

We sat on the bench in the sunlight, looking at the lake.

"Mama?"

"Yes, darling."

"Will we go to the beach this summer?"

"I don't know. I will have to work all summer. There's no more money from your father's job. And I will not take money from—" She stopped. "I don't know about the summer, Ilana."

Jakob Daw had closed his eyes and seemed to have fallen asleep. Now he said, with his eyes closed, "How serious do you think it is, Channah?"

"If Ezra is worried, it's very serious."

"I used to boast about being hated by the right people. I am not boasting now. I am very tired."

My mother said nothing.

"I am not looking forward to another sea journey."

Still my mother said nothing.

"I will not fight to remain here, Channah. I do not wish to become a cause that the Stalinists and the Fascists will turn into a circus. Nor do I wish to live in a country where I will be hounded constantly by name-less government officials. I will not permit Ezra to waste his time with this. The French will take me in. The French appreciate my writing. Malraux himself is a devoted reader. The French will certainly take me back in."

"Stop it, Jakob," my mother said.

"I detest boats and ships," Jakob Daw said, opening his eyes and looking at the lake. "I cannot begin to tell you how much I detest boats and ships. Perhaps I will write a story about it one day."

"Please stop it," my mother said.

"I think we should return to the apartment," Jakob Daw said. "I am very, very tired."

"Can I help you, Uncle Jakob? You can lean on me."

"You are a dear child. I hope someone will soon teach you how to row. Are you ready to start back, Channah?"

That evening my mother met again in our living room with the two men and the woman. They studied together. New words flew into my room: exchange value, commodities, universal money, labor power. Jakob Daw lay in his room, asleep. Later Mr. Dinn came over and he and my mother sat in the kitchen, talking. I woke in the night to go to the bathroom and saw Jakob Daw sitting at the desk in his clothes, writing, the scratching of his pen a sibilant music in the dark stillness of the apartment.

I walked home from school past the yeshiva and saw Ruthie playing in the wide front yard during her afternoon recess. The yard was crowded and noisy. A number of teachers stood along the rim of the sidewalk, forming a protective phalanx. Most of the teachers in the yard were women; two of the men were young and wore beards.

I waved to Ruthie. She came over to me. We stood in the shade of a sycamore. A car sped by close to the sidewalk.

"We heard David's father making Havdoloh in your apartment," Ruthie said. She had been jumping rope and her freckled face was flushed and sweaty. "Why did he do that?"

"Mr. Daw asked him."

"David's father said he wouldn't sing again outside his own house until after he stopped saying Kaddish."

"I didn't know."

"Are you going to keep saying Kaddish?"

"Yes."

"You don't have to, you know. Girls don't have to say Kaddish."

"I want to."

"Everyone's talking about you, Ilana."

I did not respond. One of the girls in the yard called Ruthie's name.

"Doesn't it bother you that everyone is talking about you?"

"No."

"You shouldn't do it, Ilana."

One of the young, bearded teachers was looking at me. I said, "Ruthie, does your father ever take you rowing?"

She stared at me. "What?"

"In the lake in Prospect Park. Does your father ever take you rowing there?"

"My mother takes me. In the summer, mostly."

"Do you stay in the city in the summer?"

"We go to the country where there's a lake. Are you all right, Ilana?"

"I'm not all right. My Uncle Jakob may have to leave America. The government doesn't want him to stay."

She stared at me. Once again a girl called her name.

"I have to go home," I said. "Maybe he's awake and will want something to eat. What kind of government do we have? Is it a Fascist government? David's father is trying to keep him here. I dreamed last night that he went away on a big boat, like my father."

The teacher who had been looking at me came over to us. He was a short thin man with a dark beard and he wore a brown suit and a gray felt hat. He said something to Ruthie in what sounded like Yiddish.

"Your uncle will be okay," Ruthie said. "My father says that David's father is a very good lawyer."

"I wonder if David's father knows how to row. I'll see you, Ruthie. Good-bye. I like the ocean anyway better than the lake."

I went along the parkway, turned up the side street, and walked past the candy store without looking at the newspapers. The air was warm and bright; brilliant sunlight covered the streets. On the street where I lived the brownstones seemed to be glowing in the sunlight and deep green shadows lay beneath the full-leafed trees. Baby carriages had been parked in the shade and in one of them a child lay crying. I looked up and saw Jakob Daw in the bay window of our living room.

He had the apartment door open for me before I reached the landing. I heard the final notes of the door harp. As he closed the door behind me the door harp sang again.

He asked how my day had been. I said school was boring. He looked surprised. We came into the kitchen. I brought a glass of milk and a plate of cookies to the table. He poured himself a cup of coffee. He was wearing the same rumpled pants he had worn on Saturday. He looked pale and weary. His eyes were red with fatigue, his cheeks sunken. From time to time as we sat there together, he coughed behind his fingers.

He said, in his hesitant way, that he had looked at the books in my room and hoped I didn't mind. Did I like the Hebrew books? I told him I especially liked the books about the Bible. They were good stories, I said.

"Stories," he echoed softly.

"And I like the fairy tale books. And the book about Paul Bunyan. I especially like that book." Then I said, "Uncle Jakob, why did my father die?"

He looked down into his cup, his gaunt features tight. "Because a Fascist airplane killed him."

"Why did he try to save the nun?"

"Because that was the kind of man your father was."

"If he hadn't tried to save her he might still be alive."

Jakob Daw was quiet. Then he said, "If my grandmother had had wheels, she would have rolled."

I looked at him.

"An old proverb," he murmured. "Forgive me. I do not like to play the game of if, Ilana. It gives me a headache and, worse, a heartache. No ifs, please."

"Uncle Jakob, are you a stay-at-home writer?"

"What is a stay-at-home writer, Ilana? Ah, yes, I see what you mean. Yes, I am mostly a stay-at-home writer."

"I wish my father had stayed home more. Did you see my father much in Spain?"

"I was with your father in Madrid and then in Bilbao, before he went to Guernica and I went to Barcelona. I thought I might go to Lisbon, but that turned out to be impossible. It was difficult even to travel to Barcelona. Do those names mean anything to you?"

"I know all those places. I can show them to you on the map."

"Yes," he said. "I am sure you can."

"Do you always write at night, Uncle Jakob?"

"Almost always. The day is too filled with noise. I can hear my voices better in the silence of night. The voices of the people I write about."

"Can you hear the voice of your little black bird better at night too?"

"Yes. But even at night that voice is weak. The bird is now very tired, Ilana. He is looking for a place to build a nest."

"I hope you won't go back to Europe, Uncle Jakob."

He said nothing. I watched as he went over to the stove, poured himself another cup of coffee, put in it a teaspoon of cocoa from an open tin on the counter near the sink, stirred the cup briefly with a teaspoon, and returned to the table.

"Is America a Fascist country?" I asked.

"No. But there are Americans who are Fascists."

"Is the man who wants to send you back to Europe a Fascist?"

"I do not know who wants to send me back to Europe."

"I'm afraid of you going back to Europe."

He drank from his cup and sat there staring down at the table. "I think I will lie down for a while," he said. "I am very tired. Please forgive me, Ilana."

I sat at the table, listening to him go slowly along the hallway to his room.

My mother returned from her work. Jakob Daw joined us for supper but said little. After supper my mother came into my room and stood near the door.

"Ilana?"

I looked up from my reading.

"Mrs. Helfman told me this morning that you said Kaddish in the synagogue."

I said nothing.

"You are not supposed to say Kaddish."

"I want to."

"Ilana—"

"I want to."

She looked at me and seemed not to know what to say.

"Mama, do you want me to stop saying it?"

There was a silence. She stood rigidly near the door, looking at me, her dark eyes burning, her face pale. "I don't even want you to go to that synagogue," she said finally. "But I won't stop you. Not if it means that much to you." And she went from my room.

That night I woke and heard sounds from the darkness of the apartment. I thought at first that Baba Yaga had returned, but there was no evil in the sounds; there was wind in trees and a distant sighing and the softest of laughter amidst the silken back-and-forth sliding of night surf. And softly out of the darkness, through walls that somehow always yielded to my listening ears, came a far-off rhythmic beat like the thudding hooves of stallions racing across the red sands of an endless beach.

The days passed. Sometimes in the evenings visitors would come to the apartment, people I had never seen before. Many were well dressed. They would sit in the living room, speaking respectfully with Jakob Daw and listening intently to his words. I marveled at the deference in their manner, the awe in which they held him. He seemed the shyest of people. Diffidence clung to him, a nervous reluctance to offend. He bent toward you as you spoke, inclined his ear to your words.

On occasion he and my mother went out together of an evening. He never wore anything other than baggy pants and wrinkled shirts and sometimes an old sweater if the evening was cool. His shoes were scruffy, unpolished. Color had returned to his face; much of the darkness was gone from around his eyes. He still coughed from time to time but I had come almost not to notice it.

At times my mother and Jakob Daw would go to Manhattan on their evenings out and bring back newspapers and magazines in languages I could not read. Once Jakob Daw brought me a book of stories by two brothers named Grimm.

"The brothers Grimm claimed they went out in the country among the German peasants and collected true folk tales," he said when he gave me the book. "But now we know they lied. These tales were told to them by members of their own family. Nevertheless they are very interesting stories."

Rumpelstiltskin. Sleeping Beauty. Hansel and Gretel. I found I could not stop reading.

Often Mr. Dinn would come into the apartment late at night and the three of them would sit together in the kitchen, talking.

David said to me one Saturday as we stood outside the synagogue, "Don't you know what's going on, Ilana?"

"What do you mean?"

"Don't you read the newspapers? There are petitions and all kinds of letters being sent to Washington."

"I don't read newspapers anymore."

"People are trying to save him."

"Uncle Jakob says it won't help."

"My father won't let him be sent away."

"Did you know there are Fascists in Washington, David? Can your father fight Fascists?"

"My father says—"

"David, are you going back to the beach this summer?"

"I think so. For a few weeks."

"My mother says we're not going. We don't have any money for the beach."

He looked down at the sidewalk.

"The Fascists killed my father and now they're going to send Uncle Jakob away. I wish you a good time at the beach, David. Do you know how to build sand castles? Remember the one we built together? That was nice."

"Ilana—"

"I'm tired. Did you notice that a lot of women answered amen when I said the Kaddish this morning? Did you notice that?"

"No."

"Why didn't you and your father say Kaddish?"

"We don't have to anymore. You say it for eleven months after the funeral."

"I'm going to miss the beach. We don't know where we'll be this summer. Uncle Jakob isn't allowed to leave the city. Did you know that?"

"No."

"At least your friends don't laugh at me anymore. They weren't nice when they laughed at me. Good Shabbos, David. Your father has a beautiful voice. I wish he would lead the service in the synagogue."

I felt him watching me as I walked away. The air was warm on my face and arms. I moved with care so as not to trip over the cracks in the sidewalk.

In the apartment I found Jakob Daw at the kitchen table, drinking coffee. He wore pajamas and a frayed dark-blue robe, and his hair was uncombed. He gazed at me for a moment and seemed not to know who I was. Then his eyes cleared.

"Ilana. Good morning. Is it morning? Where were you?"

"In shul."

"Shul," he said. "Yes. Your mother went out shopping. There is a note here somewhere from her. Where did I put it? Take yourself some milk and cookies and sit down and keep me company."

"Were you up all night writing?"

"Not all night. Most of the night. I went to sleep as the birds woke. Do you hear the birds in the morning?"

"Yes."

"Beautiful sounds. Beautiful music to fall asleep to. Yes, sit here. Be careful with your milk. I remember the birds on the beach. Do you remember those birds?"

"Yes."

"Some made very strange sounds. Like women laughing and crying. Is the weather nice outside?"

"It's warm."

"Perhaps we will go for a walk later. It is not healthy to be indoors so much. In Europe people walk much more than they do here. Europe is made for walking. We will go to the park and watch the rowers on the lake."

"Uncle Jakob?"

"Yes, Ilana."

"Are they going to send you away?"

"I do not know. They are certainly trying."

"David Dinn said that lots of people are writing letters and signing petitions to keep you from being sent away."

"Yes. People are doing that. But I do not think—"

I heard the downstairs door close with its loud click and thought it was my mother with shopping bags.

"Mama is coming back."

I went to the door and opened it and heard Ruthie and her parents in the hallway downstairs. I closed the door and turned. Jakob Daw had come up behind me. The music of the door harp resonated softly through the apartment.

Jakob Daw stood very still, watching the wooden balls as their motion slowed and the music died away. Then he lifted one of the balls with his fingers and let it fall on the taut wire. *Ting.* The sound echoed softly. *Ting ting ting ting ting.* He lifted a second wooden ball and let it fall. Then he began to lift them one after the other. They bounced jauntily upon the wires.

The hallway filled with the music of the harp.

I stood there watching him and then heard him say, to the accompaniment of the music of the harp, "I know now what it is that happens to our little bird, Ilana. Shall I tell you? Yes? All right." He was silent a moment, the wooden balls rising and falling beneath his fingers, the harp sending out its vibrating tones. "Our little bird flew back across the ocean. Yes, he flew and flew against the wind." The harp sang and sang as Jakob Daw's fingers kept lifting the wooden balls and letting them fall. "The wind was very strong. And cold. And the bird was burdened with strange baggage: bits and pieces of broken dreams that kept piercing his troubled heart like shards of glass. He did not care anymore about the music of the world. He wanted to rest. He flew on against the wind, straining his fragile wings. And as he flew a curious thing happened: he began to grow smaller and smaller. And soon he was no larger than the tiniest of birds and you could barely see him in the vast sky. He flew low over the ocean, skimming the water, and once or twice a wave reached up as if to pull him down. And suddenly there along the horizon was the land; and by this time the bird was no bigger than a butterfly. And still he grew smaller and smaller; and soon he was no bigger than the tip of your thumb. And he grew smaller still and now he was the size of your fingernail. And he flew slowly over a beach and across land and came to a quiet street with houses and trees and he heard a peculiar music coming from one of the houses and he circled and circled about the house and flew in one day when the little girl who lived in the house opened the door—and there was the music, rising from a bit of wood that hung from the door! It was the kind of music the bird thought he could listen to forever: sweet but not false, a comfort but not a deceiving caress; a music of innocence. And the bird continued growing smaller and smaller and then entered the circular hollow within the wood, above which the balls and wires made their music. And there he nested. And there he lived. And there he lives to this day. And there he will continue to live. In our door harp."

He lowered his hand. The wooden balls grew still. The music faded.

"In our door harp," Jakob Daw said again, as if echoing his own words. Then he turned and went slowly into his room and closed the door.

I stood very still in the silent hallway, staring up at the door harp.

The downstairs lock clicked sharply. I opened the door. The harp sang. I listened to its music and imagined the tiny bird inside, listening too. I went quickly down the stairs to help my mother.

Mr. Dinn came over that night with David and again chanted the Havdoloh prayers. Afterward we sat around the kitchen table. Mr. Dinn would not eat anything. David had a glass of milk but politely refused the cookies.

It was a hot gloomy night. Mr. Dinn kept saying he could not understand what was going on in Washington, nothing like this had ever happened to him before. The pressure against Jakob Daw was enormous. Sometimes he had the feeling it was coming from inside the White House itself. Nothing he could be sure of; nothing he could pin down. His Washington connections refused to talk to him about Jakob Daw. Sure, he was a great writer. He was also a Bolshevik. He was a Communist who had advocated revolution in speeches and articles. He was no longer a Stalinist but a Trotskyist? The fine distinction was lost somewhere in the bureaucratic labyrinth at immigration. Someone wanted Jakob Daw out of the country. Indeed, maybe it had nothing to do with Jakob Daw's communism. Maybe someone was making points with his department chief. Maybe someone was settling an old grudge. Maybe someone didn't like Jakob Daw's stories.

My mother sat staring down at the table and saying nothing.

"We have a long way to go before it's lost," Mr. Dinn said. "We have certainly not exhausted all our possibilities."

"In our time, Mr. Dinn," Jakob Daw said, "a man whose enemies are faceless bureaucrats almost never wins. It is our equivalent to the anger of the gods in ancient times. But those gods, you must understand, were far more imaginative than our bureaucrats. They spoke from mountaintops, not from tiny airless offices. They rode clouds. They were possessed of passion. They had voices and names. Six thousand years of civilization have brought us to this. Was it worth the effort? I think I shall take another cup of coffee. You are spending so much time here these days we ought to make the apartment kosher so you might eat here."

David's father smiled thinly.

"Should we organize a demonstration?" my mother said.

"Demonstrations won't affect the law, Channah," Mr. Dinn said.

"I do not want demonstrations," Jakob Daw said. "I do not want this to drag on and on and become a political circus. The left will demonstrate for me, the right will demonstrate against me. We will go to the courts and get postponements and delays and in the end the government will win anyway. I have no desire and no strength for such a battle. We will go as far as the first hearing."

"But what can they possibly find that will bring you to a hearing?" my mother asked.

"I was a wild and wanton youth," Jakob Daw said. "I relied heavily on wine as an antidote to shyness. But I have no recollection of any criminal activity."

"Jakob, this is not a time for your dark humor," my mother said.

"I believe I was on the wanted list in Barcelona," Jakob Daw said. "A few chance remarks on my part about the heroism I had witnessed by anarchist militia in the front lines around Huesca and how it might not be too difficult to sympathize with the P.O.U.M. secured for me a serious threat of arrest as a Fascist. Can you imagine that? In the eyes of the Stalinists I had become a Fascist. Why does that not qualify Jakob Daw for permanent residence in America?"

My mother and Mr. Dinn looked at each other and said nothing.

"You cannot imagine what it was like in Barcelona. They said more than a thousand workers were slain. It was a civil war inside a civil war. Workers killing workers. Machine guns, grenades, rifles, barricades, red and black flags, anarchists and Stalinists and Trotskyists. You think the Russians desire revolution in Spain, Channah? They do not. What they want is to preserve the friendship of France, and France does not wish to see a revolutionary government on its southern border. The Communists of Spain are now counterrevolutionists and are killing anarchists, who are the true fighters for a workers' revolution today. That was Barcelona, Channah. Do you hear me? I was there. These eyes saw

Barcelona. However, I do not think the people in Washington will be impressed by the fact that to the Stalinists I am now a Fascist."

My mother rose stiffly from the table, went over to the stove, and refilled her coffee cup. She returned to the table.

"Ilana, why don't you and David go into your room for a while," she said.

"Mama."

"Do you mind, David?"

"No," David said reluctantly.

"Mama."

"Go ahead, Ilana."

I finished my milk and went from the kitchen, followed hesitantly by David.

"Did you understand what they were saying?" he asked as we went along the hallway.

"Not all of it."

"I didn't understand the part about Barcelona. Your mother looked very upset."

We came into my room.

"I don't understand politics," David said. "It's very boring."

"No, it's not."

"It's boring to me."

"Wasn't the Jewish revolution that Rabbi Akiva led against Rome politics? And when Abraham destroyed all the idols, wasn't that politics? And the destruction of the temple in Jerusalem, and when all the Jews were expelled from Spain? Wasn't all that politics?"

"I didn't mean—"

"If it's American politics or politics about the world, you're bored. But if it's about Jews, you're not bored."

He stared at me. "Please, I didn't mean to make you angry, Ilana."

"I'm sorry," I said. "I'm sorry."

There was a brief silence.

"They're going to send Uncle Jakob away. How can they do that?"

David looked at me out of his wide dark eyes and made no response.

The weeks of June went slowly by. School ended. The air grew sultry; nights were hot. Terrifying rumors of polio in distant parts of the city drifted into our neighborhood. My mother would leave for work early in the morning and return to make supper. I played in the backyard with Ruthie. Her father had rigged up a swing on the sycamore and we would take turns on it. I loved the sensation of rising and falling, flying and plunging, the hot winds of the summer on my face.

One day a big car came to the house and took Ruthie and her parents off to the mountains. I played on the street with the children of the neighborhood. On occasion I sat alone in the backyard near the flowers, reading, daydreaming, waiting for Jakob Daw to waken so we could go to Prospect Park and the lake and the zoo and the botanical gardens. We went nearly every day. He had learned to row and often we went out on the lake. I sat in the boat in the sun and let him take me slowly across the smooth water. How calm the water was. How different from the churning ferocity of the ocean. And there was nothing here with which I could build a castle, no sand, no surf, only the mind-dulling calm of a mirrorlike lake.

One Sunday in early July the three of us took a train to Coney Island and went along the boardwalk and sat on a blanket in the sand. Jakob Daw would not go into the water—would not even put on a bathing suit. I swam with my mother, the hot sun on my face, the waves swelling and cresting and falling, acrid salt water in my mouth and eyes and nose. Later that afternoon I built a castle with the help of Jakob Daw and my mother; it came nearly to my shoulders. We left it there in the wet sand along the edge of the sea, glowing pink and red in the setting sun. I dreamed of the stallions that night, saw them galloping across a red beach, hooves thundering, sand flying, racing on the rim of the sea toward the horizon along which ships slowly moved beneath an evening sky.

In the second week of July David Dinn left for Sea Gate. His father remained in the city and went to Sea Gate only for the weekends. He came often to the apartment, always at night, and I would lie in my bed and listen to the three of them in the kitchen. In one of my dreams during those weeks a short, round man in a dark suit motioned to me from behind his desk, which was piled high with papers, and when I looked at him I saw his face was as vacant as an egg.

The week David left for Sea Gate Jakob Daw took me to Prospect Park. It was a hot sunny day and the park was crowded with mothers and little children. Jakob Daw took me out on the lake in a boat. I sat on the stern seat facing the sun and felt the smooth and lulling motion of the boat in the water. Jakob Daw rowed slowly and awkwardly and from time to time one of the oars would go into a skimming slide across the surface of the lake and send forth a spray of water. I saw dark water spots on his baggy trousers and wrinkled shirt. His long bony arms strained at the oars. The lake was crowded and he rowed cautiously, keeping out of the way of the other boats.

"It is clear to me," he said, "that you prefer the ocean to this lake."

"I like the lake when you take me rowing on it."

"I see that people do not swim in this lake. It is for boating only. Still it is a pretty lake and this is a fine park. Americans are capable here and there of the touches of civilization. Capitalism has not yet entirely swallowed up the land. Would you like an ice cream when we are done rowing?"

"Yes."

"So would I. I find that I have come to enjoy American ice cream. Is it too hot for you in the sun?"

"No."

"Perhaps you should wear a hat. Your blond hair will be bleached white in so much sun."

"No it won't, Uncle Jakob!"

He steered carefully between two boats.

"Uncle Jakob?"

"Yes, Ilana."

"Can I ask you something about the war?"

"Of course."

"Not the war in Spain. The big war. In Europe."

He looked at me. "The big war," he said. "Yes."

"Were you hurt in that war?"

"I was gassed. In that war both sides used poison gas, and many of the soldiers who breathed it died. I nearly died. I was not a very good soldier. I misplaced my gas mask and did not find it until it was almost too late."

"Were you in a hospital?"

"Oh, yes. For a long time." He craned his neck and steered to avoid a boat. "Many months."

"Did you go back to the war?"

"No. They thought I was well enough to go back but I would not go, so they sent me off to another hospital."

"Another hospital for wounded soldiers?"

"A hospital for wounded minds. A terrible hospital."

I stared at him. The sunlight stung my eyes.

"Move back to the middle of your seat, Ilana. You are tipping the boat to one side."

"I didn't know they did that to soldiers."

"Oh, they did worse. Sometimes they shot you."

"Did they keep you in the second hospital a long time?"

"Yes," he said. "Many years." After a moment he said, "I think I will bring the boat in now, Ilana, and we will have our ice cream. All right? Then we will go back. I am feeling a little tired."

He took me to the park twice again that week. He said nothing more about the war or his years in the hospital. On one of those days he told me another story about the gray horse who lived between the black horses of the mountains and the white horses of the plain—but I find I cannot remember it now. Sometimes in the evenings the three of us went to a movie in our neighborhood or on Flatbush Avenue. All night long he wrote; all morning long he slept. Sometimes in the night his room was empty, and I knew he was with my mother.

That was the way the three of us lived during those hot July weeks of that summer of 1937: walking, rowing, talking, working, playing—and waiting.

The wait ended one evening in the third week of July shortly after supper.

I was sitting in my room at my open window, listening to the wind in the trees and reading. A black four-door car moved slowly up the street and came to a stop in front of our house. Two men got out. They wore dark suits. One of them looked at a paper in his hand and then at our house. Some boys playing a game of stoopball in front of the neighboring house paused to regard them curiously. The two men climbed up our front stoop. A moment later I heard the loud click of the downstairs door.

My mother answered the ring of the doorbell.

I sat at my window, listening. Through the hallway and into my room came a murmurous male voice and a rush of strange words: immigration police, warrant for arrest, deportation proceeding, hearing and review.

Then I heard Jakob Daw's voice. "Who is it, Channah? Hello? Is it for me?"

Again I heard a murmurous male voice.

There was a long silence.

"I understand," Jakob Daw said. "Yes."

"I will call Ezra," my mother said in a frantic voice that trembled and seemed on the edge of panic.

There was another silence. Jakob Daw went into his room and came out a moment later.

My mother called my name. I went quickly out of my room and saw Jakob Daw and two strange tall men and my mother in the hallway near the door.

Jakob Daw said he was going away. His face was gray.

I stared at him. My mother was crying silently. The two men regarded us impassively.

Jakob Daw bent and kissed my cheek. I sensed in that moment the flooding rush of his dread and saw in his eyes an expression I had never seen before—abject helplessness. I will never forget that expression: the wide dark empty look in his eyes, the dead pallor of his face, the faintly quivering nostrils, the rigid lips, the tightened skin of his skeletal features—as if his death mask were already upon him. He said nothing more to me or to my mother. When I raised my arms to embrace him his arms remained stiffly in front of him and I felt them wedged beneath my body. I looked down and realized with a swooning sense of horror that he could not separate his arms because his wrists were shackled together with handcuffs.

Jakob Daw went out between the two men and down the stairway. My mother went down with them, leaving our door open. I stood at my window and watched Jakob Daw climb into the car with the two men.

My mother stood on the curb. The car pulled away and went quickly up the street and turned the corner and was gone. My mother came back into the apartment and closed the door. The harp sang sweetly in the silent hallway.

I sat in the synagogue and listened to the service. The air was cold. I felt everyone staring at me. I looked down at my prayerbook and thought I might pray to God, but I didn't know what to say. I kept hearing the word please. Again and again. Please. Oh please. I rose to recite the Kaddish and there seemed to fall upon the room a dense curtain of silence in which I heard my voice with a startling clarity and heard too the responses of those around me. I thought my knees would buckle and wondered why the room was so cold.

Outside I walked through the crowd and saw people still staring at me. I started home. Somewhere deep inside me the word please had nested and I kept hearing it all the way home. Please. Please. I heard it all that afternoon as I sat alone in the apartment waiting for my mother to return from visiting Jakob Daw. The hearing, which had taken place the day before, had gone badly. My mother had said something in the morning about Ellis Island and had rushed out of the apartment.

She returned home ashen-faced. I heard the word please all through that hot July night and heard too strange words from my mother as she wandered through the apartment, talking out loud, singing softly, weeping.

The next day we took the subway to Manhattan and sat huddled together through the racketing, screeching ride. A cab brought us to the river. We stood a long time in the crowd on the pier. There were journalists and newspaper photographers in the crowd.

A black four-door car pulled up. Two uniformed men climbed out of the car along with Jakob Daw. His wrists were shackled.

A second car pulled up and Mr. Dinn stepped hurriedly out. He looked gray-faced, exhausted, unshaven. His dark suit was rumpled, his dark tie was awry, and his hat had a dent in its side. He saw us and came quickly over, but said nothing.

Jakob Daw craned his neck, scanning the crowd. He found us and raised his shackled hands.

Flashbulbs popped.

The two uniformed men took Jakob Daw quickly up the gangplank and into the ship. He looked back over his shoulder once again. Then he was gone.

My mother and I stood with Mr. Dinn on the pier and watched the ship pull away. We scanned the decks for Jakob Daw but we couldn't see him. Slowly the huge ship grew smaller and smaller. I felt my mother leaning heavily against me, felt all her weight upon me, and thought I would fall. Mr. Dinn put his arm around her shoulders and drew her to him. The ship, white and luminous in the bright red afternoon sun, turned into the river and toward the distant Narrows. Would it sail past Sea Gate? Would I have seen it from the cottage as it sailed on toward the horizon and the darkness of Europe? We stood there watching the ship grow smaller and smaller until it could no longer be seen. Gulls wheeled over the sun-washed water. The crowd had gone. We stood awhile longer, in silence, looking at the wide expanse of the river. Then we climbed into Mr. Dinn's car and drove back to the apartment.

It was cold that night. I woke and went through the dark apartment to my mother's bed and climbed in beside her. She stirred and said, "Michael? Michael?" then saw who it was and said, "We won't cry, darling. There's too much to do. We will be very strong." She clung to me and I felt her softness and the heat of her breasts and thighs. We slept huddled together. Once I woke and thought I heard whispering in the apartment but it was the wind in the trees.

She took me to Prospect Park early the next morning and enrolled me in a city-sponsored summer program. She could not leave me alone in the apartment all day, she said, and she did not want me playing on the streets. I watched her go along the path out of the park. It was queer how cold I felt in spite of the sun that shone full upon my face. I jumped rope and played running games and had milk and cookies and played more games. The adults who took care of us looked to be in their early twenties. Before lunch we were taken out on the lake in boats and I put my hand in the water. Warm and silken. Why was I so cold? It was odd how detached I felt from everything around me. I saw myself in the boat on the lake; saw myself eating lunch, resting on a blanket in the shade of a tall sycamore, playing another game, then out on the lake again in a boat. There was a separate Ilana Davita Chandal watching the Ilana Davita Chandal who now sat in a boat rowed by a deeply tanned athletic-looking young man with brown hair and muscular arms and handsome features. The separate Ilana Davita Chandal saw in that boat, amidst four other girls, a thin tall ungainly girl of about nine with long flaxen hair and milk-white skin and bony shoulders that seemed bent beneath some intolerable burden. The girl, sitting in the stern, let her hand trail in the wake of the boat for a few minutes and then did a curious thing. She stood and stepped slowly out of the boat into the water. It all seemed to take a very long time: the girl rising to her feet, the boat lurching, the astonished look on the rower's face as the girl simply walked off the boat and slid almost without a splash into the water, her dress ballooning up and covering her face, her hair billowing out behind her and then closing up like the petals of a flower as she sank. There were screams from the girls in the boat and shouts from the shore as the rower went into the water and brought the girl to the surface. How warm and smooth the water felt to the girl! An embrace. "Never stand up in a boat!" the rower was saying. "I told you!" They were wrapping her in a blanket and calling her mother. Still it was cold. Still she was outside herself watching it happen, all the strained faces, all the noise, and the policeman writing things down. Her mother came with fresh clothes. A police car took them to the apartment.

Ilana Davita Chandal lay in her bed shivering with cold and in the night entered her mother's room and lay beside her mother and saw on the wall over their heads, in the moonlight that shone through the open window, the stallions on the beach and saw on two of the stallions her father and Jakob Daw, riding together. This she saw in the full and radiant clarity of her young imagination and this she continued seeing through the ensuing days when she ceased talking and would not eat and shivered with cold and watched helplessly the growing horror on her mother's face and then talked with doctors and nurses about the bird nesting in her door harp and the gray horse dead in the mountains and the witch Baba Yaga who had turned the world cold with her evil. And it was strange too that one day one of the nurses was named Sarah and walked about the apartment in slippers and knelt in prayer by the side of Ilana Davita Chandal's bed, murmuring, "O merciful God, giver of life and health; bless, we pray Thee, Thy servant, Ilana Davita Chandal, and those who administer to her of Thy healing gifts; that she may be restored to health of body and of mind; through Jesus Christ our Lord. Amen." From this nurse Ilana Davita Chandal took some food; she let herself be bathed; and the nurse permitted her to lie alone in the big bed in her mother's room beneath the picture of the stallions on the beach. She would lie gazing up at the picture hour after hour, hearing the surf and the wind and the beating of the hooves. Nothing in the picture ever moved; yet she could hear clearly even its faintest sounds.

And then one day a long shiny gray car appeared at the curb in front of the house and a man in uniform climbed out and gently helped Ilana Davita Chandal and the nurse named Sarah into the backseat. Her mother stood on the curb with Mr. Dinn. Neighbors leaned out of windows, watching. Mr. Dinn said something to her through the open window of the car but she did not respond. Her mother leaned into the car and kissed her on the cheek. Cool and dry. Why was her mother crying? The car drove away.

They drove a long time. She slept and woke and slept again. They got out of the car and slept in a big white house. She dreamed a man and a woman came into her room in the night and stood gazing down at her. The next morning they drove on again. Ilana Davita Chandal continued seeing herself in her mother's bedroom staring up at the picture of the beach and the racing stallions. The car drove onto a big boat and she became very frightened and cried and the nurse named Sarah calmed her. They slept on the boat and drove off onto shore and rode through a green country with low rolling hills and narrow roads and old farmhouses and a startling blue sky patched with ragged clouds. And sitting in the backseat of the car, Ilana Davita Chandal caught glimpses of a distant sea beyond the hills and the farms. She felt herself curious about the odd names on the road signs: Five Houses, Dingwells Mills, Dundas, Little Pond. And then, exhausted, she slept and in her sleep again saw herself looking up at the picture of the red beach and the sea beyond and then felt herself rising in the bed, slowly standing, as she had stood in the rowboat, raising her arms carefully for balance and jumping lightly into the picture and marveling at the gritty feel of the sand beneath her feet and at the abrupt lurch into motion of the tranquil landscape within the frame, like the sudden jerking into life of a frozen motion-picture scene—wind on her face, surf on the beach, a gently rippling sea, and white birds circling and calling overhead. She woke and saw the nurse called Sarah kneeling by her bed and heard, "O Heavenly Father, we beseech Thee to have mercy upon all Thy children who live in mental darkness. Restore them to strength of mind. . . ." She closed her eyes. A cool hand gently caressed her face and forehead and stroked her hair. She tumbled into a deep sleep.

Sunlight woke her, hot and brilliant. Aunt Sarah stood by the bed in her white nurse's uniform and cap.

"Thank you, Lord," Ilana Davita Chandal heard her say. "Thank you, dear Jesus."

The air was warm. A wind blew through the open window, stirring the curtains. Beyond the window lay a red-sand beach, a vast sea, an infinite sky. Birds called in the distance. I looked up at my aunt.

"Welcome, darling Davita," she said softly. "Welcome. You slept nearly two days. You look so much better. Isn't it a marvelous day? We'll get you something to eat and we'll go out on the beach. It's so good to have you here, Davita. We're going to make you well. You'll see. With the help of our Lord, we're going to make you all well."

The nearest house stood about a quarter of a mile away on the crest of a low hill and was occupied by the farmer who leased and worked the land. I could see him working the land with two other men. But no one came near us all the weeks we were there save the mailman and the delivery boy from the nearby country store in Little Pond and a neatly attired young couple proselytizing for Jehovah's Witnesses. They left behind some copies of a magazine called *The Watchtower*.

The farmhouse we lived in had been built by Aunt Sarah's grandfather before the turn of the century. It was a small two-story white clapboard house with a dark gray shingle roof and dark gray shutters and a single massive gray stone step leading to the front door. There was an open wooden porch on the side of the house that faced the sea and a wooden stairway led from the porch to a large grassy area that sloped toward the sandy beach and the water. The sea rolled gently onto the red land and only with the sudden changes of the tide would there be the rush of waves onto the beach and whitecaps upon the water. The land was so silent, save for the wind and the waves and the cries of the birds, that it seemed to have been formed by the wondrous magic of a dreamer of tales.

For much of that month I sat on the porch and watched the tides. I saw the sea move slowly back and forth upon the red earth like some breathing creature of vast and mysterious dimensions. I saw the white birds circling above the beach, wide-winged terns, wheeling, calling. I watched the mists roll in from the sea and blur the hard edges of the land and turn all the world gauzy white. I saw sunsets beyond the house and low clouds bursting into flame. I sensed it all as unreal and knew I was inside a long dream from which I would one day waken. In the distant fields men rode horses and at times horses roamed loose on the land and grazed close to the beach. I could hear their occasional whinnying and from time to time saw them break into a gallop alongside the gentle surf. I thought I might see my father and Uncle Jakob on the horses, but I did not.

I was often tired and slept at odd hours, sometimes dropping off abruptly in the midst of a sentence directed to Aunt Sarah and waking hours later alone in my bed in the dark and not knowing for a long moment where I was and thinking my father was at his desk doing his special writing or Jakob Daw was in his room in the circle of light cast by the lamp. The nights were so dark I could not see my hands. Stars burned in the sky, an infinite multitude of tiny blue-white fires in a black and boundless dome, and sometimes when I looked up at them I would burst into tears and Aunt Sarah would hold me and caress my face and pray murmurously to Almighty God or to the Heavenly Father or Merciful God or Most Loving Father or to our Savior Jesus Christ or Jesus Christ our Lord.

At first it was difficult for me to walk, I had lost so much weight and strength. When I woke in the mornings Aunt Sarah would help me dress and then lead me out of my room to the narrow second-floor landing and past the oval-framed sepia photograph of a mother and daughter that hung on the wall at the head of the steep wooden stairway leading to the hallway downstairs. The hallway was small and narrow and brought us into the living room with its large fireplace and old chairs and sofa and, on its white walls, old pictures of a uniformed band and of a tall wavy-haired handsome man in shining white knee-length stockings and tights holding a long pole and the same man rowing a long boat on a silvery lake, and a uniformed baseball team in front of a banner that read CHAMPIONS 1884. In the living room Aunt Sarah would pray, her eyes closed, her head bowed, "O God, the King eternal who dividest the day from the darkness, and turnest the shadow of death into morning; drive far from us all wrong desires, incline our hearts to keep Thy law, and guide our feet into the way of peace. . . ." She prayed before we ate and when we were done eating. She prayed when we witnessed a beautiful sunset, her longish face turned to the sky, her head arching back on her neck, her eyes pale blue in the light, "O Heavenly Father, who hast filled the world with beauty; open, we beseech Thee, our eyes to behold Thy gracious hand in all Thy works. . . ." She prayed frequently for my mother, "O God, whose fatherly care reacheth to the uttermost parts of the earth; we humbly beseech Thee graciously to behold and bless those absent from us. . . ." She prayed at night before she turned off the light in my room, "O Lord, support us all the day long, until the shadows lengthen and the evening comes, and the busy world is hushed, and the fever of life is over, and our work is done. . . ."

Often when she prayed she knelt and I knelt with her and said amen when she was done. There was comfort in the kneeling and a sense of my exhausted self yielding to the embrace of a presence I could not understand but felt all about me as I did the wind and the sea. "We are a congregation of the Lord Jesus Christ," my aunt said to me one evening as we sat watching the sun go down in a fiery sky. "You and I, darling Davita. We two out here alone. Our Lord hears us and sees us and comforts us, though we are only a congregation of two. How marvelous!" I nodded and gazed at the setting sun and listened to the birds and the wind that blew in from the sea. Marvelous. Yes. And a comfort. Yes. Oh yes.

All the furniture in the farmhouse was of dark wood. A wooden radio stood on an end table in the living room; voices and music and distant static drifted from it and faded as if borne on puffs of wind. A telephone hung from the wall near the kitchen, a party line; it rang infrequently and I never saw my aunt use it in all the time we were there.

On occasion as we sat on the porch watching the sea, she would read to me or tell me a story. Mostly she told me stories of Jesus and Mary and the disciples. She told me about Jesus healing the sick and raising the dead, about Jesus crucified and resurrected, about Paul on the road to Damascus, about Jesus and the Second Coming. She told me local tales about Prince Edward Island: an Indian maiden so lovely that angels descended to earth to gaze upon her beauty; an abandoned house occupied by mischievous elves; a mysterious white trout that appeared suddenly in one of the island's rivers; mermaids in a lake, fireballs in the sky; a phantom train, a phantom ship, a pirate's treasure, a wizard's ring. She told me wonderfully funny stories about Maine, one of them about an ocean fog so thick that a man building a fish house nailed his roof to it. And she imitated the speech of Maine as she told the story: "We was shingling the fish house when it come in to fog, and I'm telling you I never see just such a mull as that one. . . ." And when she said, "Next morning the fog lifted and carried my fish house out to sea, I was some put out. Worst fog I ever saw"—when she said that she threw back her head and laughed, and I heard in her laughter the sounds of my father's voice.

She loved telling me stories about healers and the power of faith and prayer. She told me of people given up for dead who were returned to health through prayer—through psalms and other passages from the Bible and prayers written by officials of the Church. She herself had witnessed such events—in a clinic in London, in a village in Ethiopia, in a hospital in Spain. "In Him is life," she said. "Darling Davita, when we pray we reach out to the source of all healing, we touch our Lord Jesus Christ."

Her car, a small black coupe, stood parked alongside the farmhouse and one Sunday morning we went on a long drive to a church. I remember a white one-story building with a tall white tower and a columned portico before its entrance. I sat next to Aunt Sarah on a wooden pew and followed the prayers and knelt when she knelt. An enormous cross hung on the wall behind the altar; it frightened me. The church was crowded with worshippers, all looking stiff and restrained. The hymns were quietly sung. The walls and pews were painted white and there was a smell of moist raw earth in the air. I did not understand the sermon and fell asleep in the car on the way back and was very tired all the next day. Aunt Sarah did not take me to that church again.

The weeks of August went by as if in a drawn-out and languorous dream. Slowly my strength returned. The warm sun, the vast and vaulting silence, the patient ministerings of my aunt—all was healing balm to me that month. And one afternoon I wandered off the porch by myself and went carefully across the grassy slope and down to the beach. I felt the sand on my feet, coarser than the sand of Sea Gate, and touched the water with my hands. Cool and calm and smooth. As far out as I could see were water and sky and horizon. How warm and sweet and clean all this wondrous ocean world! I began to build a castle but after a while abandoned it. I was done with sand castles at the edge of the sea. I stood there a moment longer, looking out at the water and the wheeling birds. Then I turned and started back up the grassy slope to the farmhouse and saw Aunt Sarah watching me from the porch.

Over supper that night we talked about my father and Jakob Daw and Spain. I said something about the bombing of Guernica and my aunt said it was terrible but there were many horrors perpetrated by the Communists and I told her what I had heard Uncle Jakob say about Barcelona and she said she was not surprised, nothing anyone said about that war could ever surprise her again. I asked her why she had gone to Spain and she said, "Dear child, I am a nurse for our Lord Jesus Christ. I go wherever there is suffering." I asked her how someone who believed in Jesus Christ could work for the Communist side and she said something about this being an unredeemed world and a terrible century and sometimes a person had to choose between evils. "And nothing in our century is more evil than fascism, though communism comes very close."

"My mother doesn't like to hear people talk like that," I said.

"I pray to our Lord that your mother will one day come to her senses."

"Why did my father have to try to save the nun? He could be alive now if he hadn't tried to do that."

She looked away from me and out across the beach to the sea. How like my father she was, a mirror of his gestures and features. But they were wrong on her, wrong on a woman, and she was not pretty.

"I loved my brother," she said, staring out at the sea. "He was one of the most decent people I have ever known. I pray that by that act he redeemed his immortal soul."

I did not understand, but was suddenly tired and did not ask her to explain.

My mother wrote often. She was well and working very hard. She missed me terribly. How fortunate I was to be away from the city. The weather was very nearly unbearable; even the nights were hot. Mr. Dinn kept asking about me. David was back from Sea Gate. He sent his good wishes and asked if I thought my school would still be boring next year and did I want to go to his school. Jakob Daw had written her from Paris that the sea journey had been uncomfortable and the French had received him gladly and Paris was lovely as long as you did not talk too much about the war in Spain and the disastrous Communist cause. How was I feeling? She had received a letter from Aunt Sarah saying that much of my old strength was back and there was some color in my face again and my weight was up and I was able to sleep nights without too many bad dreams. The letter had made her very happy. She was eager to see me but I should let Aunt Sarah decide when I was well enough to return. She sent me and Aunt Sarah her deepest love.

In the last week of August it rained two straight days and nights. I lay in my bed at night and listened to the rain on the windows and roof of the farmhouse and thought I heard whispering in the living room downstairs. Then the sky cleared and the sun shone and we began to take short automobile rides to nearby villages. I saw horse-driven carts and dung-heaped cow paths and piny woods and the skeletons of old cars in grassy meadows and, in a coastal village, lobster boats tied to old wooden docks and bobbing lightly in the sun-speckled sea.

We went on longer and longer rides through villages from another time, past red-sand dunes and long beaches to a coast where the sea was wild. And one afternoon we stood on a cliff near stunted, oddly shaped dead trees and watched the sea roll against a shoreline of jagged rocks, saw the wind-blown swells that were the juncture of two colliding tides crashing and boiling with furious violence, and I was awed and a little frightened.

One day Aunt Sarah took me to the nearby farmhouse and I met the farmer. He was a large, taciturn man. I saw his pigs and cows and rode one of his horses. He showed me how to sit in the saddle like a girl, how to hold the reins, how to bring the horse to a halt. It was a young horse. I rode slowly with my heart thumping in my ears, feeling the horse beneath me, its rolling motions, its powerful flanks. I smelled its heat and saw the quivering motions of its muscular skin and held its mane and felt the air on my face. When the farmer helped me from the saddle I felt I had grown wings for a long moment and flown.

That night I fell asleep to the sounds of the radio and dreamed of the stallions on the beach and saw my father and Jakob Daw on two of the horses, riding toward the sea and the darkening horizon. In all the time I was on that beach I did not once dream of Baba Yaga.

The next day I woke early and dressed and went down the steep stairway into the living room. Aunt Sarah sat on the couch, reading. We prayed together, thanking the Heavenly Father for our health and our rest. Then we ate breakfast and sat on the porch, watching the birds and the sea. When the air grew warm we put on bathing suits and went into the water. The sea was shallow for a long way out and it was like swimming in a lake. Aunt Sarah was bony and small-breasted and seemed a little ashamed of her body. She waded out to knee-deep water and then stood watching me swim. Later we came out of the water and put on clothes and sat on the porch. Aunt Sarah wore a light flowery dress and a broad-brimmed hat. She appeared calm, her long thin body slouched in a lazy curve against the back of the beach chair. She looked very like my father then, and I found myself stealing frequent glances at her.

Shortly before noon a long shiny gray car came down the macadam road toward the sea and turned into the dirt road that led to the farmhouse. A man in uniform stepped out.

"Good morning, William," Aunt Sarah called cheerfully, getting to her feet. "Did you have a pleasant drive? We shall be starting shortly. How are Mother and Father?"

I sat looking at the sea and listening to the wind and the wheeling birds. I imagined horses on the beach galloping and turning and galloping again, their hooves drumming on the red sand. After lunch Aunt Sarah and I knelt in the living room and thanked the Merciful God for the summer and for our health. Then we closed up the farmhouse and climbed into the car and drove away.

I returned to school. I sat in the classroom, numbed by vacant hours. No one talked to me. I could hear classmates whispering about me as I went by in the corridors. One morning a hall monitor put his hands on my chest and squeezed and said, "Grapes," and laughed hideously. My dreams began to return.

Letters came from Jakob Daw but I would not read them. I did not return to the synagogue.

On occasion my mother would come into my room and find me kneeling in prayer. Mr. Dinn was often in the apartment, almost always in the late evenings. David came once and heard me describe my weeks in the farmhouse with my aunt and did not come again. I saw Ruthie often but we did not play together.

One day I wandered away from my school and walked in a dreamlike haze through the neighborhood and then returned to the school a few minutes before the end of class. There was a big fuss about that.

I remember long talks with my mother and Mr. Dinn. I remember the leaves beginning to turn and the cold in the evening air. I remember coming upon my mother in the kitchen one night and seeing her at the table, her head in her hands. She was crying. She did not see me and I walked quietly away.

Again I wandered from my school and now my mother was called and we sat together in an office with a short, bald man who peered at us from behind a dark-wood desk on which papers were arranged in orderly piles. I asked him, "Is that your special writing?" They stared at me. My mother looked ill. I knelt by my bed and prayed that night and dreamed, for the first time in many weeks, of Baba Yaga. I was on the dirt road that led to the farmhouse. The door to the farmhouse opened slowly and she stepped out, Baba Yaga, and stood there, one foot on the stone step, one foot on the threshold. Then she laughed and leaped through the air and fell upon me. I woke screaming and my mother was quickly in the room.

I remember a long night in the kitchen with my mother and Mr. Dinn, but I cannot recall what was said. I remember a long talk with Mr. Helfman in the backyard near the sycamore and the bed of fading flowers. I remember long conversations with a kindly bearded man in a small musty room whose walls were lined from floor to ceiling with books.

I sat in a classroom amidst new faces and listened to a young clean-shaven man speak softly about a Jewish scholar named Rambam, who had lived hundreds of years ago in Spain. Spain was a very important country for the Jews, the teacher said. Did anyone know what was going on now in Spain? I raised my hand. "Ilana," he said gently. "Yes."

I talked. I talked and talked—as if I had never spoken before in all the years of my life; as if I had never uttered words before in all the classrooms I had attended. Faces turned to me. The teacher stood behind his desk, listening.

BOOK THREE

Six

That fall my mother left her job in Manhattan and began to work for an agency in downtown Brooklyn a few blocks from the East River and the Brooklyn Bridge. She felt she ought to be closer to home, she said. She didn't want me staying alone too long after school. And she was tired of having to travel day after day to Manhattan. I heard her tell Mr. Dinn that Manhattan reminded her too much of my father. What point was there to her being endlessly haunted by her dead husband? she said.

I wandered into my mother's bedroom one afternoon and opened my father's closet. The strong rose-petal fragrance of a sachet rose to my nostrils. My father's clothes and shoes were gone. Even the clothes hangers were no longer there. The sight of that closet—its cavernous emptiness—was shocking and sent through me a coldness that made the back of my neck tingle. The carton with my father's special writing was still on the floor near the bed; and the picture of the horses on the beach still hung on the wall. But I was haunted by the vision of that empty closet.

My mother told me that she had given all of my father's clothes and shoes to the poor. Mr. Dinn had taken care of it. What point was there to having my father's clothes and shoes moldering in the closet? she said. There were poor and hungry people everywhere who needed clothes and shoes. "Are you very upset, Ilana? I'm sorry. I did it while you were with Aunt Sarah. There are better ways to remember your father than by the suits and shoes he wore."

But each time I recited the Kaddish I would remember the look of his clothes. And I was saying it every day now, for we prayed in class at the start of each day and I was one of two students who rose at intervals and recited the Hebrew words, "Yisgadal v'yiskadash shmai rabboh . . ."

After the first morning my teacher, a kindly bearded man in his middle forties, had asked me to remain behind as the class trooped out for the morning recess. When we were alone, he said, "Ilana, a girl does not say Kaddish."

I did not respond.

"I was told that you say Kaddish in shul. I cannot do anything about that. But you will not say it in my class."

I said nothing.

"Is that understood, Ilana?"

I nodded. He dismissed me.

The next morning I rose during the morning service and quietly recited the Kaddish. I felt the teacher's burning eyes upon me, felt all their eyes, staring. But he said nothing to me about it again, and after a few days there were no more stares. All uttered the necessary responses at the appropriate places. Then one day the boy who recited the Kaddish with me did not rise, and I stood alone, saying the words—"Magnified and sanctified be the great name of God . . ."—and still all responded.

I found as the weeks went by and winter approached that my mother had been right: I was no longer clearly remembering the look and cut of my father's clothes. At times I could not even recall his face. My mother said that was natural; but it frightened me to be losing my memory of my father.

I saw David often. He was a class ahead of me. I would see him in the company of his friends in the corridors or the yard. Sometimes we would talk briefly alone together. Mostly he remained in the circle of his friends. He had an extraordinary reputation in the school. All seemed awed by his brilliance. And because the whole school knew by now that his father and my mother were first cousins, I was treated as if I belonged intimately to his family and shared in the aura of high intellect and breeding—all of this despite my mother's known political loyalties. I realized quickly enough that no one in my class snickered or whispered or laughed when I raised my hand to ask or to answer a question, to react to a book we had been told to read, or to make a point about the opera at the Metropolitan or the exhibition of paintings at the Brooklyn Museum which the school took us to see during the first semester I was there. There was much gossip and idle talk among the students; but no one in this school laughed at learning.

The school day was divided in half: Hebrew and religious studies in the morning, English and secular studies in the afternoon. I was in my regular fourth-grade class in the afternoon; but, because my Hebrew was so poor, I had been placed in the second grade for the morning hours. Ruthie, who was in my afternoon class, and Mr. Helfman, who taught sixth grade, tutored me after school hours in Hebrew. I felt myself floating and gliding and flying through this school, where no one whispered about you as you went through the corridors and no one put his hands on your chest and squeezed and yelled, "Grapes!" and no one called you a Commie Jew shit to your face.

I was busy with my studies, and my mother was busy with her work. She seemed always to be doing something: reading, cleaning, washing, cooking, writing, attending meetings, talking with Mr. Dinn, studying with the two men and the woman who continued coming to our apartment on Sunday afternoons. She went to bed long after I did and woke long before. In all the months of that fall and early winter I do not remember ever seeing her rest during the day.

We would leave the apartment together in the morning and walk to Eastern Parkway and then go our separate ways, she to work and I to school. The mail arrived after we left and I would hurry home from school and use the duplicate mailbox key my mother had given me. But the letters we waited for did not come. Nothing from Jakob Daw. Nothing from Aunt Sarah. Jakob Daw had not written us in weeks. Where was he? And was Aunt Sarah back in Spain?

In December there was a Chanukkah assembly in the school in the same large room where people prayed on Saturdays and holidays. The dividing ninon wall had been removed. A tall plywood wall stood before the ark, separating it from the room. Boys and girls sat together and one of the boys in the eighth grade chanted the blessings and lit the first candle. Another boy delivered a brief talk about the courage of the Maccabees and the miracle of the lights. "The few prevailed against the many," he said, "because they had faith in the Ribbono Shel Olom."

During supper that night I asked my mother if we could light Chanukkah candles in our house. She said no, she didn't believe in it.

"But they're so pretty, Mama. And they remind me of when Papa was here last year."

"No," she said, after a moment. "I have enough trouble on my hands sending you to the yeshiva. All I need is for someone in my section to pass by our window and see Chanukkah candles burning."

I had not realized that by going to a religious school I was endangering her position in the party.

Yes, she said. There had been a hearing. She had been given the opportunity to offer a lengthy explanation. She had reminded them of the price our family had already paid for the cause. They had listened courteously. There had been a few sarcastic remarks. The hearing had ended with no official action being taken.

I did not ask my mother again. Instead I would walk down to Ruthie's apartment just before supper and watch Mr. Helfman light the candles. Then I would go upstairs and have supper with my mother.

I knew little of what was happening now in Spain. I no longer read newspapers and only occasionally glanced at a headline. I knew the Fascists were winning the war. I did not want to hear anything more about it.

One evening my mother came back from work carrying a carton filled with house plants. She distributed the plants throughout the apartment, placing them on windowsills and tables where they could catch the sunlight. "We need some green life in this apartment," she said. "How did we go all these years without plants in the house? Aren't they pretty? And inexpensive. Would you like one for your room, Ilana?"

She attended rallies in Manhattan and party meetings in Brooklyn. On occasion groups of people would come to our apartment, quiet, serious men and women about my mother's age, and they would sit for hours in the living room and have long discussions and listen to her lectures. There was no drinking at those meetings, no rowdiness. How the door harp played to the comings and goings of those people on those nights!

I asked my mother who the people were.

They were writers and artists and theater people, she said.

"Don't they sing?"

"I promised Mrs. Helfman there would be no singing or drinking."

"I miss the singing."

"So do I," she said. "There are many things I miss now, Ilana. What can we do?"

One night after a long meeting of that group I woke and came out of my room and went along the hallway. The apartment was dark, the air rancid with tobacco smoke. I wanted a glass of water and started into the kitchen, when I noticed that the door to my mother's room was slightly ajar. Light streaming out of her room cut a sharp wedge into the hallway darkness. I moved toward the door and put my hand on the knob. Then I stopped and remained very still, peering into the room through the narrow opening of the door.

My mother stood naked before the full-length mirror that was attached to the door of her closet. I had never seen her entirely naked before. The mirror magnified the ceiling light and sent it cascading upon her as she turned her body slowly this way and that, keeping her eyes fixed upon her reflection. I saw the lovely smooth white nakedness of her, saw her slender arms and curving shoulders and the flat planes of her shoulder blades and the curving indentation of her spinal column and the deep cleavage between the rounded buttocks. I glimpsed from the side the round firm fleshiness of her left breast and, in the long mirror, saw all the golden fullness of her body, breasts and nipples and belly and the clump of triangular darkness that sent a shiver through me. She was fondling her breasts, stroking the nipples with the palms of her hands, slowly, an expression of rapt concentration on her pale and lovely face, her eyes nearly shut, her mouth open and her tongue pressing tightly upon her upper lip; then rubbing the nipples, gently, with her index fingers and thumbs, gently and slowly, rubbing. The nipples were dark and hard, her body rigid, her back slightly arched. She stood there in front of the mirror, rocking slowly back and forth. Then, slightly parting her legs, she raised herself on tiptoe. "Michael," I heard her say, in a long drawn-out whisper and in a voice I barely recognized. "Michael . . ."

I took a silent step back and then another and was in the dark hallway. I turned slowly and put my hand on the wall and went carefully back to my room. I lay on my bed in the darkness and kept seeing my mother naked before the mirror in her room. I knew that image would always remain with me, deep inside me, and return to my eyes at odd and unexpected times; like the image of the gang leader offering protection to a little girl with a penny in her hand; like the image of the boy with the cigarette asking, You Jewish?; like my father's face when he threw back his head and laughed; like the veiled look in my mother's eyes when she drifted into the past; like Jakob Daw bent over his desk, writing; like the sadness in the dark eyes of the little girl named Teresa; like the dunes and the beach and the sand castles of Sea Gate; like the birds that called *hoo hoo hoo hoo;* like Aunt Sarah on her knees in our spare room; like the candles of Chanukkah in the Helfman apartment;

like the black bird and the gray horse and Baba Yaga. Images of a childhood. My mother naked. Would my body look like that one day? Ripe and round and lovely, the boniness and angularity smooth and soft, and the forest of darkness between my legs?

I barely slept that night and in the morning could not look directly into my mother's eyes when she spoke to me. "Are you feeling all right?" she asked. I nodded. I kept imagining her naked body beneath her dress. In school I fell asleep in class and was gently wakened by my teacher, who put his hand on my forehead and wanted to know if I felt ill.

The weather turned cruel. Frozen snow lay crystal white upon the trees and grimy upon the sidewalks and streets. Cars moved cautiously across the ice, chains rattling. I began to wake in the night to the creaks and groans of the ice-laden trees that lined our street: eerie sounds that came through my window and seemed to inhabit the shadows in my room.

One Saturday afternoon in January my mother and I walked to Prospect Park. It was a cold blue windless day. The lake was frozen. Skaters glided across its smooth white surface. I stood at its edge with my mother and imagined myself stepping out of the rowboat into the water. Why had I done that? I could not imagine ever feeling bad enough to want to do that. And what if I had drowned? What if I had not been found? How deep was the lake? Would I now be somewhere in its depths, frozen to ice?

Walking with me along the frozen paths beneath the bare trees, my mother said the lake reminded her of the river where she had lived as a child. In the winters they had to break the ice to keep a channel open for the barges and ferries. She had learned to ice-skate on that river. But she had not ice-skated for a long time and probably could no longer do it.

I asked her where she had gone to school.

"In Vienna."

"No, before Vienna."

"In a little Jewish school near where I was born. It was run by a cruel old teacher who didn't like teaching girls. He taught us to read the prayerbook."

"Did your father study with you?"

"My father didn't do anything with me. My grandfather taught me

Bible and Mishnah and a little Gemora, and my mother taught me Polish and German."

"Would your father be angry if he was alive and knew I was going to a yeshiva?"

"I don't know how my father would feel about that," my mother said. "I don't know very much about my father. He was almost never home. Probably he would be angry. Yes, I think he would be very angry. He didn't believe girls should be educated."

"Was your mother very lonely because your father wasn't home?"

"Yes. So was I. My mother once told me that terrible mistakes are sometimes made in the name of loneliness. If not for my grandfather—" She broke off, suddenly lost in some memory.

"I wish your grandfather was still alive."

"So do I," my mother said. "But he's not. Shall we start back? I'm beginning to feel cold."

On Eastern Parkway, a block from our street, we met David and his father. They had been visiting a friend and were on their way to the synagogue for the afternoon and evening services. I walked with David. My mother and Mr. Dinn walked on ahead.

"It's really cold," David said. "Aren't you cold?" His face was red and he spoke through stiffened lips. "I hate this weather."

"David, did you study the Mishnah Brochos?"

"Sure."

"There's something we learned in class this week that I don't understand."

"What?"

We walked carefully on the icy streets beneath the black frozen trees, talking. Long shadows of buildings and trees lay upon the parkway. I listened to David, watched the dancing of his hands as he talked about words and ideas, listened to the high eagerness in his voice, saw the dark fires in his eyes. He was a little taller than I, and very thin. I wondered if he and his father had a housekeeper who cared for them. How did they live?

We continued along the street behind my mother and his father, talking about some problems I was having with Hebrew. After a while I began to invent problems; I liked watching him talk.

My mother took me to a neighborhood movie theater that evening and we saw a detective story and a love story. The love story seemed very long. More and more my mother went to such movies, either with me or alone. I liked the detective story and thought the love story boring. No one I knew talked so ponderously or breathed so heavily as the actors in those love stories.

Sometimes we took the subway into Manhattan to see a Russian movie, but my mother seemed increasingly uneasy about traveling to Manhattan. Manhattan reminded her too much of my father; certain streets caused searing pain. She would travel on party business to rallies and meetings; but that was all. By the middle of that winter, less than ten months after my father's death, we were no longer going together to Manhattan.

Yet she seemed tenaciously loyal to my father's memory. Often in the evenings I would see her at the desk in her room carefully going through the carton of my father's special writing: magazine articles, newspapers, journals, typescripts. My father had become a hero of sorts to a certain segment of the political world and, at the invitation of a small New York publisher, my mother was preparing a book-length collection of his serious work. And she was, at the same time, translating into English one of the stories Jakob Daw had written during the time he had lived with us. He had left those stories with my mother.

One cold Saturday night in February we saw a movie in which a young woman was attacked and badly hurt by two men. Nothing of the brutality was shown; the gaps were left to the imagination. Afterward my mother came out of the theater and hurried away as if I were not there. I had to run to keep up with her.

Later in our warm kitchen she said to me, as I sat over milk and cookies, "I had no idea it was such a movie. I'm sorry, Ilana."

"I liked it, Mama."

"Didn't it frighten you?"

"Yes. But it was a good story."

"They show movies like that to make money," she said. "They are capitalist exploiters of the working class. They should tell people in advance if such things are in a movie. Please finish your milk, Ilana, and go to sleep. It's late."

She sat staring into her cup of coffee, a dark brooding in her eyes.

Very late that night, as I lay on the edge of sleep, she came into my room and stood near my bed. She placed the palm of her hand on my cheek. I felt her caressing me, her fingers smooth and hot. Then she bent to kiss me. Her face was wet. I heard the beating of my heart and was certain she heard it too. After a moment she straightened and went silently from the room.

On occasion Mr. Dinn would come to visit, always at night and always remaining after I went to bed. From my room I could hear them talking in the kitchen. He never ate or drank anything in our house, save a glass of water or soda, because we did not observe the laws of kashruth. I didn't like that: it was strange having a guest in your house who refused to eat or drink there.

Once I heard him raise his voice and say clearly, "For God's sake, Channah, open your eyes and look at what he's doing. Those trials aren't a travesty? The country is drenched in blood. Their constitution is a mockery and their laws are a joke. The man is a murderous barbarian!" And I heard too my mother's querulous reply. "He is transforming a backward country overnight, Ezra. I trust him. Whom do you want me to trust? DuPont? General Motors? John D. Rockefeller? You know how they treat their workers. You know how they are all tied to I. G. Farben and the Fascists. Talk about barbarians! The capitalist is the true barbarian, but in a fancy suit!"

"Why do you judge socialism by its dreams and capitalism by its deeds? Is that fair, Channah? Is it logical?"

"Ezra, I judge both by their deeds. Fascism is the dictatorship of finance capitalism. If I must choose between the dictatorship of the bourgeoisie and the dictatorship of the proletariat, I will choose for the proletariat."

One night in the kitchen Mr. Dinn helped me with my Hebrew homework and seemed surprised at how quickly I was learning the language. "My mother was like that," he said.

"So was mine," said my mother.

"Did your father also never stay at home?" I asked.

He gave my mother a quick glance and looked back at me. "My father was home."

"What did your father do?"

"He owned a clothing factory."

"Is he alive?"

"No. He died when I was nineteen."

"You had ten more years of your father than I did."

The two of them glanced at each other and said nothing.

"Did you hate your father for dying?"

He looked surprised. "No. I was angry. But I didn't hate him."

"Sometimes I think I hate my father."

"Ilana," my mother said softly.

"He didn't have to try to save that nun. He didn't even believe in religion. Why did he try to save that nun?"

"Your father was a kind and generous man," Mr. Dinn said. "A gallant man. He saw a woman in danger and wanted to help her."

"He shouldn't have," I said.

They looked at me and were quiet.

"I'm tired," I said, after a moment. "I think I'll go to bed now."

I felt them looking at me as I collected my books and went from the kitchen.

Ruthie told me the next evening that she was having trouble with the composition our class had been assigned to write. I helped her with it; she helped me with my Hebrew homework. She was a serious but poor student and seemed to have difficulty remembering things.

"I wish I had your memory," she said. "You remember everything."

"Sometimes that's not so good, Ruthie."

"How far back can you remember? Can you remember to the age of five or six?"

"I remember when I was three my parents came home from a demonstration. They were all bloody. Policemen on horses hit them with sticks. My mother kept screaming about Cossacks. I remember that."

"You remember to the age of three?"

"I wish I could forget that. I wish I could forget all the different times we moved until we moved here. Have you lived here all your life?"

"Yes."

"You're lucky. This is a nice house. It looks a little like a castle."

"It does?"

"And you have a backyard with grass and flowers and a porch, and there's even a park and a museum nearby."

"My father won't let me go to the museum. He says it has pictures that aren't decent. Mr. Dinn likes our house. He once wanted to live upstairs where you live now, but his wife liked the other apartment better, so they didn't move. You know, Mr. Dinn and your mother knew each other before they were married. I heard Mama tell Papa they once were in love, but he wouldn't marry your mother because she didn't believe in religion and was a Communist. Why did your mother become a Communist?"

"I don't know."

"I'll bet Mr. Dinn knows. He's a smart man. He knows everything."

"He didn't know how to keep the Fascists in the American government from sending Jakob Daw back to Europe."

"Papa said Mr. Daw wouldn't let him do anything."

"He should've done something anyway. Smart people know how to do something even when they can't."

"Papa says if you tell your lawyer not to do anything, the lawyer—"

"They're all ending up in Europe, and they're all going to end up dead. Jakob Daw is in Europe and he doesn't write us anymore. And my Aunt Sarah is in Europe and she doesn't write us anymore, either. She went back to Spain. She's a nurse and a Christian missionary. She tries to make everybody believe in Jesus Christ."

"Don't say that word!"

"Which word?"

"You know."

"Jesus Christ?"

"Don't say it, Ilana! Papa told me you're not supposed to say his name. If you don't say his name it means he doesn't exist."

"I don't understand."

"That's what Papa told me."

"But why can't we say it?"

"Papa said that Christians believe that he's their God and that the Jews killed him."

I stared at her. "I don't remember that in any of the stories Aunt Sarah told me. We killed him?"

"Papa said that Christians have been killing Jews for thousands of years because they say we killed their God."

"I don't understand."

"I don't, either," Ruthie said.

We were both frightened.

I asked my mother about it during supper that night.

"They accuse Jews of crucifying Jesus," she said, and explained the meaning of the word crucify. I had never thought to associate the crucifixes I saw on Christians with a slow and horrible kind of execution. "All of Europe believed it in the past and most of Europe probably believes it today. It's one of the ways the capitalists and the Church control the working class—by turning them against the Jews. That's the true reason Jews are hated. And that's the true reason for all the pogroms." She explained the meaning of the word pogrom. "An organized killing of Jews. It's a Russian word."

"I think Ruthie told me about that once. Were you ever in a pogrom?"

"Yes."

"Were your parents in it too?"

"My mother and my grandfather were in it. My father was with the rebbe. Please, Ilana, let's not talk about it any more tonight. Are you done with supper? Then finish your homework."

Later I lay awake in my bed and listened to the howling wind. Ice cracked and snapped and tumbled from the trees. After a while I fell asleep. There was a heavy rain that night and toward morning it turned to sleet and fell with an irregular drumbeat upon the street. In the pale light of morning a film of gleaming crystal-white ice lay upon the street and clung to the trunks and branches of the trees. It seemed as if the lake had overflowed and now covered all the neighborhood. I walked carefully to school on the ice.

In March a letter arrived from Jakob Daw, written in German. My mother read it to me.

Paris was cold, wet. His flat on the rue des Solitaires was small and damp. He could see from his bedroom window the chimney pots of the Nineteenth Arrondissement and the little rivers of rain on the narrow streets below. France was glutted with right-wing exultation and left-wing despair over the Fascist victories in Spain. Now and then he got together with Max Jacob and Picasso and Jean Renoir. He had seen Picasso's *Guernica*. It was a knife in the heart of the human species that would turn and turn forever. He himself was weary and dispirited but still writing. On cold nights in his flat he remembered their days together in Vienna, and that warmed him. The cough was bad. He thought he might go south to a warmer climate. Perhaps Marseilles. How was Ilana Davita? "Please tell her the bird still nests in our harp. Do not ask her what it means. It is between me and your lovely daughter. Frequently I run across someone who remembers Michael. It is astonishing how many people came to know him during his months in Spain. Now I am tired and will lie down and rest. Jakob Daw."

We were in the living room. My mother sat very quietly on the sofa, looking at Jakob Daw's letter.

"Mama?"

"Yes, darling."

"Why did your father let you go to Vienna?"

She colored slightly and did not respond.

"Mama?"

"I went to Vienna to study."

"But why did your father let you go?"

"My mother wanted me to go."

"And your father?"

"He wanted me to go too."

"Mama, was it a bad pogrom?"

She hesitated. "There are no good pogroms, Ilana."

"But was it very bad?"

"Yes," she said, after a moment.

"Did the Russian soldiers hurt you?"

"Yes. They hurt me and they killed my sister."

"I didn't know you had a sister."

"I had two sisters. One died of pneumonia, the other was—she was killed; she was killed by those Russian soldiers. So was my grandfather. He tried to stop them from hurting me and my sister, and they killed him." She gazed out the window at the late afternoon winter light. "Is it snowing again? What a long winter this is." She turned her gaze back upon me. "A father should protect his daughters, don't you think? A father shouldn't leave that to a grandfather. My grandfather was an old man. He tried to help us, and a Russian soldier shot him. Then they left us in the forest and my mother and I came back to the town. It was my mother's idea that I go to Vienna."

"But why did your father let you go?"

"He was ashamed to have me in the house."

I stared at her.

"They hurt me very badly, Ilana."

I was quiet. We sat together awhile in silence.

My mother broke the silence. She said, looking down at the letter in her hand, "The years in Vienna were beautiful. It took a long time for the bad memories to begin to fade even a little. Jakob Daw helped me. Then he went to war and was hurt. This is a terrible century, Ilana. So many people are being hurt in it. I was so happy when the Russian government was overthrown. How I hated those soldiers! I remember one of them wore a cross on top of his tunic, and when he—when he—" She broke off for a moment, and then continued. "When I came back home to my parents from Vienna, it was impossible to live with my father. Then my mother died of influenza, and I came to America."

"Did you become a Communist in Europe?"

"No. Your father introduced me to that after we met. I stopped being religious when I lived in Vienna. But I was not very political. I wanted to be a writer, an—an intellectual. How pretentious that sounds! But I would have become political soon enough. You can't be an intellectual in Europe and not be political. Do you understand any of this, Ilana? I think you understand enough. Look at the snow! And so late in March!"

"Is that why you don't like religion, Mama? Because of your father?"

"That and other things. It made a slave of my mother."

"Not everyone is like your father. Mr. Helfman isn't. Mr. Dinn isn't."

"I only know my own life, Ilana. In my life there was my father, not Mr. Dinn or Mr. Helfman. You can't forget the bad things that are done to you by telling yourself that the world isn't all bad. We really can know only the people and things that touch us. Everything else is like words in a dictionary. We can learn them but they don't live deep inside us. Can you understand that, Ilana?"

"I think so."

"Religion is a dangerous fraud, Ilana, and an illusion. It prevents people from seeing the truth and expressing their discontent, and sometimes it inflames the heart so that people follow horrible ideas like fascism."

"But I like my school and the shul."

"I know you do, darling. It's all right. They keep your mind working and that's very important. It's fine to learn the grammar and the words and the stories and to be with people. It's very important to be with people, Ilana. You don't have to believe in God in order to understand a verse in the Bible or a passage from the Talmud. You can study it as literature. You can learn how the Jews were oppressed the way so many other people were and still are. It's all right that you like the school and the shul, Ilana."

"I especially like the shul."

"Yes. I know."

"I like the singing."

She said nothing.

"I don't like the wall in the middle."

She grimaced but was quiet.

"Mama, David said the law is that you're supposed to stop saying Kaddish after eleven months."

"I know," she said.

"Will you come to shul with me the last time I say Kaddish?"

"No," she said. "I don't go to shul. I haven't been in a shul in almost fifteen years. Are you done with your homework, Ilana? Yes? Then I think you can help me make supper."

I went alone to the synagogue that Saturday morning. Mr. Dinn led the service. The synagogue was crowded and warm and filled with the rhythms and songs of the service. Afterward I returned home and heard the singing of the door harp. I found my mother in the living room, rereading the letter from Jakob Daw.

That week my mother completed her work on my father's book. The day after she journeyed into Manhattan to deliver the manuscript to the publisher, she was invited by another publisher to write an introduction to a collection of the stories of Jakob Daw, some of which were to be translated by her. She seemed a little dazed by that and immediately sent off a letter to Jakob Daw.

She began to work far into the nights on that book. I wondered when she slept. I would get up in the middle of the night to go to the bathroom and the light would still be burning in her room. Once she fell asleep at the kitchen table during supper and I woke her because I was afraid she would fall off the chair. She opened her eyes with a start and spoke some words in a language I did not understand. Then she looked at me and smiled shamefacedly and asked if I had finished my homework and would I help her with the dishes.

She had always been neat and caring about her housework, save for the few months that had followed our move to this apartment. Clothes were meticulously folded, beds carefully made, floors swept and washed, corners dusted free of cobwebs, shades raised to the same level in each window, books arranged in straight lines on their shelves, newspapers set down in their separate piles on the living room coffee table, street clothes and shoes placed in orderly fashion in our closets. My father had been the careless one in our family and had gone about leaving trails of his presence throughout the apartment: parts of newspapers in the kitchen and bathroom, magazines on the floor of the living room, books face down on the kitchen table, pages of his writing strewn about the bedroom; once I found a small packet of some sort in the bathroom sink and brought it to my mother and she blushed scarlet and said it belonged to my father.

Now she became strangely uncaring about the apartment. Books, magazines, and newspapers lay strewn about everywhere. I found her underwear beneath the bathroom sink, kitchen towels in the living room, an unopened bar of laundry soap on her desk, one of her berets on the hallway floor, a box labeled Kotex on the bookcase in her bedroom. She would wear the same dress three or four days in a row. She had taken to wearing house slippers in the apartment and shuffled about in a way that reminded me of Aunt Sarah. And she began to put on weight: I found her late one night in the living room letting out one of her dresses. She looked embarrassed.

Vaguely, I wondered if I would ever again have a father. I asked her about that one day that spring and she laughed in a high nervous way and said she wasn't thinking about that, no man could ever take the place of my real father.

She was busy, very busy. People continued coming to the apartment for meetings; the two men and the woman kept showing up on Sundays for the study sessions on the writings of Karl Marx; she went out to meetings, worked at the agency, labored over the collection of Jakob Daw's stories. Yet a strange sort of leadenness had settled upon her; a shadow had entered her eyes. At odd moments—at night before I turned off my light; in the morning on Eastern Parkway as we were about to go our separate ways; on early Saturday afternoons just as I got back from the synagogue—she would suddenly embrace me and cling to me suffocatingly and kiss my face with her cool, dry lips. The frantic quality of those embraces frightened me a little.

One Saturday morning that spring I went to the synagogue and recited the Kaddish for my father for the last time. I pronounced each word with care, my eyes closed so I would not be distracted. All around me women uttered the appropriate responses. As I left the synagogue I thought I saw the pale, haunted face of my mother. Then the face was gone into the crowd. I came outside and threaded my way quickly through the mass of people milling about in front of the building and looked up and down Eastern Parkway. I saw no one who resembled my mother. I ran to the corner where I normally turned off the parkway and saw a woman in my mother's brown coat hurrying up the side street. I ran and came alongside her and it was my mother. I took her hand. Her skin was hot and dry. We walked in silence together back to the apartment. That night I woke and listened to her crying and lay quietly in my bed and let my own tears come too.

Mr. Dinn's visits became more frequent as the weeks went by. It was a little annoying to have him sitting at the table in our kitchen and never eating anything and drinking only water or soda out of a glass. Always he came in a suit and a tie and a hat, and would take off his jacket and hat only at my mother's insistence. In place of his hat he would wear a small dark velvet skullcap. Sometimes he would remove his vest and loosen his tie. He was a tall, angular man, loose-jointed, with strong, bony features, a smooth, prominent forehead, and a jutting Adam's apple whose up-and-down dancing movements above the knot of his tie fascinated me. His deep baritone voice would echo throughout the apartment and often woke me long after I had fallen asleep. He seemed comfortable in our apartment and it was clear that my mother was at ease in his presence.

One Saturday night he came to the apartment and he and my mother went out together. "We're only going to a movie," she had said to me earlier. I had said nothing.

I wandered through the silent rooms, opening closets and drawers. My father's closet echoed with emptiness. The only object in it now was the carton of his special writing. I bent down and opened the carton; it was filled with magazines and newspapers and pages of typescript. A notebook lay on top of the pages, small and with hard dark cardboard covers. I held it and carefully opened it and saw on its first page, in the handwriting of Jakob Daw, the words *Eine Geschichte*. I turned the pages slowly. The writing was in a language I could not read. I replaced the notebook in the carton and went from the room.

I was in bed when they returned. The door harp sang in the hallway. They went into the kitchen. My mother laughed softly at something Mr. Dinn said. It was a lovely sound, high and girlish. I had not heard her laugh in a long time.

My mother left the apartment early the next morning and took the subway into Manhattan to attend a rally. It was the first day of May, one week after Passover. We had not observed the festival; and my mother had politely but resolutely turned down Mrs. Helfman's invitation to their Seder. "I don't really believe in it," she had said to me afterward. "And there are too many memories of Sedorim when my father was with the rebbe instead of being with us. Why should I sit at the Helfmans' Seder and spoil their night with my bad memories?"

"David and his father will be there."

"We won't," she said. "I don't need it. I have enough memories for now."

Her color was high, her mood buoyant, when she returned to the apartment that Sunday afternoon. The rally had been a great success. Thousands had marched, many thousands. She packed food and an old blanket into a shopping bag. Her mood continued high all during our walk along Eastern Parkway. She talked on and on. You could sense the effect that the party was having on American life, she said. Union legislation, an awareness of horrors like Georgia chain gangs, laws to protect the working man, the efforts of writers and artists for the people of Spain. The capitalists who thought they could do whatever they wished with America should have come out to that rally. She was still in this exuberant mood when we turned into Prospect Park and walked along the curving path beneath spring trees past the lake, with its boats, and past playing children and adults on blankets under the trees, to the edge of a long stretch of young green grass where her friends waited for us.

There were about a dozen of them, men and women her age and a little older, and four children, all younger than I. Most of the adults I knew from the meetings in our apartment, but I had not met the children before now. We sat on blankets and ate. It was a warm and brilliant day. The sun shone on the lake and the trees. I lay on the blanket and listened to them talking about the rally and the brief skirmish with the police somewhere along their line of march and about the war in Spain and the Popular Front and the coming revolution and Comrade Stalin and someone called Robert Epstein who had enlisted in the loyalist air force and was leaving that Tuesday for Spain. I caught glimpses of the lake through the trees. They seemed an ardent and intense group; the air vibrated with their talk. My mother was their center, their magnetic pole. She looked radiant with her long dark hair, white blouse, red beret, and brownish red skirt. I wondered idly what she and Mr. Dinn had talked about the night before. I had not even asked her what picture they had seen. How could someone as religious as Mr. Dinn go out with someone as irreligious as my mother?

I lay back on the blanket and put my hand over my eyes and listened to the happy noises in the park.

Normal days of school followed, and dismal spring rain. That Saturday night my mother went out again to a neighborhood movie—this time with one of the men who came periodically to the meetings in our apartment. And a week later I lay again on the grass of Prospect Park and listened as my school happily celebrated Lag Ba'omer, the holiday that commemorates that day, about two thousand years ago during the Jewish revolution against Rome, when a raging plague that had been killing the students of a great sage had begun to ease. The sage, Rabbi Akiva, had been a leader of that revolution: a scholar like my mother and a fighter like my father.

I lay beneath a tree in a beam of sunlight and listened to schoolmates playing on the grass. Some were off on the side with bows and arrows. Others were in running games and in a tug-of-war. Their noises drifted over me, dreamlike, gossamer, an illusion. The air was soft and warm. Far above us in the blue sky, so small it seemed a dark stiff-winged bird, an airplane flew slowly by, its engines droning lazily. I could feel the vibrations on my skin and in my ears. A voice called to me to join the game but I closed my eyes and lay very still in the beam of warm light. It seemed then that someone came and stood over me for a long moment, concealing the sun. Give us a hug, my love, I heard a voice say. A big hug. It has to last a long time. That's right, my love. *That's* a hug!

I opened my eyes and sat up on the grass. Schoolmates played at their games and teachers stood about, watching. The lake glistened through the trees. A boy stood at the edge of the lake, tossing stones into the water. Someone called my name. I sat very still, watching the boy toss the stones at the lake. The stones struck the water with little splashes and disappeared into its depths. Again someone called my name. I rose and brushed grass from my skirt and joined my classmates in a game of tug-of-war.

That summer we stayed in the city. My mother enrolled me in the city-sponsored day camp in Prospect Park. They didn't want to take me back at first; there was a fuss, and my mother prevailed. I played with others on the grass and went boating in the lake. In the early weeks of the summer a counselor sat next to me in the boat. Then they let me sit with a camper. I trailed my hands in the wake of the boat and looked down into the water. Warm and darkly golden on the surface and then dark and cold and darker still. I remembered the farmhouse and the beach and the horses of the previous summer and wondered if it might not somehow all have been a dream. Where was Aunt Sarah?

My mother was going out often with two or three of the men who came to the meetings in our apartment. Very early one Sunday morning Mr. Dinn pulled up in his black sedan and we drove out to Sea Gate and spent the day with him and David in the house next to the cottage where we had once lived in the summers. Another couple lived there now with many children. It felt a little strange, peering over at that cottage from the screened-in porch of the house where David now lived. From the porch I looked out across the dunes and saw my mother and Mr. Dinn walking together in bathing suits on the crowded beach. Mr. Dinn's tall frame was bony and pale; my mother seemed so small beside him, her hair loose and long, her skin white. David asked me if I wanted to build a castle and I said no, I was not in a mood for castles. Nor did I want to swim. I walked with him down the beach and watched him in the water, swimming skillfully, his long tanned body flashing in the sunlight, and wondered who had taught him. "My father," he said, shaking the water from his dark hair and drying himself with a towel. "It's in the Gemora. A father is supposed to make sure his child learns how to swim."

In the third week of July my mother received a letter from Aunt Sarah inviting us to the farmhouse. She had returned from Spain and was remaining in America. She would be at the farmhouse all summer and would love us to join her there. But I didn't want to go without my mother, and my mother couldn't go because of her work. She wrote back, regretfully declining the invitation.

In August, amidst the usual letters in our mailbox that were appeals for funds for labor defense committees, for refugees from Spain, for assistance to striking workers, was a letter from Jakob Daw. He was now in Marseilles. His health had improved somewhat in the warm air of the Mediterranean. He lived in a flat that looked out on the sea. He could dream of Dakar and Martinique as nearby places of refuge if Hitler ever came to France. Yes, he was still writing. A small collection of his stories would soon appear, translated into French. He was grateful to my mother for her work on the English edition of his stories. He had dreamed of that once: the two of them writing together. But in the dream he had neglected to specify that they not be separated by an ocean. Another of the many ironies of our century: it played with human dreams as a child played with sand. He lived now off the generosity of his publishers and friends. How much did one man need in order to live? And a sick man at that. If Hitler came to France he would leave Marseilles. He would need an exit visa, a transit visa, a final visa. That would require a bit of money. Did it sound insane, Hitler coming to France? As insane as had once been the possibility of Franco taking all of Spain. At any rate, he would be prepared. He would go to Martinique and Santo Domingo. That was the route. He had made the necessary inquiries. He would not be trapped again as he had once been trapped in Spain. How was Ilana Davita? "Tell her our bird still nests peacefully in our harp and listens with pleasure as she recites her Hebrew lessons. Who would ever have believed that the daughter of Michael and Channah Chandal would one day attend a yeshiva? Nothing I write can be as astonishing as life, which is indeed the strangest story of all. Jakob Daw."

At the end of August, Ruthie returned from the mountains with her parents, and in the first week of September we were back in school.

My mother had begun to go out regularly with one of the two men who used to come to the apartment on Sunday afternoons for the study sessions on Karl Marx. He was a short thin man with sparse blond hair, angular features, and gray, unsmiling eyes. He wore tweed jackets and chain-smoked. His name was Charles Carter and he was an assistant professor of modern history at Brooklyn College. He had an intense air and a high voice. He talked a great deal and used words I could not understand, and once when I asked him to explain some words he grew annoyed and impatient, and I did not ask him again.

My mother asked me one night if I liked him.

"No," I said.

She looked hurt and upset. "Why?"

"I don't know."

"He's a brilliant person, Ilana, and a loyal member of the party."

I said nothing.

She said, in a quiet voice, "Do you think you might like him as your father?"

I stared at her. A chill darkness moved through me.

She said, after a long moment, "You have no idea what it's like to be alone, Ilana."

Mr. Dinn came over one Saturday night that fall and took my mother to a theater in Manhattan. How dignified he looked in his dark coat and suit and hat. They returned home very late. The door harp woke me. I heard them go through the hallway to the kitchen. I fell back asleep and was awakened sometime later by their loud voices. They were in an argument and were making no effort to conceal their anger.

"Think of what you're doing, for God's sake!" Mr. Dinn said. "Isn't one mistake enough? Think!"

"You have no right to meddle in my life, Ezra," my mother said. "No right whatsoever."

"Then think of the child, Channah. What's the matter with you? You're a brilliant woman. You solve the whole world's problems, but you can't solve your own. You're so filled with anger at your foolish father that you can't see how you're hurting yourself and the child."

"I don't want to hear you talking that way, Ezra. I'm a grown woman. I'm not your little cousin from Europe. Don't preach at me!"

"You'll take the child from here and move with her to Chicago? Where is your head, Channah? We don't live forever. The mistakes we make now are harder and harder to clean up. Who will clean up this one in Chicago? You have no one in Chicago."

"Michael was not a mistake, Ezra. I loved him. You know that. And Charles won't be a mistake. Don't treat me like a child. He's a brilliant man. And he writes and—"

"And you'll help him with his books and his monographs. You'll raise Ilana as a nice midwestern girl. You'll organize for the party in Chicago. You'll bear his children."

"I don't want any more children."

"My God, Channah. What are you doing to yourself?"

"I don't want any more of this conversation."

"I will not stand by and let you—"

"Ezra, stop. Please stop."

"Think of your mother. Think of your grandfather."

"Don't do that to me, Ezra. You tried that once before. Don't—do—that—to—me!"

There was a long silence.

"All right," Mr. Dinn said in a drained voice. "All right. Good night, Channah."

I heard a chair scrape against the kitchen floor and his footsteps in the hallway. The door opened and closed and the harp sang.

My mother remained in the kitchen, sobbing.

I got out of bed and went through the dim hallway in my bare feet. My mother sat at the table, her head in her hands. I squinted in the light.

"Mama?"

She looked up, startled, and quickly wiped her eyes with the palms of her hands. Her face was puffy. Strands of wet hair lay upon her cheeks. Her lipstick was smeared.

"Are we moving again, Mama?"

She stared at me through the sheen in her eyes.

"I don't want to move again."

"Ilana—"

"Can I live with the Helfmans if you move with that man to Chicago?"

Her mouth fell open. I saw her face go white.

"Go to sleep, Ilana."

"I don't want to move to Chicago. I'm happy here. Why are we moving to Chicago when I'm finally happy?"

"Ilana, I haven't the strength to—"

"Papa wouldn't want you to move."

Her lips stiffened with sudden flashing anger.

"I won't go to Chicago with you and that man. I don't like that man. I think he's—"

"Young lady, don't you dare! *Don't you dare!*" She raised her hand to strike me. I drew back. She had never raised her hand to me before. Her eyes had a dark, wild look. She stopped and lowered her hand and sat at the table, breathing heavily, staring.

I went back along the hallway to my room. My feet were cold. I lay in my bed in the darkness, frightened by the hate I felt for my mother.

I wrote to Jakob Daw in Marseilles and to Aunt Sarah at the farmhouse. I attended school. At the end of October I was asked to see the head of the Hebrew Department, an elderly man with gray hair and moist lips. He informed me that I was being moved up one grade in Hebrew. I saw David in the yard during the morning recess and told him. He let out a whoop of joy and encircled me with a crushing hug— from which he immediately retreated in red-faced embarrassment. Ruthie jumped up and down and squealed with delight. My mother nodded absently and said, "Very nice, Ilana." She had other things on her mind.

She was seeing Charles Carter very often now. He had accepted an associate professorship at the University of Chicago and would be leaving New York the following summer. He tried hard to become my friend by showing an interest in my Hebrew studies. He had no religion and was not Jewish. When he came into my room he smoked and often left ashes on my floor. As soon as he got to Chicago he would start his research for the new book he was planning on the rise of the labor movement in America.

"Will you write about strikes?" I asked him one night.

He stared at me. It seemed always to be difficult for him to reconcile my questions to my age. "Certainly," he said. "You bet."

"Do you know how many different meanings there are for the word strike?"

He squinted at me through the smoke of his cigarette and appeared not to know what to say.

"You're showing off, Ilana," my mother said.

"My father used to write about strikes. When I was a little girl he used to go away to strikes and write about them for his newspaper. Did you ever write about strikes for a newspaper?"

"No," he said, and exhaled a cloud of cigarette smoke that rose slowly to the ceiling of the kitchen.

"Were you in the war in Spain?"

"No."

"Will you be going to Spain?"

"No. I teach, you see."

"What do you teach?"

"Modern history."

"About wars and things?"

"Wars and things. You bet."

"My mother was in the big war. She was in a pogrom."

"Ilana."

"Are you going to marry my mother?"

"Ilana!"

"We've talked about it."

"You can marry my mother if you want, but I won't go to Chicago!"

"Ilana!"

"I think I'll go to bed now. I'm very tired. Good night. I hope you write a good book about strikes."

I left them in the kitchen and went to my room.

Some days later my mother received a letter from Jakob Daw. It was in German and she would not translate it for me. She read it at the kitchen table, her face slowly stiffening. She looked at me. "You had no right," she said angrily. "I have my own life to live."

"Can't I write to Uncle Jakob?"

"Write to him about the weather. Write to him about your school or his stories. Don't write to him asking him to change my mind."

A letter arrived from Aunt Sarah addressed to me and my mother. She was working in a Boston hospital and living in Newton Centre. She

wished my mother well. She planned to spend the last ten days of
December at the farmhouse. If my mother and I could somehow manage to break away for a few days we would be welcome. The beach had
a special loveliness to it in the winter. She understood that Chicago was
a raw and bitterly cold city with little culture and a pervasive odor from
the slaughterhouses. Still, she wished my mother all the luck. Was it at
all possible that we could come up in December?

"Whom else have you written?" my mother asked.

"No one."

"You will not write anyone again about this."

I said nothing.

"Do you hear me, young lady?"

"Yes."

A letter arrived for me from Jakob Daw.

"Dear Ilana. I understand. But you must understand that your
mother is young and beautiful and deserves her own life. You will be a
good girl and not cause her sorrow. She has had at least two lifetimes of
sorrow already. She is the kindest and gentlest of little birds, the sort
whose suffering is almost never noticed. We must care for her and be
gentle with her. Write to me again. Uncle Jakob."

I was at my desk one night that November doing my Hebrew homework when the apartment door opened. I heard the harp and waited for
my mother's greeting. Always she called out, "I'm home!" Now, instead, she went with urgent steps through the hallway. The door to her
room opened and quickly closed. The apartment was silent.

I went from my room into the kitchen. The newspapers which my
mother always brought home with her lay on the table. I looked at the
headlines and read a few paragraphs about a vengeance shooting of a
German embassy official in Paris by a seventeen-year-old Polish émigré
Jew whose parents had been expelled by the Nazis from Germany back
to Poland with nothing more than a few articles of clothing.

I read some of the paragraphs again. Then I looked up. How silent
the air had suddenly become, how hushed—as if all the world were
holding its breath.

I went from the kitchen and stood for a moment outside the door to
my mother's room. I heard nothing. I returned to the kitchen and read
some more. I was slowly reading the piece in *The New York Times* when

my mother came into the kitchen. She put on her apron and stood at the sink.

"Will it hurt Uncle Jakob?" I asked.

"I don't know," she said. Her back was to me. "I don't think so."

"The Jewish man shouldn't have done that."

"He shouldn't have, Ilana. You're right. But sometimes if you hurt a person badly enough, you cause him to do crazy things. Are you done with your homework? Can you help set the table?"

Three days later, as I walked past the candy store on my way to school, I saw on the front page of *The New York Times,* NAZIS SMASH, LOOT AND BURN JEWISH SHOPS AND TEMPLES UNTIL GOEBBELS CALLS HALT. A second headline on that page announced, ALL VIENNA'S SYN-AGOGUES ATTACKED; FIRES AND BOMBS WRECK 18 OUT OF 21.

My briefcase felt very heavy. I put it down and stood in the cold November air, reading.

"BERLIN, Nov. 10.—A wave of destruction, looting and incendiarism unparalleled in Germany since the Thirty Years War and in Europe generally since the Bolshevist revolution, swept over Great Germany today as National Socialist cohorts took vengeance on Jewish shops for the murder by a young Polish Jew of Ernst vom Rath, third secretary of the German Embassy in Paris."

I read it again. I picked up my briefcase and walked quickly to school.

David said to me during recess, "Did you see the papers? We have relatives in Germany."

"I'm frightened, David."

"Do you have relatives in Germany?"

"No. Won't it happen in America?"

"What?"

"All the breaking and the burning and the hurting of Jews."

"The government won't let it happen here."

"But there are Fascists in America. They demonstrate in the streets of New York. I'm really scared, David."

My mother said to me that evening during supper, "The Nazis are barbarians and must be stopped. Do you understand now why I let your father go to Spain?"

I did not respond.

Faintly, through the walls, drifted the Shabbos songs of the Helfmans from the apartment below. Didn't they know what was happening? Why were they singing? I wondered if the Jews in Germany and Vienna were singing Shabbos songs. Broken windows, plundered synagogues, burned Torah scrolls. Later in my room I looked out my window and imagined broken glass everywhere on our street and when I lay in bed I imagined broken glass all up and down Eastern Parkway and the windows of my school smashed and the synagogue thick with smoke and flames. Everywhere fire and glass; tiny glistening slivers along the sidewalks and in the branches of the trees and on the winter grass in Prospect Park and in the lake. I remembered a story I had read in a magazine one summer in the cottage at Sea Gate. POGROM IN SEPTEMBER! Someone had patented a special weapon called the Kike Killer. What had he said? "We're not going to drive the Jews from this country. We're going to bury 'em right here!" That was where I had first seen the word pogrom. But I had been too frightened then to ask my mother what it meant. Pogrom. I fell asleep and woke in the morning, tired and chilled with sweat. I pulled aside the curtains and raised the shade. Brilliant sunlight entered my room. I dressed quickly and walked along tranquil streets to the synagogue.

The room was unusually crowded by the time I arrived and my seat near the dividing curtain with the small tear in the ninon had been taken by an elderly woman. One of the few empty seats left was in the first row. I sat down and found myself facing the bare front wall of the room and with a hazy, distorted view of the other side.

The service sounded subdued, the singing restrained. A boy read the Torah, hurriedly and with no errors. When the Torah was returned to the ark, all sat down. Silence filled the room.

The synagogue did not have a rabbi. From time to time one of the men would deliver a brief talk before the Silent Devotion of the additional service.

Now a man began to speak and I recognized immediately the deep, slightly nasal voice of Mr. Dinn. I saw him vaguely through the curtain. He stood at the lectern in his dark suit and long prayer shawl and dark felt hat. I looked through the curtain for David but he sat among tall adults and I could not see him.

"We are confronted by a new Haman," Mr. Dinn began, "one far deadlier than the Haman of old. This new Haman does not require the approval of a higher authority for his acts of brutality. This Haman is himself the highest authority in his land. Germany has returned to the age of Teutonic barbarism.

"Today's Torah reading tells us about the destruction of Sedom and Amorrah. What terrible sins were committed by those cities? Our sages gave us a long list of their sins. But one sin appears to stand out above the others. The people of Sedom and Amorrah hated strangers who entered their cities. These were wealthy cities that refused to share their good fortunes with anyone unknown to them. The stranger would be defiled, dishonored. He would be given no recourse to the law. He would be killed. How would all this be done? Our sages tell us that when a stranger entered those cities he would be set upon and beaten. Bleeding, he would go to a court of law and ask for damages. Whereupon the judge would tell the poor victim to pay his attacker for the medical treatment of bloodletting! Indeed, a story is told by the rabbis about Eliezer, the servant of Abraham, who one day visited Sedom and was injured, and sued for damages in the court and was told by the judge to pay his attacker a bloodletting fee. Whereupon Eliezer picked up a stone and struck the judge and said, 'The money you now owe me for this bloodletting you can pay to the one whom I owe.' "

Soft laughter rippled across the room. Mr. Dinn waited a moment, then continued.

"Law that is used to victimize the stranger, the one who is helpless—that is the law of Sedom and Amorrah. Jews have lived in Germany for a thousand years. Still the Germans look upon us as strangers because we worship a different God, came to the land from the warm south rather than the frozen north, had our beginnings in a desert rather than on a tundra. We now know the true nature of Nazi Germany. It is Sedom and Amorrah. And it will be destroyed as were Sedom and Amorrah."

He paused a moment. The room was very still. He went on.

"I'm not a politician. I'm a lawyer. But this much I do know. There are times when people must choose sides and tell themselves, 'That's my enemy, and the enemy of my enemy is, at least for now, my ally and my friend.' Let us now find who our true friends are and join ourselves to them. Together with them, and with the help of God, we will destroy this brutal twentieth-century Sedom and Amorrah."

A murmur of approval swept through the large room. Mr. Dinn sat down. I saw David lean forward out of the adults around him and hug his father. People were shaking Mr. Dinn's hand. An elderly man rose and walked over to the lectern and resumed the service.

Later I told my mother about Mr. Dinn's talk, and she said soberly, "The Fascists won't destroy only Jews, Ilana. They will destroy decency everywhere. That's why I work so hard for the party now. That's why your father went to Spain. Who else is trying to stop the Nazis today? England? France? America? Who else?"

"I'm very scared of the Nazis, Mama."

"Yes," she said. "There's good reason to be scared of the Nazis."

A letter arrived from Jakob Daw.

The recently published French edition of his stories had been well received by all who were not involved in politics. And since nearly all the French were involved in politics, the voices of approval had been few, indeed. The right had called him a Marxist obscurantist and his writings a threat to moral decency, and the left had labeled him a voice of the decadent bourgeois class. Still, there were some who read his stories and understood. Here and there small islands of sanity were still visible in the fog of madness descending upon Europe. "How is our Ilana? Well, I hope. How old is she now? Ten, I believe. Tell her our bird still nests peacefully in our harp. Is it still your intention to move to Chicago? If so, I wish you well. The cough is bad and seems not to be helped now by the Mediterranean air. What a strange darkness I feel about me everywhere in this sunlit city! It is as if a curtain is being drawn across the entire vault of heaven while a drum beats a distant barbarous rhythm. I grow weary and must lie down now. Please remember me to Ezra Dinn. Jakob Daw."

The winter months wore on. At the social work agency, my mother had begun to work mostly with Jewish immigrants, recent arrivals who were trying to bring the rest of their families out of Germany. Her days were filled with the desperation of frightened people. She came home, made supper, worked at her desk, went to bed. The party meetings continued. On weekends she went out with Charles Carter. Mr. Dinn no longer visited us. Ruthie told me that he and David planned to move into our apartment after we moved out.

That spring my mother was asked by her agency not to leave until the end of the year. She had a special ability with refugees, and the agency sorely needed her. They were short of people with her talents. They asked her to use the additional months to train the woman who would replace her. My mother agreed. Charles Carter would be leaving for Chicago in August, and we would follow a few months later—not in August, as had originally been planned. My mother explained it all to me again and again. I said yes, I understood, I understood. But I did not really understand. I did not want to leave for Chicago, especially in the middle of a school year. There were fights between us. Our kitchen became a battleground.

The days were longer now and the winds warmer. I walked alone often in Prospect Park along the rim of the lake, gazing at my reflection in the water. Trees were returning to life, tiny shoots of grass were springing from the earth. Did the trees and grass grow green in Germany too? Somehow it seemed to me that Germany should be covered with darkness: black sky, black grass, black leaves, black trees, black sun. I didn't want to share the loveliness of a green spring with Germany, my last spring in this neighborhood. Everything I saw now I was seeing for the final time. I thought of the Lag Ba'omer day of games that had taken place here last year. Had a year gone by already? Was it two years since my father had died? I had been told by the head of the Hebrew Department of my school that if I continued my good work I would be moved into my regular Hebrew class in September. I did not want to go to Chicago and live in an apartment somewhere with my mother and Charles Carter. Would they sleep in the same bed? Would I have to share a bathroom with him? Papa, why did you have to try to save that nun? For once, only once, couldn't you not have done the decent thing, and stayed alive?

I walked slowly back through the park to the botanical garden. I had gone with my class to the garden during the past week and a man had talked to us about the different kinds of flowers that grew there. It was lovely in that garden in the spring: beds of flowers, a banked hill glowing with yellow daffodils, winding paths, scented air—an enchanted magical kingdom. My mother had not come to the park or the garden in a long time. Too much work to do. Too much to think about. Too much. A haunted brooding had settled upon her like a garment of mourning.

We rarely talked now. She was reading the galley proofs of the book of my father's special writing and translating into English the stories Jakob Daw had written while he had lived with us. She worked at the desk in her bedroom, in a nightgown, and often her door was shut. Sometimes she would wander out of the room with papers in her hands and sit near the living room window where she could look out upon the trees, and I would be able to see the tips of her breasts through the thin cloth of the nightgown and the vague hint of the triangular darkness at the juncture of her legs. I wondered when I would begin to look like that, breasts and nipples and hair between my legs—and a faint stirring would begin somewhere deep within me. My mother seemed no longer to care how she looked as she walked about the apartment or that, in her nightgown, as she stood by the window or before the living-room floor lamp, she was almost naked to my eyes. She would sit looking out at the trees or reading and playing with her hair, twisting long strands of it in her fingers. She would turn on the radio to listen to the news or to music. She listened often to the news. And the news was always bad.

Late that spring on a warm and sunny day I climbed into a bus along with my classmates and rode to an art gallery in Manhattan. I think it was named the Valentine Gallery; I am not certain. We did that sort of thing from time to time: went on trips to museums, the theater, the ballet. But this was our first visit to an art gallery. We had been told by our English teacher that the gallery was showing a very special painting; she knew someone who worked there and had obtained permission for this class visit.

I remember the ride through the tunnel and along the river and up narrow streets thick with people and traffic. There were only about twenty of us on that trip and we walked in a huddled mass about half a block through the heart of Manhattan and into the entrance of a tall building. I think it was a tall building; I am not certain. I remember my English teacher being greeted by a handsome, dapper-looking man in a dark suit, and how we all quietly tittered at that. I remember carpeted rooms with paintings on the walls. Then the man led us into a room that was dominated by a huge painting on one of its walls. I do not remember if there were other paintings in the room; there may have been drawings and sketches on the other walls. Ruthie, standing next to me, eyed the painting and giggled. "Look at it," she whispered. "Isn't it crazy?" The teacher began to talk to us about the painting.

I had to crane my neck in order to see it. We stood near the wall across the room from it and still it was enormous and I could not see all of it at one time. I had never seen such a painting anywhere. It seemed inhabited by monsters and was not even in color but in black and white and gray. Most of my classmates seemed bewildered and bored. The teacher kept on talking and I stood there trying to see all of the painting at the same time and could not. She had mentioned the name Pablo Picasso a number of times and I was trying to remember where I had heard that name before. And then she said something and I grew very still and I stood looking at the painting and took a step toward it and stood very still, staring at the painting.

The teacher had said the painting was called *Guernica.*

A slight shiver ran through me. I could not stop staring at the painting. It was odd how silent the room had become, the teacher's voice slowly fading as if absorbed by the walls. *Guernica.* Black and white and gray. Grotesque bodies of women and a horse and a bull. A woman with a dead child, screaming. A woman with naked breasts, running. A woman with arms raised, burning. A black and white bull, staring. A lamp clutched in a disembodied hand. And a light overhead. And bits and pieces of a dead soldier. And what was that in the darkness between the screaming head of the horse and the staring head of the bull? A bird! A small gray bird, head upturned, beak wide open, crying. And all in black and white and gray. How easy it was to do now what I had done once before—a bending of the knees and an upward thrust and lightly through the air and landing effortlessly beside the bird and gently scooping it up and running with it away from the bull and the horse and through the rubble of blasted streets and fallen houses and fires and pieces of bodies to the river and the bridge at the edge of the town where my father was and helping him carry the wounded nun so his hip wouldn't crumple beneath her weight. People were shouting at me and I responded but I did not know what I was saying. I ran back and forth through the town, holding the bird to me, and I could not find my father. Fires and bombs and airplanes and screams and a bridge somewhere and a river. He was here and I could not find him. I turned a corner—and there was the bull, staring, and the horse, screaming. I held the bird, felt its warm and terrified pulsing.

Ruthie was talking to me. My teacher was talking to me. I stared at them. I was fine, I said. Sure. I was okay.

My mother was talking to me. "What is the matter with you? You haven't eaten a thing. How can you waste food this way?"

How did I get back to my house? And my room? It should have been easy to find him. Guernica was a small town. Only a few thousand people. Where was the river and the bridge?

I lay in my bed with the gray bird in my hand and when I woke in the early morning the bird had grown tiny during the night, tinier than a thumbnail; but I could still feel its beating heart and its warmth. Outside it was raining. I saw the rain in the leaves of the trees and on the street, a gray rain that ran in rivulets along the gutters, and I wondered if all the rains in all the world could ever put out the fires of Guernica. I got out of bed and went silently through the hallway, the tiny gray bird still in my hand. And I placed the bird in the circular hollow of the door harp next to the black bird nesting there. Then I dressed and ate breakfast and left early for school.

We lived in the city that summer and Mr. Carter came often to the apartment. Sometimes he stayed very late. Once he and my mother were in her room together for a long time. I played in the park and sometimes I imagined myself in Guernica, saving my father. David and Ruthie were away and Mr. Dinn no longer visited us. I went to the synagogue on Shabbos mornings but no one I knew well was there. My father's book would be published in September. My mother was sad when Mr. Carter left in early August for Chicago.

It was a sweltering summer. I slept naked and sweating in my bed. Often I dreamed of all the ways I would save my father and the nun. Sometimes I prayed that my mother and I would never go to Chicago. Let something happen, I prayed. Not anything terrible. But enough to keep us from going. I did not know whom I was praying to. But it was good to think and whisper the words in the darkness of my room. I did not pray on my knees.

Letters arrived from Jakob Daw, all in German, and my mother would not read them to me. They were personal, she said. Yes, he sent me his good wishes. No, he was not well. Would I please stop pestering her; she was definitely not going to read me Jakob Daw's letters. And she would grow angry and sometimes shout at me. We had become strangers to one another. At times I thought I hated her, and that frightened me terribly. After each of our quarrels I would journey into the painting, searching for my father.

Always somewhere in our lives that summer there seemed to be a radio. On weekdays I played in the park with others in the day camp program and went rowing on the lake. There was a radio in the small house that was the camp office and the news would come from it like some dark utterance from a region of fire and pain. It would move across the grassy meadows and through the trees and over the lake. And in the nights the news would enter my room from the radio in the kitchen and become caught in the corner shadows and I would hear it there, vibrating softly with words I was listening to for the first time: mobilization, war of nerves, brink, hostilities—words of impending war. It was over that radio that the news first came to us of the treaty between Hitler and Stalin.

We heard it during supper one night in the last week of August, the announcer's voice calm and smooth: Germany and Russia had signed a nonaggression pact. He talked about it at some length, then went on to other news. My mother turned off the radio.

"Capitalist lies," she said. "What they go through to slander us!"

"What does it mean?" I asked.

"Never mind."

"What does nonaggression pact mean?"

"Finish your supper, Ilana. Filthy lies. Even the radio news is corrupt."

The phone rang. She went out of the kitchen to the hallway. I heard her talking in a low, tight voice, but could not make out her words. Some minutes later she returned to the kitchen and poured herself another cup of coffee. She spilled coffee on the table as she set down the cup and washed it off with a towel. Her hands were trembling.

"Mama?"

"Leave me alone, Ilana."

"Mama?"

"Ilana!"

I went out of the kitchen. The phone rang again. From my room I heard my mother's voice, low, urgent. Later that night I went back into the kitchen for a glass of water and saw the radio was gone. I stood at the closed door to my mother's room and heard the voice of a news announcer softly through the darkness. In the morning the radio was back on its shelf in the kitchen. We listened to the news. My mother stared at the radio, her face a clear mirror of her emotions: anger, pain, disbelief, bewilderment. She would not respond to any of my questions and left quickly to go to work.

On my way to the day camp I stopped at a subway newsstand and looked at the headlines. I read, GERMANY AND RUSSIA SIGN TEN-YEAR NONAGGRESSION PACT. I asked the news vendor what it meant and he told me to get out of the way, I was keeping him from taking care of his customers. In the park I listened to the radio and, later, in the rowboat on the lake I asked the counselor at the oars what nonaggression pact meant, and he explained it to me. He was the same counselor from whose boat I had jumped two summers before.

"I don't understand," I said.

He explained it again. The others in the boat were giving me queer looks.

"You mean the Communists have become friends with the Fascists?"

"That's right," he said. Then he said, "Ilana, sit still and stop rocking the boat."

"I don't believe that," I said.

"I don't care whether you believe it or not. Sit still!"

I sat very quietly. I believed none of it. He was a liar and a capitalist tool. I hated him and wished he would hurry and bring us to shore so I could get out of his boat.

I did not go rowing with him in the afternoon but sat beneath a tree and read a copy of the *Times* that I had found in a trash can. I read:

"MOSCOW, Aug. 24.—With the meticulous punctuality of a perfectly staged arrival, two huge Focke-Wulf Condor planes conveying Joachim von Ribbentrop, the German Foreign Minister, and his thirty-two assistants, landed at the Moscow airdrome on the stroke of 1 P.M. yesterday.

"Adequate but not excessive police precautions were taken at the airdrome. For the first time the Soviet authorities displayed the swastika banner, five of which flew from the front of the airdrome building, but were placed so as not to be visible from the outside. . . ."

I put the paper back into the trash can.

There was a party meeting in our apartment that night. People arrived angry. I could hear the anger in their tread as they came up the stairs. The harp sang and sang. I sat at my desk and listened to the shouting in the living room. "With that murderer?" someone was screaming. "That barbarian? I shit on the whole thing! You want to know what I think of it? I'll tell you what I think of it. You can take this card and shove it up your ass!" Angry footsteps sounded through the hallway and then the slamming of our front door. The harp sang.

There was an explosion of voices in the living room. A woman was shouting. I did not hear my mother. Some more people left, slamming the front door. The harp sang and sang.

Two nights later there was another meeting. A man I had seen only once before came to the apartment that night, the bald-headed man who had spoken at the memorial meeting for my father. I heard his quiet, authoritative voice through the walls of my room. He talked about the need for discipline, for buying time, for secure frontiers. I heard a man's voice suddenly shout, "Fuck you, comrade! You think I'm going to kill myself for the party when it—"

"Sit down!" a woman shouted. "Listen to what he has to say!"

"To hell with it!" the man shouted back. "We're being played for suckers. Can't you see it?"

"I see breach of discipline," a second man shouted. "That's what I see."

"To hell with all of it!" the first man shouted. "I gave you years of my life to fight fascism and now you give me this shit! To hell with all of it!"

Again, angry footsteps sounded through the hallway and, again, the door harp sang.

I said to my mother at breakfast the following morning, "Mama, what are you going to do?"

She gave me a look of pain, a look that implored me to ask no more questions of her—and I finished my breakfast in silence and went off to the day camp.

She went to a meeting that night and to another meeting a few nights later. In the middle of September, about two weeks after I had returned to school, yet another meeting took place in our apartment. Again, I heard raised voices and angry imprecations. And again, others shouted their demands for total adherence to party discipline: there was a reason for the move; it was a life-or-death choice; it was needed to buy time for the world revolution; sometimes you were forced to make an alliance . with an enemy for the sake of a—

And then I heard my mother's voice and I turned cold and felt the skin rise on the nape of my neck. I had never heard her sound like that before: strident, coldly raging, gulping some of her words, and the words pouring from her in a torrent of unrelenting fury. She understood everything, she said. It all made perfect sense, the treaty, the opportunity to increase the security of Russia's borders, to augment the power of the Russian people and strengthen the hand of Comrade Stalin. It all made perfect sense, and yet it made no sense at all. It had nothing to do with the Communist cause. It was a pure geopolitical act having to do with national security—and as far as she was concerned Russia was no longer the leader of world communism. No truly Communist state could ally itself with the absolute enemy of communism, no matter what its self-interest might be. She for one could never live at peace with any person or state that tied itself to Nazi Germany. She began to quote from the writings of Marx and Engels. She quoted from Lenin. She even quoted from Stalin. She went on and on in that coldly furious high-pitched voice—and then I had the feeling that she was no longer making any sense. A deep silence had settled upon the meeting, and still my mother continued talking. How can one justify this theoretically and morally? she asked again and again. How can one explain it? It defied elementary morality. An alliance with Hitler, who had helped Franco conquer Spain, whose aircraft had destroyed the town of Guernica, who persecuted Jews. How is such an act even remotely justifiable, no matter what geopolitical reality is taken into consideration? Again, she quoted Marx. She was beginning to sound hoarse. Suddenly someone said, "Anne, please, enough, enough. Sit down." Someone else said, "What are you talking about? How can you have world communism and revolution without Russia? You're babbling!" A third voice said, "Listen to her, for heaven's sake!" The first voice said, "We don't have time for this. There's work to be done. Without discipline we're nothing."

My mother fell silent.

I was asleep when the meeting ended and did not hear them leave the apartment or the door harp singing.

My mother slept late the next morning and did not go to work. I went out of the apartment and walked to school. She was in her room when I returned in the late afternoon. I found her on her bed, staring up at the ceiling. She told me to close the door and leave her alone.

In the weeks that followed she seemed to grow old before my eyes. Her face sagged and became strangely dull, her eyes took on a pinkish, inflamed look, her mouth became a hard, ragged line between perpetually pursed lips. An odor began to rise from her, sour, fecal. Her skin became dry and flaky, her long hair scraggly. She seemed to be growing smaller and smaller. She went to work, prepared our meals, wrote letters, worked on Jakob Daw's book—but all the light was gone from her, and I barely knew who she was.

There were no more meetings in our apartment.

One day in early October I went shopping with her, and in the grocery store we met the woman who had regularly attended the Sunday afternoon study sessions. The woman—short and thin and plain-looking, with straight brown hair and moist brown eyes—turned on her heel and walked off without a word. My mother's face reddened; her lips trembled.

There were no more study sessions in our apartment.

A letter arrived from Charles Carter. My mother read it and read it again and then went with it to her room. I heard her choking sobs through the closed door. When she emerged she looked ill.

"Mama, shall I ask Mrs. Helfman to—"

"We will not be going to Chicago, Ilana," she said.

I stared at her and felt a slow turning of the world.

"Can you make supper by yourself? You'll find things in the icebox. No, we won't be going to Chicago after all. What shall I do now? I think I'll go out for a walk. Can you take care of yourself for an hour or so, Ilana?"

Every weekday morning she went to work. Every evening she returned. At night she would wander about the apartment like a shade. She favored the darkness and would sit for hours in the living room without a light. One night I went into the living room and turned on a light and saw her in her nightgown in an easy chair. She jumped, startled, and threw up her hands before her eyes. "Turn off the light!" she screamed. "Turn it off!"

Sometimes she would begin to hum melodies I had never heard before. She fell asleep over books and newspapers. "What shall I do?" I heard her say at times as she wandered about the apartment. One day I realized that she was no longer listening to music. I went by the bathroom once and saw her, through the door she had left open, asleep on the toilet, her panties pushed down to her ankles. She sat there in her nightgown, which had been pulled up over her knees, her hands clasped together in her lap and her knees slightly apart. Her head had fallen forward over her left shoulder. I did not wake her. I went quietly to my room and closed my door and lay on my bed and put my hand over my eyes. Some minutes later I heard the toilet flushing and my mother's footsteps in the hallway to her room. The image of her on the toilet asleep would not go away. Like the image of her naked. Like all the other images burned into me over the years.

It was autumn now and cold. My father's book had been published, but its birth had gone unnoticed in the aftermath of the Nazi-Soviet pact and in the din of death now coming from Europe. Germany had invaded Poland in the first week of September, and the Second World War had begun.

I remember the frenzy into which the neighborhood and the school had been thrown by that invasion. Nearly everyone in the school had relatives somewhere in the war zone. What had Jakob Daw written? Yes, I remembered—and I lay awake at times imagining the curtain of darkness being drawn across the sky and the barbarous drums beating to the rhythm of war. I hated that word. War. How many bits and pieces of arms and legs would now litter the world?

A letter arrived from Jakob Daw. It lay for days on a shelf in the kitchen. My mother would pick it up, stare at it, and put it down. Finally she opened it one evening and sat at the kitchen table, reading. She wore her nightgown. Her hair was scraggly, uncombed. A strange dry stale odor rose from her. I wondered when she had last bathed.

"What does Uncle Jakob say?"

"He says he heard someone mention that on the day Germany invaded Poland all the lakeside beaches in Berlin were crowded. He says that Goebbels told the Berlin Philharmonic Orchestra that war is the father of all things, and a musician must play and not be silent. He says other things too, but they're personal."

I asked who Goebbels was and she told me.

"Jakob Daw is not well," my mother said. "He was in the hospital for a while." She was silent and sat staring down at the letter. "It's all ended," she said. "All the dreams. And what shall I do now?" She slumped in the chair and let the letter fall to the top of the table. "I think I'll lie down now, Ilana. I'm very tired."

"You didn't have supper."

"I don't want supper. I'm not hungry. You ate enough for both of us."

She went to her room.

I noticed that she was eating little and losing weight. She drank a great deal of coffee. Her face was haggard. Tiny wrinkles had appeared in the corners of her eyes and around her lips. She continued to grow smaller and smaller.

Mr. Dinn had begun to visit us again. He would sit in the kitchen with my mother late into the night, talking. She cried a great deal when he was alone with her. Often they talked in Yiddish.

In the first week of November my mother collapsed in the office where she worked and was taken by ambulance to a nearby hospital. Mrs. Helfman rushed to the school to tell me about it; the police had come to the house, looking for a relative. I moved in with the Helfmans and shared Ruthie's room. In the synagogue a prayer was said for my mother's health and people told me they wished her a speedy recovery.

The Helfmans were warm and kind. Mr. Helfman loved to tell stories about famous rabbis and Jewish heroes. He told about the Maharal of Prague who created out of clay a huge manlike creature called the Golem to protect the Jews from persecution; about the Gaon of Vilna who would study Talmud with ice on his head so he would not fall asleep; about Rabbi Amnon of Mayence who wrote religious poetry and accepted torture and death rather than let himself be converted to Christianity.

"Where is Mayence?" I asked him.

"In Germany," he said.

One day when Ruthie and I were alone in the apartment, I wandered through the rooms and on top of a wooden file cabinet in her parents' bedroom found a pile of newspaper clippings with stories and pictures of the past few years of Akiva Award winners. The stories talked about the award as the ultimate recognition of achievement given by the school, as a mark of permanent membership in the annals of the yeshiva community. All the winners were boys.

My mother returned home from the hospital in the middle of November. She would not eat. I was afraid to look at her eyes, they seemed dead. She began to talk to me one night about dead dreams being like dead children. Her words frightened me.

That Friday night before supper she saw me light candles and asked me brusquely what I was doing. I had set candles in two small glass dishes, first heating the bottoms of the candles and fixing the molten wax to the glass.

I said I had seen Mrs. Helfman light Shabbos candles when I had stayed with them and weren't they pretty.

"I don't want those candles in my house," my mother said.

"Shall I blow them out?"

"No," she said, after a long moment.

"I'm sorry, Mama. I didn't think they would upset you."

She said nothing. From time to time during the meal she glanced at the candles. She fell asleep at the table. I helped her to her room and into bed. How white and gaunt she looked. I was very frightened. Her life had suddenly swerved, and she was bereft. Had something like this happened to her in Poland and Vienna, this kind of bewilderingly abrupt change?

I asked her one night why none of her old friends came to see her and she said she had no friends, she was no longer a member of the party.

"You didn't have any friends outside the party?"

"Friends outside the party? Real friends? No. Who had time for that, Ilana?"

The days went by. She grew thinner and weaker. One night she fainted in the kitchen as I sat eating supper and I ran to call Mrs. Helfman.

It seemed to me that my mother was slowly dying of loneliness.

I read and studied a great deal. I talked with Ruthie and her parents. I talked with David in the corridors of the school and on Shabbos mornings outside the shul. I wrote a letter to Aunt Sarah.

Late one night in December Mr. Dinn came over and was in the kitchen with my mother for a long time. I heard the rise and fall of their voices, and at one point I heard my mother laughing. It was a strange, harsh sound.

Mr. Dinn came to see my mother two more times that week.

The next Sunday morning he pulled up to the house in his black sedan and helped my mother inside. She was dry-eyed and looked docile, defeated. Mr. Dinn loaded her bags into the trunk. Then he kissed my cheek. I stood on the curb with Mrs. Helfman and watched the car pull away. My mother looked at me through the window, her eyes wide and haunted. I stood on the curb, crying. Later that day I moved in with the Helfmans.

Mr. Dinn drove my mother to Newton Centre, and Aunt Sarah brought her from there to the farmhouse. Aunt Sarah had asked for and received a leave from the Boston hospital where she worked. A family emergency, she had explained.

Aunt Sarah wrote me often; my mother wrote infrequently. I imagined my mother in my bed in the farmhouse, the silence, the vast sky, the quiet sea, the long red curving beach, and the birds circling, skimming the water, calling. She was being cared for by my Aunt Sarah as my father and I had once been. I hoped they prayed together. I thought my mother needed the comfort of words uttered in prayer.

Aunt Sarah wrote, "Your mother is ill but she will be better soon, I promise. Davita, how can you know what it means to have your dreams collapse all about you? Your mother has the soul of a poet. Such souls are easily broken by the real world. She is in great spiritual pain. We will help her. She loves you very much. Be patient. Such illnesses take time before they are healed. She speaks a great deal about you and your father and about her mother and grandfather. And about Ezra Dinn, whom I found to be a most decent gentleman, indeed."

She wrote, "Your mother has begun to take walks with me along the beach and through the little forest near the house. Remember the forest? It is deep in snow but the farmer cleared a path for us and we are able to walk and see the sky through the dense bare branches. How lovely it is up here in the snow—a white world of untouched snow stretching as far as the eye can see; and the ocean, gray and wintry-looking and rolling on and on to the horizon that seems to be on the very edge of the world. I am taking good care of your mother, Davita.

You take good care of yourself. Your mother is a very special person and I am glad she is in my family. I will send her back to you healed."

My mother wrote, "Darling Ilana. With every passing day I grow stronger and stronger. What a remarkable individual your Aunt Sarah is! If only all Christians were like her. She is so kind, and very devout. She tends to my needs, is strict with my diet and medication, and listens to me talk. And I talk a great deal. I do love this place—especially the quiet all about us, the utter silence. I can *feel* the silence. It is like an enormous and very gentle healing hand. I am so sorry to be away from you and so happy to hear of your grades. Your Aunt Sarah prays for you very often. She believes with all her being. I envy her. I had such belief once. It is the finest of comforts. I love to watch the birds over the sea. I sit at the window and watch them circling and calling. Some of them make strange sounds, like *hoo hoo hoo hoo*. A flight of gray fowl flew by yesterday afternoon low over the water; a beautiful sight. Horses often come down to the beach and wander about. They remind me of the photograph in my room, the one with the running horses that your father loved so much. I don't know when I will be coming home. Aunt Sarah will tell me. I am tired now and will conclude with words of love to my darling Ilana. Your mother."

My mother remained at the farmhouse with Aunt Sarah all through December and into the second week of January. Mr. Dinn brought her back in his car. She had regained most of her lost weight and looked rested and well. Much of the light was back in her eyes.

"Your Aunt Sarah is a magician," she said to me one night after supper. "Wasn't it clever of your father to have such a sister? I love her."

We settled back into our lives. As the winter wore on Mr. Dinn was in the apartment more and more frequently. One day my mother brought home a set of glass dishes and some new pots and pans and silverware. A sale, she said. How lucky! That evening Mr. Dinn and David joined us for a fish dinner in the apartment—my mother shy, a little flustered, worried about the fish; Mr. Dinn shedding a little of his austere and courtly manner and looking gracious, solicitous, relaxed. David and I kept glancing at each other and not knowing what to say.

One Friday evening my mother lit Shabbos candles without saying the blessing and covered her eyes and stood there in the flickering light and wept. The candles burned evenly in their tall twin silver candelabra—a gift from Mr. Dinn, who had brought them to her the day after she told him she wished to light Shabbos candles. I will never forget the images of that night—the candles, the weeping, my mother holding me, and our meal together afterward. The next morning we walked together to the synagogue and she sat next to me near the curtained wall. I noticed that she did not pray but sat with her head slightly inclined toward the wall, listening. People kept glancing at her but she seemed not to notice. I showed her the tear in the curtain and how she could see through it to the other side, and she laughed softly but would not use it.

In the weeks that followed, David and I saw each other often in the synagogue and in school—and not once did we talk about my mother and his father. There seemed something fragile and wondrous about it all, and I think we felt that we might spoil it if we put it into idle words.

Nor did we speak to each other about what our parents separately told us one day that spring. We communicated with looks and glances and with the language of our bodies: a wave of a hand, a turn of a shoulder, a raising of the eyebrows, a light skip, a wide smile. Words of congratulations washed over us in the synagogue. Ruthie chirped and bubbled; her parents beamed. Nothing but darkness was coming out of Europe: Germany had invaded Denmark, Norway, the Netherlands, and France. But at least here in our little Brooklyn neighborhood there would be a moment of light.

Painters came and redid our apartment. One of them took a look at my father's books and muttered angrily under his breath. "You have to know who your enemy is," my mother said quietly. He looked at her, grunted, and went back to his work. Rugs were brought from Mr. Dinn's apartment and placed on the bare floors of our living room and my mother's bedroom. All of Mr. Dinn's dishes and silverware were moved in, along with a new kitchen set and a large new bed that was divided down the middle and was like two beds with one headboard and footboard. New linoleum was put down in the hallway, new fixtures were hung from the ceilings. My father's books were moved to new shelves in the hallway and living room. Additional shelves were built in the bedroom and living room for Mr. Dinn's large library: volumes and journals of law, folios of Talmud, holiday prayerbooks, a many-volumed set of Bible commentaries. There were no books of stories in Mr. Dinn's library.

Paintings appeared on the walls, mezuzahs on the doorposts. The four of us worked together. My mother was like a young girl, Mr. Dinn like a courting youth. The picture of the horses on the beach was moved to a wall in my room. There it hung, over my bed, and sometimes at night I would wake and imagine I could hear the hooves of the horses on the sand. Mr. Dinn did not think he wanted the harp to remain on our front door and helped me hang it on the back of the door to my room. I felt in a trance. I was inside a dream in a story written by Jakob Daw and knew I would soon wake. But the story went on spinning itself out, though I didn't really understand it all, and one day in June my mother, shy and blushing and dressed in white, married Mr. Dinn in the midst of a large crowd of celebrants. David and I stood by, glancing at each other and not knowing what to say. Aunt Sarah was there too, in a white dress and a white hat—not her nurse's uniform. After the ceremony I held her for a long time and cried.

My mother and new father went away for a few days and then returned. I searched my mother's face and saw in it a new light. Happiness seemed to dance in her eyes like tiny specks of sunlight on the surface of a sea.

David moved into the room once occupied by Aunt Sarah and Jakob Daw. I helped him put his clothes and books away. He had many books, and his bookcases had been placed along the wall across from the window that looked out on the cellarway.

In my room the harp sang each time I opened and closed the door. I thought often of the two birds nesting in the harp and wondered if Uncle Jakob was still writing stories.

Seven

July was cruel with heat and news of the war. Summer rumors of polio seeped into our lives, evoking dread. David spent most of his days studying Talmud with a small special class formed by the yeshiva. I read a great deal and went to the day camp in Prospect Park. My mother had taken a part-time position with the agency in which she had worked before; she was still helping immigrants and war refugees. My new father worked in a large law office somewhere in lower Manhattan near Wall Street.

The days went slowly by. There was little rain and from time to time I watered the flowers planted in the backyard by Mr. Helfman. Evenings I often spent beneath the canopy of the sycamore, reading. Nights were sultry with damp heat. The heat rose from the streets in shimmering waves. On my way back from the day camp I could see the trees and fireplugs wriggling.

My new father said to us during zemiros one Friday night in the middle of July, "Could I interest anyone here in a few weeks at Sea Gate? I think I should get my family out of this heat."

He used those words often. My family. He seemed to like the sound of it and said it with pride.

"I don't know, Ezra," my mother said hesitantly. "Sea Gate has too many memories."

"You can't run away from your memories, Channah," my new father said. "Say good-bye to them if you have to, but don't run away from them."

"I'll have to tell Rav Hammerstein we're going away," David said uncertainly.

"He'll forgive you," my new father said. "He won't begrudge you a few weeks in the sun. My family needs it."

"What will happen to Mr. Helfman's flowers?" I asked.

My new father smiled indulgently. "We'll pray for rain," he said.

"Will we live on the beach?" I asked.

"I'll see what's available. You're all interested, yes? Good. Then it's settled. Let's continue with zemiros."

He found a house on the beach. Early one Sunday morning we loaded up the car and climbed in and he drove us through silent tree-lined streets and past elegant houses. My mother sat very still in the front seat, gazing out the window. She wore a pale yellow cotton summer dress and she looked lovely, her eyes calm, her long hair moving in the warm wind that blew into the open windows of the car. I sat with David on the backseat. I was still not used to all this newness: a car, a father, a brother.

Familiar scents entered the car: ocean water, briny air, the gas works. And suddenly there was the silver sheen of the sea, and the security gate, and the embowered streets, and the tide of memories like an inundation.

And so that August we lived in a cottage in Sea Gate a few blocks from the cottage my parents used to rent years before. Everything seemed the same. The dunes were the same: dwarf hills beyond the screened-in porch sloping gently to the beach and the sea. And the ocean was the same, though a little choppier near this cottage, noisier. A stone jetty extended deep into the water to the right of the cottage, and waves crashed against it, loudly, endlessly.

One day I wandered along the beach to the cottage where I had once lived. There was another family in it now. I stood on the beach and gazed at the screened-in porch. The cottage lay stark white in the hot sun and was the same as it had been before. I looked across the beach and imagined my parents swimming together and Jakob Daw in baggy pants and wrinkled shirt standing on the sand and gazing up at the wheeling birds. Give us a hug, my love, an ocean of a hug. I walked down to the tidal pool where I had once built castles along the rim of the sea. Waves rolled and foamed and broke upon the shore. The surf moved back and forth monotonously across the smooth wet sand. I whispered good-bye to the cottage and the castles and did not return again to that part of the beach.

The beachside cottage we lived in that August was a large red-brick structure with bedrooms along both its sides separated by a spacious living room and a large, open kitchen. Exposed beams spanned the length of the living room, and the white cathedral ceiling ended in a bank of floor-to-ceiling oceanfront windows through which the sun shone all morning long. There were drapes on those windows to protect us from the sun and the gaze of passersby, but we almost never used them during the day. Somehow in my imagination the morning sun was diminished that summer, changed. I told myself that each dawn was dimmed by what the sun had witnessed on its journey across bleeding Europe. The sun would gather strength as it climbed into our sky. But mornings seemed pale as the weakened sun glided into my room and woke me slowly to the day.

I would lie in my bed in the early sunlight and listen to David. We were separated by a thin wall and I could hear clearly his breathing, his movements as he turned in his bed, his footsteps, his soft chanting of the prayers. He was not yet a bar mitzvah, would not be required to observe all the Commandments until he turned thirteen next June. There were certain things he could not do until then: lead a service in the synagogue, chant the Torah portion for the congregation, lead the Grace After Meals. Yet he was as meticulous as his father in the performance of those commandments that he could observe.

He told me that August that he wanted to be a rosh yeshiva one day —the head of an academy of Torah learning. He said it during a long moment of openness between us: a night when we sat together on the porch, gazing out at a starry sky and the distant lights of the curving shoreline. He said it softly and wonderingly, his voice shy and hesitant, as if he doubted what right he had to attempt so lofty a calling. He seemed very self-conscious that summer. He was growing; his voice was changing, deepening. I saw the beginning of hair on his legs and under his armpits and soft down on his cheeks. I made it a point never to look too long at the nipples on his chest or the bulge in his bathing suit as we sat together or lay on the sand after a swim.

Every morning after breakfast he studied Talmud. He sat at the table on the front porch with the folio open before him and chanted softly in the intonation that accompanies the flow of a talmudic argument: a kind of music of the mind that I found enchanting. I would sit on the steps or walk back and forth on the hot sands of the dunes, listening. His deepening voice was taking on a nasal quality. I found myself humming along with his sing-song melody. One morning I asked him if he would teach me a passage of Talmud, and he looked a little surprised, then said sure, why not. We studied together for a while and then went swimming. In the afternoon we studied together again. My mother came out of the kitchen and stood in the doorway, listening, her face expressionless. She brushed a hand over her dark hair and went back inside.

We studied together from time to time in the days that followed. I found it very difficult to keep up with him. He seemed impatient with my inability to understand ideas that he grasped immediately. Also, I had the feeling he was a little uncomfortable about teaching a girl. Often he studied with his father. Mostly he studied alone. He was already many pages beyond the quota of summer study assigned him by his Talmud teacher.

"Can a girl become a rosh yeshiva?" I asked him one day.

The question startled him. "I don't think so. No, she can't."

"Why not?"

"There are no girls in the high yeshivas."

He looked so uncomfortable that I did not pursue it and went on to talk of something else.

He seemed to grow easily embarrassed in my presence. I had the feeling he had been so long without a woman in his family that the presence of me and my mother was now often overwhelming to him. Once, in the apartment before we left for the beach, I walked out of my room in my underwear and ran into him in the hallway near the bathroom. He looked shocked, his pale face flamed, he averted his eyes. My mother gave me a brief lecture that night about proper garb outside one's room now that there were men in the house.

I read a lot that summer. The world of the novel began slowly to open itself to my imagination. I haunted the local public library, spent hours searching its shelves. I found I was too bored by the books in the children's division and too young for the books in the adult division. I talked to my mother. She gave me her library card.

"Who is this book for?" the librarian, an elderly lady with spectacles and gray hair, asked me one day.

"My mother told me to take it out on her card."

She knew me well and looked at me for a long moment. "I am not supposed to give it to you," she said.

I said nothing.

She held the book open beneath the rubber stamp affixed to the end of her pencil. "This is a very serious work."

Still I said nothing.

"I always suggest to people that they owe it to such a work to invest in it between seventy-five and a hundred pages before they decide whether or not to go on reading it."

She stamped the book and handed it to me. I thanked her.

I brought it to the cottage and sat on the porch, and after a hundred pages was gone deep inside it and heard only distantly David's talmudic music, the wind and the waves, the news of the war on the kitchen radio, my new father calling out, "Hello! It's me!" as he came home from his day's work in Manhattan. He came out onto the porch, his hat tipped back on his head, his tie loose, and his shirt collar open. He patted David lightly on the shoulder, patted me on the head, looked at us for a moment, and said, "I thought school was over. Why are we in a beach house if all you do is read? Why doesn't your mother chase you out, for God's sake?" He smiled broadly and went inside.

He seemed a happy and relaxed man. Much of the stiffness had left him since his marriage to my mother. He was proud of his family, solicitous and soft-spoken, with a courtliness of manner that resembled somewhat the old-world habits of Jakob Daw: a slight bow when he met someone new; a way of listening seriously to all sides of a conversation; a moment of thought before responding to a question; a vague note of irony that at times crept into his words; a restraint even when all around him were loudly laughing. But when it came to ritual practice, his strictness with the Commandments brought an exactness to my life that was quite new. He insisted on the careful observance of the law: Shabbos began each Friday night at sundown and not a moment later; kosher meat was to be bought from a specific butcher and no other; the Havdoloh service at the end of the Shabbos could take place only from this moment on and no earlier; this or that act was permissible on Shabbos and festivals, and this or that was not. Sometimes he sat relaxed in an easy chair, one of his legs draped over an arm, and I saw in his sprawled form a ghostly reminder of my father. He read *The New York Times,* the *Wall Street Journal,* and a Yiddish newspaper. He read law journals, the *New Republic,* and a magazine having to do with government service. His newspapers and magazines were arranged in neat piles on a table in the living room near the bookcase that contained his law library. He was orderly and self-disciplined. He rose, prayed, ate, left for work—each act at a fixed time every weekday morning. On Friday afternoons he came home with flowers an hour before the start of Shabbos. Often on Sunday mornings he went shopping with my mother in a neighborhood grocery store run by an observant Jew. He did not read the Sunday comics or stories or novels, but was never disdainful toward those who did. He treated my mother with tenderness and respect. I liked him, my new father, Ezra Dinn, and was not sorry my mother had married again.

I had asked my mother, shortly before she remarried, what her new name would be.

"Dinn," she said.

"And my name?"

"Ilana Davita Dinn."

"Why?"

"That's the way it will be, Ilana."

"Not Chandal?"

"No."

"I don't want to lose Papa's name."

"Your new father will adopt you and you will have his name."

"What does adopt mean?"

She explained it to me. To take as one's own child. Papers and courts and signatures and—a new name. I found I could not reconcile myself to no longer carrying my father's name. I told myself I would do something about that one day.

In the library at Sea Gate I asked the librarian one day if she knew the meaning of the word Chandal. She knew my name had been Chandal and was now Dinn. She searched for it in the dictionary on her desk and could not find it.

"Perhaps it hasn't any meaning," she said. "Sometimes words and names refer to sounds and not to things or ideas."

I went to the shelves, found two more books by the author of the book I had read and returned, and brought them to the librarian. She stamped them and said, "I found your word. Chandal. I went to our largest dictionary. Not precisely that word, but the one closest to it."

She pointed to the huge dictionary she had brought over to her desk. I followed her finger and read, **"chandala:** an Indian of low caste: OUT-CAST; UNTOUCHABLE; esp.: the son of a Sudra by a Brahman woman."

"I don't understand what that means," I said.

She explained it to me.

"But Chandal can't mean that," I said.

"That is all I can tell you, Ilana. That is the closest to Chandal that I am able to find."

Chandala. Chandal.

I told my mother.

"No," she said. "It can't have any connection to that. How could it?"

It seemed strange not to know the meaning of your own name, even if it was a name you were no longer using.

"What does our name mean?" I asked my new father one Shabbos that August on our way back from the little synagogue where we prayed —the synagogue to which I had once followed David and his uncle. "Din means law in Hebrew, doesn't it?" I added.

He smiled. "I don't think it's connected to that, Ilana. Dinn is a town in southern Germany."

"What does it mean?"

"I don't know," he said.

One Sunday afternoon my mother and I went swimming together while David and his father sat on the porch studying Talmud. We came dripping out of the water and lightly toweled ourselves and lay on our blanket with our faces to the sun. I began to tell my mother of the dreams I had been having that summer.

"No more dreams about Baba Yaga?" she asked when I was done.

"No."

"Good-bye to Baba Yaga. I'm glad. Only dreams about birds falling into the ocean and a gray horse chasing you through the school and Jakob Daw coming to America and David jabbing you with his fountain pen. That's all?"

"Yes."

"How busy you are at night, Ilana." She raised herself on one elbow and gazed at me, squinting in the sunlight. Over her face seemed to come a sudden startling realization. "Your body has begun to change," she said very softly. "Perhaps soon you will begin to menstruate."

I sat up and looked at her and heard the beating of my heart. I knew that word from school. Menstruate. Unwell. Got your period.

"Come with me, Ilana. I want to show you something."

She took me to the wet sand along the edge of the sea. There she drew with her finger the outline of a female body. "Listen to me, darling. Let me explain this to you." And she gave me a dictionary lecture about the word menstruate, its origin and meaning, and a biology lecture on what would soon be happening inside my body. She went on for what seemed to me to be a very long time. I listened to her and heard also the thumping of my heart. "When it starts," my mother said, "you will have become biologically a woman. I'll show you how to take care of yourself."

She fell silent. I stared at the figure in the sand. The surf rolled in from the sea, licking at the drawing as it had once licked at my castles.

"Does it still happen to you, Mama?"

"Of course. It stops when you become pregnant."

I looked at her and saw the color rise in her cheeks. She shook her head with a smile. "No, darling, I am not pregnant. Shall we go back in for another swim? It's very hot today."

I marveled at my mother. She seemed so easily to have become once again an observant Jew. She still read the *New Masses*—for the fine writers it published. She remained a fervent advocate of the working class and an opponent, as she put it, of the greed and rot of capitalist exploiters. When she spoke of Stalinist communism her voice shook with anger and bitterness, with her sense of having been used and duped and betrayed. She had been brought up well by her mother and grandfather and was familiar with the details of those parts of the Commandments a woman needed to observe. She lit candles on Friday evenings and was scrupulous with regard to the laws of kashruth. Her household was neat, clean, orderly. She had two pasts now. On occasion I saw returning to her eyes the old dark brooding look. During her years with my father she had thought often about her religious past; now she reflected upon her Communist past. She seemed unable to bring together those two parts of herself. And that haunted her.

I realized, as we sat together week after week in the little synagogue in Sea Gate, that she never prayed. One Shabbos during the service I quietly asked her about that.

"A woman is not required to pray," she said.

"What do you mean?" All around us women were praying.

"A woman may pray if she wishes. But she is not required to pray. That's the law. Ask your father. I don't wish to pray. I prefer to read the Bible instead."

The women's section in that little synagogue was even more confining than the one in the yeshiva synagogue. A heavy muslin curtain had been drawn across the last few rows from wall to wall, forming a space that resembled a large cage. We could hear the service and see nothing. I found no holes or tears in that curtain. My new father was leading the service. I enjoyed hearing his deep baritone voice and wished I could see him.

Two days later he brought back with him from the city a letter from Jakob Daw. A brief note inside the envelope told us that someone had carried the letter from Marseilles to Dakar and had mailed it to us from Mexico.

We sat around the kitchen table in the cottage and waited as my mother read the letter. She read very slowly, then looked up.

"Is Uncle Jakob all right?" I asked.

"He's been in the hospital again."

"Can he leave Marseilles?"

"He's trying very hard."

One night soon after they were married I had heard my mother and new father talking about Jakob Daw. Now I imagined him in his flat in Marseilles. A small, dark, bug-ridden room on a narrow, dirty street.

"Papa, can't you get Uncle Jakob to America?"

My new father looked down at the table and slowly shook his head.

"The Fascists in the government won't give him a visa?"

"Ilana," my mother said.

"They're not Fascists," my new father said. "Don't throw that word around so easily, Ilana."

"Papa," David said quietly. "You can't do anything?"

"All the doors are closed. When I knock no one answers."

There was a brief silence. Through the open windows came the sounds of the ocean and the warm evening wind.

My mother stood up, folded the letter carefully, and put it into a pocket of her apron. "I'll wash my face and we'll have supper. All right? Whose turn is it to set the table?"

Later I walked alone on the beach, watching the eastern horizon slowly pale and darken in the aftermath of a lovely sunset. I walked along the edge of the sea and saw, farther down the beach, a man in rumpled trousers and a creased shirt. I came up to him and he turned to me with a sad half-smile and said, "You see what people will do to you when they do not like your stories?" I stared at him, my heart thundering. But of course he had not said that; all he had really said was, "It's a pretty night, ain't it?"

I had never seen him before and wondered who he was and how he had got through the guards onto the beach.

"You live here?" he asked in a very quiet voice. His face looked blurred in the fading light. He was thin and pale and had straight dark hair and dark glittering eyes.

"Yes. In that house."

"A pretty house. Would you like to take a walk with me?"

I looked at him.

"We could take a walk and I could buy you an ice cream. Would you like that?" His voice had risen slightly. "Wouldn't that be nice?"

"No," I said, and felt myself shiver.

"I could buy you a pretty doll. And we could see a nice movie. Wouldn't you like that? There's a Charlie Chaplin movie playing in Coney Island. That's not far. What do you say?"

I turned and walked quickly away from him up the beach toward the house. The wind blew suddenly hard and the ocean seemed very loud and my heart beat so fast I thought it would burst. Was he following me? On the dunes outside the cottage I turned and looked back. He was gone. Had I imagined it? For a long moment I felt a swooning sense of weakness, a blurring of lines between real and imagined worlds. The feeling was still with me as I climbed the stairs to the screened-in porch where David sat chanting a passage of Talmud.

Two days later my new father brought back with him a second letter from Jakob Daw. It had been mailed to an address in Casablanca, where the letter in its original envelope had been placed in a fresh envelope and mailed to an address in Rio de Janeiro. There the letter in its two envelopes had been put in a third envelope and mailed to our apartment.

The letter was addressed to me. I read it in the strong light of the late afternoon sun while sitting on the dunes and facing the sea and a warm east wind.

"Dear Ilana Davita. Are you well? I am quite ill. I lie in bed and remember the stories I told you. Do you remember them? I am never certain what happens to my stories. Your new father—your mother's letter reached me after a few weeks of wandering—is a good man. I thought to cross Spain to Lisbon and go from there to South America. But it appears that I am too ill. The doctors here do not look directly into my eyes when they speak to me. Do you wear your glasses when you read and write? Always remember to do that so you can see the world sharply and truthfully. Truth is often very painful, but it alone will save us. How is our little bird? Does it still nest peacefully in our harp? Ilana Davita, sooner or later birds grow weary and close their eyes. Some fall from the heavens while in flight, dropping like stones to the earth, others run into a mountain, a house, a tree. Still others are caught in the talons of a bird of prey. And still others simply fall asleep, and sleep on and on and on. Care for our bird and do not let it close its eyes. It is wrong to face this world with one's eyes closed, no matter how deep the weariness. It is a world of mountain-dwelling black horses. Keep your eyes open, wide open, Ilana Davita. Of what use is a bird with its eyes shut—save to be cooked and eaten? Are you on the beach this summer? I remember your castles as dreams in the sunlight, each with its own story. Now I think I will rest again. Try to remember the stories of your Uncle Jakob."

In the kitchen my mother and new father were talking quietly together. David was somewhere in the cottage. I walked along the dunes, holding the letter in my hands and listening to it jerk and snap in the wind as if it were alive.

Later I showed the letter to my mother. She read it and began to cry. I let David and my new father read it.

"I admire that man," my new father said. "But he should have let me fight for him. He might still be here."

My mother said nothing.

That evening I walked on the beach for a long time. At a distant jetty I saw a solitary figure standing barefoot in the surf, gazing out across the sea. He wore baggy trousers and a long-sleeved shirt. Gulls wheeled overhead in wide circles, screaming. I saw the man begin to walk slowly into the surf. I watched as the water lapped at his knees and thighs. Waves broke against him. And then, as I watched, he disappeared: the bobbing light that was his face winked out, vanished. I stood very still, looking for the man, but saw no one. I ran back to the cottage and told my parents what I had seen.

My mother stood at the sink, staring at me. My father called the police.

I walked with my father across the beach to the edge of the surf where I had seen the man enter the water. The waves rolled and crashed in the hot wind.

Two policemen came across the sand, burly men, walking steadily and deliberately toward me and my father.

One of them said, "You the party that called?"

"Yes," said my father.

The other took out a pad and asked for my father's name.

"My daughter saw it happen."

"What's your name?"

"Ilana Davita Dinn."

He wanted to know my age and where I lived. He wanted to know what I had seen and if I could describe the man. He put away his pad.

The four of us stood there, staring out at the sea.

"We'll call it in," one of the policemen said.

They walked off, going back across the sand to the street where they had left their car.

My father and I stood there a moment longer.

"Was that what he really looked like?" my father asked.

"Yes."

"You're sure?"

"Yes."

He sighed. "All right. Let's go back. It's late."

My mother said to me later that night, "Are you well, Ilana?" She put her hand on my forehead. "You're running a fever."

I lay in bed gazing up at the ceiling and wishing I had not left the door harp in the apartment.

I was in bed four days. David came into my room on the morning of the first day and stood at the foot of the bed. He looked shy and would not gaze at me directly.

"How are you feeling, Ilana?"

"Sick. I wish I could read, but my eyes hurt."

"Did the man on the beach really look like that?"

"Yes."

"They haven't found anybody yet. They're looking as far as Brighton."

I said nothing.

"Please get well soon, Ilana."

He went quietly from the room.

I lay in my bed and watched dust motes dancing and whirling in the beams of light from the diminished sun that daily witnessed the blood of Europe. I fell asleep and dreamed of sand castles on the beach.

We returned to the apartment at the end of August. Two months later, a few days after Simchas Torah, the festival in which men dance joyously with scrolls of the Torah to mark the end of the annual Torah reading cycle, we received word that Jakob Daw was dead.

The news reached us in a strange way. From the hospital in Marseilles where he died of pneumonia it made the brief trip to a local newspaper, then the longer journey to Paris by an underground courier, and then to London by illegal radio. In London it was picked up by the wire services. Aunt Sarah heard it on an early morning news broadcast as she was preparing herself for her daily trek from Newton Centre to

Boston. She called my mother. She was so sorry, she said. So deeply sorry.

Sorry about what? my mother asked.

Hadn't my mother heard the news?

What news?

And she told her.

We were all in the kitchen having breakfast. The phone stood on a polished dark-wood stand in the hallway between the kitchen and my parents' bedroom. We heard clearly my mother's gasp. My father rose quickly from his chair and went from the kitchen.

I heard them talking in the hallway about Jakob Daw and heard myself say to David, "Uncle Jakob is dead." A tremor went through me. I looked at my hands. They were shaking.

My mother came back into the kitchen, her arm supported by my father, and sat down. Her face was waxen.

"Shall I get you a cup of coffee, Channah?"

"Please." Her voice trembled.

"Is it Uncle Jakob?" I asked. "Is Uncle Jakob dead?"

"Yes," my father said. "Your Aunt Sarah heard it on the radio."

"Blessed is the righteous Judge," David said in Hebrew.

"Shall I turn it on?" I asked.

"Please," my mother said. Her voice still trembled and she was taking small deep breaths.

I switched on the radio. My father brought over a cup of coffee and put it on the table in front of my mother.

We sat there listening to the news of the war in Europe and heard nothing about Jakob Daw.

My father turned off the radio.

"Maybe it was a mistake," I said.

"I think you and David should start your day," my mother said. "You have school and I don't want you to be late."

On the way out of my room I whispered to the two little birds in my harp, "Uncle Jakob may be dead. Don't close your eyes. We have to keep our eyes open."

It was not a mistake. His obituary, as well as articles about him, appeared in all the afternoon newspapers. We heard about it again on the evening news. My mother wept. My father comforted her. They were together in their room a long time.

Two days later my mother began to go to the very early morning service in our synagogue to say Kaddish for Jakob Daw.

There had been a brief discussion over the supper table about my mother reciting Kaddish for Jakob Daw. We were done eating and were sitting at the table, listening to the news: German aircraft bombing England; 16 million American men registered for the draft; Jews beginning to be deported from Alsace-Lorraine and the Rhineland; Hitler and Franco meeting at the French town of Hendaye on the Spanish border. After the news my mother turned off the radio and announced that for the next eleven months she intended to get up very early in the morning to go to synagogue to say Kaddish for Jakob Daw, and did we think we could make our own breakfasts?

We all looked at her in a long moment of silence.

"Why?" my father asked quietly.

"No one else will say it."

"Ask one of the men to do it."

"I want to say it."

"You're not part of his family, Channah. You were not related to him."

"I want to say it anyway."

"But you don't have to. You shouldn't. It falls into the category of a Commandment that doesn't need to be performed. It has no meaning in the eyes of God."

"It has meaning in my eyes, Ezra."

David and I sat quietly, glancing at one another.

"A woman is not supposed to say Kaddish," my father said very quietly to my mother. "You'll upset the shul. Especially if you go to the daily minyan."

"Should I go to a Conservative or Reform synagogue?"

He gave that no consideration at all and shook his head.

"Then I'll go to our shul."

He shrugged. "All right. It will be awkward. There will be a fuss about it, that I can promise you. But if that's what you want, go ahead. We'll manage with breakfast. This family will manage, Channah. If that's what you really want."

She would leave the apartment before David and I woke and return after David and I had left for school. Weeks went by that way. I saw my mother only at night. The weather turned cold. Leaves fell. Roosevelt was elected president for a third term. Winter came and with it snow and sleet. Still my mother continued to leave the apartment every weekday early in the morning for the morning service and before sunset for the afternoon and evening service. She said Kaddish on Shabbos as well, and all around her women responded.

On our way back from the synagogue one Shabbos I asked her why she was saying Kaddish for Jakob Daw.

"I was really a child when I met him," she said. "He opened my eyes to the world. I owe him a great deal. And I loved him. Are those enough reasons, Ilana?"

It became part of our lives, my mother reciting Kaddish for the memory of Jakob Daw.

My father would prepare breakfast; David and I would help. "Stubborn woman, your mother," he would say often in his courteous and respectful way. "She was stubborn when I knew her twenty years ago and she's just as stubborn today." David and I would leave for school, sometimes together, sometimes separately. Then my father would leave for his office, most often by subway, at times taking the car.

In a corridor in the school one day I overheard some talk, and on a cold gray morning soon afterward I left the house early and followed my mother to the synagogue. An icy wind blew along the parkway. The building seemed to be empty; it was more than an hour before the start of school. The front double door yielded to my push. My footsteps echoed in the empty hallway. I opened the door to the large room that was the synagogue and stopped. The room was empty.

I stood in the doorway and stared into the room. The ninon curtain was gone. Rows of neatly arranged empty chairs filled the room. The ark with its Torah scrolls stood unseen behind a high plywood wall, which enabled the room to be used for secular purposes, such as school assemblies, a rehearsal hall, and graduation ceremonies. I had forgotten for the moment that the room was not used as a synagogue on school days.

Where was my mother?

I came back out into the central hallway and listened. The building was silent. I walked up and down the floors and corridors of the school, listening. I heard nothing. Then I went quickly downstairs to the basement, pushed open a heavy metal door, and heard immediately the murmur of chanted prayers.

Adjacent to the furnace room was a small room, its door open. About a dozen men sat in wooden folding chairs, praying. This was the weekday minyan, which met early so as to enable the men to get to their jobs on time. At the lectern stood a roundish man whom I immediately recognized as Mr. Helfman. A small ark stood against the wall that faced the lectern. The room was painted a pale green and lit by a small dusty ceiling fixture. The air smelled of furnace heat and damp earth. In a dark corner rested what looked like a slanting bamboo wall. I glanced quickly around and did not see my mother.

I went back along the corridor to the metal door. Then I stopped and stood still a moment and turned and went back to the room, a queer pounding in my chest. Inside the room I went silently behind the last row of chairs and peered behind the bamboo wall. There, on a single chair, her back to the wall, sat my mother, a prayerbook in her hands. She wore a dark blue beret and a dark blue woolen dress. Her coat was draped over the back of the chair. There was little light and she was bent over the prayerbook.

I stood very still, staring at her.

Then she sensed my presence and glanced up. A look of astonishment filled her eyes. "Ilana?" she whispered. "What's wrong?"

"Mama? Why are—?"

I heard people rising from their chairs. My mother rose and stood quietly as one of the closing prayers of the service was said. Mr. Helfman repeated the last words of the prayer. A number of the men began to recite the Kaddish. My mother stood behind the bamboo wall and said the Kaddish in a clear, steady voice that was audible throughout the small room. She said it once more in that same clear, steady voice before the service came to an end.

My mother put the prayerbook on the chair and picked up her coat. I followed her through the room. A few of the men nodded at her; most remained impassive; one looked visibly annoyed.

Mr. Helfman said, "Good morning, Ilana. Aren't you up early? Is everything all right?"

I nodded, feeling my face hot and my heart pounding.

In the corridor I said, "Mama, why are you sitting like that?"

"It's all right, darling. They didn't want to build a wall just for me. Someone found that piece of bamboo."

"It's like being in a prison."

"What else can I do? They didn't want me there at all. With the bamboo wall they can have their service, as long as I stay out of sight."

I said to my father that night, "Is that the law, Papa?"

"Yes, Ilana. That's the law."

"I think the law isn't decent."

He gave me a patient smile. "Let me explain something to you, Ilana.

We pray separately as a group. If there were no separation between men and women, the men would not be able to hold a service. And then no one would be able to say Kaddish. Women don't have to pray because they're involved in family responsibilities. It's your mother's choice, Ilana. The men were very decent to put up the bamboo. That solved the problem and enables your mother to say Kaddish."

I raised the issue in my Hebrew class. The teacher, Mr. Margolis, was tall, middle-aged, clean-shaven, with fleshy cheeks and a paunch. He wore a dark suit and tie. Across his vest, in two roller coaster loops from pocket to button to pocket, rode the gleaming chain of his pocket watch, which he regularly pulled out, snapped open, consulted, and put back. On his thick dark hair was a tall dark skullcap. He listened to me patiently and said, "What do you want them to do, Ilana? Let your mother sit in the same room with the men?"

I nodded.

A murmur rose from my classmates. Shocked eyes stared at me. Ruthie, three seats to my right, threw me a startled look.

"That's the way all the Reformers and the Conservatives sit," Mr. Margolis said sternly. "Such a synagogue is not a holy place, and we may not pray in it. It is a Christianized synagogue. Do you want us to become like the Conservatives and the Reformed?"

It was not a question that required an answer. I sat very still at my desk and said nothing. How they all stared at me! My heart pounded and my throat was dry.

At the end of the class he asked me to stay behind for a moment. I came up to his desk as the others were filing out for the afternoon recess in the yard, some of them glancing at me pityingly. When we were alone, he said, "I tell you this directly, Ilana. You are probably my best student. Don't cause trouble in class. You will set a bad example for the others."

I stood in front of his desk, frightened.

"Tell me, who is your mother saying Kaddish for?"

"Jakob Daw."

"How were they related?"

"They were good friends."

"They were not related?"

"No."

He looked at me out of narrow eyes. "Where did your mother know him?"

"In Europe. In Vienna. They went to school together. And he was in America awhile."

"Ah, yes. Now I remember. Jakob Daw. The writer who was deported."

"Yes."

"You knew him too?"

"He was like an uncle to me. I loved him."

Mr. Margolis was silent a long moment, looking at me intently. Then he lightly cleared his throat and said, "Listen to me, Ilana. Everywhere in the world, wherever you go, there are rules and laws. If we did not have rules and laws there would be anarchy. Do you know what anarchy is? This school has rules and laws. No one here forces you to come to this school. But once you do come, you must obey the rules and the laws. You are a very good student, but your head will not help you if you do not understand the rules and the laws. In a year and a half you will graduate. There are awards and prizes. Keep up your good work and we will all be proud of you. Do I make myself clear? Good. Very good. Now you can go and join your friends."

I had learned a strange lesson: walls are laws to some people, and laws are walls to others.

I went out of the room and did not again talk to anyone in that school about the cage in which my mother daily sat to say Kaddish for Jakob Daw.

We were studying the Book of Genesis, the stories of the Patriarchs and Matriarchs. That was the winter of early 1941, when German planes were daily bombing England, and Franklin D. Roosevelt was inaugurated for his third term as President of the United States.

I loved the stories in Genesis. Mr. Margolis taught slowly and with some impatience. We were studying the Hebrew text along with the commentary of Rashi, a great French rabbi who lived in the period of the First Crusade. Always I got myself ready for class by studying the text in advance, even when Mr. Margolis did not assign it. I had learned that method of study from David, who always prepared in advance whatever page of Talmud would be studied next by his class.

We were in the twelfth chapter of Genesis. God tells Abraham— Abram was his name at the time—to leave his country and the place of his birth and his father's house for a distant land. Abraham journeys with his household to the land of Canaan. There he travels as far as a site called Shechem. And the text says, "The Canaanites were then in the land."

Mr. Margolis wanted to know if there was any problem in that verse with the Hebrew word *oz*, then.

He stood behind his desk, tall and dark, one finger in a pocket of his vest, waiting.

No one said anything.

Eyes stared at the Hebrew word. Who paid attention to a small word like that? *Oz*. Then. "The Canaanites were then in the land." I had gone over the text before class but had not thought to stop on the meaning of that word.

Then. At that time. That's what it meant. At the time when Abraham came to Shechem there were Canaanites in the land. But why did we have to be told that? Obviously there were Canaanites in the land. It was called the land of Canaan.

"I want you to think about it," Mr. Margolis said.

I raised my hand.

"Ilana."

"Rashi says the Canaanites were conquering the land from the children of Shem."

"Very good, Ilana."

"But if the Canaanites were conquering the land from the children of Shem, why was it called the land of Canaan?"

He stood tall and dark behind his desk, fingering his pocket watch, and looked at me. "What should it have been called, Ilana?"

"The land of Shem."

"The land of Shem." He looked down at the open Bible on his desk and scanned the Rashi. The top of his skullcap formed a dark shiny satin moon as it caught and reflected the winter sunlight that came through the windows. Steam hissed softly in the silver-painted radiators. There were cracks in the pale green walls and flaking paint on the white ceiling. The room was overheated. *Oz*. Then. What could that little word mean? Clearly the then of the story was the time of Abraham. But, again, why did we have to be reminded that there were Canaanites in the land of Canaan? Perhaps—perhaps—

Something hung elusively on the edge of thought, but I could not grasp it and it was gone.

Mr. Margolis looked up from the Bible on his desk and gave the class a thin smile. "Ilana asks a good question. Why was it not called the land of Shem if, according to Rashi, the Canaanites were not actually living there but were conquering it?"

Along the periphery of my vision I saw Ruthie raise her hand.

"Ruth?"

"Maybe the Canaanites were living in it a long time already and were still trying to conquer the rest of it."

Mr. Margolis's thin smile widened. "Very good, Ruth. Very good. The Canaanites had no doubt been living in it a long time already. Like America. It was called America even while Americans were still conquering the west. Very good, Ruthie."

Ruthie, her face suddenly a shade of high color that accentuated her freckles, looked astonished at having stumbled upon the answer wanted by Mr. Margolis.

I talked about the verse during supper with my father, and he said Ruthie's explanation made sense to him. David said there couldn't be any other explanation. My mother sat at the table looking very tired and said nothing. Her early risings to get to the synagogue, her half-days at work, her journeys to the synagogue for the afternoon and evening service—all had put her in a state of permanent fatigue.

Later I lay in my bed reading a novel my mother had taken out for me from the Brooklyn Public Library on Eastern Parkway. On the other side of the hallway, David was softly studying Talmud in his room, the chanting reaching me through the walls that separated us. I thought again of the word and looked up from the novel at the harp that hung on the back of the door. It lay in the shadows cast by the bed lamp. Suppose Jakob Daw had used that word in a sentence in one of his stories. What would it mean? I tried to imagine it in his story about the bird who went wandering through the world in search of the source of the world's music. Suppose it left its land, its flock, its nest, and found a land of tall hills and fertile valleys. And suppose Jakob Daw had then said, There were Canaanites then in the land. What would that mean? It would mean—it would mean that at the time Jakob Daw was telling me the story—or was writing the story—there weren't any Canaanites in the land. And if it was important for my understanding of the story that I know of the existence of Canaanites in the past, he would have to remind me of it. And he would do that by saying or writing, There were Canaanites *then* in the land.

What was that? Had a wooden ball lifted of itself and fallen upon a string of the harp? Had the birds stirred? I was in a dream, of course. I had drifted off to sleep for a moment and had been in a dream. I put the book on the night table, removed my glasses, and snapped off the light.

The last thing I thought I heard as I slid into sleep was the faint singing of the harp blending with the quiet music of the Talmud that came from David's room.

The next day I raised my hand in Mr. Margolis's class and waited to be called.

"Yes, Ilana."

"May I go back to yesterday and give another explanation of *oz?*"

"Of course."

We had been on a difficult verse. I could sense the class relaxing all around me. My mouth was dry, my heart beat loudly.

"*Oz* can mean that at the time this story was written down, there were no longer any Canaanites in the land; and the writer of the story is reminding the reader that at the time the story took place there *were* Canaanites, because Canaanites are important to the story."

Mr. Margolis stood very still behind his desk, gazing at me. He asked me to repeat my explanation.

I repeated it, slowly, my heart thumping wildly. Why was he looking at me like that?

He said, solemnly, "You mean to say, Ilana, that a writer wrote this story?"

"Yes."

"And who was this writer?"

"I don't know."

"You don't know. And when did he write this story?"

"When there were no longer any Canaanites in the land."

"There were always Canaanites in the land, Ilana."

"When there were no longer any Canaanites near Shechem."

The room was strangely hushed, as if all had long ceased breathing.

"Ilana," Mr. Margolis said, after a pause that seemed endless, "we do not study the Torah this way here."

I sat very still, my heart thundering.

"God wrote the Torah," Mr. Margolis said. "Not a writer. God. It's the holy word of God. Do you understand?"

I had never seen him so dark and stern. He seemed to be growing in darkness before my eyes.

"If people wrote the Torah, why should we bother with it? Why should we sacrifice ourselves for it? Why should we read it in shul every Shabbos and yom-tov? Why should we be willing to die for it? God spoke every single word of the Torah to Moses, who wrote it all down, every word. Even his own death Moses described, with tears running down his face."

He paused for a moment and took a breath, then went on. "The Torah is not stories, Ilana. The Torah is not a piece of make-believe. It is not like Shakespeare or like—what is his name?—James Joyce or like your good friend Jakob Daw. The Torah is God's stories. God's! The truth of God. The eternal truth given to us by the Master of the Universe. Rashi has the correct understanding of the verse. And that is the way we will learn it here. I want you to think about that, Ilana. I want you to remember that. All right? Very good. Now let us continue reading."

I sat in a pall of confusion and shame and heard nothing of what went on for all the rest of the day in that class.

My father had an English commentary in his library in the living room. I went to it that evening after supper. The commentary was by a modern English rabbi named J. H. Hertz. I found the verse and read the commentary:

> *the Canaanite was then in the land*—i.e., was already in the land. 'Before the age of Abraham, the Canaanites had already settled in the lowlands of Palestine—Canaan, be it noted, signified Lowlands' (Sayce). The interpretation of this verse as meaning that the Canaanites were *at that time* in the land, but were no longer so at the time when Genesis was written (an interpretation which misled even Ibn Ezra), is quite impossible. The Canaanites formed part of the population down to the days of the later kings.

I read it again.

Ibn Ezra, I knew, was one of the greatest of the Jewish commentators of the Middle Ages. He had been born in Spain and wandered throughout Europe. I had ventured a guess—and had come up with Ibn Ezra's answer! I wondered how Ibn Ezra would have responded to Mr. Margolis's questions. Would Ibn Ezra have sacrificed himself for the Torah? I couldn't understand why Mr. Margolis seemed fearful of there being more than one way to understand the meaning of the Torah. Was he afraid he would lose control over our thinking? Why did he need to control the way we thought? Did he believe that God wrote stories with only one kind of meaning? It seemed to me that a story that had only one kind of meaning was not very interesting or worth remembering for too long.

The harp sounded muted that evening as I came into my room and sat down at my desk to my homework. I looked at it, wondering if something was wrong with its strings. Across the hallway from me David softly sang his talmudic music. In the living room my parents were listening to a symphony on the phonograph. Outside an icy wind moaned in the trees, rustling bare branches in a sad music of its own.

Winter slipped away. The days grew warm. Trees began to bud. Mr. Helfman planted his garden.

That spring of 1941 was a dream time for me, an idyll, the loveliest time of my young life. I felt untouched by Europe and its war, freed of the dark burden of politics and history. My body was changing. There were long, shy, intimate conversations with girls in my class about boys, menstruation, brassiere sizes, clothing styles. Some of the girls seemed ashamed of their growing breasts. Boys began to look at me in awkward masculine ways.

My father marveled at my growing. "You're a beauty," he kept saying. "Isn't she a beauty, Channah?" And from time to time, in the kitchen or the living room, I would feel David's eyes upon me, and something would begin to turn warm inside me, and I would feel it moving slowly between my legs, a warm and gentle throbbing, and I would turn my eyes to David and see him blush scarlet and turn away. And the image of my mother naked in her bedroom would return to me, and I would see her standing before the mirror, rubbing the hard nipples of her breasts and whispering, "Michael? Michael?" She slept now with my new father. What was it like to have slept in the same bed for years with my father and now to sleep with my new father? I could not bring it into my imagination.

My mother continued going to the synagogue twice a day to say Kaddish for Jakob Daw. She kept on with her half-time job at the social work agency. With the coming of the warm weather she seemed to gather strength. Two or three of the acquaintances she had made in the synagogue became her friends and discovered that she knew her way through certain rabbinic texts which she had been taught by her grandfather. They would meet once a week on Sunday evenings in our living room and study together. I would hear the music of their voices from my room. My father would retire to the kitchen with the Sunday *Times* or to his desk in the bedroom where he did some of his law work. Only women came to those study sessions, three or four of them, week after week, from late winter and into the early weeks of summer.

From my room I would hear, too, David chanting talmudic texts and also the Torah portion he was learning for his bar mitzvah in June. His graduation, too, would be in June. He had been told at the start of the year that he might qualify for the Akiva Award if he maintained his English grades, but he seemed indifferent to the award and was concentrating all his energies on Talmud. He wanted the Talmud prize, the award that would gain him automatic entry into the highest and best talmudic academies of learning. All kinds of music filled our apartment that spring.

There were other kinds of meetings in our apartment that spring, meetings conducted by my father. During those meetings my mother would sit in the kitchen, reading, or go into the bedroom and work at the desk. She was trying to complete her translation of the stories Jakob Daw had written when he had stayed with us. I would sit in my room and listen to those meetings with my father. New words flew through the air like strange birds: controlling votes; Agudah people; fanatics; Hungarians. And a harsh-sounding guttural word that I could not pronounce and did not know how to spell. I would imagine other meetings, in cold apartments, and other words that had flown about—and it seemed as if it all had happened in a distant time and had been witnessed by someone other than a girl named Ilana Davita Dinn. And perhaps it had. Perhaps the girl who had listened to those distant words had been someone named Ilana Davita Chandal. Was I two people? What connected me to my past? Memories? Save for certain sharp images, they seemed to be fading. Stories? Yes, stories. I still remembered the stories. Even though I didn't understand them. I remembered. A bird and music and a gray horse. And the girl on the slope along the river who sold her ground-up flowers in the nearby village. And, yes, even Baba Yaga. What stories had Jakob Daw written while living with us? I would have to ask my mother about that one day.

Ruthie came over to me in school one morning and told me she had overheard her father telling her mother that David was receiving the Talmud prize. But I was not to tell him, she said. We sat in class, glancing repeatedly at each other and filled with our secret, and Mr. Margolis wanted to know what we were smiling about so much and why weren't our eyes in the book.

David told us the news at the kitchen table that evening.

"That's my boy!" my father said, and thumped him on the back.

"I'm so proud," my mother said.

"Congratulations," I said.

David smiled shyly, his face crimson.

He became a bar mitzvah on a Shabbos morning at the end of the second week of June. My parents had very little family in America—on my father's side, the Helfmans, some cousins, and his late wife's brother's family; on my mother's side, no one—and so almost everyone in the synagogue that morning was a member of the school and synagogue community to which we belonged. There were also present lawyers and social workers who knew my parents at their jobs. My mother and I sat up front in places of honor reserved for female relations of the bar mitzvah.

David chanted the morning service in a voice that was changing timbre and growing deep. I listened to the music of the service. He read the Torah, slowly, carefully, the melody flowing across the curtained wall. I saw him dimly through the curtain; he was standing at the podium in his dark suit and tie and dark skullcap and prayer shawl, swaying slowly back and forth as he chanted the service. My mother sat very still, her eyes on the Bible in her hands. She looked lovely in a pale yellow dress and a white beret, her face smooth and high with color. We sat together, listening to David. I wished I could see him clearly. I wished I could watch clearly his eyes and his lips and the movements of his body. I wished I could be near him when he finished. Some minutes later he completed the final blessing and was deluged by a cascade of candies. There were cries of "Mazol tov! Mazol tov!" I saw dimly through the curtain my father embracing David. Around us, women shook my mother's hand. Then I heard my father's voice. He had stepped to the podium and had begun the second portion of the service.

A few minutes later David stood before the congregation and began a lengthy talk based on the Torah reading. He talked about the future of Yiddishkeit in America, about the need to build more yeshivas, about the importance of the law in the life of the Jew. He quoted repeatedly from the Talmud. He thanked his father. He thanked his mother, of blessed memory. He thanked my mother. He even thanked me for being a kind sister, and I felt my face go hot. He thanked his teachers. He uttered a prayer for a speedy end to the war and for the coming of the Messiah. It was an involved talk and I remember the music of his voice —strong and clear and shading into the deep baritone he would one day have. How I wished I could see him clearly!

He was done. A loud murmur of approval filled the room. People seemed awed. My mother sat very quietly, her head high. And then I saw her nod slowly to herself. She was looking off into a corner of the synagogue, where no one sat, where there was only the juncture of floor and walls—and nodding slowly and faintly to herself. Her face was serene and there was a light in her eyes. I had the feeling she was telling herself she had made the right choice for her life and was now finally content.

My mother rose to her feet three times to say Kaddish. She was the only one in the women's section to do that. A few of the women responded in the appropriate places. Most were silent, impassive.

Afterward there was the crowd outside in front of the school, the tumult of congratulations, the exhilaration of successful achievement. David was thumped and pounded and congratulated. His face was flushed; he seemed in a state of astonished disbelief over having accomplished it all so successfully and being forever done with his childhood. I looked at him as he stood surrounded by his classmates and felt for the first time the gnawing touch of envy. Nothing like that for me when I'd leave my childhood. All I had to look forward to was menstruating every month, bleeding and sanitary napkins and discomfort.

David was graduated the following day. The Akiva Award went to an eighth-grader named Joshua Langner. I had seen pictures of him in the newspapers, a silent and sullen boy who was reputed to possess a photographic memory. He delivered a boring talk in a low and barely audible voice.

David's name was announced. He rose to the podium to receive the Talmud prize. Loud applause followed. The winner of the Akiva Award seemed to have been forgotten. David was the center of a joyous communal festival. All seemed to sense that his future achievements in Talmud would reflect upon them, their school, their synagogue, their small Torah world.

That night I was unable to sleep. Images of the day crowded my eyes. I lay awake and listened to the apartment settle into the deep silence of the night. Still I could not sleep. I got out of bed and turned on my desk lamp and stood squinting in the light. There was the picture of the beach on the wall and there was the harp on the door. Carefully, I opened the door and stood in the hallway, listening. The harp sang briefly and grew still.

The apartment was dark and silent.

I went quietly to the living room, snapped on a table lamp, and took down from a bookshelf the first volume of my father's *Jewish Encyclopedia*. It was a large book, bound in thick dark red buckram and very heavy. I turned off the lamp and went back to my room.

I put the volume on my desk and sat in my chair. I had on only a nightgown, but the air was warm and I did not feel chilled. An odd throbbing sensation filled my throat. I opened the book and began to search through it for the name Akiva.

It was not there.

I thought there might be a different spelling of the name; that happened often when Hebrew words were spelled out in English.

I found the name Akiba. There were ten entries under that name. I did not know what to do.

I began to read each of the entries.

The first was about a medieval talmudist and mystic named Akiba Baer ben Yosef. The next three were references to other entries. The fifth was about someone called Akiba ben Joseph. I read the first paragraph and knew I had found the name I was seeking.

He had been born about the year 50 of the common era and had died a martyr about the year 132. The article called him the father of rabbinical Judaism. It said that he marked out a path for rabbinical Judaism for almost two thousand years.

The second paragraph was more difficult to read than the first. Akiba was an ignorant shepherd, it said, and began to study when he was forty years old. I read that again. Forty years old.

The article was difficult to read. But certain words and phrases leaped out from the densely clustered language and small print: Akiba's political followers; numerous journeys; modesty; kindness toward the sick and needy; moral worthiness; could not be cowed by the greatest. Quickly the article became highly technical, and I could not read on. I skipped to the end and saw a section titled In Legend. I read a story about the sudden change in his life from shepherd to student: He noticed a stone at a well that had been hollowed out by drippings from the buckets, and said, "If these drippings can, by continuous action, penetrate this solid stone, how much more can the persistent word of God penetrate the pliant, fleshly human heart, if that word but be presented with patient insistency." I read that he owed everything to his wife, who was the daughter of a wealthy and respected man and who married him on condition that he devote himself to study. When her father discovered the marriage, he drove his daughter from his house. They lived in terrible poverty. She had to sell her hair to enable him to continue his studies. He spent twenty-four years away from her, studying, and returned a great and famous scholar, escorted by 24,000 disciples. When his poorly clad wife was about to embrace him, some of his students, not knowing who she was, tried to restrain her. He said to them, "Let her alone; for what I am, and for what we are, to this noble woman the thanks are due." I read that his favorite saying was, "Whatever God does, He does for the best," and that when someone asked him, "Why has God not made man just as He wanted him to be?" he answered, "For the very reason that the duty of man is to perfect himself."

I began to read a section titled Akiba and the Dead, and fell asleep over the book. I woke hours later and for a long and fearful moment did not know where I was. The air felt cool. I went out of the room with the volume and returned it to its place in the living room bookcase. I climbed into my bed and lay awake in the darkness, thinking of Rabbi Akiba.

The following week Germany invaded Russia.

"I hope they destroy each other," my mother said as we sat in the kitchen, listening to the radio. "I hope they eat each other alive."

Hot darkly joyous vengeance lay upon her face and in her eyes.

"But what if Hitler wins?" David asked.

"No one can defeat Russia," my father said somberly. "Hitler has just lost the war. But millions will die before it's over."

We spent the summer in the red-brick house in Sea Gate. Every morning and evening my mother walked to the little synagogue to say Kaddish for Jakob Daw. I swam and went about with young people my age and took long walks on the beach and the Coney Island boardwalk. I read a great deal—short stories and novels and a book I found in the Sea Gate library on Rabbi Akiva.

We returned to the city in the first week of September. David began traveling daily to a prestigious yeshiva high school on the Lower East Side of Manhattan, where there was a talmudist who had received a law degree from Columbia University and with whom his father wanted him to study.

I entered eighth grade.

In the early fall the Kaddish period for Jakob Daw ended. I came into the kitchen one morning—and there was my mother, preparing breakfast. Our family returned to its normal state.

Some weeks later my mother told us that she was pregnant. She announced it at the kitchen table during supper. "I would like to tell all of you that the woman of this household is expecting a baby early next summer."

My father, normally reserved, coughed, put down his knife and fork, stared at her, and nearly burst into tears. He was overjoyed and seemed not to know what to say. Never demonstrative in his affections toward my mother when the children were around, he now embraced her and gave her a long kiss. He opened a bottle of wine and we drank to life. He could not contain his joy. My mother sat quietly, smiling and serene.

David and I glanced at each other; his cheeks colored slightly.

I told Ruthie about it in school the next day. She whooped with joy and immediately went and told her father, who was now teaching eighth grade and was our Hebrew teacher as well as the head of the Hebrew Department. He smiled at me when we trooped back into class after the recess and mouthed at me the words mazol tov.

Mrs. Helfman came upstairs that evening and visited with my mother awhile in the kitchen. From my room I heard them talking quietly and laughing. Later there was a meeting in the living room: my father and some people from the synagogue. I heard strange words again, and voices raised in anger.

The harp lay still on my door. Over my bed the stallions galloped in silence across the red-sand beach.

On occasion my parents would go out in the evenings to the theater or the movies and David and I would be alone. One night he tapped on my door and came inside, leaving the door open behind him. I looked up from my books. The balls of the harp danced softly upon the taut strings.

"Am I disturbing you?" he asked. "Are you still studying? It's so late."

I told him to come in and sit down.

He advanced hesitantly into the room and sat in the chair next to my bed. His eyes were narrow, tired. He seemed in an odd trancelike mood.

"I need to talk to you about something," he said.

I sat at my desk and waited.

"About—girls," he said.

I looked at him. He was very pale. He spent about an hour each weekday morning on the crowded subway. Then school all day. Then about an hour on the crowded subway home. Then homework. He looked worn.

"I have dreams," he said. "About girls. Do you ever have dreams about boys?"

"Sometimes."

"I see them," he said, then stopped. "They're—" He stopped again. Then he said, "Do you like me, Ilana?"

"Of course I like you. You're my brother."

"No I'm not."

"What do you mean?"

"I'm not your brother. I'm your stepbrother. There's a difference."

"I don't think about the difference."

"You should."

"Why?"

"Because—" He stopped again and passed a hand over his eyes. His face was set with determination. "I dream about you a lot, Ilana. Is that terrible?" He looked ashamed.

"No. Why should it be terrible?"

"It's a sin to have dreams like that."

I didn't understand what he meant.

"Do you dream about me?" he asked.

"Sure. Sometimes."

"What do you dream?"

"I can't remember."

"Tell me."

"I really can't remember."

"Do you ever see me in your dreams without my—without my clothes?"

I stared at him. My heart moved inside me in a strange and frightening way. "No. I can't remember."

"I see you that way sometimes," he said. "You're very pretty. I'm proud you're my stepsister. I tell you that in my dreams. How proud I am that you're my stepsister."

I did not say anything.

"Are you angry at me?" he asked plaintively. "Please don't be angry at me."

"I'm not angry, David." My voice trembled. I kept my knees tightly together.

"Everyone thinks I'm a saint. Everyone thinks all I do all day and night is study study study."

I said nothing.

"I really like you, Ilana. I needed to tell someone about my dreams. Sometimes I think I'm going to explode."

"Can't you tell Papa?"

"No. I don't think so. Something inside me tells me I can't talk to Papa about this. Something inside me said you were the only one I could talk to."

"I won't tell anyone."

"Sometimes when I'm asleep I wake up in the middle of the night and —and—" He stopped. "It's a sin," he said. "It's against the Torah. But what can I do? I can't control it. What can I do?"

I sat at my desk looking down at my books and was very quiet. I wondered if he could hear the wild beating of my heart.

"Maybe I ought to go to my rosh yeshiva," he murmured, talking to himself. "But I'm afraid. I'm afraid he may throw me out of the yeshiva. There's no one to talk to, Ilana, if everyone thinks that you're a saint."

"You can talk to me, David."

"Can I kiss you?" he asked suddenly.

My heart lurched. I stared at him.

"On your cheek. Can I kiss you?"

I nodded. I thought my heart would tear itself apart. He came toward me and put his lips on my cheek. I felt his fear and his heat and his breath on my face. His lips were smooth and hot. He backed slowly away, his eyes strange and a little wild-looking.

"I'm glad you're my sister," he said very quietly. "I'm glad you let me talk to you."

He went slowly from the room, closing the door behind him.

The harp sang softly in the ensuing silence.

Later, after my parents returned and the house was dark, I heard David in his bed. I lay very still, listening. I felt the nipples of my breasts gently beneath my fingers, felt the slow throb of warmth between my legs. David sighed and was silent. I fell asleep and woke in the darkness to a muted cry. "Nothing!" came David's voice in Yiddish through the walls; I knew enough Yiddish by now to understand that.

"It's all worth nothing!" I lay awake a long time that night before I let myself go back to sleep.

One day that November my English teacher asked me to remain after class. She was a tall thin woman in her late thirties with short blond hair and blue eyes. She reminded me a little of Aunt Sarah. When we were alone in the classroom, she said to me, "Where did you get the idea for your story, Ilana?"

"From my imagination."

"It's a marvelous story. Have you actually seen the painting?"

"Yes."

"In a book?"

"No. In a gallery a few years ago."

"Here, in New York?"

"Yes."

"And the little girl going into the painting and running through the town during the bombing—you imagined that?"

"Yes."

"How marvelous! Does she ever find her father?"

"No. He got blown up by a bomb. But I don't want to put that into my story. I want her to keep trying to find him. Rabbi Akiva said it's our duty to help make the world more and more perfect. So it's better if you keep trying. Isn't it?"

"Yes," she said, after a moment. "I suppose it is."

"My father was killed in Guernica," I said.

Her mouth fell slightly open. "Your father?"

"My real father. Mr. Dinn is my stepfather."

"I didn't know."

"My real father was a journalist and was killed trying to save a nun. I think it's important not to forget. And stories help me to remember."

She looked at me intently and said nothing.

"Do you know any of the stories about Rabbi Akiva?"

She shook her head. It occurred to me that she might not be Jewish. Some of the teachers in the English Department were not Jewish.

"He was a scholar and a fighter and a good person. He believed in justice for poor people. His wife helped him to become a great man. The Romans killed him. They tore off his flesh with iron combs. I think of him sometimes when I think of my father."

She did not say anything.

"Yes," I said. "The story is all from my imagination. All except the part about the little girl's father running toward the river with the nun. That part happened. Will I get an A for the story?"

"Yes," she said. "Of course. It's a marvelous story."

"Thank you," I said.

I walked home alone in the fading afternoon sunlight through the sea of leaves that covered the streets.

In the winter the Japanese attacked Pearl Harbor and we were suddenly at war with Japan and Germany. Some of the men in the synagogue went away for a while, returned briefly in uniform, and then were gone again. Stars began to appear in the windows of our neighborhood. Ruthie told me that some of her cousins were in the army.

My father was asked by the government to do some special sort of work. He traveled to Washington and was away a few days. I asked my mother over supper, "What's Papa doing in Washington?"

"Something having to do with the war," my mother said.

"It's supposed to be a secret," David said.

"Papa is doing secret work for the government?"

"I don't know," my mother said. "We'll find out when he returns."

"Is it dangerous?" I asked.

"I don't know, Ilana."

"Do you want Papa to do it?"

"We're fighting a war against fascism," my mother said. "We'll do what we have to in order to win it quickly."

"But do you want Papa to do it?"

"Yes," my mother said.

My father returned from Washington. He refused to talk to David and me about what had happened, except to say that he would not be working for the government. But I could see that in his reserved and gentlemanly way he was furious.

"I don't understand why they won't let you work for the government," David said.

"Is it because Mama was once a Communist?" I asked.

They all looked at me. My parents said nothing.

"Papa?"

"This is not anything I want to talk about, Ilana."

"The Fascists in the government—"

"Please don't use that word like that," my father said, his voice rising. "Not everyone who disagrees with you is a Fascist."

"But why won't they—?"

"Ilana," my mother said. "Enough."

"But Mama—"

"Enough, Ilana. Enough!"

We did not talk about it again. My new father did not go back to Washington.

I remember lying in bed at night and trying to think of the whole world at war. I could not grasp it; it was beyond imagining. My classmates and I thought little about the war during the day as we talked and gossiped; but the nights were a difficult time for me, a time for touching the world, a time for flying birds and galloping horses and singing harps and long red-sand beaches in a green and distant land. How I missed my father, my real father, on those nighttime journeys into history and memory! How I missed Jakob Daw!

Sometimes at night I thought of Rabbi Akiva. I imagined him tall and powerful, with a long flowing beard and a strong voice and dressed in a long robelike garment. I imagined him embracing his wife, Rachel. I imagined him urging the Jews on in their rebellion against Rome. I imagined him journeying to collect funds to help the poor. I imagined his skin being torn off by the iron combs.

One morning Mr. Helfman asked me to stay behind during recess.

"Ilana, your Hebrew essay on Rabbi Akiva is wonderful. You wrote it by yourself?"

"Yes."

"Where did you get the words he said to his wife?"

"From my imagination."

"Your imagination? Wonderful!"

"He was away from his wife twenty-four years, studying Torah. I thought he would say those things to her when he came back."

He looked at me out of his cheerful round eyes.

"I like Rabbi Akiva," I said. "I like the way he started to study the alphabet very late in his life and wasn't ashamed to sit in class with young students and the way he cared about poor people and the way he died for the things he believed in."

"It is an excellent essay," he said delightedly. "Go over my corrections in your spelling and the mistakes you made in grammar. Yes, an excellent essay, Ilana."

"I like his optimism," I said. "I like the way when he and some other rabbis saw a jackal in the ruins of Jerusalem, and the others began to cry, he laughed and said that just as the prophecy of the destruction of the temple was fulfilled, so the prophecy of the rebuilding would also be fulfilled. I like that."

Mr. Helfman nodded, smiling.

I went out of the classroom, the essay in my hand. On the top of the first page was the grade, written in red ink in Mr. Helfman's characteristic slanted and sprawling style. He had given me an aleph, an A. I joined Ruthie in the front yard in a jump rope game.

My American history teacher, a thin bald-headed man with smooth-shaven features and small dark eyes, said to me one afternoon, "Where did you get this information for your essay, Ilana?"

The others had left. We were alone in the classroom. I could hear through the closed door the sounds of students in the corridors and the emptying of the school building.

"From a book."

"Which book?"

I told him.

"That's a novel. I can't accept a novel as a source for this assignment."

"But the novel has stories that are true. The part about Centralia is true."

"I prefer that you stick closer to the subject we're studying. I asked you to write about one of the robber barons, not about the Wobblies."

I said nothing.

"And, Ilana, it isn't necessary for you to be quite so—graphic."

"I was telling the truth, Mr. Mandel."

"Stick to the subject under discussion, Ilana. Do you understand?"

"Yes."

"I'll want another essay from you in place of this one."

He handed back the paper. I went from the room and walked home alone in the early darkness of the winter day.

In Mr. Helfman's class we completed studying the Book of Numbers. The next day there was a siyum, the traditional party that follows when a group completes the study of a sacred Jewish text. We brought candies and cookies and chocolates to school, and Mr. Helfman gave a little talk about how the study of Torah had kept the Jewish people alive all through the centuries.

The siyum lasted about half an hour. Then Mr. Helfman called the class to order and stood behind his desk and began to talk to us about the Book of Deuteronomy, its first-person style, its lofty poetry, its ethical and moral themes. I listened and at the same time read quickly through the first verses. Names and dates. In the fifth verse I read two words that I remembered having read before, and I went back to the beginning of the book and found the words in the first verse: *b'ever ha-Yarden*. I glanced at the Rashi on the verse and found that Rashi had not bothered to explain the words—which meant that they were very easy to understand. Mr. Helfman went on with his introduction to the book, and a moment or so after he was done, the bell rang for the morning recess.

In the school library I found an English translation of the Bible and turned to Deuteronomy. The Hebrew words *b'ever ha-Yarden* were translated as "beyond the Jordan." The text read, "These are the words which Moses spoke to all Israel beyond the Jordan . . ."

What did those words mean? Beyond the Jordan.

It was snowing when school let out. I walked home with Ruthie in a wind that blew the snow in a steep slant across the parkway and was piling it in drifts against fences and homes.

Inside the apartment I found the verse in my father's copy of the Hertz commentary. There the words were explained as meaning at the crossing of the Jordan or on the banks of the Jordan or as referring to a fixed geographical name.

But what if there was another explanation? I thought of Jakob Daw writing this as a story. What would "beyond the Jordan" then mean? What if Jakob Daw were living on this, the Israelite, side of the Jordan? And what if he were writing this story? Wouldn't he simply write "beyond the Jordan" to indicate where the action of the story was taking place?

And wouldn't that mean that the writer of the story in the Bible had lived *after* the story had taken place, because he was on the Israelite side of the river and in the story the Israelites had not yet crossed the river? I thought that made sense. You didn't have to change the simple meaning of the words. I liked the idea that a human being had thought to write those words; it made the text seem more real to me.

The next day, when we came to that verse, I raised my hand. Mr. Helfman called on me. I recounted my explanation of the words *b'ever ha-Yarden.* I talked for what seemed to me to be a long time. Mr. Helfman let me go on. He kept looking at me and nodding. Behind me the class was very still.

Then I was done and sat back in my seat, listening to the drumming of my heart.

Mr. Helfman quietly cleared his throat. "Where did you read this explanation?" he asked.

I told him I hadn't read it anywhere, I made it up.

"You made it up," he echoed.

There was a silence. An airplane went by high overhead. The windows rattled faintly.

"It is the explanation given by Ibn Ezra," Mr. Helfman said. "Do you know who Ibn Ezra was?"

"Yes."

"It is not an acceptable explanation. It creates more problems than it solves. What problems does it create?"

I looked at him and did not know what to say.

Two rows to my right a boy raised his hand. This was Reuven Malter, the son of a Talmud teacher in a nearby Jewish parochial high school, a dark-haired, good-looking boy who was very popular and very smart.

"Reuven," Mr. Helfman said.

"If this verse was written by a person and not given by God, then how do we know other verses weren't written by a person, including verses that deal with the law?"

"Yes, indeed," said Mr. Helfman. "And what does that do to the Bible, Ilana? You understand, don't you? That is why the explanation of Ibn Ezra is unacceptable. Now, let's go on with the text."

I saw Reuven Malter glance at me out of the corner of his eye. His face wore a look of triumph. He was smart and had his own clique of friends; lithe and fast-running and athletic; the only real competition I had in that class for the Akiva Award.

I sat with my eyes on the text, listening to Mr. Helfman.

Ruthie told me one day in January that she had overheard her father tell her mother that Reuven Malter and I were the two best students in the class and the faculty would have a difficult time deciding which of us would get the Akiva Award.

David said to me one evening, "You're working too hard, Ilana. Even I don't work this hard."

I motioned him out of my room and heard the harp sing as he closed the door.

My mother came into my room one night and said, "It's very late, Ilana. I want you to go to sleep."

I looked up from my books.

She stood near my desk, thick now about the waist, showing the baby she carried.

"Ilana, you're going to make yourself sick," she said. "Go to bed."

"You're interrupting me!" I said in a furious voice. "Please leave me alone!"

She gasped. I looked away, astonished at my anger, my heart thundering.

After a moment she turned and went from the room. The harp sang quietly in the stillness.

My father said to me over breakfast one morning in early February, "Are you awake, Ilana? Hello? Is anyone there?"

"I'm awake, Papa."

"I wasn't sure. When someone's eyes are closed, you can't be sure if they're awake or not. I won't ask you what time you went to sleep last night. What time did you go to sleep last night?"

"I don't remember."

"Your light was still on when I turned mine off," David said.

"You don't look too wide awake yourself," my father said.

"I'm awake," David said.

"A family of night owls," my father said. "A family of book eaters." He smiled and dug into his grapefruit. "A nice family."

"You're all going to be late," my mother said. "Finish your breakfast." She was very large with the child now and no longer working. Her face was rounder than it had been before the pregnancy, fleshier. Her eyes seemed to dominate her other features: they were radiant with expectation. She stood near the sink, the bulge of her body against the counter. Is that what happened? You grew larger and larger with the life inside you, and then you squeezed it out and held it and nursed it?

Ruthie told me in school that day, "Ilana, I heard my father telling my mother that—"

"I don't want to hear it, Ruthie."

She laughed. "All right."

"What else do you hear your mother tell your father?"

She blushed scarlet. "You don't have to be mean, Ilana."

"I'm sorry."

"Are you all right?"

"My head hurts and I have a stomachache."

"Are you sure you don't want me to tell you what—?"

"Ruthie!"

She laughed and raced away along the corridor.

My English teacher said to me later that afternoon, "I like your essay on Abraham Ibn Ezra, Ilana. A scholar and a poet and an astronomer and a doctor. He sounds like a very remarkable person. I especially like your description of his wanderings. Did he really travel so much?"

"Oh, yes. And he did most of his writing while he traveled."

"It's a fine essay, Ilana. Are you all right?"

"I'm a little tired."

"You ought to go home and get some sleep. You look exhausted."

"Yes, ma'am."

"You don't want to weaken yourself and become ill, Ilana. There's a lot of flu going around this winter."

"Yes, ma'am."

I walked home alone in a cruel winter wind. There was little traffic on the icy parkway. The side streets were deserted. My head hurt and there was a pain in my stomach. At home the pain was severe and I went to the bathroom and pulled down my panties and sat on the toilet. Then I looked down and saw the blood. I felt a trembling shock of fear and a sudden soaring sense of excitement. Sitting there, my panties down around my ankles, I called out, "Mama!"

We had no lock on our bathroom door. The family rule was: if the door is closed, knock before entering. No one had yet violated that rule.

My mother knocked on the door. "Ilana? Are you inside?"

I told her to come in and she did and stopped in the doorway, then stepped quickly inside and closed the door. How big she was with the child she carried! Would it be well? Would we need Aunt Sarah again? She came over to me and I showed her the panties. I slid them off my feet and closed and flushed the toilet. She held me then and kissed my cheek. I felt the firmness of her belly. She showed me how to use the sanitary belt and napkin, and hugged and kissed me again. I went to my room and lay on my bed. Blood and discomfort month after month for as long as I could look into the years ahead. My heart beat dully. I gazed at the picture of the stallions on the beach. In his room David sat over his folio of Talmud, softly chanting.

My mother must have told my father, for he gave me the gentlest of looks at the start of supper that evening and kissed my cheek. "My family is growing up," he murmured.

David seemed to notice nothing. He was in an arduous self-imposed regimen of study. I had the impression sometimes that he was trying hard to stifle the demons within him. He had yet to talk to me again as he had the night we were alone months ago in my room.

I came over to Reuven Malter one cold morning in March during recess and said, "Can I talk to you?"

He was standing in a circle of his friends. He looked a little surprised. "Sure," he said.

We walked a few steps away from his friends. I could feel them all staring at us.

"I'm having trouble with that problem we had today in algebra. No one else seems to understand it. Can you explain it to me?"

He was the best mathematics student in the class. "Sure," he said, and explained it quickly and clearly.

"I get it now," I said. "Thanks."

"Okay," he said. "Sure. Listen. I liked your essay about Rabbi Akiva and his last thoughts before he died. Where did you get the idea for that?"

Mr. Helfman had asked me to read the essay aloud to the class.

"From my imagination."

"Really? That's pretty good. I wish I could write like you do."

"I wish I could do math like you do."

He smiled, looking a little shy and embarrassed. "Well, anytime you need help with algebra, let me know, Ilana."

"Thanks."

He went back to his friends.

My English teacher said to me later that day, "I'm afraid I didn't understand much of what you wrote in your essay, Ilana. Was Rabbi Akiva really a mystic?"

"Yes."

"Tell me what a mystic is."

We talked about that for a while.

"But what does the word mean, Ilana? What does mystic mean?"

I had meant to look it up and put it into the essay. It had been so late. I had forgotten. I didn't—

"You shouldn't write on something you know nothing about, Ilana."

"I thought it was like the stories of Jakob Daw. That's why I made the connection. I thought—"

"It's not at all clear to me what the connection is. How do you know about the stories of Jakob Daw?"

"He lived with us once for a while."

"Jakob Daw?" She looked astonished.

"He was a good friend of my mother's. They went to school together in Vienna. He was together with my father in Spain—my real father, I mean, who was killed in Guernica."

She was having some difficulty taking all this in. She regarded me for a while in silence. Then she said, "This isn't another of your flights of the imagination, Ilana."

"No, ma'am."

"All right. In any event, have a look at my comments. And pay more attention to your spelling. Especially words like weird and eternal and journey. And it isn't necessary for you to be quite so—um—explicit in some of your descriptions, Ilana."

"Yes, ma'am."

I walked home alone in a cold winter wind.

The winter was coming to an end. Purim arrived, the holiday that celebrates the deliverance of the ancient Jewish community of Persia from the hands of Haman. There was a carnival in our school and we all came in costume. I came as Queen Esther, Ruthie came as Vashti, wife of King Achashverosh of Persia, and Reuven Malter came as Mordechai. All the classes assembled in the large hall that was the synagogue during Shabbos and holidays. It was a happy and rowdy time.

Reuven Malter came over to me. "You look nice," he said.

"So do you," I said.

"Should we wish each other good luck?"

"About what?"

"About the Akiva Award."

"I guess so."

"Good luck," he said.

"Good luck."

He walked away, looking very handsome in his turban and flowing robe.

Then the final weeks of winter and the early weeks of spring went by and suddenly it was Passover.

We had the first Seder at the Helfmans'. For the second Seder the Helfmans came up to us. We chanted the Passover story, the account of the deliverance from slavery in Egypt. We talked and sang and ate and sang some more. David drank a bit too much wine the second night and fell asleep at the table after the meal. Ruthie and I giggled as we listened to his soft snoring. He looked so gaunt and was slightly flushed from all the food and wine he had taken in.

I noticed during both Sedorim that Mr. Helfman kept giving me piercing glances from time to time as if he were studying me. It made me a little uncomfortable.

My mother sat queenlike in her chair, large with the child she carried, calm, radiant, at peace with herself. My father and Mr. Helfman talked a little about the war in Europe. Mostly they traded insights into the text of the Haggadah, the story of Passover.

That was a lovely time, a dream time, those days and nights of Passover with my family. It continued on after the holiday as the days lengthened and grew warm and flowering trees came to life and the hyacinths and crocuses and daffodils gleamed in the sunlight in the backyard and tiny leaves appeared on the sycamore and in the tree outside my window.

One afternoon in the middle of May, Mr. Helfman sent a note to my English teacher, asking her to inform me that he wanted to see me in his office the following day about twenty minutes before the start of school. I noticed that she did not have any message for Reuven Malter.

At eight o'clock the following morning I stood in front of the door to Mr. Helfman's office at the end of the corridor on the third floor. On the frosted glass rectangle that was the upper half of the door were the letters M. HELFMAN, HEBREW DEPARTMENT.

I knocked on the door.

There was no answer.

I waited a moment, then knocked again, a little louder, and heard Mr. Helfman's voice. "Come in."

I opened the door and stepped inside. Behind me the door closed with a soft click.

I waited near the door.

Mr. Helfman sat in a low-backed swivel chair behind a small desk piled high with papers and file folders. Behind him a window looked out onto the trees and traffic of Eastern Parkway. There were books and papers on the two chairs near the desk. The office was small. Two glass-enclosed bookcases stood against a pale green wall. Paint was peeling from the ceiling. Near the door stood a table heaped with papers, text-books, and examination booklets. The air was musty with the odor of yellowing volumes and old linoleum.

I stood in front of the door and waited.

Mr. Helfman motioned to me.

"Come here, Ilana. Come. Sit down. Move the books and papers to the other chair. Yes."

I sat down in one of the chairs, arranged my dress over my knees, and put my hands in my lap. My heart beat dully, loudly, the sound like the rush of ocean water in my ears.

Mr. Helfman, short and round and clad in a dark suit and a black skullcap, sat in the chair behind the desk and gazed at me. Behind him the early morning sunlight lay soft and golden on the parkway. Soon we would be back at the beach. Soon. After graduation and the birth of the baby. Soon. Please please oh please.

"Ilana, I have nice news for you," Mr. Helfman said. "News you will be happy to hear."

I sat in the chair and waited.

He smiled, enjoying the moment.

"The faculty has decided to award you the English prize and the Bible prize," he said.

I looked at him, my heart thudding. "Thank you," I said.

"We are very proud of you," he said.

"Thank you," I said again.

"This is the first time in the history of the school that these prizes are being given to the same student," he said.

I did not know what to say to that and remained quiet.

"You are one of the best students we have ever had, in spite of your—how shall I put it?—unusual background. Two prizes. *That's* an accomplishment!"

"Thank you," I said.

"You are very welcome, indeed," Mr. Helfman said.

He sat behind his desk, smiling at me.

A moment passed.

"How is your mother?" he asked.

"Fine, thank you."

"Soon you will have, with God's help, another brother. Or a sister."

I nodded and said nothing. Morning traffic moved back and forth in the sunlight on the parkway. The branches of the trees were stirred by a warm wind.

Another moment passed.

Mr. Helfman leaned forward, his round belly touching the edge of the desk.

"You can go to class now, Ilana," he said.

I stared at him. A chasm of sadness opened up within me. I had lost. No Akiva Award for Ilana Davita Dinn. Well, maybe it had been crazy to think I could have won. I had come late into the school. How could I have won over someone like Reuven Malter, who had been in it since first grade and whose father was a teacher of Talmud? I had tried. I had really tried. That was some consolation. Still it would have been nice to have won that award and to have been able to hang it on the wall of my room and have it there together with the picture of the horses on the beach and the door harp. And to have been able to say good-bye to my father and to Jakob Daw in front of all of those people, the people in the community that was my new home. How sweet and nice that would have been! The door harp from my father's brother, the picture from my father's and my aunt's grandfather—the old past of my family, the past of the Chandals; and the Akiva Award from the new past into which I had thrust myself, the past of the Dinns. Yes, that would have been nice. Well, I had really tried.

I got to my feet and started toward the door.

From behind the desk Mr. Helfman softly called my name.

I turned.

"Sit down, Ilana. I want to tell you something."

There was a sudden sad quality to his voice, a strange heaviness.

I sat down again in the chair.

"You will find this out anyway," he said, staring past my head at some point on the wall behind me. "I know how you all go about comparing your grades. Besides, Ruthie will no doubt overhear me saying it one day to Mrs. Helfman. She has very big ears, my Ruthie. So I will tell it to you now."

I did not understand what he was saying.

"Actually," he said, still not looking at me directly, "actually you have the highest average in the class. Yes. That's true. The highest average."

I sat very still in the chair, my heart pounding.

"Most of the time—not always, you understand—most of the time the Akiva Award is given to the student with the highest average." He shifted slightly in the chair. "Well, no, that isn't quite correct. Actually, to be entirely honest with you, Ilana, it has really been given until now to the best student. You earned it and you deserve it. But the Hebrew faculty felt you should not get it because it would look bad for the school if we announced to the world that a—how shall I put this without hurting your feelings?—that a girl is the best student in our graduating class. It would not be good for the name of the school, for its reputation. What would all the other yeshivas think of us?"

I sat there staring at him and did not understand what he was saying.

He let his eyes move across my face, then looked away. "The faculty was sure you would understand. We will give the Akiva Award to a boy, and you will have your two prizes. That is what was decided."

There was another long silence. I felt myself beginning to sweat. I kept my knees tightly together.

He looked at me.

"Ilana?"

"Yes."

"Is the prize worth a fuss? It's after all only a prize, and you don't study for the sake of a prize, do you?"

I was quiet.

"We would be the only yeshiva with a girl as head of the graduating class. Your name and picture would be in the newspapers. What would the world think about our boys? It would not be nice."

I said nothing. Sweat trickled down my back and sides. I could not believe what I was hearing.

There was a long silence.

Mr. Helfman sat back in his chair and looked at me.

"You may go to class now, Ilana," he said from behind his desk.

I slid off the chair and went to the door. I felt his eyes on my back. The door closed behind me with a soft click.

I stood in the corridor. It was noisy and crowded with students. I found I was trembling. I went to the bathroom and sat on a toilet. I felt vaguely nauseated and stood with my head against the cool tile wall. I closed my eyes and felt the floor slowly move beneath my feet. I opened my eyes and washed my face and went to class.

Mr. Helfman stood behind his desk. I slid into my seat. He gave me a brief glance. We were studying Deuteronomy, chapter 16, and were about to begin verse 18. He called on Reuven Malter to read. I sat with my eyes on the text, listening to the words. "You shall appoint judges and officers for your tribes, in all the settlements that the Lord your

God is giving you, and they shall govern the people with due justice."
Reuven Malter read the Hebrew text and translated the words flaw-
lessly into modern spoken Hebrew. "You shall not judge unfairly; you
shall show no partiality; you shall not take bribes, for bribes blind the
eyes of the discerning and upset the plea of the just. Justice, justice shall
you pursue. . . ."

I closed my Bible and rose from my desk and started slowly toward
the door.

"Ilana!" Mr. Helfman called.

I did not turn. It was like rising and stepping slowly out of the boat
into the lake. Slowly and deliberately and who cares what they think or
say. I could feel them all looking at me as I opened the door and went
out of the room and closed the door behind me.

I walked quickly home in the sunlight and golden air of that warm
spring morning.

My mother was in the kitchen. She was astonished to see me home so
early. I told her about the meeting with Mr. Helfman.

She stared at me. "You must have misunderstood what Mr. Helfman
said, Ilana. I want you to go back to school."

I went into my room and lay on my bed.

Soon after my father came home that day he knocked on the door of
my room. He stood in the doorway, frowning, and said, "Tell me exactly what happened, Ilana. Word for word, if you can remember. Everything."

When I was done he stood in the doorway looking at me for a long
moment. Then he turned and went from the room.

David came home and passed by my door and said hello. He poked
his head inside. "What's the matter?"

I told him.

"I can't believe it," he said, and went up the hallway to the kitchen.

I lay on my bed and heard the three of them in the kitchen, talking.

After supper my father went downstairs to talk to Mr. Helfman. I
was in my room when he returned. I heard him in the kitchen with my
mother. The two of them came into my room.

I lay on my bed and looked at them standing near the door.

"What did Mr. Helfman tell you?" I asked.

"Exactly what you said," my father told me.

"I'm furious about this," my mother said. "They are not going to get away with it. It's absurd and petty and stupid!"

"I intend to look into it, Ilana," my father said. "No one is going to do this to my family, I don't care who he is."

They went from my room. The harp sang sweetly from the door.

My father brought a chair over to the phone in the hallway and sat there, making calls. When I fell asleep that night, he was still on the phone.

He told us over breakfast the next morning, "There's someone on the board of directors who's responsible. I don't know who it is, but I'm going to find out."

"Can one member of the board do this?" David asked.

"It depends upon who it is. And how much he gives the school."

"You mean money?" David asked.

"Yes," my father said.

I sat there looking down at the table and said nothing.

By the end of the day my entire class knew: Reuven Malter would receive the Akiva Award. Only Ruthie knew what had happened between her father and me.

"I'm going to tell him," she said to me during the afternoon recess in the front yard.

"Who?" I said.

"Reuven."

I shrugged. "I wouldn't take it now even if they changed their minds."

She stared at me.

"It's not worth anything anymore, Ruthie. It's—it's shit."

She gasped. Her mouth fell open. I left her standing there and walked away.

Mr. Helfman said to me a few days later, "You didn't hand in your weekly essay, Ilana."

I said nothing.

He said to me from his perch behind the desk, "I want you to bring it in tomorrow."

We were alone in the classroom. I stood in front of the desk, looking at him and saying nothing.

"Ilana, are you listening to—"

Someone knocked on the door. Mr. Helfman turned. The door opened. A man stepped quietly into the room and closed the door behind him.

Mr. Helfman took in a deep breath and rose quickly to his feet and stood staring at the man near the door.

He was a small, thin-shouldered man in his early or middle fifties, with pale gaunt features and dark eyes. He wore a dark gray striped suit and a gray felt hat. He looked tired and his eyes seemed red and weary behind his silver-rimmed spectacles, as if he had not slept in a long time. He coughed lightly and held his hand to his lips.

"Did I come at a bad time?" he asked quietly.

"No, no," Mr. Helfman said in a deferential tone I had never heard from him before.

"You were not in your office, and I thought—"

"It's all right, it's fine," Mr. Helfman said. He turned to me. "You can go now, Ilana."

I went from the room. The man near the doorway looked at me as I went past him. I felt his eyes on me. He reminded me vaguely of Jakob Daw.

In synagogue that Shabbos Mr. Helfman said to me, "Good Shabbos, Ilana. How are you?"

"Good Shabbos," I said politely, and turned and walked away from him.

He said to me in school, "You still haven't turned in your essay, Ilana."

I said nothing.

"The term isn't over yet," he said. "I don't want to threaten you."

Still I said nothing.

For a long moment he stood behind his desk, looking at me. Then he dismissed me with an abrupt wave of his hand.

My father said to us that night during supper, "It had nothing to do with Mr. Helfman. He was against it from the start."

"What do you mean?" my mother said.

"He was against the decision not to give the award to Ilana. The faculty voted for it because word came down from the board."

"I don't understand," David said.

There had been secret figures behind the decision, my father said. Authorities in high academies of learning who had let it be known through intermediaries that they would look with disapproval upon a yeshiva where a girl was publicly shown to be the best student of a graduating class that had boys in it. This had not been a mean and petty decision, my father said, but a statement of strong policy from some of the most powerful figures in the Torah world. What sort of future students of Torah would come out of a class where the best student was a girl? And how could a high academy of Torah learning accept any boy from such a class? But no one would say with certainty who those mysterious authorities had been.

"I don't believe it," my mother said.

"That's what I was told," my father said.

"Some of the boys in my yeshiva heard about it," David said, "and are laughing because a girl is graduating first in the class. They're calling it a school for wives."

"I cannot believe this is happening," my mother said.

When had I heard her say that before? When my father had disappeared in Spain? When Jakob Daw had been deported? I cannot believe this is happening.

"Mr. Helfman wanted me to get the award?" I asked.

"Yes," my father said.

"Thank you," I said.

I went to my room and was up most of the night and handed the essay to Mr. Helfman at the start of class the next day. He took it without a word and returned it to me the following day. I had titled it with the Hebrew words "Justice, Justice Shall You Pursue." It was an analysis of the comments of Rashi on that verse: "Seek after a proper court of law. . . ." He returned it without comment and I saw on top of its first page, in red ink, the Hebrew letter aleph.

My father stopped making phone calls and inquiries. In the end the issue, such as it was, faded away. Even Ruthie stopped talking about it. How long could anyone be expected to remain upset over such a small indecency?

I was graduated from that school on a sunny day in the middle of June. The large room was crowded. All our family was there. Aunt Sarah had been invited but wrote that she couldn't come because her mother was very ill. I wore stockings and white shoes and a white short-sleeved dress with a square neck, a cinched waist, and a flared skirt. I wore a corsage of roses. My long hair was pulled up at the sides and caught in the back in a barrette. It was a hot day and people sat fanning themselves with the program, which carried in bold type the names of all who were receiving awards and prizes.

To my surprise, Reuven Malter's name was not listed as the recipient of the Akiva Award; it was given to another male student in the class. I had avoided looking for the pictures and announcements in the newspapers. Reuven Malter received the prize in mathematics.

I do not remember what the boy who received the Akiva Award said in his farewell talk.

I was given the English prize and the Bible prize and an honorable mention in history for an essay I had written on the Spanish Civil War.

Reuven Malter came over to me immediately after the graduation ceremony.

"I don't want anything I don't earn, Ilana," he said. "It wasn't mine, it was yours. What they did wasn't right. If that had happened to me . . ."

He left the sentence unfinished.

Later I saw him walk up to a small, thin-shouldered man. The two of them embraced. It was the same man who had come into Mr. Helfman's classroom some weeks back, the man who had vaguely reminded me of Jakob Daw.

Some hours after the graduation ceremony I lay on my bed listening to the sounds of the wind in the tree outside my open window. It was early evening. Soft light lay upon the street. My parents were in the kitchen, listening to the news. David was in his room, studying Talmud.

I lay in my white graduation dress with my hands over my eyes, thinking about the day. The dense crowd milling outside the school building. Handshakes and congratulations and smiles and noise, and the glances of my classmates—some sad, others smirking—who knew what had happened. I lay very still and felt the anger rising within me. How sweet it could have been! How proud I could have made my family! And it was mine, really mine. And it had been stolen from me for a reason I could not control: I was a girl. What else would they steal from me in the coming years? I would accomplish something, and they would tell me I couldn't have it because I was a girl. I had made this community my home, and now I felt betrayed by it. It was like turning a corner in one of the neighborhoods where I had lived as a child and never knowing if that gang leader with the pimpled face and glittering eyes would suddenly come upon me. How could I be a part of such a community? I felt suddenly alone. And for the first time I began to understand how a single event could change a person's life. I could understand something of my mother's terrible moment in that forest and my father's in Centralia and Jakob Daw's in the gas attack. How do you fight faceless phantoms? What would the westering women do now? What would Uncle Jakob do? They would use their imaginations. Uncle Jakob would write a story. I didn't want to write a story. I only wanted to say a few words of good-bye. That's all. A few words of good-bye.

I lay on my bed and kept going over the day again and again. You can't call it back. It's gone. Like my little baby brother. Gone. Like Papa. Gone. Like Uncle Jakob. Gone. Like Guernica. Gone. Like everyone who is dying in the war. Gone.

I felt the wind blowing into the room, felt it warm against my hot face. How I raged inside myself! I had wanted to show that I could be a Jewish hero—a scholar. I had wanted to enter Jewish history. I had wanted to be part of that warm and wondrous world—and they wouldn't let me. They had denied it to me because of a circumstance. An injustice had been performed by a world that taught justice. How could I live in that world now? How could I be part of its heart and soul, its core? Why should I continue to be part of something that behaved this way? How could I trust it?

I lay very still with my hands over my eyes, feeling the anger like a boiling juncture of tides. The wind moved through the room, stirring the wooden balls of the harp. The harp sang softly in the stillness. . . .

That was strange. How could so gentle a wind stir the harp to music?

I opened my eyes and sat up on the bed.

The harp hung on the door, covered by shadows. The softest of music was coming from it, faint, as if borne on wind, and an odd distant fluttering as of a waking bird shaking and fluffing and stretching its wings. I sat on my bed, listening. . . .

And then—and then Ilana Davita came down from the bed and walked slowly to the harp and stood very still, gazing up at it, and quite suddenly the harp began to grow before her eyes, quickly, growing and growing. And then with a start she realized that it was not the harp that was growing larger but she, Ilana Davita, who was growing smaller. In her white shoes and white dress and stockings, smaller, quickly smaller, so that the balls of the harp were suddenly like huge boulders and the strings thick, the size of the trees that Paul Bunyan used to cut down. And then she was suddenly lifted by the wind that blew in through the window and brought gently into the circular heart of the harp—and there she found herself between the black bird of Jakob Daw and the gray bird of Guernica; Ilana Davita, in her white graduation dress, between birds that were now fully awake and stirring. Wings brushed against her, beaks pecked gently at her arms. The birds stood, wings outspread, and began to grow. They stood on the edge of their circular nest, craning their necks, pecking into their feathers, stretching. Then they flew off, each to one side of the harp, and grasped the harp with their talons and lifted it off the door. The harp yawed and swayed and sang as the birds flew it carefully through the room; and, from the circular heart of the harp, Ilana Davita saw the wall near her bed and the picture of the beach and the stallions. The wall and the picture came closer and closer, and in a moment she could see nothing but the picture, and suddenly she was through some kind of unseen wall and inside the picture, and she could hear the wind that blew in from the water; and the birds, their wings fluttering, brought the harp down ever so gently on the grass near the front stone step of the farmhouse and lifted her out and set her down on the wooden porch.

I stood on the porch, facing the beach and the sea and the stallions that grazed quietly on the summer grass. How sweet the wind was! And everything so still. And the gulls circling the beach and softly calling.

Behind me the door to the porch opened quietly. I turned—and it was my father, Michael Chandal.

Hello, my love! he said gaily. You didn't think we wouldn't show up, did you? Look how you've grown! Hasn't she grown, Sarah?

My Aunt Sarah stepped out onto the porch, smiling. She most certainly has. She is a young lady.

Give us a hug, Davita. A big hug. That's right. Say, you *are* a big girl!

He grinned broadly and ran his hand over his curly brown hair. How young he looked, my father.

May we begin? said a voice from inside the house. And my father said, Come on outside, Jakob. It's too beautiful to hold a graduation inside on a day like today.

Jakob Daw came out to the porch, carrying a folding chair.

Hello, Ilana Davita, he said. How are you feeling? You took good care of our bird, I see. You even added a bird of your own. A wise girl. Then he smiled and said, You see? Stories may have some use after all.

They sat on chairs on the porch, waiting. How radiant they looked! How alive! Waiting. On the beach one of the stallions whinnied, the sound carrying clearly through the silence.

I only wanted to say a few words, I said. That's all.

Say them, my love. That's what we came all this way to hear. Say them. We're listening to you.

I stood there, facing them, sunlight on my face.

I began to talk.

I told them that I wanted to speak to my family and my friends, to the world and to this century. I wanted to say that my mother was once badly hurt in Poland because she was a Jewish woman, and my father was killed while trying to save a nun in Guernica, and my uncle died in part because of his politics and in part because he wrote strange stories. I wanted to say that I'm very frightened to be living in this world and I don't understand most of the things I see and hear and I don't know what will happen to me and to the family I love. I wanted to say that I would try to find and join with the side of America that wouldn't hurt people like Wesley Everest, and I would also try not to let this century defeat me. I wanted to say good-bye to Papa and thank him for his love and his laughter and for the way he used to hug me, and also for teaching me about Paul Bunyan. And I wanted to say good-bye to Uncle Jakob and thank him for his stories and for the way his glasses used to shine in the light when he wrote at the desk in his room and for the way he didn't care much about his clothes and walked on the beach with his hands clasped behind his back. And I wanted to thank Aunt Sarah for her kindness. And I wanted to show everyone the harp so they could see where the decent music of the world comes from. And I wanted to use some quotes from the Bible and from Rabbi Akiva. That's all I wanted to say. It wasn't very much. I couldn't think of anything original like one of Uncle Jakob's stories. But they wouldn't let me say it.

There was a long silence.

I liked those words, my father said quietly.

They were very fine words, Uncle Jakob said. Good words.

You are quite a young lady, Aunt Sarah said. I thank our Lord for bestowing upon you His favor.

I'm going to applaud that speech, my father said.

As will I, said Uncle Jakob.

And I, said Aunt Sarah.

There were only the three of them on the porch—but it seemed the beach, the birds, the sea, and the sky all joined in the applause. And above all the noise was the harp, singing and singing, for all the Ilana Davitas who never had a chance to speak their few words to this century.

My father rose from his chair. It's time to go, he said. Give us a hug, my love. A whole world of a hug. A century of a hug. It's got to last a long time.

I held him and was crying and closed my eyes.

That's a hug! he said loudly and cheerfully.

Good-bye, Ilana Davita, said Uncle Jakob. You will take care of our birds, yes?

And take care of that harp, said my father. Good-bye, Davita. Give your mother my love.

I stood there, crying, and could not open my eyes.

Then I heard the sudden thunder of hoofbeats. I opened my eyes and there were my father and my uncle racing across the beach on the stallions toward the sea. The water splashed all about the galloping horses, rose in white foaming waves to their knees and flanks and shoulders and necks. Then they were suddenly all gone, but the sea still foamed and boiled. And then, very slowly, it settled back into calm and watery silence.

Overhead the gulls circled and wheeled and called. Aunt Sarah stood with her arm around my shoulder. We looked out at the silent sea.

Where will you go to school in September? she asked.

A public high school. A very good one.

Are you very angry, Davita?

Yes.

If you continue to be angry at the world, you're in for a lot of trouble.

I'm getting used to trouble, I said.

She smiled. My brother and Jakob Daw didn't know it, she said softly, but they were possessed of sacred discontent. Oh, yes. Especially my brother. That's why I loved him.

Near the farmhouse the birds stirred faintly as they waited alongside the harp.

It was a good talk, my Aunt Sarah said. They should have let you give it.

I was quiet.

Good-bye, Davita. Be discontented with the world. But be respectful at the same time.

Good-bye, Aunt Sarah.

She kissed my cheek.

I walked toward the harp, the wind on my face and the silence in my ears. The birds rose from the grass, their wings beating. The harp ascended into the air. There was the sea and the farmhouse far below me and my Aunt Sarah, waving. And then it was all gone, and I sat on my bed, gazing at the picture on my wall and at the harp on my door, and listening to my mother calling me to help her set the table for supper. **P06**

In early July my mother gave birth to a baby girl. My father walked around dazed with joy. David went about smiling broadly and for a few days even neglected his studies and kept going with me to the hospital to visit our mother and stare at the baby.

I remember when they brought her home. She lay small in the crib in my parents' bedroom. I didn't think anyone could be so small—though my black and gray birds were smaller still as they nested once again in my harp.

That Shabbos morning my father was brought up to the Torah and I heard him chant the blessing and saw him at first dimly through the ninon curtain and then clearly through the rip in the fabric. The Torah was read by David. My father chanted the closing blessing. Then I heard the baby being named—after my father's mother, the aunt with whom my mother had lived when she had first arrived in America from the wars and pogroms of Europe. Rachel daughter of Ezra and Channah Dinn. There were shouts of "Mazol tov! Mazol tov!"

That afternoon I watched her nursing at my mother's breast. Sunlight came into the living room through the wide bay window and fell upon my mother and sister. Later my mother let me hold her. I sat in the sunlight with my sister in my arms, warm and nestling against me. My mother stepped out of the room. I held my sister and rocked her gently back and forth and smelled the scents of her tininess—oil and powder and milk—and I thought, in a moment of bitterness, Enjoy your childhood. They'll take it away from you soon enough. And then I said, softly, my mouth close to her ear, speaking so softly that only my tiny birds and my tiny sister could hear, "I want to tell you a story. It's a strange story. It doesn't have an ending. But you might find it interesting anyway. It's a story about two birds and some horses on a beach far away. Are you listening, little Rachel? And it's about a door harp. . . ."

5/18/85